BACK-UP
(Book 1 of the Back-up Series)

By:

A.M. Madden

Back-Up
A.M. Madden

Published by A.M. Madden

Copyright ©2013 A.M. Madden

First Edition, ebook-published 2013

ISBN: 9780615857275

www.ammadden.com

Chapter 1-Leila

Calm down, Leila…

Nervously tapping my foot, I keep repeating the same words over and over in my head. I have never been this anxious or nervous in my entire life. I can't believe that I am here, sitting in a recording studio and waiting to audition for a real live rock band. Devil's Lair, a band I love and have been following for years!

Every child is asked the rhetorical question, "What do you want to be when you grow up?" Since I was a little girl, I've wanted nothing more than to be a rock singer.

Most answer and change their minds hundreds of times before they become adults. Not me. My answer has always been the same…singing rock and roll. That's always been my dream, mission, and goal. Two key factors played a huge role in my career choice. First off, I can sing. Secondly, I grew up in a household that loved to listen to classic rock. I think I knew the words to *Born to Run* before I knew *The Itsy, Bitsy Spider*. Singing rock makes up as much of my DNA as being Italian does.

This audition is huge for me. It seems so surreal that I'm having a hard time wrapping my head around it. I want this so badly that I'm not sure how I'll survive the disappointment if I don't get this job. The optimist in me tries to reason with the pessimist. Obviously getting this job would be my first choice. But if I *don't* get the job, this is a great experience for me that can easily open other doors and opportunities. I believe in fate and I believe things happen for a reason. There's a reason that I'm here.

It was a lucky tip that got me here. It's very hard to get your foot in the door. I don't have a rich famous record producer as an uncle. American Idol isn't my thing. Hoboken, New Jersey isn't exactly the birthplace of rock singers either. I constantly scour the papers for opportunities to get my voice heard. I've entered competitions and won many of them. Besides what I've been doing, I'm at a loss for other ways to put my dreams into motion. These last few years have come up empty and I've been increasingly becoming more frustrated.

Last weekend, I was singing at our regular gig at a bar called The Zone in Hoboken. I sing with four guys I've known for most of my life. During our break, a petite girl with long blonde hair and big blue eyes strolled over to me and held her hand out.

"Hi, I'm Patti." The way she measured me up immediately put me on the defensive. I was a pro at declining propositions from men, but getting hit on by a woman would be a first for me.

Cautiously I introduced myself while I shook her hand. "Leila."

She smirked and answered, "Of course you are…that's just perfect."

Thinking…what the hell does that mean? I smiled politely, while I slowly extracted my hand from her grip. *The wacko alarm was ringing loud and clear in my head.*

"Excuse me…I have to use the lady's room."

She grabbed my wrist and said, "I'm dating Scott Malone. He's the guitar player in the band Devil's Lair. Do you know them?"

The mention of Devil's Lair snapped my focus from her hand up to her pretty face and captured my attention.

"Yes, I saw them perform in the city last year. They are fantastic." I chose not to divulge how obsessed I actually was with this band, especially with the lead singer.

"Well, they're looking for a female back-up singer. I'm here with friends tonight, and I saw your show. I think you'd be perfect. In fact, they are holding auditions next week. Would you be interested?"

OH MY GOD!

I was trying very hard not to bend over and start hyperventilating in front of this total stranger. I secretly said a silent prayer thanking the bar gods for sending Patti to The Zone this night. Maybe a guardian angel was responsible…or perhaps it was fate? Either way, a higher power *was* involved.

Patti gave me her phone number and asked for me to call her on Monday. So, here I am three days later and about to audition as back-up singer for Devil's Lair.

Hopefully it will open some doors for me and give me the kick in the ass I need to make my dreams come true.

My dad wishes that my dreams weren't so ambitious. He feels that as long as I'm choosing singing as my profession, my voice is perfect for Broadway and is constantly trying to push me in that direction. Dad tries hard to be supportive. Being his only daughter, he is naturally over protective. Inexcusably, he still uses every opportunity he has to sway me. To quote him verbatim, "Living a quiet life in New Jersey, while commuting to Manhattan to star in a successful Broadway show would be a very honorable way to make a living, Leila."

Ugh!

A tiny, *tiny* part of me can't blame him for trying. Having done the school glee club thing, the church choir thing, and having really good range, my voice can easily acclimate to any musical genre…whether it's rock and roll or Broadway.

Dad finally conceded that he lost the battle. All things considered, he is taking it fairly well. Other than my decision to skip college and my career choice, I've rarely disappointed him. Dad wanted me to go to college to get a degree and have a back-up plan. I simply couldn't justify having him spend all his money on exorbitant college bills. I wouldn't have learned anything that I didn't already know. I know I can sing, and I don't want or need a back-up plan. Cocky as that may sound, I'm good at what I do. Whether it's as a famous rock singer or its continuing on the path I'm on now as a back-up singer in a bar band, it's what *I* want to do.

P.S. – for the record, the famous rock singer would be my preferred choice.

Unsurprisingly, Dad wasn't very happy hearing about Patti's fateful visit to The Zone. I dropped it on him during our weekly Sunday brunch. I know he loves me, and that he's happy for me, but his eyes couldn't conceal his trepidation. I'm a master at interpreting my dad's looks. After spending way too much time explaining who Devil's Lair was, I decided to show him a video clip that I took of them a few years earlier, and a few songs I have on my iTunes account. He reluctantly admitted that they had talent.

Coincidentally, my friend Evan and I saw Devil's Lair perform in a dive bar in lower Manhattan. We were as far back from the stage as you could get and it was dark. Even from a distance, the lead singer Jack Lair looked edible. Looks aside, his voice had me swooning. His voice oozed sensuality. At the time, if you would have told me that I'd one day be auditioning for them, I would have said, "Shut the eff up."

I've seen a lot of bands perform, but none have impressed me as Devil's Lair had that night. I became a touch obsessed at the time. It wasn't the kind of obsession that had me searching where he lived or stalking him. It was the kind where all I wanted was to listen to his voice while imagining all sorts of other stuff. What can I say? My sex life has been somewhat stagnant.

Jack finally strolls into the lobby and walks over to where I'm sitting.

Holy hell...he is gorgeous!

I am really nervous, and my nerves are already wreaking havoc on my insides. Unfortunately, as I stand here and stare at this breathtaking specimen, I can now also throw my raging libido into the fray. The combination has my stomach roiling and my lady parts throbbing...definitely not a good mix.

Seeing him on stage was nothing compared to seeing his beauty just a few feet away. In the flesh, he is simply stunning.

"Are you Leila?"

"Um, yes... I'm Leila." My response sounds completely winded.

Sweet Jesus... he is so pretty.

I've never been hypnotized before, but I'm guessing this is as close as it gets. I literally fall into a trance, staring at Jack while he pins me with his penetrating gaze. A few seconds later (or maybe even minutes?), my stupefied state causes him to call my name for the second time.

"Sorry...yes, I'm Leila. Um...my dad loves Eric Clapton, but mine is spelled differently, my mom didn't like Clapton's spelling..." I pause uncomfortably. "Um...sorry. Yes, I am here for the audition."

Oh crap! Shut up Leila! A stinging blush rises from my toes and creeps up my entire body.

Smirking he says, "So do I."

"Excuse me?"

"Love Clapton."

"Um...oh."

Um...oh? *Really?*

I sound like a complete moron.

He's got me all flustered. Using the word *handsome* to describe Jack Lair seems inadequate. Dark brown hair that is shorter on the sides, and is floppy, sexy, and screams *touch me* on top. I have to hold my hands behind my back to avoid the impulse of doing just that. His eyes are just WOW. They are a smoky grey and completely mesmerizing. The light stubble on his face subtly defines the cleft in his chin, which is square and masculine. He's absolutely gorgeous.

I continue to devour him with my eyes and commence a mini sex dream that plays in Technicolor glory in my mind.

His body is long and muscular. I'm guessing he's six-two or three? His long legs seem to go on forever in his dark denim jeans. Levi's…God, I *love* Levi's on a man.

Bulging biceps are straining the sleeves of his t-shirt, which is charcoal grey and a shade darker than his eyes. It also happens to be tight enough to show a spectacular upper torso. There is a tattoo that is barely visible under his left sleeve and I'm dying of curiosity to know what it is.

Jack smiles kindly and asks, "You ready to get started?" Not trusting my voice to respond in a calm and normal manner, I simply nod.

Somehow remembering how to walk, I follow Jack out of the lobby and down a long hallway with posters of famous bands covering the walls. The band I am auditioning for today is on the precipice of fame. They just signed on for a three album record contract. They have a tour starting this fall in North America only. The shows are at small to medium sized venues. With Jack as their lead singer and the way they sound, they are going to be huge. It's definitely a great time for me to get on their *bandwagon*, so to speak? That's if I get this job. Which I now sincerely doubt since I just basically eye-fucked the lead singer in the lobby.

At the end of the hall is a small recording studio where three guys are patiently waiting for our arrival. Behind the drum set is a really cute guy with spiky light brown hair. His one ear is heavily pierced. He has a lip piercing and he has a really nice smile, too. I think his name is Hunter.

To the front, left side of Hunter is a tall, very rocker looking dude. He has lots of tattoos and is dressed entirely in black, even sporting black sunglasses, black hair pulled back into a short ponytail, and a black bass guitar. I don't remember his name, and maybe that's because when I saw them perform, he scared the hell out of me? I doubt this is Patti's boyfriend. They are the yin and yang to each other in looks.

To the right is a guy of average height who looks more suited to be Patti's boyfriend. Clean cut, strawberry blond hair, nice smile, and he is holding a guitar. It's probably Scott. It's funny though, he does not look the rocker type at all.

Jack strolls right over to a microphone that is facing a plate glass window that separates us from the control booth. A few guys are sitting at a huge panel with all sorts of buttons and lights. Unfortunately they all look bored and it makes me nervous. I have no idea what number I am in the revolving door of auditions and I hope they haven't been doing this for days.

Standing behind them is a stunning blonde who is assessing me coolly with piercing blue eyes. She looks like a runway model in a black fitted suit without a blouse underneath. The way her arms are folded effectively displays her impressive cleavage.

Noticing another microphone positioned next to Jack, I can only assume it's meant for me. Panic stricken, I stand frozen. My feet won't cooperate and they feel like they're cemented to the floor.

"Leila, do you think you can actually stand in front of the mic so we can hear your audition?" Someone provokes Jack to laugh by chuckling, which then causes my face to turn tomato red.

Turning back to me he says, "None of our songs have back-up vocals, so we'll try something else. Do you know *Come Undone*, by My Darkest Days?"

Thankfully, I know this one. "Yes, I know it."

Jack signals Hunter, who hits his sticks together twice. This prompts Scott to start playing his guitar. The song begins with a short guitar intro, and then Hunter and the bass guitarist join in when Jack begins to sing. Goosebumps appear all over my body from hearing these fantastic musicians playing a few feet away. I'm captivated as I watch Jack's reflection in the glass. He has both hands on the mic, and his eyes are closed. He looks like he is making love to the music.

During the chorus, the female vocalist sings a solo and I smoothly pick up at my mark. Jack intently watches me in the reflection of the glass as I'm singing. It's a bit unnerving, and I keep looking away…but he never does. I can feel his eyes on me the entire time.

The song ends with Jack and I singing vocals together as the music fades. Turning towards me, a grin slowly spreads across his face revealing his…DIMPLES?

Of course he has dimples! Are you freaking kidding me?

My crotch clenches instantly!

How can a smile make my crotch clench?

Moreover, how have I not noticed his dimples before?

There is no way I wouldn't remember them because dimples are a complete turn on for me.

"That was good Leila, really good." He continues to stare into my eyes while smiling. Everything north of my belly buttons goes numb and everything south bursts into flames.

I vaguely remember Jack complimenting me, and I manage to mumble a pathetic "Thank you." Every eye is focused on me and I feel like I am standing here with nothing but a red nose and clown shoes on.

"So, Leila, can you sing something else? Something that can show us your range?"

Oh crap.

Crap...Crap...Crap!

As I look around the room, the guys are blatantly checking me out from head to toe. Deciding to change my strategy, I try to envision them all naked instead and this seems to work.

"Of course, what would you like me to sing?" I'm clearly stalling for time.

"What do you know?"

Ok, that is easy...I have a song I can belt out with no problem. "Do you guys know *Dream On* by Aerosmith?"

Jack smirks, "Dream On? You can sing that song?" It's obvious he doesn't believe me.

"Yes...is that ok? It's one of my favorite songs." His doubt in me hits a nerve. I'm about to wipe the smirk off his face.

"Um, yeah, absolutely." Jack shakes his head and adds, "Ok, let's do it." He grabs the mic stand with one hand, and glances back at Hunter to give him a signal. Hunter nods and hits his drum sticks together twice, leading the band right into the song. These guys are very much in tune to each other. I quickly take a few deep breaths trying to corral my nerves.

Closing my eyes, mainly to avoid eye contact with Mr. Sex God, but mostly to channel my talents, I sing my song choice like my life depends on it. Not far into the song, I morph from the dim-witted dork to the rock singer I am meant to be. This is my opportunity to nail it.

Feeling confident enough to open my eyes, I quickly scan the room for signs of disapproval. What I see instead is complete awe. I think I *AM* nailing it. I can tell by the faces in the control booth, (except for the hot blonde). I can tell by watching Jack's reflection in the glass. I can tell by the goosebumps that run all over my body. I feel that I am making quite an impression. I hold nothing back and let it all out.

Towards the end of the song Jack surprises me by joining in. His reflection once again watches me while showing his CCDS smile. From here on in that's how I will refer to the Crotch Clench, Dimple Showing smile. I really wish he would look away because internally I am freaking out.

After what feels like hours later, Jack breaks our eye contact and turns to face his band still grinning like a fool.

"Dude that was so fucking outrageous! I'm hard from that song." Words of wisdom from Hunter. The guys start laughing and my jaw drops.

Jack turns back to look at me and laughs when he sees the expression on my face. "That was most definitely a compliment Leila. Hunter's right. It was very impressive. Actually, I'm blown away." He turns towards his band. "Have you guys heard enough?"

They all agree and Jacks asks me to leave my contact info with Sally at the reception desk. "We will be in touch." Smiling, he puts his hand out towards me. A tiny seed of optimism begins to cultivate as I shake Jack's hand.

His touch sends a jolt right through every internal organ I have. His hand is warm and his grip is firm as his long fingers wrap around my entire hand. Shit…I never want him to let go.

One handshake has me yearning for more of his touch. How can a complete stranger have such an effect on me? The pull I feel towards this man doesn't make sense. This is the most bizarre thing I have ever experienced in my life.

"Thanks for the opportunity." I murmur quietly as Jack releases my hand. My body feels like it's been doused with lighter fluid, and someone struck a match. Just as I turn to leave the room, my heel catches on an electrical wire and I stumble backwards.

He immediately reaches out and pulls me flush to his body with his strong grip, his eyes showing unmasked concern.

"Careful, are you ok?"

I can't speak and instead barely nod while gnawing on my bottom lip. Our faces are inches apart and I have an overwhelming impulse to close the distance between our lips. The buzzing sensations that are coursing through my lower region continue and shoot straight up, accelerating my already pounding heart. My breath expels loudly in short pants.

I step back, but he is still gripping my arms. He leans in and whispers "Don't sweat it. You did really great today."

Managing a very weak smile, I pull away from his hold and thank him again before bolting out the door. I sprint down the hall and break right in front of Sally, the scary girl at the reception desk. She has midnight black hair with a single purple streak, a nose-ring and a tattoo on her exposed cleavage. She looks very bored as she reads a magazine and barely glances up at me.

"Hi, I'm Leila. I need to leave my contact info with you." She wordlessly passes me a piece of paper and a pen that I use to scribble my name and cell phone number on. She then takes it from me with a look of complete disgust and resumes reading her magazine.

She is scary as hell.

I mutter a thank you and then sprint out the front door to make my way to my car. Once inside, I slam my head against the steering wheel and set off the horn. The hysterical part is that I am parked directly in front of the studio, and I can see Scary Sally watching me out the front door. Ha…Ha, right?

Could this get any worse?

As I drive my humiliated ass back to Hoboken, I try to analyze what the hell happened in that studio. I'm almost afraid to hope for this job. Let's fast forward and assume I get hired…then what? Can I survive being in his presence daily, when I couldn't make it through a twenty-minute audition?

What am I saying? Of course I want this job. Plus, I don't even know this man. He probably is a complete jackass. As I try to convince myself that Jack is indeed a jackass, a tiny voice in the back of my demented brain says, *"You'd better hope so."*

***

It's now Friday, day three of waiting for "the phone call." I'm sitting at my little table poking my phone, actually willing it to ring. We have another show tonight, and I've been sitting here for four, five, eight hours? I have no clue. Since Tuesday, I have completely lost track of time. I know I have to go on with my life or I can simply call them. But after my embarrassing behavior, I would rather stick needles in my eyes.

16

I'm running late *again*, so for the third night in a row I mechanically go through the motions of getting ready for our show. I feel like a zombie sucked my will to live and has turned me into a zombie. The audition and waiting for them to call me has me completely unhinged. I have never been so consumed by my thoughts as I have these last three days. My anxiety has festered into a constant pounding in my chest. I know I impressed them, but I guess my ridiculous conduct overrode my performance.

My phone is now sitting on the floor outside my shower. I keep moving back the curtain to stare at it, and still nothing.

Damn it.

I need to put my ass in gear. At least my beauty routine takes hardly any time at all. My hair is brown, long and wavy, and I usually dry it slightly and then let it finish drying naturally. I start on my makeup next, which takes two minutes since I only wear mascara and lipstick. My eyes are an ordinary golden brown in color, but I have thick black lashes that help them out a bit. Having typical Italian coloring, just like my dad, affords me to never have to wear foundation or blush. That's a plus, because I hate the stuff.

I numbly start to look for an outfit to wear while still gripping my phone. Tonight I decide on a short skirt, high heels, and a funky top. I am five-six, but in heels my legs appear fairly long, and they become my best asset. This is my typical performance uniform. I call it a uniform because I wouldn't be caught dead wearing it in my everyday life. The normal, everyday Leila dons a ponytail, jeans and sneakers.

I leave my apartment well after nine and head to my car. We perform every Wednesday through Saturday at The Zone. Sundays are reserved for private parties while Mondays and Tuesdays are our days off.

Since the audition, my nerves had me acting somewhat robotic during my performances. The good news is no one really noticed, except for my band. The bad news is tonight we will have a big crowd. We always do on Friday and Saturday nights. I really need to snap out of it.

The bar is only a few minutes away. We don't start until ten and I usually like to get there early to chat with the girls. Alisa and Lori are two of the bartenders and my closest female friends. Since I am once again late though, I'll have no time to chat.

When I pull into the lot, I can see the familiar pick-up truck that belongs to Matt Rizzo, our lead singer. The Jeep that Logan drives is not here yet. He's our guitarist and Matt's older brother. He usually picks up our drummer and bassist, Joseph and Evan.

Matt can't be bothered chauffeuring anyone around. Logan always offers to pick me up as well, but I prefer to drive myself. I don't drink while I'm working, and I like to high tail it out of there as soon as we are done.

This is our band singer, guitarist, bassist, drummer, and I as back-up. I also play keyboards when the song requires it. We call ourselves Cliffhangers. I personally think it's a really dumb name.

We are pretty good. The Zone is jammed most weekends and we all like to believe its Cliffhangers that brings in the crowds. The pay is decent, and I can survive on it just fine most of the time. I am pretty low maintenance. The boys play at weddings and bar mitzvahs every so often on Sundays. I hate working private parties. I feel they are complete and utter torture. I'll work them only if I need to supplement my salary from The Zone when I'm having a financially rough month. My dad always offers me money, but he works hard and I'd rather he spend it on himself. He doesn't, of course. Except for his baseball games and his CD obsession of old rock bands, he saves every penny he makes.

On my salary, I can afford to live in a nice apartment in Hoboken. It's small but really cool, and I love it. It's close to work, the city, and my dad's house in Cliffside Park, the town where I grew up. Cliffside faces New York City and overlooks the Hudson River. That's where I met the boys. Cliffhangers is a tribute to the streets we all lived on that overlook those cliffs. Like I said, it's a dumb name.

Most of my expenses are just the rent and utilities. I drive an old Honda that's in good condition and gets me where I need to go. My wardrobe is Jersey Mall. Even my food bills are minimal because I tend to mooch a lot of meals off dad.

Dad did a great job raising me. My mom Marie died in a car accident when I was ten, and I miss her every day. We had a normal, happy family life. Mom worked hard as a nurse yet always found time for my extracurricular activities. She never missed a recital or spring pageant. Mom was my biggest fan. She said I had the voice of an angel. It pains me today that she is not here with me, but I know she is in spirit. I like to think she was the guardian angel who sent Patti into the bar last weekend. I wear her wedding band every day to feel connected to her even after all these years.

I look a lot like her, but my personality is strictly Anthony Marino's or dads. Quiet, shy, cautious, and naturally a skeptic. Mom was more a free spirit and impulsive. Going for that audition on Tuesday was the craziest thing I have ever done.

Anthony is the best dad a girl can ask for. He works for a newspaper in the city. He's been there more than twenty years. I feel as if he never took a risk because of me. He probably doesn't love his job, but it's stable. Being a huge Yankee fan, this job affords him a chance to see a game every few weeks during baseball season, pay the mortgage, and to live comfortably.

Dad was a hottie years ago. Still an attractive man at fifty, he has aged a bit since mom died. I'm always looking for a nice woman to set him up with, someone to care for him and love him. He deserves it. Dad says he already found the love of his life. He wonders if there is another waiting for him. The hopeless romantic gene I definitely inherited from him.

As I make my way through the parking lot, Ace, our trusty bouncer, sits on his usual perch. I love Ace. He is a security guard during the week, but moonlights as Sal's bouncer on Friday and Saturday nights. He is saving up to start his own security business.

Ace is as intimidating as they come, but deep inside he is a softie. He has a sweet wife named Cindy, a little girl who adores him and a boy on the way. The day Ace found out, he was already handing out cigars. Seeing him with his family makes it hard to see him as a brute that could bash someone's face in. Thank god I never witnessed Ace in action, but I've heard plenty of stories.

Ace looks up as I walk towards him. "Here she is. How are you doin' gorgeous?"

"Hi Ace. I'm ok, trying to keep myself sane." I give him a brief hug before apologizing to my friend that I'm running late and can't stay to chat.

He shakes his head and laughs at me. He knows my story and is just another one of my friends who feels I have nothing to worry about. I really wish I felt the same. I did so many things wrong during that audition. I'm sure I'll be the butt of jokes at Devil's Lair parties for years.

The Zone is my home away from home. Sal the owner is my dad's best friend and has known me for most of my life. I spent a lot of time in this bar, even before I sang here. Dad played a huge part in convincing Sal to hire us and add entertainment. At first Sal scoffed at the idea but then jumped full steam ahead once it grew on him. He built a stage and added the proper acoustics. It was a good idea, and business has boomed ever since. This meant less weddings and bar mitzvahs, thank God.

There is already a decent crowd filling The Zone. My buddies Alisa and Lori wave from the bar. They are a team and always work the same shifts. Once Sal added the entertainment, he went all out with the advertising. Alisa and Lori are pretty girls with perky breasts. They show off the bold white typeface "THE ZONE" nicely on their black t-shirts. Well-placed advertising is Sal's forte. Along with the t-shirts that the staff wears, mostly by busty cutie pies, he has placed "THE ZONE" flyers on every inch of northern Jersey.

The Zone was a dive. Now it's a dive with rocking entertainment. Those are Matt's words, not mine. Speaking of Matt, the self-proclaimed "god's gift to women" is sitting at a booth flirting with Kelly, one of the waitresses.

At the bar, Alisa is busy filling a pitcher with beer. Alisa is a brunette with big brown eyes, a pretty smile and really nice boobs. She is shorter than me and prefers her converse sneakers to wearing heels. Lori is mixing a fancy looking cocktail while watching Matt. Lori is a stunning redhead with emerald green eyes, freckles on her nose and even nicer boobs than Alisa. Even though Lori is tall, she has absolutely no problem wearing heels. When she and Alisa work the bar, Lori towers over her.

As I approach, they both immediately start chatting at the same time. Alisa is rambling about the best time she had with her boyfriend Logan the previous night. They make a perfect couple. Logan is nuts about her.

Lori is sulking about Matt not giving her the time of day. She wants him to be her boyfriend desperately and really can't take a hint. I wish she would move on because he simply is not worth it. I have firsthand experience in that subject.

The girls and I met freshman year of high school and we have become the best of friends. Alisa did not go to college. She hated everything about school and wanted no part of continuing. Instead she started to work for Sal as a waitress and quickly realized that this was also something she despised. She decided to take a bartending course and effectively found her calling.

Lori, on the other hand, went to college and graduated with a business degree. She says The Zone is just a stop on the way to the perfect job. She won't settle and doesn't care how long it takes. We all know Lori doesn't have a clue what that perfect job is. Alisa convinced Lori to take the same bartending course, as it wouldn't hurt her to make decent tips while waiting for her dream job to appear. So here they are, and so far it's worked out for both of them, as well as for Sal.

Listening to them both as they speak tandem, I am barely able to interrupt long enough to excuse myself.

"Girls, I gotta go." These are the first words I've uttered during our ten-minute conversation. Neither of them seemed to notice. They are a bit self-involved, but if I needed them for any reason, they would be there for me in a heartbeat. They ignore my stress levels because they both feel I'm being absurd and that I most definitely got the job. Everyone I know seems to think that but me.

Listlessly, I head to the back room with my purse and jacket. Sal keeps a table and chairs back there for our breaks. Some lockers line the back wall. The rest of the room serves as an overstocked storage closet.

With my phone firmly wedged in the back pocket of my skirt, I pull it out to curse at it. "Fucking ring already!"

"Have you taken your meds today Leila?" Matt says while walking into the room.

"Shut up Matt, I'm not in the mood." I say, frowning into my uncooperative piece of shit phone. He smirks at me without sympathy. He can be such a jackass.

"Yeah, shut up Matt." Joseph our drummer walks into the room and immediately pulls me into a big hug. "They will call Lei. Stop stressing…I know they will."

"You're making her head even bigger than it is." Matt retorts. While watching us, he sits at the table. The man with a Thanksgiving Day Parade balloon as a head has the nerve to say I'm big headed. That's actually funny. Rolling my eyes at him, I turn back to Joseph.

"Put it out there Lei and it will happen." Joe kisses my temple and throws Matt a look before walking out the door.

Joseph Torrone is the teddy bear in our group and a total sweetheart. You wouldn't know that by just looking at him. He is kind of scary with his buzzed crew cut, tattoos and dark brown eyes. Shoulder to shoulder he's built like a linebacker. You'd probably be afraid to bring him home to meet your mom and dad. But then once your mom got to know him, she would be hoping he proposed to you by dessert… not so much your dad.

Our lead singer Matt and I have history. We dated in high school until I realized he was a jerk. All Matt Rizzo wanted was sex. He was my first, and I thought I loved him. Since he didn't have a job, he would make excuses that we could only afford to hang out in his basement and have sex. That got real old for me and after nine months, I dumped him. But the attraction continued to be there between us. He is gorgeous and cocky as all hell. We reconnected again a few years later. The second time we were together was shorter than the first. Six months later, I dumped him again, after realizing he was now an even bigger jerk and also a dick. The second time around all Matt Rizzo wanted was sex from me, as well as from others.

Truth be told, he hurt me. So now we are just friends…I guess. I say the term loosely though, because there is a definite attitude he has towards me. He teases me a lot and sometimes it's bordering on being mean. Evan thinks it's because he hasn't gotten over me yet. I find that ridiculous as it's been years since we were together. Besides, *he* is the one who cheated on me and broke *my* heart.

Matt needs to have his heart broken just once. Maybe this will help him become less of a jerk. I would buy tickets to see it happen. Hell, I'd even bring the popcorn.

When he bothers me, Logan, Joseph, and Evan always jump to my defense. We all tolerate Matt because he has a great voice. He can belt out a rock scream like no one I've ever met before. That and his looks give us plenty of female fans. We do have a nice clump of male fans that show up every week just to see me. Some have tried to get my number, or even put their moves on me. I am not interested at this point in my life. As horny as I am, I'd rather be single and successful, than attached and miserable. Relationships and I don't get along very well.

I've only been with two guys. My second boyfriend was perfect or so I thought. Good looking, good job, good family. I loved him and was a bit blind to his extremely over-bearing, controlling, cave man ways. Having come to see our show one night, he made a scene because of the outfit I was wearing. Long story short, he was the second jewel in my pathetic relationship crown…and both jewels were cubic zirconium at best. I often wonder why I'm not lucky in relationships. It seems easy. I watch Logan and Alisa, and hope for that in my life one day. They have such mutual respect for each other and are so crazy about one another. They are best friends. Alisa is a lucky girl to have Logan.

Logan, our guitarist, is also sort of the manager of our little group. He is the oldest and tries to keep his brother Matt and the rest of us in line. They may be brothers and share the same height, shade of brown hair, and smile, but that's where the similarities end.

Matt has beautiful hazel eyes. Logan has warm brown eyes. Matt is a jerk, dick, and a heart breaker while Logan is sensitive and kind. How the same woman gave birth to these two is beyond me.

There is just something about Matt that is irresistible. I fell for his charms twice, and I'm trying to protect Lori from the Matt Rizzo experience. She has been dying to hook up with him since I dumped him the second time, only after she made sure I was ok with it. She knows our story. I've tried to tell her he isn't worth it, but she won't listen. She feels she can rehabilitate the dick-ness right out of him.

It doesn't really matter because Matt is just not interested. Not because Lori isn't hot. She is very pretty and has a great body. Evan claims Matt was done dating girls who are also friends. I felt that was good news for her.

Evan Miller, our bass player, is also my best friend. He is absolutely adorable with the nicest green eyes and shaggy, golden brown hair. More importantly, he is quiet and sweet and has a heart of pure gold. As a bass player, he is phenomenal. Cliffhangers is lucky to have him. Don't get me wrong, all the guys are talented. But there is just something about Evan.

I love him dearly but not in a romantic kind of way. He's the brother I never had. I also feel dad thinks of him as the son he's never had. He spends a lot of time with us, especially since his parents got divorced. He is an only child, too, and he has a lot in common with my Dad.

Evan is one year older than I am. We lived a block away from each other in Cliffside, but hadn't met until my first day of sixth grade in public middle school. Until then I had only attended a catholic grammar school, and felt like a fish out of water. Having recently lost my mom, I was very quiet and introverted. I noticed him in the cafeteria and thought he reminded me of someone. Unconsciously, I stared at him from across the room while eating my lunch. He noticed and came over to sit down at my table.

I should have been embarrassed, but I wasn't. The minute I looked into his eyes, I knew we were going to be good friends. Since that day he took me under his wing, and the rest is history. Evan's had a few fights for me, broken up with a few girls because of me, and is my biggest fan.

He bursts through the door just as Matt and I are about to walk back out to the bar.

"Matt, give us a minute, please."

"Sure, Evan, anything for you." He replies while batting his eyelashes and then turns to walk out the door.

Rolling his eyes, Evan comments, "He can be such a prick." I can't help but laugh. The word "prick" coming out of Evan's mouth is just wrong.

Taking my hand Evan asks, "Lei, what number did you give Devil's Lair to call you on?"

"Um, my cell…why?"

"Well, they have a wrong number for you and have been trying to call you all day."

Oh, hell no…

"What did you say? Are you freaking kidding me?" *It is probably that damn scary receptionist, Sally!* I tell him as much.

"She probably changed my number on purpose. She looked at me like I was a bug."

"Well fuck her. Jack Lair just called Sal. Patti gave him the bar's name and he needs you to call him ASAP." Evan passes me a bar napkin with a phone number scrawled on it.

"OH MY GOD!" I squeeze Evan's hand so tightly that he winces.

"Go out to your car and call him now."

"Wait, what about the set?"

"Just go. We will wait, Lei." He kisses me on my forehead and shoves me out the door. As I run to my car I dial the New York number. I force myself to breathe normally and to stop panting like a phone sex operator.

"Hello?" Hot male voice, most definitely Jack.

"Um, hi, this is Leila… Leila Marino. I was told to call this number."

"Well hello, Miss Marino." He croons through the phone in a voice so sexy I feel a quiver down below. "This is Jack Lair. I've been trying to reach you to discuss your future with Devils Lair, if you're interested."

"Wait…what!?"

He chuckles and repeats himself, and I go completely silent until he clears his throat.

"Oh, um, yes. I am absolutely interested!" Going from one extreme to the next, I am now practically screaming into the phone. He chuckles again, and it is almost like I could actually feel his breath in my ear. The quiver becomes a clenching.

So now I am apparently clenching from the sound of his voice too?

"Can you come to the studio at eleven am on Monday?" he asks.

"Yes. No problem."

"Great…and Leila? Try not to break any limbs before you get there."

I blush into the phone and squeeze out in a tiny voice, "I'll try."

He chuckles and hangs up leaving me with a vivid fantasy...sheets, legs, arms, all tangled together, and Jack chuckling into my ear. Unable to move, I sit in my car for a full twenty minutes. It's a good thing I got this job, because I may lose my current one for being twenty minutes late.

Devils Lair…damn! Thank you universe!

Since I'm already late, I might as well call my dad.

"What's wrong? Aren't you supposed to be on stage?" No hello, no greeting, this is so typical of dad.

"Hey, dad. Nothing's wrong. I just wanted to tell you that they called me back." There is a two second delay. Most wouldn't even notice it, but I do.

"That's great Lei. I'm so happy for you."

But?

I was waiting for the *but* and say as much over the phone.

"No but. I truly am happy for you. I just worry about you, you know that."

"I know dad. I have to go. I just wanted to let you know." We decide to talk more at Sunday brunch. That's when and where I would hear the "But" I was sure.

Devils' Lair…this is crazy!

Chapter 2-Jack

These past few weeks have been fucking crazy. The band is most definitely on its way. As this has been my one and only goal for most of my life, I couldn't be more prepared. I was destined for this and I risked a lot for it. My name is Jackson Henry Lair and I'm the lead singer of Devil's Lair.

I knew I was meant to be a rock star, even if my parents weren't on the same page as me. They knew that I had a great voice, I liked to write songs and constantly hung out in the city to watch bands play, but they thought it was only a hobby.

Denial maybe?

They didn't listen when I complained about school all the time. I was in the Pre-law program at NYU and hated every minute of it. Many find it hard to believe that I do have an intelligent brain in my head. My parents feel I am totally wasting it. Dad was grooming me to follow in his footsteps to be a lawyer.

I just couldn't do it.

Even though it terrified me, I had to tell my parents that I was dropping out. I couldn't keep pretending that a law career was going to be my future. I had visions of living on the streets while homeless and penniless and without either of them speaking to me. Of course, that was just my vivid imagination running wild. I wasn't raised to think that way. But I was about to drop a bomb on them of catastrophic magnitude. Although, my parents have been nothing but loving and caring to my sister and me, my scenario isn't that farfetched.

My dad is Peter Henry Lair, Esq. of business law. It's super boring, but that's dad. He is very even keeled, level headed, sensible, and smart.

I may be taller than he is, but otherwise we look a lot alike. We have the same dark brown hair - had, rather, as his is now grey at the temples, same deep grey eye color and smile, dimples included. Otherwise, that's it. I am not even keeled, level headed, or sensible.

My personality is definitely more like my moms, or Renata Cornwell Lair, homemaker and ex-beauty queen. Mom was, and still is, simply stunning. She is tall and slim and has long blonde hair and green eyes. In her early fifties, she could pass as someone twenty years younger. Growing up, it was a bit embarrassing having a hot mom. I remember her getting looks from men wherever we went. Little league, school functions, the friggin' supermarket…it didn't matter where she went. Parent-teacher conferences were always interesting. The same hard-ass, male teachers that would bust my balls on a daily basis would suddenly become babbling idiots after meeting my mom. My female teachers had the same reaction to dad. He can be quite a charmer. Sometimes that worked to my advantage.

Mom is passionate, impulsive, and headstrong and has a great sense of humor. I've heard stories of her and her wild past. My parents met in college where they fell madly in love and got married a year later. They were complete opposites when they met and have slowly morphed into one personality type, each equally changing in subtle ways like two chameleons. Where my mom became more practical and prudent, my dad went from bookworm to party animal. Well not *really* a party animal, but mom said he has most definitely "loosened up" over the thirty-one years that they have been together.

Thirty-one years…that's a very long time to be with one person. I don't think I believe in soul mates, but watching my parents is a constant contradiction to my beliefs. They feel that they were meant to be together and fate played a huge role. The whole thing baffles me… love, eternity, forever after? Is there really one person out there you are meant to be with? Or is it all random luck?

Together my parents have built a loving, safe, upper middle class life for us. We had a pretty normal childhood that included a center hall colonial, pool in the back, and a golden retriever. All of it was quite boring. My career choice doesn't fit into the *boring, suburban, cookie-cutter world* we grew up in.

I have a younger sister, Elizabeth Ann Lair, or Lizzy. Lizzy and Mom look like sisters, except Lizzy's hair is not blonde but light brown in color. They also act like sisters and get along very well. Like mom, Lizzy is aware of her beauty, but doesn't use it to her benefit.

Beauty means nothing to my mom. Mom didn't encourage Lizzy to model and to fall victim to such a cold, hurtful industry. Like they did for me, my parents insisted that Lizzy go to college and get her degree. She obeyed without objection. The difference between my sister and I was that she was on the same page as my parents.

Lizzy graduated from Columbia University with a Masters in Psychiatry. She is now working towards her PhD. My sister is the perfect trifecta. She is attractive, intelligent and has a heart of pure gold. The man who wins her heart had better be something special, or he'll have to deal with my temper and me.

Having a psychiatrist in the family will most definitely help with my many issues. As a teen I was like a bull in a china shop doped up on Viagra. My temper has calmed down quite a bit since then, yet my libido - not so much. I've been a walking hard-on since I was twelve. For some stupid reason I ended up having a girlfriend in high school for almost two years. Her name was Jessa Perez. In hindsight, that was fucking dumb. Don't get me wrong, she was gorgeous, and we had a really good time, until we fought that is. My temper pales in comparison to hers.

Jessa and I were very immature and needed to grow up. We argued, made up, and then argued again. For two straight years, that was our relationship in a nutshell. At the time I thought we were in love.

I was so wrong.

In all fairness, I do suck at relationships. I am a serial flirt. That doesn't seem to bode well when you have a girlfriend. So her retaliation was to cheat on me. Well, she denied the rumors that she cheated on me. I didn't have proof, and my gut didn't believe her. I finally got tired of all the fighting and rumors and so I ended it right after graduation.

Jessa didn't have a problem replacing me when I dumped her. With her long black hair, chocolate brown eyes and her killer body, she is a complete knockout. She's dangerous too. She can persuade the pope to run naked through the streets of Rome.

I was determined to get over her. Once at NYU, the girls were the only thing that helped me get through. They were everywhere, and they made the hell I was in more bearable. I more than made up for those two years with Jessa. I guess I was trying to sow all the wild oats I missed in junior and senior year…and I still am.

I have not committed to a relationship since high school, and I don't see myself doing so any time soon. I just can't deal with the drama that comes with it. Being with Jessa was nothing but drama that was wrapped in a hot sex burrito.

Dumping her didn't stop her from wanting to get back together with me. There was no way I was doing that. She claimed she wasn't looking for a relationship, and only missed our sex life. She had a point. That was the only part we were good at. I caved a few times…twice to be exact. Our reunions have always been the same. There was hot sex, arguing, me screaming at her, her throwing something at me, and then me walking out. Not much had changed since we were together in high school. No one can push my buttons like Jessa can.

The last time we got together was a few days ago. We "ran" into each other at a club and ended up in her bed because I was drunk and horny. I'm not proud of the fact that I tend to think with my cock more than I should. By the end of the night, she had changed her story about only wanting sex. I barely remember what she was ranting about. Something about me being a bastard and needing to grow up. She is convinced we belong together, and after listening to her go on and on, I had a sick feeling that running into her wasn't an accident. She's delusional and a bit unstable.

That night was a huge mistake. To say that I regret it is an understatement. Hunter had to pick me up because I was so wasted. He told me to stay away from her. Actually he threw a fit and treated me like a child the entire drive home. Trey told me to get the fuck over it. His exact words were, "Shut the fuck up. So you had to fuck a complete knock-out, poor you."

Dick-head.

Hunter gets it. Trey doesn't get it.

It was a stupid move. Especially since I don't need Jessa to fuck a knockout. I am not lacking in that department. Short of obtaining a restraining order, I've done everything I could to cut her out of my life. Like a bad penny, she keeps showing up.

I should have listened to Hunter. Hunter Amatto is our drummer and my best friend. He plays the role of band manager, and keeps our asses in line. About eight years ago, we met at a bar in the city while listening to a band and hit it off immediately. I spilled my guts about wanting to ditch my law career and start a rock band. It took exactly five minutes that night for Hunter to jump into my plan and run with it.

I owe him a lot. He got me through my intimate relationship with tequila after I told my parents that I was dropping out. I thank god that Hunter had the guts to dive head first into my plan, because his push lit a fire under my ass that has gotten us where we are today. He's been an awesome friend and an even better "manager". He even came up with the band's name. It was a lucky day when I met Hunter.

So, for the record I am a firm believer of LUCK. I'm not trying to downplay how good we are as a band, but luck definitely had a part to play in our success.

Hunter's roommate moved out soon after I dropped my nuclear bomb on my parents. The timing couldn't have been more perfect, and I moved in. My mom was not happy with me, but I needed to get out of Long Island and away from them. Seeing my dad come home every day from his office was a constant reminder of what I was supposed to be doing and how I disappointed them.

It felt cathartic to move from suburbia to Brooklyn. I love where we live. We are in the Dumbo section, and it is one of the trendiest neighborhoods in the city. Our rent is hefty, but still a fraction of what an apartment of the same size would cost in Manhattan.

Our apartment is nothing special. We have a decent sized living room with a TV that's way too big, but boys *will* be boys. Our kitchen is small and a half bath sits off the main hall. Our tiny bedrooms each have their own bathroom. That's the entire apartment.

The best part is the roof. We are on the top floor of a six-floor building, and we have access to the roof. For some reason none of the other tenants ever go up there. We threw around some plastic tables and chairs. We invested in a cheap plastic couch. We put up some Christmas lights. We carry up our portable speakers. Voila'… instant hang out. It's a great quiet place where we can chill out, or more specifically where I can *entertain*. Hunter doesn't *entertain* as frequently as I do, so it's a perfect hangout for me. I fucking love it up there.

It's not like Hunter never has any girls over. I guess he is handsome by most women's standards. He is tall with spiky hair, a few piercings, and one on his lip. I don't get the attraction to piercings, or why chicks love them so much. His killer smile and blue eyes makes him a hot commodity, but he is shy as shit. It's weird how he's cocky and confident in every other aspect of his life, other than trying to pick up a chick. He waits for them to make the first move. What a waste of time.

We put an ad in the Village Voice and advertised for a guitarist and bassist. We found our guitarist first. Scott Malone is a nice Irish boy who is also from Long Island. Hunter and I were a little skeptical when we found him. He just looked too nice. Does he look like a rock star? Not so much. He has a clean-cut look that is more suitable for a cereal commercial. But damn, his talent blew us away. After hearing him play guitar, we hired him immediately.

Scott has a girlfriend named Patti Wells. Actually they are practically married. She is a petite, blond who's cute but somewhat annoying and a little too enthusiastic for my tastes. Hey, I'm not the one screwing her. It just seems Scott can never get a word in edgewise with her.

Finding our bass guitarist was quite an ordeal. Initially we hired a guy who I grew up with and who I'd rather not name. He was crazy years ago, which should have been a red flag to me. Don't get me wrong - we all like to think of ourselves as bad boy rockers, with the exception of Scott - but this guy took it to another level. That fucker almost got us arrested one night, and I really don't want to be some dude's bitch. We fired "him" and luckily we found Trey.

Trey was born and raised in New York City and had just recently moved back from California. We knew we had found our guy when we saw him playing at a bar in SoHo. He looked the part perfectly. Quite simply, Trey is dark. Tattoos everywhere, chin length black hair, black clothing, black shades, and black guitar. He is the opposite of Scott, which is good because we need him to level out the "Opie looking" field.

Trey not only looks the part, he is one awesome bassist. If we hadn't found him, someone else would have any second. He rarely cracks a smile. If he does he gets quite the reaction from our girl fans.

Yes, we all have fans. Our fans uploaded our performances on the Internet and now we get recognized even more than ever. It's freaky when we it happens, it shocks the shit out of us.

Some of our fans are extremely aggressive. I've had sex with some of them. Most of the time they move on when they see my road is a dead end. There is a constant stream of gorgeous women throwing themselves at us, more specifically at me. I always treat them with utmost respect, and I always use a condom! These women chase me and who am I to disappoint? I am not forcing any of them to do what they weren't planning on doing any way. It's amazing how many women will have a one-night stand with a complete stranger.

I lost count of how many women I've been with, and I am a little embarrassed of my promiscuousness. It hasn't stopped me though. I enjoy being in the company of a woman, for one night, maybe two, a week tops. That's as far as I'll take a relationship, for now. I don't have time to waste energy or even brain cells on relationship drama. I have more important things to worry about. My career is finally taking off and I plan on enjoying this wave. The next year of our lives will be recording an album and then touring.

Fuck yeah!

We are so ready for this. I don't regret all the dirty, sleazy, seedy bars we've played in over these last few years. Those dives made us who we are. We don't take anything for granted. Each one of us appreciates what is happening and we are loving every goddamn minute of it.

Two years ago we were playing in a band competition and won. The super famous band MACE saw us and caught a few more of our shows. They were about to start a small tour and asked us to open for them.

Except for living with a bunch of smelly guys on a bus for months, touring with MACE was fantastic. It definitely gave us tons of experience for our own tour. I had the fucking time of my life…literally.

While in LA, we were approached by a tall gorgeous blonde with ice blue eyes. She introduced herself as Jennifer Baxter. I prefer brunettes, but she is stunning. After our segment, she stalked right over to me and thrust her hand out. She looked like she wanted to eat me alive. I was just about to put my moves on her until she introduced herself as an agent and said she wanted to represent us. This is just how she works; there is simply no beating around the bush for Jennifer. Not having an agent and liking her balls, we went for it. What could it hurt?

We trusted Jen, and luckily it was the best move we made. In the past year, she got us signed by the same record label representing MACE.

Jen is not exactly a veteran in the music business, but damn she is as tenacious as they come. That definitely works in our favor. She was having drinks with a friend while on a business trip to LA on the night she found us. We trusted her and she came through.

The guys made me swear on a stack of bibles, a box of condoms, and a case of beer that I would NEVER DO JENNIFER! Jeez, I really wasn't planning on it anyway, but she sure hasn't made that easy on me. Yes, she has been the utmost professional. However, I am a master at interpreting looks and I was convinced she wanted me.

Jen has been seeing someone for almost a year now. Malcolm Reynolds is also an agent, and if you look up agent in the dictionary, it would show you Malcolm's picture. He is as tenacious as Jen, but in a sleazy sort of agent way. He's very successful at what he does, so I guess it works for him.

You would think that having a boyfriend would curtail her flirting with me, but nope. I've met him a few times. He has quite a wandering eye himself, and I wonder if Jen's tactics aren't to try and get him jealous. I guess you could say they make a perfect couple.

Now we have a three-album record contract. We have just about two albums worth of songs already, so hitting the three-album requirement will not be a problem. I am constantly writing songs. Hunter and the boys put my words to music effortlessly. They always know exactly what I'm feeling in my lyrics. Along with that, we're also under contract to rehearse in the studio for the next few months to prepare and record album number one. We will then be going on our US tour beginning in September to promote it. The tour will run from coast to coast over five months. Most of the venues are a few thousand seats. Jen feels it's better to start small and sell out. I think we could have started a bit bigger since we have a nice following now. I guess I understand her mentality.

One night while hanging out in a bar and listening to another random band, Hunter came up with a great idea. He suggested that we add a back-up singer to create a different sound that would make us stand out more. Rock bands are a dime a dozen, and we can easily get lost in the mundane. He felt my voice begged for a female companion.

He was right. It was fucking brilliant! Jennifer did not agree. This was our first disconnect. She wasn't thrilled with the idea. Once we checked with the studio and got the green light, we overrode her and went for it. There aren't many other rock bands that utilize the female voice all that much. We are creating a sound that is practically missing in the rock band world. Last week we held auditions, and one girl blew us away. Many we saw had the perfect voice. Many had the perfect look. This chick had it all.

Leila Marino.

She has a very sultry sexy voice, and her range is outrageous.

Her look is also *perfect*. She has a fucking hot, killer body with nice legs. Long, brown hair that has a natural wave extends to the middle of her back. Her eyes are a stunning golden brown, fringed in thick black lashes. Her full lips are the kind you want to suck on for hours. She did a lot of staring at me, so I was able to get a good look at her. She's perfection. She had on tight jeans with black boots to her knees. Her blouse was black and sheer and fitted, revealing some nice curves underneath.

When Leila walked in, she looked dumbstruck. My first impression was, "What a ditz!" She was gawking at me like a star struck groupie. At first, I couldn't get her to focus. She gets this "deer in headlights" look on her face that makes you want to laugh. I attributed her skittishness to nerves.

When we finally made it to the studio for her to actually sing for us, FUCK ME! She blew us away. She sang one song as back-up, and I desperately needed to hear more. Her song choice was *Dream On*, by Aerosmith. Do you know how hard it is to sing that song? She nailed it. When she belted out the rock screams, my cock twitched. It was so fucking hot.

Her audition song choice was a work of art. I joined her towards the end, and we complimented each other perfectly. Her voice is the female version of mine.

Patti, Scott's girlfriend, found Leila singing in a bar in Hoboken. I was a little skeptical about Patti's find since she tends to over react. Patti's opinion was dead on. Why this girl hasn't been discovered yet is baffling. She will need some work. She has absolutely no confidence in her talent, little self-esteem and is a klutz. The confidence and self-esteem issues aren't a problem. I can help her ten-fold in those departments. The klutziness could be an issue. However, I simply don't care. Hell, I'll put her in a padded suit if necessary.

We finally tracked Leila down yesterday and we are now waiting to meet with her. I really hope she accepts our offer. She is perfect.

A loud "Fuck you" drags me out of my daydream. This crew can be so annoying. They are arguing away about utter nonsense. I suddenly feel real antsy and stand to stretch. Damn, it feels like my ass has been in this chair for days.

"Let's grab some food and hang out at my place." Scott chimes. He is content in playing our gigs, hanging out with us and snuggling with his chick Patti, all in the same night.

"Nope. I'm heading home." I look up to see three sets of eyes staring at me. "What?"

"It's Saturday dude. What the hell?" Hunter on the other hand, can go out to a different bar every night without fail.

"As much as I'd love to spend a romantic evening with you three, I'm going to work out, get something to eat and then call that chick from last weekend, Ella? Emma? Whatever the hell her name is. I'm going to invite her over and relax." I emphasize "the relax" with air quotes.

"Relax my ass." Hunter smirks. "Make sure you close your door dude, and stay out of the living room. I don't need to see your junk again when I get home."

Last night Hunter walked in on my friend Heather and me having sex on our couch. Heather calmly pulled herself off of me and without flinching sauntered to my room while smiling at Hunter. In the process, she left me completely exposed in all of my own naked glory. Hunter grabbed a potholder and threw it at me to cover up. Really, what did he think that would cover up? So I left it on the floor and followed my friend into my room. The look on his face was priceless.

"That wasn't my fault. Heather is an exhibitionist. She likes to do it in every room and doesn't care who is watching." I give them my full dimple smile. It really only works on chicks and the guys hate it when I lay it on them, so I do it often. I am a bit of a ball buster.

***

After my workout, I scroll to my Ella/Emma entry on my phone and dial the number. When she answers I smoothly announce, "Hey babe, it's Jack. How are you?"

"Hi Jack. What a nice surprise. I'm so much better now hearing your sexy voice." She seductively says into the phone.

"Want to come over?"

"I'd love to. Be there soon."

I guess she doesn't have plans or she's ditching whomever she's with. Ella or Emma is a gorgeous, leggy brunette that I met last weekend at our gig. She was up against the stage and stared at me the entire time. I walked up to her once our show ended. Before long she was in my bed. We didn't have a lot of conversation, which is why I can't remember her damn name. The sex that night was mind-blowing. Also, I pegged her to be about a one and a half on her "relationship scale". The combination of the two is the only reason I called her tonight.

First off, I usually don't see one night stands for a repeat. I have really good relationship-seeking radar. I can usually tell if a woman is in search of a relationship within fifteen minutes of meeting her. I don't want to lead anyone on, or raise her expectations. There are certain red flags and I am a pro at detecting them. At a one and a half, Ella/Emma definitely passed the test.

Secondly, obviously the sex has to be good.

I have just enough time to grab something to eat, jump into the shower, and wrap a towel around my waist when the intercom buzzes.

Anxious to get down to business, I answer the door in just a towel. Why get dressed when I will be naked in a few minutes?

"Hey gorgeous, how are you?" Leaning in, I give her a kiss on her cheek. She is wearing a black mini skirt that barely covers her fine ass, a black tank top that is showing off her assets nicely and black heels with the sharpest point I have ever seen. They look like weapons; they also make her very tall.

While I'm checking her out, she is checking me out and focuses on my towel.

"Thanks, Jack. I'm so glad you called. Tonight is looking to turn out much better than I expected." She flashes me her super white smile, probably fake. I know her boobs are most definitely fake. I prefer natural, but it doesn't matter in the least to me since she is smoking hot.

"I hope I didn't pull you away from something important."

"Nope, no worries."

Wasting no additional time with pleasantries, she rubs up against me and kisses me flush on the lips. Dipping her finger inside the edge of my towel and running it from side to side, she instantly has my attention. It's less than ten minutes later when we find ourselves in my bedroom and Ella/Emma is giving me a noteworthy blowjob.

This is exactly what I needed tonight, and I'm relishing in the feeling of her lips wrapped around me. Lying back, I close my eyes and I see… Leila.

LEILA??? WHAT THE FUCK?!!

I am so surprised by seeing Leila inside my head that I actually call out her name.

Hot chick lifts her head and says, "Leila? Who the fuck is Leila? I'm Ella."

Oh crap!

"Sorry baby, I meant Ella." Placating her, thankfully she continues with her task while I remain baffled by my vision. It must be because I spoke to her yesterday, right? I was just remembering her audition earlier, right? That can be the only logical explanation for seeing Leila while I'm getting the best fucking blowjob from Ella!

Deciding to not waste a good blowjob, I close my eyes and settle back to enjoy what Ella is determined to finish. And I might as well continue with my fantasy because I am so *going* to hell.

Chapter 3-Leila

This week's Sunday brunch with dad is interesting, to say the least. We are both purposefully avoiding the elephant in the room. I have no new information to share with him, since my meeting isn't until tomorrow. My silence on the topic of my new career is the only encouragement dad needs to ignore it and wish it away. But he keeps zoning out. His gaze shifts nervously from his plate to his coffee and back again. I'm completely aware of the turmoil swirling in his head. He can't fool me.

"So Lei, Sal said Saturday was the largest crowd he's ever had. That's amazing." He slowly chews on a piece of bacon and zones out again.

Saturday was amazing. It was standing room only. I don't know if it was because I was on such a high from hearing about my audition, or if we rocked the place, but I had one of the best nights ever. I even allowed myself to hang around afterwards and have a few drinks with the entire gang. We were celebrating my "phone call" as well as having the best turnout we have ever had at The Zone. Sal was so happy that he bought us all a round of shots. That has *never* happened before, *ever*. I chose not to tell dad the details of our little celebration. I don't want to add fuel to his "denial" fire.

"Yep, it's pretty amazing. The boys just loved the standing room only crowd. I hope their egos don't get too big for the bar."

"Nah, they are good kids. I'm sure they'll take it in stride." Dad loves the boys in the band, and they feel the same about him. Having known them for years, he is proud of the men they have become, even Matt. In all fairness, dad would have killed Matt by now if he were aware of the details of our relationship.

Dad would have preferred it if the guys had gone to college and gotten degrees. But he's proud that they are not into drugs, or squandering their time doing nothing. They may be in a rock band, but these boys work hard.

Dad levels his gaze on me, and I know what's coming. It's here and he is finally going to address the issue. Clearing his throat, three times, he mumbles, "Um, so, I know this band that is interested in you is due to tour soon. I guess that means you would be gone too?"

Oh boy.

"Um, dad, let's wait and see what they have to say to me tomorrow? I really don't want to jump to any conclusions." I look down into my bowl of yogurt and granola. I'm afraid to make eye contact with him. I'm afraid of the look I will see in his eyes. I know this is his way of prepping himself for what's to come, but I simply can't discuss this with him yet.

We finish our meal with some awkward silence. This is rare for us, as we can usually discuss just about anything. It's times like this when I wish that Evan were here. He has a knack for shifting the focus away from me when I need that the most.

After I kiss dad goodbye and I let him hug me a bit tighter and longer than is normal, I jump into my car and drive home. I can't seem to swallow the huge lump that has firmly lodged itself in my throat. He's going to be lost without me. It's not realistic to think I can be here for him and never leave the confines of northern Jersey. This is when I wish he had other children, or at least a girlfriend to keep him busy. I worry that he'll be permanently molded to his recliner watching the Yankees or Food Network. I'll have to have a chat with a few key people in his life to be sure to keep tabs on him.

Trying to re-direct my thoughts, I begin to think about my meeting tomorrow and I immediately see Jack's face, his legs, his arms, his chest and his mighty fine ass. Remembering the comatose, stupefied, idiot that I became, I struggle to figure out how I'm going to be able to act normal when I face him tomorrow.

UGH! It's embarrassing how much this man turns me on. Since my audition, I've thought about him so many times I've lost count. I find myself constantly wondering what he is doing. Pathetically, most thoughts of him come at night as I'm settling in to fall asleep. My relationship dry spell isn't helping my Jack Lair crush. I couldn't be hornier if I tried. My said situation is in dire straits, and I'm not the type of girl to sleep around or to take matters into her own hands.

So instead of succumbing to my yearnings, cravings, desires, I decide to clean my apartment, bake enough cookies to supply a grammar school bake sale, and watch *The Notebook* for the three-hundredth time. Glaring at the clock like it is responsible for my lack of orgasms, I literally grunt to see it's still only five pm. I decide to call Evan and ask him to come over and without hesitation, he's on his way. He only lives in Weehawken and is at my apartment in less than fifteen minutes.

Evan is all ears as I unleash every detail of my breakfast with dad over bad Chinese take-out. He is quick to defend dad and reminds me how hard this is on him. He also makes sure that I know he gets where I'm coming from as well. Evan is diplomatic, if nothing else.

"Damn Lei. I'm going to miss the hell out of you. How am I ever going to get through all those months without you?"

Leaving Evan will be harder than leaving dad will be. "I'm going to miss you so much Ev. I am scared to death. I am on the verge of freaking out about this whole thing."

I reluctantly tell him all about Mr. Sex on Legs. At some points, Evan's face looks like he is about to hurl.

I know what he is thinking. "How the hell can my dad, and he himself, allow me to tour with that man, for months and months if he is walking sex?"

But he doesn't say it.

Because just like Evan has the knack to support me and tell me things I do need to hear, he also has the knack to keep to himself what I don't need to hear.

***

On Monday morning I shower, pluck, shave, primp and polish every inch of my body. I stare at my closet as I always do, in hopes that new, expensive, trendy clothes have miraculously generated overnight. I'm left disappointed by my selection. In desperation, I pull out one of my best professional outfits. I don't own many, as much of my wardrobe is either casual stuff or performance uniforms. I finally choose a black pencil skirt that falls right above my knees with a white cotton fitted blouse and my black patent stilettos that make me feel like a naughty schoolteacher. In all of my excitement, I didn't think the clothing part through. There's really nothing I can do about it at this point, since a trip to the mall isn't possible.

With a deep breath, I grab my bag and run out the door.

The ride into the city feels like an eternity. I've released the f-bomb more times during my commute than I have my entire life. I allowed plenty of time for traffic but it was horrendous, and I manage to arrive only a few minutes early.

Of course all the spots on the streets are taken, and I don't have time to circle, so I pull into a lot as close as possible and hope it won't cost me a small fortune. I pluck the valet ticket out of the attendant's hand and sprint towards the studio in my stiletto's as I pray to the heavens not fall. A few whistles and catcalls later, all of which I ignore, I slow my pace a half block from the studio, check my face in a window store front and take another deep breath.

I grab the door handle just as a firm grip grabs it as well without ever knowing that *he* was watching this entire episode. Surprised, I flip my head to the left and gasp out loud as I come face to face with Jack. Feeling that same jolt of electricity zip up my arm and down to my crotch as I experienced during my audition, I quickly pull my hand free from his grip as he smiles down at me.

No doubt, I am beet red from running and seeing him. He looks directly into my eyes, and cajoles, "Nice to see you in one piece Miss Marino. I'm impressed you can run in those shoes." He winks and pulls the door open for me.

Oh God…he did see me.

It's funny how I could sprint three city blocks in these heels, yet one look at Mr. Pretty, and I can't seem to balance on them while standing still. I carefully make my way into the lobby, surprisingly without injury.

"So, are you ready for this?" I can feel his breath on me from his whisper and it sends goosebumps all over my entire body…and yep, here comes the clenching.

He smells so good. It's clean and masculine and it's overwhelming me. I quickly step away so I can clear my thoughts. I can't walk into that room stupefied again.

"I'm ready." I nod my head and attempt to ignore my raging hormones. Jack is smiling while assessing my outfit. The tables have turned, and it's now his turn to eye-fuck me in the same lobby. His gaze makes me feel exposed and naked. I have to summon every fiber of my being to ignore the electric pulses running through my body, specifically my lower body and to force my legs to literally move and follow behind him.

As we walk past evil witch Sally, Jack greets her and of course she smiles for him. I don't spare her a glance, but I doubt she even notices my indifference. Out of the corner of my eye, I can see her eyes firmly glued to Jack's ass.

Jack leads me down the hall, but this time we turn right into a small conference room. The same familiar faces are in the room. The band lines one side of the table. The stunning blonde is at the head. This leaves the side that is closer to the door with three empty chairs. Jack turns and motions for me to sit. I pull out a chair closer to the blonde, and he pulls out the chair that's to my immediate right.

All eyes in the room are on me and my nerves jump-start my annoying foot tapping habit.

The blonde says, "Hello, Leila. My name is Jennifer Baxter, and I am the agent for Devil's Lair. Can we get you anything to drink?"

Yes, a shot of vodka please.

"No thank you. I'm fine."

As I size Jennifer up I am feeling dreadfully inadequate. She is truly striking. Her blonde hair looks like silk. I'm certain she's never experienced Jersey frizz on a hot July day. Her eyes look and feel like ice. They're not warm and fuzzy at all. Her red painted lips are turned up at the corners is an amused smile. Her nails are perfectly manicured. Her clothing screams power. I sit up straighter in my chair in a pathetic attempt to shake the intimidation I feel.

Jennifer turns to her left and says, "This is Hunter Amatto, and he's our drummer." Hunter is gorgeous. I didn't get a good look at him during my auditions. He definitely looks rocker enough with his piercings and spiky hair, but not in a scary way.

"Hey, Leila. Nice to meet you." Hunter smiles warmly at me and I return the gesture. I have a gut feeling that I'll like him. He reminds me a little of Evan.

"Then we have Scott Malone, our guitarist." He waves and grins as well.

"Hey, Leila." I can see him with Patti, although it looks as if he wouldn't get a word in edgewise.

"This is Trey Taylor, our bass player."

Trey…that's his name.

He doesn't lift his shades. He doesn't smile. He simply nods his head and for some reason this makes me blush awkwardly.

"And lastly we have Jack Lair, our lead singer." I turn towards Mr. Sex God and he is smiling the CCDS smile.

Crap…

Pressing my thighs together causes me to shift uncomfortably in my chair. What shade comes after bright red? Purple? Because I'm sure that's the color my cheeks are right now.

His eyes are so beautiful and hypnotic. I don't realize my gaze is still focused on Jack's eyes until I hear Jennifer clear her throat.

"Leila, as you know the band feels you would be the best fit for their back-up singer. We are trying to change our sound and we feel your voice is the right complement to Jack's. This meeting is merely an informal presentation of contract. We will proceed to Mr. Crowse, our band's attorney, for the formal signing should you accept our offer.

"The band is due to tour in September. Until then, there will be grueling rehearsals, almost every day of the week. Jack is quite the work horse, and expects all his members to be one hundred percent committed to the integrity of their music." She smiles warmly at Jack.

Hmmm…so she *can* be warm and fuzzy?

"Devil's Lair is on the cusp of super stardom." she continues. "Your commitment to this band will bring a huge change to your life. We want you to be as prepared for that as possible. This contract is a detailed account on what those obligations entail. Although Devil's Lair is more recognizable than they were last year and will be playing in major cities across the country, the studio cannot afford to contract three buses. We want you to be completely comfortable with the traveling arrangements during the tour. You will be roommates with these four gentlemen and their drivers. There will be another bus following that will contain our tour manager, our equipment manager and the rest of the stage staff. I will not be traveling with the band, but I will be meeting up with them at key locations throughout the tour."

I internally sigh with relief. Thank God for small miracles.

"This contract is also here to protect you from any unfortunate events or situations that can occur, as well as protect the band in the same right. Leila, this isn't intended to scare you. This is a mere precaution and necessity to ensure your safety, as well as ours. Please understand, all your actions and decisions are secondary to the band's success if you sign. We will terminate your contract and part in the most peaceful of ways if you decide that you cannot continue with your commitment, or we deem you are unfit for the band at the end of the tour. If for some unforeseen reason, you or we terminate your contract before the end of the tour, you will leave the band and immediately sever all affiliations to Devil's Lair. Your compensation will continue for thirty days after your termination date.

"Salary, benefits and insurance details are all in the contract as are tour dates and the schedule of cities we will be playing in. The band will cover wardrobe requirements and personal grooming. The band has full authority to present you in the best manner they feel represents Devil's Lair." She pauses to ensure that I understand her words.

My head is swimming with all this information. My heart is pounding frantically through my chest wall, and externally I do everything in my power to try and remain cool and calm. My attempts aren't working very well. I have my legs crossed, and I'm subconsciously jiggling my foot again, which causes my skirt to ride higher than I'd like.

A sideways glance at Jack reveals that he is staring at my exposed thighs. His heated gaze causes my cool and calm façade to slowly burst into flames. I'm hoping we are almost done here, because I will not be able to keep up this act for much longer. Turning back towards Jennifer, I internally beg, *please be done...please be done.*

I gratefully watch as she slips the thick contract towards me and I quickly reach for it with shaking fingers.

"Thank you for this opportunity. I will review it with my lawyer and get back to you as soon as possible." I could very easily sign it right here, right now and screw all the legal mumbo jumbo. I don't have a doubt in my mind I will be taking this job, but I can't show my cards this quickly and I really need to get out of this room.

Jennifer looks at Jack and asks, "Gentlemen, is there anything you would like to add?"

Jack smirks and says, "Nope. I'm good."

He looks at his band mates, and one by one they agree with him.

Jennifer plasters her fake smile on her face and puts her hand out for me to shake. "It was great meeting you. I ask you to please have this signed and returned to us in seventy-two hours. Of course if you choose not to proceed with us, please let us know within that time frame as well, as we will have to continue our search."

The way I abruptly stand, prompts everyone but Trey to follow. Hunter glares at him and he callously shrugs. He should hook up with Sally, as they would make a nice *couple from hell.*

Thanking them again, I turn to leave the room and hastily forget the contract on the table. Jack snaps it up for me. "I'll walk you out."

We walk side by side in silence until we reach the lobby. Jack holds out the contract for me and our fingers touch sending another jolt of electricity right through my arm down to my sex.

"Leila, you already have my cell number. Call me if you have any questions. Jennifer can come off a bit strong, but she only has our best interests at heart. If you need to talk to someone less intimidating, call me."

Less intimidating? Is he serious?

I nod and thank him without attempting to shake his hand. The last time I did, his grip almost caused me to almost fall flat on my ass. Today I'm wearing a skirt and the last thing I need is for Jack to become acquainted with my clenching crotch.

With a shy smile, I walk out of the studio and wait one block before I bend over and hyperventilate violently.

Feeling a bit better by the time I get back to my car, I analyze the meeting on my drive back to Hoboken. I managed to remain somewhat professional and controlled. Sure my nerves were a bit obvious, but there was definite improvement from the last time I was here. Of course I have no idea how I'm going to be on a tour bus with Mr. Sex God or be in his company twenty-four hours a day and not get fired in the process. I'm pretty sure inside this thick, fat contract there is a clause stating that attacking Jack or his junk in any way is cause for immediate termination. Some super models insure their legs or boobs. I wouldn't doubt the studio has insured Jack's penis. I actually giggle at that thought. I wonder how much it's worth. I can't wait to get home to read this thing and find out.

All in all, I'm ecstatic with my new job offer. Life is so unpredictable. Who would have imagined a week ago that *I* would be a member of Devil's Lair? My dreams are finally coming true.

Chapter 4- Jack

That girl is very attractive. It was very distracting, to say the least. I can still see Leila very clearly in my mind as I walk back to the conference room. She looked so damn sexy in her outfit. The way her legs looked in her short skirt and heels and how her tight blouse hugged her curves, not to mention how she would pull her bottom lip in between her teeth when she got nervous, or the random flush of her cheeks was all very distracting.

Overall, I do think that went well though. Jennifer was a bit intimidating, but Leila held her own. There were moments when she did look terrified. I just hope she doesn't get home with that contract and run in the opposite direction. Seeing it all on paper can most definitely scare the hell out of her.

As I get to the conference room, I can overhear Jennifer voicing my concerns. For some reason it irks me hearing her saying it. "She is very inexperienced and not in a good way."

"We were all inexperienced at one point, Jen." I quip back while walking into the room and taking the chair I sat in earlier.

Catching my tone, she turns to look at me and narrows her eyes. "Yes, we were, but she hasn't a clue about what she's going to sign on to. I worry her inexperience and insecurities will be a hindrance to the tour."

"Hindrance? Oh, just relax, Jen. You're overreacting."

The guys all sit quietly watching our exchange. I know Jennifer doesn't like this whole idea so her comment is nothing new to me. But does my band feel the same way?

I ask them as much.

Hunter looks over at Jennifer and shakes his head. She has never intimidated him and he never had a problem standing up to her. Adding Leila was his idea, after all.

"Nope, I think she is perfect. I told you this. She is sweet and shy, but gorgeous and sexy as hell. The fans are going to love her. Plus her voice is the best we have heard. She'll be great."

Wait a minute… Hunter thinks Leila is "sexy as hell"?

I turn to the other two members of my band. "Scott? Trey?"

Scott looks over at Jennifer and it's clear that he is struggling with what he's about to say because his skin suddenly turns pink.

"I get Jennifer's concerns. We wouldn't want her to bolt two weeks into the tour because she can't hack it. It wouldn't hurt to make sure she understands the commitment before she signs." Scott says playing devil's advocate.

I look over at Trey and he shrugs. "Whatever man. She can sing and she has the goods. Cut the drama." His words come out in the typical - I don't give fuck, just let me play my damn guitar - Trey fashion.

Hunter looks over at him and shakes his head, before he turns to Jennifer. "Jack will call her. He'll make sure she doesn't have any concerns or questions that she wasn't comfortable voicing in this room. Cool?"

Me? Why am I calling her?

Jen nods. "Fine. Obviously you feel that she would open up more to Jack than to me, so Jack, make the call."

Yes ma'am.

She grabs her copy of the contract and heads for the door. Flipping her hair behind her shoulders and giving us her full-on Jennifer charm, she smiles sweetly and touts, "Ten am, tomorrow morning. We have a lot to do."

She saunters out of the room knowing we are most definitely checking out her ass.

I stand to close the door so I can have an honest pow-wow with my band. "Does anyone have any concerns that I haven't heard yet?"

No one speaks. "Now or never. Excluding Hunter, do you two feel Leila is it, or do we keep looking?" Still nothing. I point to the door and add, "Jennifer has her reservations, and I get that. But if the four of us aren't on the same page, this is a huge waste of time."

I focus my gaze on Scott until he finally speaks. "I agree with Hunter. I just think she looked terrified in here, and I worry she's going to run out on us."

"Scott, there are no guarantees. Hell, how do I know one of you won't run?" I know damn well that would never happen, but I just want to make a point.

Scott stands and retorts, "None of us are running. I get that there are no guarantees. I think we made the right choice and I'm not changing my mind. I just feel like the poor girl was scared to death in here." He points to the door for emphasis. "That woman can be as scary as hell. Someone should make sure Leila isn't sitting in a corner shaking from this experience. That's all I'm sayin'."

Ok, he has a point. I decide not to bother with Trey again, as I'm sure I won't get any more from him since he already gave such a poignant statement.

With a loud exhalation I concede. "Fine, I'll call her to make sure she is ok. Not sure she would even open up to me, but I'll give it a shot." I'm done with this conversation. "I need food and lots of beer. Let's get out of here."

We pile into Scott's van, and he drives us towards his apartment in midtown. We may have to start bright and early tomorrow, but we can chill the rest of this gorgeous day. Scott lots the van and we walk over to the pub that has decent bar food a few blocks away from his place. We eat and drink and laugh for hours. Even though all the stuff happening to us is fantastic, it's still been a stressful few weeks. It feels good to act normal. Even Trey is relishing in the normalness of our afternoon.

We are a little buzzed by the time we stumble out of the pub. We draw attention to ourselves because we are loud and obnoxious and noisily head over to one of our favorite rock bars called Granite. They have a rooftop bar, the music is awesome, the personnel know us well and I know one particular waitress intimately. I haven't seen her in a while.

Scott finds a corner table facing the stage, and we sit like we own the place. Trini our favorite waitress makes her way over and straddles my lap. She is a pixie of a thing with spiky black hair, a few tattoo's, piercings that are visible, others that aren't (which I've seen firsthand), and an attractive face.

She once showed me her high school graduation picture, and I couldn't believe it was the same person. Her natural hair color is light and fair. Her parents weren't thrilled with her transformation, but it didn't stop her. This is who she is and you gotta love that. We've had a few romps in the sack and she never expects more. She is a free spirit who goes with the flow. My kind of girl.

"Hey guys, I haven't seen you in like forever. Where have you been?"

"We've been a little busy getting ready for the tour Trin." My hands are on her ass as she continues to straddle me, and the contact with her crotch is really turning me on. I lean in to whisper in her ear, "I definitely have missed you. Are you free tonight?" Nibbling on her earlobe, she responds by rubbing herself against me in a very suggestive manner. It's such a turn on.

Leaning in she whispers back, "Yes and if you continue doing that you are going to get me fired. I get off at ten. I did the day shift today."

"I don't know if I can wait that long."

She slowly licks my top lip and gets up off my lap leaving me hard as a rock.

Hunter is watching me with amusement. "Does she ever say no to you?"

Smiling I say, "No, and I haven't said no to her either. It's mutual you know. We each scratch an itch that needs scratching."

Shaking his head he simply says, "Sometimes I hate you."

Sputtering out my beer from laughing out loud, Hunter picks up a coaster and flings it at my head.

Over the course of the night, several girls make their way to our table. Quite a few pass me their phone numbers. Once they walk away I pass their numbers over to Hunter.

After the fourth time he wads it up and throws it at me. "Fuck off. I don't need your leftovers."

Attempting to stand, I wobble over to Hunter and pat him on the back. "Just tryin' to help a friend in need, and you my friend need to get laid."

"Fuck you."

"No thanks. You're not my type." I lean over to give Hunter a nice wet kiss on the cheek and he turns to take a swing at me. Laughing my ass off, I stumble backwards to avoid his fist. I am thoroughly buzzed and goad him even further without remorse. "You sure are pissy."

Trini appears just in time. "Trin get him out of here before I kill him."

Trini grabs my hand and says, "Ok, let's go Romeo."

Hunter and Scott are staying. Trey disappeared an hour ago.

I turn toward the guys and slur, "See ya' mañana."

"Don't be late Jack. I mean it."

What the hell? Who died and left him boss?

With a wide smile I blow him a kiss and watch him flip me the bird. Trini pulls me out of the bar. On our way out, we get a few looks from some of the girls who passed me their numbers. It's funny seeing their reaction to Trini. I love that she couldn't give a shit.

She has a studio apartment across town. The minute we jump in a cab, we are all over each other. She immediately has me worked up into a frenzy. I barely remember throwing money at the cabbie or climbing the three flights of stairs to her apartment. By the time we reach her door, she's already torn my shirt off and is working on my belt.

We walk and make out and walk our way to her bed. She pushes me hard so that I land on her bed on my back and I laugh out loud from the way my aroused body bounces. I'm definitely drunk, but hopefully not enough that it will hamper my performance tonight.

Trini immediately strips for me and my laughter quickly fades. She has a very hot little body. She's not well endowed, but her proportions are perfect. If at all possible, my excitement grows seeing her in a sexy red bra and stringy thing.

"Were you expecting me tonight?" My eyes devour her from head to toe.

"A girl can dream. I definitely missed you and I've had a crappy week." She straddles my hips and begins sucking on my lips. Make-outs aren't my thing, yet making out with Trini is always hot and steamy. We are completely breathless by the time she pulls away. She pulls my pants off and trails her fingertip down my length, causing my cock to twitch beneath her touch.

"Commando?" she asks with a smirk.

"A guy can dream."

Trini straddles my waist and slowly rubs against me causing me to lose all conscious thoughts.

"Oh god…"

Pulling her pierced nipple in between my lips elicits her own moans. The more I suck, the more she rubs.

"Trin, you're torturing me."

Smiling deviously, she quickly kisses my lips and turns her body so she is now straddling my chest, but facing the other way. Trini loves having oral sex almost more than regular sex. It's her thing.

This is gonna be fun.

She bends her body until her ass is in my face. Tracing her tattoo on her lower back with my tongue, she responds by wrapping her lips around my cock.

"Oh fuck…" I am wound so tight, and I am so ready, it's going to take every conscious thought and effort not to explode too quickly.

Trying to focus on her, I move the red strap of her thingy over to slip a finger inside simultaneously pulling her between my lips. She moans so deeply that I can feel the vibrations through her mouth around my erection. She enthusiastically does her part as I try to do mine.

Until a quick flash of Leila's face halts my efforts.

Fuck…not again.

Because of the lack of oxygen to my brain and the visual in my head, it's almost impossible for me to concentrate on pleasuring Trini. Her mouth, all the beer I consumed, the fact she worked me up to frenzy before we even hit her bed, Leila's face in my thoughts, all of it culminates and I release with a very violent orgasm all too soon.

Throwing my head back, I grunt, "Oh, fuck."

She doesn't stop until the last shudder leaves my body. I can feel her smile against me, as I lay lifeless and try to regain my senses.

Trini attempts to turn around, but I grip her hips immobilizing her so I can finish what I started. This prompts her to continue her oral skills on me in a leisurely manner, bringing the blood flow right back to my flaccid dick.

Wanting to return the favor, I keep my eyes open, not wanting to picture anyone but Trini at the moment. She deserves an orgasm. More importantly she deserves my focus.

I tug her other piercing between my lips as she gasps around my cock. Soon after my lips, mouth, tongue and fingers bring her to the brink, her legs start to shake from her own orgasm that rolls on and on.

Collapsing on me, Trini pants trying to catch her breath. Neither of us moves for the longest time. Guiltily, I welcome the interruption so I can process what the hell is going on inside my demented head. I suddenly feel exhausted.

Trini slowly turns and stretches leisurely on top of my body, pulling me from my thoughts. "MMMMmmm…that felt so good."

Having a hard time keeping my eyes open, I think I nod, but I can't be too sure. Trini kisses me erotically to capture my attention. "I'm not done with you yet."

She moves to her nightstand to retrieve a condom and rolls it on while I'm still fighting sleep. Since my cock has a mind of his own, her hands on me stirs him up even though I'm still extremely dazed and confused.

"I hope I can do this." I mumble and she giggles.

With her panties still on, she straddles me and says, "I have faith in you, Jack."

She's good. It's a short while later when she has me wide-awake and on the brink again. I grab her hips and flip her onto her back. She arches and I thrust hard and fast and Trini keeps pace. It's quick and effective. She climaxes first and I follow soon after.

As we are lying on our backs and panting side-by-side, she purrs, "So good, Jack."

I nod and focus on a spot on her ceiling. Suddenly I want to leave. It's not Trini. It's me. I'm coming off my buzz and I'm really, *really* tired and *really* confused.

"Do you want a beer?"

"Do you have a coke? I'd rather that." I remove my condom and drop it gently to the floor.

"You got it." She hops off the bed, picks up the condom and disappears into her kitchen.

"Trin, I would have thrown that out."

"No worries." She calls out.

My mind starts to wander to Leila again as I'm lying here waiting for my coke. I wonder what she is doing right now. Is she kinky? Is she strictly missionary? Why am I thinking of Leila again, anyway?

Trini returns and hands me my coke as I continue to stare into space. "Hey, where did you go off to?"

I wrap my arm around her waist and pull her closer. "Just a lot on mind, sorry." She turns on her side and examines my face.

"Spill it, Lair. I've known you for a long time. The Jack I know would be taking me from behind right now and not lying here thinking."

I turn on my side to face her.

How do I explain something, when I don't even know what's happening myself? How do I explain I keep thinking about a girl who I barely know, and I have no idea why I keep thinking about her? How do I explain to Trini that I've pictured Leila's face now during sex with two different women, including with her?

I know I can tell Trini because this is just the kind of relationship we have. There have been many times after we screwed each other's brains out, that she would unleash her latest guy problems on me. She has been pining over this asshole at the bar for months and the idiot isn't biting. I told her he was probably gay.

But what the hell am I admitting to? Damn it…I have no idea what this is.

"Well?"

Maybe voicing my bewildered thoughts will help me understand them better?

Taking a deep breath, I lie on my back and stare up at the spot on the ceiling again. "We wanted to hire a new back-up singer. The girl we decided on is fantastic. She is so fucking talented. She is reviewing the contract as we speak, and we hope to God she accepts our offer. Her name is Leila and she is beautiful." I turn on my side again and look into my friend's eyes. There is no judgment there, just concern.

"Trin, I can't stop thinking about her. I barely know her, but there is something about her. I don't know what the hell is wrong with me."

She continues to look at me. "Does she know how you feel?"

I scoff, "Feel? We hardly know each other. There's no *feel*? I just keep thinking about her."

"You're attracted to her…so?"

I push my hand through my hair. I've been attracted to women before, and have never spent even thirty seconds thinking about them. It's not just an attraction with Leila. I really don't know what it is.

"So? So we have to work together."

"If she gets you all hot and bothered, come see me. I'll help you." She deadpans and I smile weakly.

"Nothing? Huh, now I'm worried." Settling in the nook of my arm she adds, "Stop stressing. Once you get to know her you may hate her."

Sighing I nod, not feeling all that confident in Trini's words of wisdom to me. Truth is, the more I get to know her, the more I want her.

Chapter 5- Leila

The same contract that gave me complete joy yesterday is now causing me to sweat under my boobs. There is a section that details the possibility of having companions in our bunks. They can travel with the band as long as the rest of the members are okay with it. So I get to say yay or nay to Trey's indiscretions? Yeah, I don't think so. I'd rather walk on hot coals.

On the flip side, they would have the same rights over me. I'm sure that will not be a problem, as I don't sleep around or plan to. But what if I meet "the one"? What if he is head over heels in love with me and can't be apart from me for even one minute? Those guys get to toss him off the bus if they want to? That might suck.

My phone rings as I'm sitting here staring at the stack of papers as if they would explain themselves to me and jolts me back to my apartment. My heart starts pounding like a drum from the ringtone that is playing loud and clear. When I saved Jack's phone number into my phone, I assigned a song called *Tie Me Down*. It's a very sexually explicit song. I thought it was apropos and the perfect choice. I can *NEVER* have him hear it or know about it!

Carefully monitoring my breathing, I answer, "Hello?"

"Hey, it's Jack. How are you?" His tone is too cheerful.

"Hi Jack. I'm great. A bit overwhelmed, but great. What's up?"

"Just checking in to make sure you don't have any questions." He did tell me to call him if I had questions or concerns. The fact that he is calling me first tells me that he's thinking about me. This pathetically puts a firm smile on my face.

"Well I have tons of questions, but none that you can really answer." I laugh to show him I am kidding, sort of. How can I tell him that I'm concerned with where I'll be storing my tampons on the bus?

"Are you sure? I am more than happy to help."

Oh boy…he has no idea how much I would like him to help.

"Well I am putting together a list for my lawyer. Once I review with him, I'll call you with any other questions he can't answer. Is that ok?"

"Sure Leila, that's fine. Whatever you need. But I just wanted to let you know I meant it when I said I'm here for you if you have any concerns and or questions. This can be a bit daunting, but I want to remind you how talented you are. This is going to be great, for all of us." He pauses and I'm too moved to respond.

He chuckles at my silence, and says, "Well, have a great day. I hope to hear from you soon."

I finally respond lamely, "Ok, thanks. Bye, Jack." He promptly hangs up and it takes me a few minutes to wake up from my daydream.

As a distraction, I decide to call my dad to discuss what time we were meeting for dinner tomorrow. I was going to bring the contract with me, but decided against it. I don't want to freak him out unnecessarily, and I know he will be tormented from just hearing the details. By the time we meet, I would have seen the lawyer and maybe I would have some intelligible information I could relay to dad. Not sure it matters, short of telling him I've changed my mind, there really is nothing I could say to alleviate his stress.

I already made an appointment with an attorney that Evan's mom, Barb, recommended. I immediately called her when I realized I needed one. We are set to sit down tomorrow morning at his offices in Fort Lee. His name is Mr. Morrow, and Barb said he is a good lawyer and would help me with anything I needed. He asked if could have the contract picked up today, so he would be able to review it before our meeting.

Barb is a very sweet, kind person. I have never met Evan's dad, Doug. He took off when Evan was a baby, and never speaks to him. Barb raised Evan alone and still lives in the house where he grew up, one block away from my dad.

There was a time a few years ago I thought of my dad and Barb together. She is attractive enough, in a motherly kind of way. She is neither skinny nor overweight. Her strawberry blond hair is cut into a stylish bob, and she has very nice blue eyes. They crinkle in the corners when she smiles and light up her whole face.

Dad and Barb have been friends for a long time, both having grown up in Cliffside. He doesn't elaborate on details of their friendship. I don't have any memories of Barb or Doug being friends with my parents. Dad did say Barb and mom were friends, but they were not BFF's. I thought that was strange. With Barb being such a warm friendly person, I would've assumed that she and my mom got along perfectly. Apparently Dad didn't care for Doug at all, and had no desires to socialize with him.

I asked my dad why I didn't know Evan earlier than when I met him in school. It seems that the lives of our parents were somewhat intermingled. Dad explained that he and mom avoided them at all costs when Doug was in the picture.

He was not a nice man. He was not abusive towards Barb or Evan in any way. He was simply indifferent.

Evan became very ill when he was a baby. Mom being a nurse helped Barb through the entire ordeal. Barb and Doug only married because of her pregnancy with Evan. Their marriage had been strained prior to his illness. During it, Doug was unsupportive. Thankfully Evan's infection was treatable, but there was still stress in their marriage. It wasn't long after that when Doug took off.

Barb kept her distance once he left. Mom and Dad would check in with her to make sure she and Evan were ok. Evan and I rarely talk about his dad. He doesn't want to waste brain cells on him.

We became friends after mom died and my dad started socializing with Barb on occasion. They never did anything even remotely romantic. It was only a lunch at the diner, a trip to the mall, a Yankee game every so often.

It seems too perfect, though. Here are two old friends, who are both single, living a block away from each other, and their kids are best friends. Maybe Dad just doesn't find Barb sexually attractive? I understand you can't force an attraction, and I don't feel that way towards Evan either, but neither of them has made any efforts to meet someone else.

I've since stopped obsessing over it. Evan would laugh at my matchmaking schemes. Some of them were doozies! I would confess to him how perfect it would be for all of us to live together, as one big happy family. He, being a typical guy, had no desire to "set his mom up" with my dad or any guy. I felt differently and I've told him so, over and over. I also mentioned he was selfish and he said I was a hopeless romantic…men!

Once I finally get my act together, I start a list of questions and concerns to bring to the lawyer. It wasn't a very long list, since I have no clue what I am doing. I am depending on Mr. Morrow to help in this area.

I feel like a caged animal after being cooped up for hours. I need to get out of this apartment. It is a beautiful day outside and fresh air will do me good. Kicking my ass into gear, I throw on some workout clothes, pull my hair up in a ponytail and take off out the door.

Living in Hoboken affords me the greatest view of the city. There is a pretty walking path along the river only a few blocks from my place. I set out for it and I feel better already. Distracted by recent events in my life, I walk and lose myself in my thoughts.

I have so much running through my head. The same thoughts keep me up at night. The problem is that I start to panic when I allow myself to spend time in the cluttered corners of my mind.

I'm a just normal girl from Jersey. Is this really something I am prepared to embark on? Where will it lead for me? I know where I want it to go, which is singing in my own band, but I am absolutely not ready for that. I ask myself shouldn't I be in the back ground for now? I am only twenty-five and I need to mature before taking on such ambitious plans, right? But then again, I've lived a very sheltered life in Jersey and I need to push my comfort envelope.

This back and forth going on in my brain is giving me an aneurysm.

Then there are the stupid issues, like how much do I pack for a six-month tour? I was only partially kidding when I worried where I would hide my tampons. Do we get to stop at a mall to shop in between shows? How will I do my laundry? When will I be able to pick up on more shampoo and mascara? Will I be getting that stuff myself or will someone be shopping for me? A roadie?

Oh God. Does that mean they will also be buying my tampons?

Who would I even ask these questions to? Jack? Um no! Jennifer? Hell no! Can I Google it?

After walking for hours, I am exhausted and my head hurts. The thought of walking all that way back, continuing the battle in my own head makes me want to throw up. I pull out my cell phone and make a better choice. I call Evan.

"Hey, can you come get me?" I plead into the phone.

"Where are you?"

"Edgewater. I'm at the Starbucks."

He huffs, "Fine, I'll be there soon." He doesn't even ask why I'm all the way in Edgewater without a car. Evan knows better.

I can relax now. I will not torture my brain or feet for the rest of the day. Instead, I grab a latte and sit at a table facing the river. Every sip calms me and gives me a moment of clarity. This is what I was born to do. I need to quit whining and show everyone, including myself, what I am made of.

***

On Wednesday morning my newfound confidence is missing. I lost it somewhere in the middle of the night. I don't get it, though. After my "ah ha" moment and the ego stroke from Evan, I was convinced that I was good to go.

Damn it!

I force myself out of bed to get ready for my appointment with Mr. Morrow. I search through my closet for another professional outfit and find a basic black dress, my mom's pearls, and sensible black heels. It's the perfect outfit for meeting with lawyers and/or funerals.

The drive to Fort Lee is quick and it's less than a half hour later when I'm sitting in Mr. Morrow's outer office waiting to meet my legal guardian angel.

An angel is exactly who steps out from his office to meet me. He is a very pleasant looking man and has rosy cheeks and a portly middle. He looks like a grandpa. His mere presence comforts me.

Shaking my hand he ushers me into his office. "It's very nice to meet you Miss Marino." He smiles and gestures to a wingchair positioned in front of his antique wooden desk. "Ready to secure your fabulous future?"

"Please call me Leila. And yes, I'm very ready."

"Well, Leila, this is quite an opportunity for you. You must be extremely excited."

"Oh, yes I am, but equally nervous. It's a huge change in my life. I want to make sure I am ready for it."

Since he had sent a messenger to pick up the contract yesterday, he assured me he would be totally prepared for our meeting. He glances down to retrieve his reading glasses and replies, "Well, this is why you are here. We will make sure you are comfortable with this information and the expectations this band requires from you. Let's get started."

Two hours later, I feel much better. We discussed what I was okay with and what I wasn't. He prepared me with amendments to the contract that I should insist on. He explained, in layman's terms, all the legal mumbo jumbo that I had no clue how to interpret. He discussed salary and whether I was content with their offer, which I was. My new salary was a significant increase over what I was making, even with the weddings and bar mitzvahs. This contract covered the first album and tour only, with re-negotiations required for future salary and royalties.

Mr. Morrow said his secretary would make the necessary changes and that she would fax a revised contract over to the studio by the end of the day. For my part, I was to request a meeting with Devil's Lair to review. If we all agreed, I should be prepared to sign. If not, back to the drawing board.

Ok, I can do this. I thank him, and leave his office feeling like I have someone on my side. I make a mental note to call Barb to thank her, as I loved Mr. Morrow and am grateful she recommended him.

Needing to make another phone call, a very important one, I wait until I am inside my apartment to call Jack's number.

"Hi Leila." He answers on the first ring. He *saved* my number?

HE SAVED MY NUMBER!

"Hi Jack. I'm ready to discuss the contract." I say trying to sound confident and calm. "My lawyer has a few minor adjustments we would like to make. He will have a revised copy to you by this afternoon."

"Great, we are anxious to get this ball rolling. Why don't you come by tomorrow at noon? This will give us a chance to review it with Jennifer and our own lawyer as well."

"Ok, I'll be there."

See? Easy…except for my palms are drenched.

Chapter 6- Jack

It was minutes after my warped confession to Trini when I fell into a very deep sleep. The smell of coffee wakes me and it is heaven.

"Thanks for letting me crash, not that you had a choice. What time is it?"

"It's before nine. I know you have to be at the studio, so I set an alarm. After you passed out on me last night, I got a lot of sleep." She carries a hot cup of coffee over to me in bed, while smile and I stretch. She has gotten dressed in short shorts and a tank top. Her hair is adorably messy. She removed her piercings and make-up at one point during the night, and it makes her look so young and sweet. She really is very pretty.

"Remind me, why I haven't proposed to you yet?" I ask as I grab the cup from her hands.

"You can't keep up with me, Lair." She says before bending to kiss me on the lips.

"You are awesome Trin. Thanks for listening last night." I say while looking down into my cup of coffee.

"I owe you for all the times you listened to me crying like a girl over some dick." She says smiling warmly. "It will work out Jack, have faith."

I look up at her and smile back. "I hope so."

After my coffee I am a new man. Showered, dressed and out the door in record time, I arrive at the studio by nine-thirty and thankfully am the first one in. I grab another two cups of coffee on the way, and look forward to sitting in peace while quietly drinking my drug of choice. I still have to complete the little task of calling Leila, but it's way too early for that now. It will have to wait until later.

My time alone goes by way too quickly when I hear Hunter and Scott coming down the hall arguing annoyingly on what time I will show. They have twenty bucks riding on me. Scott has me for ten-thirty, Hunter for eleven.

Douchebags.

I can be very responsible when I want to be, or have to be.

When they walk through the door they both stop in shock. "What, did you sleep here?" Hunter asks.

"Zip it dickhead, I heard you both betting on how late I would be. I got here a half hour ago."

"No shit. Well we both lose then." Hunter says smiling his annoying smile.

"Fuck off." I fume, flipping him the bird.

"You sure are pissy." He repeats my words from last night.

"How was your night, Jack?" Scott says trying to make peace.

"Awesome. How did your date with Hunter go?" Now it's Hunter's turn to flip me the bird.

Trey walks in wearing the same clothes as yesterday. I am too. An exchanged glance is the extent of our conversation on both of us getting lucky last night.

Once Jennifer arrives we get right to work. We need to lie out the album sequence, and fax it to the studio heads by the end of the day. This is going to be agony as we all have an opinion.

Three torturous hours later, we are taking a short break and Hunter remembers my homework assignment. "Did you call Leila?"

"It was too early when I got here. I'll call her now." I need to get this over with. Jennifer looks over at me, as I am about to walk out of the studio and moves to follow.

75

I hold up my hand. "Stay here."

Stopping her in her tracks, she gives me a look.

"I want to talk to you when I am done calling her. You need to ease up on her. She'll be one of your clients if she signs and she deserves the same treatment as you give us. Just think about it." I turn and walk out of the studio leaving a stunned Jen behind. Suddenly I want to protect Leila from Jennifer even more.

Ducking into the conference room, I shut the door and dial her number. Why the hell is my heart pounding through my chest?

"Hello?"

"Hey there, how are you?" I say trying to sound normal.

"Hi Jack. I'm great. A bit overwhelmed, but great. What's up?" She sounds like she is
surprised to hear from me.

"Just checking in to make sure you don't have any questions." This *is* a legitimate reason to call, right?

"Well I have tons of questions, but none that you can really answer." She laughs into the phone. Her laugh is adorable. God she is too cute.

"Are you sure? I am more than happy to help." I really would like to help her in any way she wants me to.

"Well I am putting together a list for my lawyer. Once I review with him, I'll call you with any other questions he can't answer. Is that ok?" She asks tentatively.

"Sure Leila, that's fine. I just wanted to let you know that I meant it when I said I'm here for you if you have any questions or concerns. I'm sure your head is reeling right now and I want to remind you how talented you are. This is going to be great for all of us." I pause. I better stop now. "Um, well, have a great day, and I hope to hear from you soon."

There is silence on her end before she answers, "Ok, thanks. Bye, Jack."

She does not sound as if she's about to bolt. I'm sure her lawyer will put any other reservations she has at ease. Jennifer and Scott are just overreacting. I feel better as well, plus it was really nice hearing her voice.

Shit…

Chapter 7-Leila

Dinner with Dad tonight should be interesting. I wonder if he will continue to ignore the situation. I'm meeting him at his favorite restaurant. Well, it's actually just a pizzeria, but they serve a mean chicken parm. I'm barely two feet into the restaurant when the entire front staff yells out, "LEILA!" in varying degrees of Italian accents. I love this place.

"Hi guys. How's it going?" I call over to them, heading for my dad's table.

Angelo, the owner smiles and says, "Bellisima." as I walk by.

"Hi Dad. I hope you haven't been waiting long." I bend to kiss the top of his head.

"Nope, just got here. How's my sweet girl?" He seems chipper and is showing no apprehension at all. This is good. I know he and Evan have a heart to heart talk. I may owe Evan big time, once again.

"I'm great. I have had a few busy days. I'm really excited about this."

"Ok, let me have it. I want all of it no matter how much it will hurt."

I begin to fill him in on all the details of my meeting with Devil's Lair. I tell him about my audition, since I held back a lot of details when I saw him last week, but I still leave out details of Mr. Sex on legs. I tell him about my meetings with Jennifer and the band, and with Mr. Morrow, and how I will be re-meeting with the band tomorrow to finalize the contract.

I talk as we eat and he rarely interrupts me at all. After he knows almost everything, he lays it on me.

"You really want this, right babe?"

"Yeah dad, so much."

He closes his eyes and nods. I guess that was his last attempt to sway me. "Ok. I get it. Lei, first I want you to know that I am extremely proud of you. You have been the most wonderful daughter a man can ask for. I know your mom is smiling down on you right now, and I so wish she could be here for you. I'm sure being raised by your dad was challenging and inadequate at times."

I'm about to interrupt, but he puts up his hand and tells me to hush. "Through it all, through all my insecurities, I managed to raise a beautiful young girl and watch her become an even more beautiful young woman. I look at you now and know I did something right."

He is freaking killing me…

"I want you to know that I support you wholeheartedly. I am not going to lie. I am terrified about this tour thing. I expect a phone call every few days, even if it is for ten seconds. Texts won't count, as I will need to hear your voice. If anyone hurts you in any way, I will find that bus and I will kill them. I know plenty of places to hide a body."

Oh jeez, he's only half joking about this I'm sure.

"I want you to relish in every minute of this awesome experience. Most would kill for this opportunity and you need to constantly remember how fortunate you are. I want you to take care of yourself and most importantly stay true to yourself. That's all I ask of you."

"That's it?" I'm smiling now from ear to ear.

"Yep, that's it. Your dad is done ranting. I will be fine. Don't you worry about me for one minute." The way his eyes moisten with unshed tears rips at my heartstrings and causes my eyes to betray me as well.

"Dad, I'm not leaving for a few months. You can't keep making me cry."

"Sorry sweetheart, I can't make any promises." He says while squeezing my hand. He reaches over and wipes away my tears and kisses my forehead gently.

"I love you so much, baby girl."

"I know dad. I love you too."

That could have gone a whole different way. This man always has me guessing. When I expect him to freak out, he doesn't. When I expect him to be cool, he freaks out.

Relief floods my veins. I was absolutely dreading this conversation with Dad, more than anything in the world. I don't look forward to having the same conversation with my band. With this behind me, though, I feel much more confident and able to get through the rest.

I have an awesome support system. I am a lucky girl, in so many ways. I have so many great people who love me unconditionally, a talented singing voice, and a chance to pursue my dreams of becoming a rock star.

**

Jack, Jennifer and an older gentleman are in the conference room when I arrive. "Welcome back Leila." Jennifer says with a forced smile. She is once again dressed to kill. From what I've seen of her wardrobe, it looks to be very expensive. I have on the same dress that I wore yesterday to my meeting with Mr. Morrow, except I lost the pearls and traded the sensible heels for funky ones. Even so, it still feels more appropriate for a funeral than a business meeting.

"Thank you." Since we are going to be spending a lot of time together, I might as well kill her with kindness.

She barely smiles back. It's obvious that she doesn't feeling the same way as I do. Yet her eyes aren't as cold as they were during our first meeting.

As she turns away, I'm hit with a realization. I think I understand her attitude towards me. She was probably queen of the Lair and I'm possibly going to muddy the estrogen-to-testosterone ratio with the band. Well this should be interesting…

"Leila, this is Mr. Crowse. He is the attorney for Devil's Lair." She says while motioning to the gentleman standing next to her.

He reaches over the table to shake my hand. "Nice to meet you Miss Marino. "

"Please, call me Leila." I reply while shaking his hand. He seems nice and not at all intimidating.

Jack leans closer and whispers, "Welcome back."

Two words and nothing remotely sexy, hot, or seductive about them.

SO WHY THE HELL IS MY CROTCH PULSING?

Thankfully, Mr. Crowse takes over and interjects, "Well, Leila, we have reviewed the new contract containing the revisions you and Mr. Morrow have made, and we feel all amendments are acceptable." I make a tiny sigh of relief.

One of the amendments states that I can still continue to perform with Cliffhangers, even after Devil's Lair rehearsals begin. I asked for this to be added to the contract. I thought they were going to veto that request, but they obviously didn't have a problem with it. Rehearsals will run daily Monday through Friday. As long as I can manage both commitments, there is no reason that I can't continue with Cliffhangers on weekends until our tour begins. I'll catch up on my sleep during the nights that I don't perform.

I'm fine with it and can definitely handle it. I will only perform at The Zone, which is definitely an upside. This will also give me a chance to wean myself off my boys and vice versa.

My mind wanders as we briefly discuss some more details. The contract effective date is the First of June. That gives me less than a month before rehearsals begin. This will give me a chance to spend quality time with dad, and for Cliffhangers to replace me. I need to have a conversation with them regarding that and I am not looking forward to it.

"Do you have any further concerns, or questions for us?" Mr. Crowse question yanks me back to our meeting.

"No, Mr. Crowse, I am all set. I am extremely excited about joining Devil's Lair, and I am definitely ready to get started." I speak only the absolute truth.

"Well, it would be our great pleasure to request for you to please sign on the dotted line." He responds while smiling at his own rhyme.

The contract is passed around the table, and we all add our signatures. I suddenly feel like I just literally signed over my soul to the devil as I write my name. I look over at Jack to see the mentioned devil staring directly at me.

Grinning as he watches me, I can't help but beam right back. Wow! I am a member of Devil's Lair. It's almost anticlimactic. I expected to hear a choir of angels, or see fireworks erupt over Jennifer's head.

Mr. Crowse rises and announces, "Leila, we will have a copy of this contract Fed Ex'd to your home tomorrow. Please feel free to call me if you have anything else you would like to discuss. It was a great pleasure meeting you today. Devil's Lair has gotten themselves' quite a beautiful addition."

"Thank you, that's very nice of you to say." I thank the kind man standing next to Jennifer, as well as Jennifer and Jack. I grab my bag and turn to leave the conference room just as Jack holds my elbow and asks if I'd like to get a cup of coffee or something to eat.

The zing is running right through my body and hitting every erogenous zone along the way.

Nodding is the only form of communication I can muster.

I sneak a glance over to Jennifer, but she is quietly discussing something with Mr. Crowse. Relieved she didn't hear what Jack said, I follow him out of the conference room. I really don't want to get on her bad side even more than I already seem to be.

Jack leads me out of the studio and down the street. The silence stretches between us, and builds the kind of tension that only comes from being in the company of a perfect stranger. The more I wrack my brain for something to say to him, the more it goes completely blank.

Jack doesn't seem to notice the angst, or the trail of girls he leaves in his path panting over his handsome face. He turns to a small coffee shop tucked in the middle of the block and guides me towards the door with his hand on my lower back.

"This is it."

The warmth of his touch penetrates the fabric of my dress and burns right through to my skin.

An involuntary gasp escapes my lips and prompts him to look at me with concern. "Oh, is this ok? I eat here quite a bit. It looks like a dive, but the food is decent. They make a mean grilled cheese."

"Um…yeah, this looks great. I love grilled cheese." I smile weakly trying to control my erratic breathing. Internally I'm chastising myself for my lack of control, once again.

The dinette looks like something out of a movie set. Stainless steel panels line the walls behind the back counter. A glass carousel sits at the end of a long counter and revolves the day's selection of pies and desserts. Dessert glasses are stacked as well as plastic tumblers, coffee cups and saucers. There is even the uniform clad waitress with the typical bouffant hairdo, snapping her gum very loudly. I almost expect her nametag to read "FLO".

She comes over with a carafe of coffee in her hand the minute our butts hit the booth. There are already cups, and saucers on the table. She immediately starts pouring coffee for us without asking if we wanted decaf, or tea instead. FLO's actual name is Doris, which would have been my second guess.

"Hey cutie pie. How's my handsome boy today?" She looks at Jack like she wants to eat him alive. It's funny actually because she must be sixty.

"Hey Dee, I'm great. This here is Leila. She just joined the band." There is something in his eyes. It can't be pride? He barely knows me.

Doris gives me the once over. "Well aren't you adorable. It's nice to meet you Leila. Be sure to treat my boys real well, or you will have to answer to me." Though she speaks with a smile, I can see the threat in her eyes.

"I will do my best." I am more concerned with how they will be treating me.

Jack orders for both of us. Dumb as it sounds, it's actually very sexy. We are only in a greasy diner and he ordered me a grilled cheese and fries, but it's kind of romantic. He asks me if I want anything else to drink, and I request ice water. He orders a Coke. Doris jots it down, winks at Jack and makes her way to the kitchen doors.

"So, tell me about yourself, Miss Marino." He ventures after taking a sip of his coffee. He drinks it black. I cannot, so I start to add cream and sugar to my own cup.

"What do you want to know?"

"How old are you?"

"Why do you ask?"

He shrugs, "Just curious."

"Twenty-five. Is that ok?"

Chuckling he responds, "Of course. I just thought you were older."

"Definitely not something a girl wants to hear."

"No, no, it's a complement. You are very mature and responsible. I was impressed with how you handled Mr. Crowse."

"Thanks?"

He smirks and explains, "It's a compliment."

"How old are you?"

"Twenty eight."

Nodding, I take a sip of coffee, looking up to see Jack frowning. "What's wrong?"

"What, no compliment for me?" He teases.

"Oh…um, yes you are very mature also?" An apologetic smile accompanies my response.

He chuckles again and shakes his head. "You sound so convincing, Miss Marino. I have another question. Where do you see yourself in five years?"

"Wow. Didn't I already get the job? I feel like I'm on an interview."

He laughs. "You did get the job. But I'm still curious."

"Five years…that's right around the corner. I was just in high school." Stopping to take a sip of my water I scramble my brain for an acceptable answer. Truth is I see myself touring the country as the lead singer of my own rock band. Being in a relationship would be nice too. "Um…I see myself singing in my own rock band." I say hesitantly, watching his face for his reaction. "Am I fired?"

"No, you aren't fired. I appreciate your honesty. I get it. Your voice definitely screams for solo success. It's flattering that you are choosing Devil's Lair to begin your career."

"*I'm* flattered you chose me to join your band. I'm a big fan."

"What other bands or artists do you listen to?"

"Well my dad played a lot of music while I was growing up. I love Springsteen and..."

"Wait…" He immediately cuts me off. "I knew you were going to say that. It's like every Jersey girls' birth-right to like Springsteen."

"That's not true. I have a lot of friends who prefer Bon Jovi."

Jack lays his full blown CCDS smile on me in response.

Oh my god…

"What?" I ask breathlessly.

"I knew you were going to say that too."

"Why don't you like Springsteen?"

"He's alright."

"He's a poet. Have you ever listened to his lyrics?" Pure conviction fills my voice.

"They're alright." He throws back at me.

WHAT?

I shake my head in disbelief. "Have you ever heard the lyrics to Jungleland? You can argue that his lyrics can be considered Shakespeare's modern day Othello. They are poetic genius."

He shakes his head while smiling widely. "Ok you get an A+ for that literary reference, but poetic genius? You are definitely insane."

"Uh…ok, we need to agree to disagree about Springsteen. I just signed a contract to spend a year with you and I really don't want to hate you already."

"Hate me? Wow, that hurts." He grins while holding his heart, and he takes my breath away yet again.

The filter in my brain malfunctions, and I blurt out, "You have a really nice smile."

My comment takes him by surprise. "Why thank you. You have really nice eyes."

Out of embarrassment, I look down to avoid eye contact while biting on my lip. An awkward silence looms between us. Jack notices my uneasiness and brings the conversation back to music.

"Ok, so keep going, who else?"

Doris appears just in time with my water. I take a long sip and carefully watch him gazing at me over the rim of the glass. He waits patiently. My guess is that he most definitely is onto me and knows I am stalling.

Clearing my throat, I try again. "Um, ok, I love Pat Benatar. Her range blows me away. I love Fleetwood Mac, and The Eagles, and Boston, and Foreigner, and The Who, and Journey, and Zeppelin and…"

"Wait." He interrupts me again.

Rolling my eyes I complain, "What?"

Suddenly he laughs…a deep, throaty, sexy as hell laugh.

Oh lord.

We will never finish our conversation if he continues to do this to me during this lunch, and I will end up getting fired.

I grab my water and take another sip to cool down.

Jack has been talking, but I have no idea what he has said. I tune back in to hear him say, "…of your dads' influences, I'm sure. What about modern bands? Who do you listen to that aren't over the age of thirty?"

At that exact moment our food comes and he dives right in. I take a bite out of my own sandwich and moan. He's right it's delicious.

At once he glances up with an intense, smoldering gaze. "I take it that you like?"

It's the look that hypnotizes me, puts me in a trance, and turns whatever brain cells I do have into mush. Nodding as a reflex reaction, he repeats my motions just before he shoves more of the sandwich into his mouth and calls Doris over.

"Dee, can I get a… "

"I already put it in doll."

This must be a pattern for him.

With a face full of fries, he asks, "More?"

I again shake my head pathetically out of reflex. I've apparently forgotten the basics of the English language. Doris nods and walks away.

Jeeze, he even looks pretty while shoving food into his face. Anyone else would look like a total buffoon. His hands picking up his fries, his sandwich, his coke, have me completely mesmerized. They are so masculine. This is a first. I don't think a pair of hands has ever turned me on. There is a long scar on the back of his left hand that makes me wonder what happened to him. Was it a fight? I need to ask him about it one day.

"Ok, keep going. Who else?"

"Are you going to interrupt me again?"

With a look of complete innocence, he crosses his heart. "No. I promise."

"Ok…I love Cliffhangers." I smile sweetly at him. The look he gives me makes me giggle. "They are the band I play with in Hoboken."

"Oh, I am definitely coming to Hoboken to hear them play. So who else?" He finishes his sandwich and continues with his fries.

I bat my eyelashes. "You know how much I love Devil's Lair. They sound so hot!"

Jack blinks a couple of times disoriented. Then he smirks at me while his smoldering gaze sets my insides on fire. "You already signed the contract Leila, so there is no need to butter me up, unless you want to that is."

Holy hell…he's wrecking me.

"Hello? Are you still with me?" he asks. Sometime during my internal orgasm Doris delivered the second grilled cheese sandwich and he has already taken a bite.

"Um…" I pause. "I love Every Avenue. I think they are awesome. I have most of their music downloaded. I also love My Darkest Days, Linkin Park, and MACE."

"Much better. MACE is very cool. We loved touring with them last year. My Darkest Days is also cool. Not many know who they are yet, kind of like us. I also love Every Avenue. They have a great song called, *Tie Me Down*. Do you know it?" He glances down but grins devilishly.

That's my ringtone for him. It's a song about being tied down and fucked and I suddenly feel very, very warm.

My blush tells him that I know the song well.

"Who else do you like? Who influences Devil's Lair?" I try to throw the conversation back to his court. I need time to sit and process.

"The usual. The Stones and Zeppelin. I love the Doors. Morrison was a freaking genius. I also love U2, and Aerosmith, as you already know. Coldplay, Linkin Park, and Kings of Leon are cool. Oh, and Bob Marley."

Now it's my turn to interrupt him. "Reggae? I wouldn't peg you as a fan."

"The beat is fantastic. Bob Marley is a legend. I like to relax and listen to reggae. It doesn't influence my own music too much, so I can purely enjoy it without worrying its seeping into my artistic subconscious."

He explains when he sees my eyebrows pulled together in confusions. "When you write your own songs, it's hard to listen to a lot of the competition. Other music and lyrics tend to influence what you want to create. I avoid other rock bands when I am in a zone and writing lyrics to a song, so my music is purely me." I knew he was a talented musician, but this bit of information he shares with me has me very impressed.

I am about to tell him so, when a very giddy young girl interrupts us.

"Oh my god!!!! You are Jack Lair!!!" She hops up and down at the end of our booth.

"Um yes, I am. How's it goin'?" He looks clearly discomfited. Mr. Sex God is not quite used to fame yet.

She asks for a picture and without waiting for a yes or no response slides into the booth next to him. Shoving her phone at me she asks, "Please, can you take this?" while never taking her eyes off Jack.

"Um, sure. No problem." Jack raises his left arm to wrap around the girl's shoulders, and she beams at the phone. I barely snap the picture when she scoots out of the booth and starts texting it out to someone.

She calls out, "Thank you!" and practically skips away. We look at each other and burst out laughing.

"You aren't used to getting recognized yet, I see."

Jack shrugs and says, "Nope, not yet. None of us really are yet. It doesn't happen often, but it is very surreal when it does." Jack fiddles nervously with his silverware while quietly contemplating something in his mind. I surprisingly see a different side of Mr. Sex on Legs. He isn't the cocky, *look at me I'm a hot rock star* type that I thought he was. He actually seems more unassuming than arrogant.

When he put his arm around "giddy girl" the sleeve of his t-shirt rode up, exposing a small part of his tattoo. Dying of curiosity, I decide to ask him. "What do you have tattooed on your arm?"

He glances down to his left arm, twisting his body and lifting the sleeve enough to reveal the whole thing. It's the band logo in gorgeous vibrant color. On the bottom running in straight block letters is "Devil's Lair" with multi-color flames of red, gold, and orange, shooting up out of the words. It's beautiful and I tell him as much.

"Thanks. Shortly after we got signed we worked with the studio on our logo. This is what the graphic department came up with. It was such a defining moment for us that I felt it was necessary to honor it." He's gives me a shy half smile.

"Do any of the other guys have it also?" I ask worrying this is some sort of rite of passage into the band.

"No, just me. I'm not sure Trey could find the space on his body for this. Hunter wants to get something similar tattooed one day. He thinks he wants his drum set with the logo on the bass drum, but he hasn't made up his mind yet. Scott's not the tattoo type. Do you have any tattoos?"

"Nope, no tattoos. I never had the desire for one actually. Maybe one day something will mean enough for me to put it on my body."

Um, did I just say that out loud?

Amusedly he opens his mouth to comment, yet decides not to.

Instead, he looks over at my uneaten fries.

"Would you like some of my fries?" I tease.

"Yep." He reaches for some and dips them into my ketchup.

"I have a question. Is Jack Lair your real name?" I just need to know.

"Yeah, why?" he asks looking amused.

"Oh, I don't know. Jack Lair. Seems too perfect for a rock star." I say exactly what I am thinking.

"Kind of like Leila is for a rock singer?"

"Touché."

"So what's your favorite movie?"

"The Notebook." He rolls his eyes and groans.

"What?"

"I hate that movie."

"Ok, so far you hate Springsteen and my favorite movie. I quit."

Chuckling he shrugs. "Sorry, it's just such a chick flick."

"Ok Mr. Macho, what's your favorite movie?"

"Platoon." Now it's my turn to roll my eyes and groan. Shrugging he adds, "I'm all MAN."

That he is.

"So have you always lived in Hoboken?" He shoves more fries into his mouth.

"No, I grew up in Cliffside Park. It's about twenty minutes away from Hoboken, closer to the George Washington Bridge than the Lincoln Tunnel. Where are you from?"

"I'm from Long Island…Massapequa. I've lived there my entire life until I moved in with Hunter eight years ago. Our apartment is in Brooklyn." He throws the ball back in my court. "How do your parents feel about this tour?"

Oh damn… he's going there.

"Well, it's just my dad. My mom died when I was ten."

"I'm sorry." He simply says, staring intently at me.

Uncharacteristically, I end up breaking our eye contact first by shrugging and looking away. "It was a long time ago."

"So how does Dad feel about all of this?"

"Dad is very happy that I'm happy, but he's not thrilled with my career choice." I am not able to hide the uneasiness I feel with this line of questioning.

Jack doesn't seem to notice. "What would he rather you be doing?"

"He supports a singing career, just not a rock band one. He prefers Broadway or a vocal teacher."

We stare at each other for a few seconds, and I feel my pulse quickening. Jack starts to say something, and I cut him to the quick. "What about you? How do your parents feel about you being a rock star?"

"Oh they are just thrilled." He says sarcastically. My confused expression prompts him to continue. "I was supposed to follow in dad's footsteps and become a lawyer. I'm an NYU dropout." He stops and smiles when he sees the surprise on my face.

Jack a lawyer?

Jack at NYU?

A model or an actor or most definitely a rock star? Yes! But an NYU lawyer? Mr. Pretty is also smart?

This man is killing me.

"I was actually studying pre-law at NYU when I dropped out. They were most definitely not happy with me. But they are more supportive now than they were a few years ago. Thanks to my sister, they now realize this is what I am meant to be."

"How old is she?"

Doris appears with more coffee, filling our cups without asking for permission. She looks down at my plate and asks. "Didn't you like it, hon?"

"Oh, it was the best grilled cheese I ever had. I'm just full."

Doris goes to lift my plate. "Leave it Doris. I'm still working on it. But I'll take my pie now. Leila would you like some pie?"

"No, I'm good. Thanks." Doris winks again, and makes her way to the dessert display.

"They also make a really good apple pie." He grins and I can't help but return a grin of my own. He looks adorable, like a little boy waiting for his ice cream.

"So how old is your sister?"

"She's twenty five."

"What's her name?"

"Elizabeth, but we call her Lizzy. How did you become a singer?" Again he throws the conversation back to me. He really is good at that.

"I have been singing since I was a little girl. I grew up with the guys in my band. They immediately asked me to join them when they started. I share vocals with our lead singer Matt. We started off singing at weddings and bar mitzvahs, but thank God we got the gig at The Zone a few years ago. I was really happy about that since I hate singing at private parties." I didn't mean to ramble and share so much.

"Oh I don't know. Private parties can be a lot of fun." He raises his eyebrows and smirks suggestively. It's unfair how this man exudes sensuality, especially to warm-blooded females who've been on an exceptionally long unprovoked sexual dry spell, like me.

Doris appears with the biggest piece of apple pie I have ever seen. Jack sees me eyeing it and says, "I usually don't share. But you really need to try this."

"I'll take your word for it."

"Nope. You need to try it. Trust me." He cuts a huge piece off with his fork and shoves it into his own mouth first. "Mmm…damn it's good." He cuts another huge piece and stretches his arm towards me. "Taste."

I lean back in the booth and shake my head while he nods his.

"Oh come on, I don't have cooties. Try it."

I widen my eyes at the huge hunk of pie sitting on his fork. Jack licks his lips while watching me intently.

Fuck…I really need to have sex.

The bastard is doing this on purpose and he's not going to let me off this hook.

Well, two can play at this game.

"Fine." I lean forward, open my mouth wide, and take the pie from his fork, running my lips along the prongs to wipe them clean. Instinctively, I close my eyes, lick my lips and moan suggestively as I slowly chew.

"Wow…that is good." I open my eyes to see Jack staring at my mouth, with his fork still suspended in the air between us. In turn, I do the same in an effort to go tit for tat with him by visually devouring his chin, his stubble, and his lips before glancing back up to his eyes. I feel like we are playing chicken with each other. I'm not sure where this newfound confidence is coming from. I blame the Jack Lair voodoo. I haven't acted like my typical self in his presence once since meeting him.

Jack slightly shifts in his seat and shoves more pie into his mouth to break our eye contact.

Game. Set. Match.

One point two seconds later, by merely watching as he slowly chews his pie, my internal switch is flipped causing me to squirm in my own seat from the throbbing in my lower region.

95

Close game.

There is an uncomfortable silence between us buzzing with sexual tension. I nonchalantly pick up my water as Jack consumes the rest of his pie.

He finally breaks the silence by asking, "Um, how many guys are in your band?"

"There are four guys and me. I am really proud of them. They have come a long way since playing in Logan and Matt's basement."

"Matt is your co-lead. Who's Logan?"

"He's our guitarist and Matt's brother. Then there is Joseph our drummer, and Evan our bass player and my best friend."

He looks up at me. "Best friend? How did you and Evan become BFF's?"

I pause and try to answer his question without giving him my life story. "Well, we met in middle school. Evan is a year older than I am. We connected and have been inseparable ever since. He's very close to my dad as well."

"Oh, so Evan is like family?" Jack says this like a clarification. "How does Evan feel about your new career?" He takes another sip of his coffee while intently watching me.

"He is my biggest fan, even more than dad. He'll miss me, but I know we will speak every day and nothing will change between us. We simply won't let it." I admit with complete honesty.

He stares at me until I break the connection and look down to take a sip of my own coffee.

"So Leila, besides Evan, is there anyone else that would be missing you terribly when we go on tour?"

Is he asking me if I have a boyfriend?

"My dad." I shrug.

Jack smirks smugly and nods. "Got it. Well, I'm glad we did this. I feel like I know you better already."

I glance at my phone and am shocked to see we have been sitting in this booth for over two hours. Jack motions for Doris and she makes her way over and says, "All done cutie pie?"

"Yep, we are good to go. Thanks, Dee." He reaches into his back pocket and pulls out his wallet. I reach for my bag and open it as well. He gives me a look and says, "No way. It's on me."

"Thank you."

He nods and hands Doris the money. Once he slides out of the booth, he puts an arm around Doris and kisses her cheek. She looks like he just made her day.

I follow Jack and slide out of the booth as well. Doris pats my arm like she has known me my whole life. "You take care of yourself Leila. Good luck with this crew. You'll need it." She says with humor.

"Hey Dee, what the hell?" Jack throws his hands up just as she swats at his ass. It's obvious Doris feels very comfortable with Mr. Sex on Legs.

Jack puts his hand on my lower back as we walk out of the dinette and back towards the studio. I'm not even sure he is aware he is doing it. I'd like to think he is a gentleman and it's just a habit instead of some cheesy move. It's chivalrous and sweet and I like it.

"Where are you parked?" He looks around as if he would be able to spot my car at a glance.

"I'm over a few blocks." I point behind me.

"Do you want me to walk…"

"No, not necessary." I cut him off. "I'm fine. Thanks for lunch Jack. I had a nice time."

"Me too, Leila. I'll touch base with you in a few days and let you know what the next step is." He steps towards me and pulls me into a hug.

He *smells* so good. He *feels* so good.

Jack releases me, way too quickly for my liking. Waving as he turns and walks into the studio, he leaves me rooted to my spot near the front door. Through the glass I watch as he strolls over to Sally and she smiles at him. The woman can smile, so what do you know? He says something to her and she holds up a magazine. I wonder if Sally is a friend, or an ex? God, I hope not.

I walk back to the lot where my car is parked, not remembering anything along the way except for Jack, and specifically that hug.

***

I call Evan on as I drive home.

"I can't wait to hear all the details."

I am really going to miss him.

"I thought I would make dinner for everyone tonight." I ventured. "Sort of wine and dine them, to help soften the blow."

"You sure you want to do that? It could get messy."

"Yeah, I'm sure. There are a few things I want to talk to you guys about, and I'd rather do it on my home turf. Can you ask the guys to come by around seven? That will give me a chance to pick up some stuff. Would you mind coming earlier though?" I don't mean to turn him into my secretary, but I know Evan doesn't mind.

"How about I meet you at the store? I'll help you get what you need."

We agree to meet in an hour.

I arrive a few minutes earlier than Evan and make my way down the aisles to get my ingredients. I know I'm making them pasta, so I start throwing all I need into my cart. As I put the last few items in, I feel two hands cover my eyes from behind… Evan. He has been doing this since we were in middle school.

Turning towards him, he brings me in for a hug. "Hey, Lei, I missed you."

I laugh and reply, "Ev, we saw each other yesterday."

"I know. Just sayin'."

He grabs my cart, and we start walking side by side down the aisles. "So how did it go?"

"It went well. Contract is all signed, and we are starting rehearsals on the First of June."

"Not much time, huh?" His tone makes the lump form in my throat.

"Well the good news is I will still be playing with you guys until we go out on tour in September. I had them add it to the contract. Rehearsals are in SoHo during the week. There is no reason I can't continue playing at the bar on the weekends."

He stops the cart to face me. "Lei, won't that be too much on you? Juggling two bands at once?"

"No, Evan. I can handle it. I want to do this." My words come out defensively.

He sighs. He knows he will lose this battle. He could easily keep arguing with me on the subject, but he chooses to change it.

"Ok, what are you making us tonight, because I'm starving?" This is the "Evan Miller" way of handling stress.

"My specialty, penne with vodka sauce."

"Well then stop wasting time, woman." He pushes the cart further down the aisle and then turns suddenly.

"Can you make us some of your brownies too?"

"Now you're just taking advantage of me."

"Damn straight." He doesn't deny my accusation. "Make a double batch so I can take some home." He grins as he walks away, probably knowing I can't deny him.

"Jerk." I call after him and hear him laughing from the next aisle.

Chapter 8–Jack

I walk back into the studio after my lunch with Leila to see Sally is busy doing what she does best - nothing.

"Busy at work Sal?"

She looks up and beams. Sally is a little rough around the edges. If I weren't in this business, I would probably be afraid of her. But truth be told, she is a sweetheart. She can act all badass, yet beneath it all she is a mush.

"I am working hard, smart ass. I am researching." I lean over the counter to see what it is she is researching. Lying on her lap is a playgirl magazine open to the centerfold.

"And what research would that be for?" I ask quickly looking away. I have no desire to stare at some dude's junk.

"My next tattoo." She says, as if it's obvious. "Look, he has a cute little tattoo on his hip." She lifts the magazine to show me and I turn away.

"Ugh, get that thing out of my face. I'm out of here."

"Oh, don't leave. Come see page forty five, his tattoo is on his…"

I leave a laughing Sally behind as I sprint down the hall. She can be such a ball buster. Like her, the guys are all sitting around the studio doing absolutely nothing.

"Working hard boys?"

"Where've you been? I texted you twice." Hunter is at the drums playing with his sticks. He was born to be a drummer. It doesn't matter where we are. He always sees a drum set and a beat to be found.

"You did?" I pull out my phone and sure enough there are two texts. "I was with Leila." Three sets of eyes gawk at me.

"WHAT?" I know what they are thinking.

"Jack, what are you doing?"

"Really, Scott?"

It's annoying how these douche-bags blatantly don't trust me around girls. Granted, I don't have the best track record, and I *have* been thinking about Leila constantly…but still.

"Really, Jack?"

"Cut the crap. I don't screw every girl I meet." They continue to stare at me like I just announced I wanted to have a sex change and Trey lets out a single laugh.

"Fine. I admit it. I banged her in the back alley."

Scott raises his eyebrows like he believes me, the dickhead. I'm about to blow my fucking fuse. "Christ. I took her to Leo's and bought her a grill cheese. Give me a goddamn break."

"Calm down." Scott counters. "I'm just sayin'."

Hunter ignores my irritability and announces, "So while you were gone wooing Leila, we decided we need to have a party."

"Where?" I grunt in irritation from these idiots.

"Our place, genius. We can't have it at Scott's because it's too small, and there isn't a person on earth that would go to Trey's neighborhood willing." We all look over at Trey and without even looking up from his guitar he flips Hunter off. This causes me to laugh out loud.

"Our place? Really? How many people do you want to invite to this party?" I like going to parties, not throwing them. Not to mention I really don't want us to lose roof privileges either. I love my roof.

"We thought it would be cool to invite Leila, and see if she wants to bring some friends." He rambles on a few other names, but I'm no longer listening.

Leila?

I don't know how I feel about that. I guess we do need to start including her. She is part of the band. But inviting her to a party at our apartment? Not that I would hit on her while she was in my apartment, but do I want anyone else to?

NO!

Wait…what??!!

With a sigh, I impassively respond, "When?"

"Sunday. Leila is off on Sundays."

"Fine, but the roof is off limits. No one goes up there. Got it?"

"Yeah, yeah, whatever Dad."

Party, alcohol and Leila? Fuck.

I feel like these dicks are setting me up for failure. Stupid, I know. I'm about to spend a lot of time with her, and I'll have to learn how to deal with it. Still, I'm a textbook procrastinator and I need to work up to that.

We decide to call it a day and head for one of our regular hangouts after we unproductively rehearse for a few hours. Walking the short distance to the bar, I can't help but feel these moments of complete normalcy may soon be rare, if non-existent. Where we can walk down the street inconspicuously and anonymously. I can't help but wonder what will happen when we take this exact path a year from now. Hopefully, we will be running from hoards of screaming fans or better yet, driven from place to place in a big-ass-obnoxious-stretch Hummer.

We stop on the way for a quick bite. It's still fairly early once we arrive at the bar and it's not long before several females make their way over to our corner and rudely invade our private party. Normally, I'd be fine with mooching girls looking for a good time. I'm not in the mood tonight. I'm exhausted. Plus, I'm still freaked out from my Leila induced wet dreams and the fact she is invading my thoughts. Not to mention how bad I wanted to suck the remnants of pie off her lips at the diner.

Shit…

Scott's whole demeanor stops any girls from approaching him at all. It's funny actually. He looks so wholesome and sweet, but he sends out this vibe that clearly says, "Fuck off, I'm taken." Shortly after his second beer, he takes off to meet up with Patti.

Trey is also gone. We have no idea where he went, and probably will not see him until tomorrow. That's Trey. No goodbye, he just disappears. I would love to know if he hooks up every time he disappears or if he just finds us so boring that he can't be bothered.

That leaves Hunter, two chicks and me who have hitched their tents. I quietly drink my beer and decide to ignore everyone around me. Hunter on the other hand is talking to the brunette with long curly hair. I notice her for the first time and I am impressed. Turned up nose, plump lips, and a nice body. She's cute. She seems very shy, which means Hunter is the initiator and is actually engaged in a conversation with an attractive shy female. There must be pigs flying by outside.

Her friend is a perky blonde with a killer body. She seems opposite to the brunette in every way. I'm curious why they are friends. The blonde persistently bumps her ass up against my hip as she chats with Hunter and her friend. After the third time, she turns towards me and apologizes.

"Oh, sorry."

"No worries."

She leans in close enough to give me a juicy view of her impressive cleavage and asks, "So, you guys are in a band?"

Oh *brother*.

"No, I'm a mortician." I wink and take a swig of my beer. It takes her a few seconds before she giggles at my joke and stealthily places her hand on my wrist.

My humor opens her floodgates. Blondie morphs into a cartoon character, albeit with big boobs, and starts animatedly yapping, touching, leaning in, winking, and licking her lips. She pulls out all the stops.

As she drones on and on, my brain quickly assesses the situation. Yes, she is attractive and definitely has a hot body. She's kind of annoying and is flirting heavily with me, but she's asking too many questions and that's definitely a red flag.

I decide if Hunter wants to take her friend home then I'll do the same. I firmly place our fate in his hands while knowing damn well that his track record with bringing home girls downright sucks.

The name of Hunter's chick is Amanda. The blonde is Rachel. We buy them a round of drinks, then another. The more Rachel drinks, the more she touches me. What seems like hours later, they finally excuse themselves to go to the ladies room.

The minute they walk away I ask, "So, are you taking her home tonight?"

"I don't know. What do you think man, should I?"

"Damn it, Hunter. Just go for it! She is obviously into you. She's hot. What the hell is the problem?" I want to smack him upside his head. I don't know what his issue is when it comes to picking up girls. He is normally one of the most confident guys I know. Yet he's pathetic when it comes to this.

"Do you like Rachel?"

"No. She's annoying."

Amanda is more my type, but I decide to keep that bit of info to myself.

Hunter laughs. "Annoying? That never stopped you before. She's gorgeous. What's your problem, Are you off your game tonight?"

His arrogant comment hits a nerve.

"No, jackass. I'm just not in the mood."

"Not in the mood? You?"

"Don't worry about me. I'll hook up with Rachel if it helps you to hook up with Amanda." Hunter turns his body to give me a scathing look.

"What?"

"Hell man, don't do me any favors."

"Sometimes you need a little push. I'm just trying to help you out."

"Fuck you."

"Whatever. There's no need for hostility."

Hunter gives me the silent treatment until the girls return from the ladies room. He never holds a grudge, and is back to his normal self in no time.

Watching Hunter and Amanda interact so comfortably with each other is my deciding factor. In my buzzed state I stupidly convince myself that hooking up with Rachel would only help Hunter. Regardless of what he thinks, he needs me to seal the deal. If I were to back out right now, Rachel would be gone with Amanda in tow. So I guess I'm taking one for the team. After the four of us consume several more rounds of beer and a round of shots, I decide I've had enough.

"Let's get out of here."

Normally, I am very diligent in choosing the women I hook up with. I like those who seek the exact same thing as I do, aren't looking for a commitment, want a good time, and whose company I enjoy. I don't appreciate women like Rachel who are annoying, yappy, and make me want to slit my wrists.

I regret my decision by the time we arrive to the apartment.

Something has my radar all messed up. There were too many red flags during the night that I ignored and now I am worried this is a huge mistake.

After a quick tour, a quick beer, and a quick coin toss that I rigged, Hunter is now on the roof with Amanda while Rachel and I get comfortable on the couch.

She unleashes question after question after question about our tour, our album, the rest of the band…blah, blah, blah. I feel like my ears are bleeding.

I really need to shut her up. Contradicting my gut instincts, I move closer and start nibbling on her ear. Thankfully this does the trick, and she finally shuts up.

Unfortunately, I've now started something I really don't want to finish. As she starts to kiss my neck, I quickly play out two scenarios in my head. Either, I tell her I'm not in the mood and call her a cab now or I let her finish what she is about to do, and she goes on her merry way.

As I'm debating these two scenarios in my head, Rachel is making it very clear why she came home with me tonight. Since my cock has a mind of his own and is at full mast anyway, I might as well make him happy.

Moving us to my room gives Rachel the green light she's been waiting for. She effectively has me prepped and ready in no time. I quickly roll on a condom to give Rachel what she came for.

By closing my eyes, I actually manage to have a very pleasurable experience after all. My vision, fantasy, or dream, whatever the hell you want to label it, is very real and vivid in my mind.

Leila.

Where previously her face caused me panic and confusion, tonight it's a welcome sight.

I can taste her lips on mine.

I can feel my fingers wrapped in her silky hair.

I can feel her breasts pressing against me with each thrust.

I can taste her skin as I run my lips and tongue down her neck.

Rachel speaks and I quickly kiss her lips to stop her from ruining my fantasy.

Three deep thrusts later result in a very satisfying release. Leila, I mean Rachel, follows immediately after.

For a few long minutes we both lay on our backs, fighting for breath, neither of us saying a word.

"Wow. Jack that was fantastic."

I can only nod in response.

She has no clue I used her body to fulfill my fantasy. Nausea hits as the shame I feel slowly slinks through my digestive tract. I regret using Rachel. Unfortunately she fell short in capturing my attention.

Totally oblivious to my inner turmoil, Rachel cuddles up to me and I unconsciously stiffen. I don't do the cuddle thing, not even with girls I like.

"Round two?" she asks as she nibbles on my neck.

Um…no.

"Rachel, I'm exhausted…you wiped me out." A partial lie.

Taking my comment as a compliment, she picks up right where she left off, and starts to run her mouth a mile a minute, kissing me intermittently. She's quiet only when she stops to take a breath. I pretend to listen until I can't take it any longer.

I can excuse myself and arrange for Scott to call me with an emergency.

Or I can start a small, contained kitchen fire.

Or I can stab myself by accident.

Holy hell…I need to get her out of here.

I sing the lyrics to about a dozen of our songs in my head and then decide that I've waited an acceptable amount of time.

"I'm sorry Rachel. I have a really early appointment tomorrow. Can I call you a cab?" The look on her face unleashes a barrage of guilt, so I lie to soften the blow. "I'll call you."

This is why I rely on my "relationship scale" technique. It's foolproof. By ignoring my meticulous system, I am now feeling all the crap I try so desperately to avoid - guilt, shame, and pity.

Damn it…And I've broken at least ten of my own rules. The most important one being, *"Never tell a chick you'll call her…ever!"*

This whole night was a huge mistake.

I feel like I just spent the last few hours babysitting a child with severe A.D.D. by the time I close the door behind Rachel. Her attention span is the size of a pea. It took most of the forty minutes to talk her out of going up to the roof to tell Amanda she was leaving. I wasn't about to let her ruin Hunter's night. I paid for her cab and promised I would tell Amanda personally that she had left.

Now I feel gross and add that to my fucking list. The minute she leaves I hide in my room to work out like a mad man before showering and falling into bed exhausted.

Chapter 9-Leila

Evan is sitting on my couch, drinking a beer and watching me in the kitchen. He offered to help, but I shooed him away when he kept eating my ingredients. Now he's pouting.

My apartment is on the third floor, and it's one big rectangle. From my door you can see the entire space. Past the kitchen on the left is a short hallway with a bedroom and bathroom adjacent to each other. To the right is the living room and small dinette table with four chairs.

The best part of the space is the windows. The living room is in the front part of the apartment. There are windows from floor to ceiling that look out onto the street. You can see a fantastic view of the city if you sit in my favorite chair in the front corner of the room. Next to the chair is a media cabinet with a modest sized TV. The wall facing the chair and TV has a long, comfortable, squishy couch. A coffee table some pictures on the walls and a lamp complete my furnishings.

The guys usually crowd onto the couch and watch TV when I have them over, while I sit in the chair facing them watching the view. They love hanging out here, especially when I cook for them.

There was a reason I decided on making the penne with vodka sauce. It's one of their favorites. I also have garlic bread and a salad, which they won't touch. I picked up a huge chocolate cake and the soft packaged chocolate chip cookies that Joseph loves, my brownies, along with lots of beer. It's the perfect meal for "buttering them up."

It's after six and I have some alone time with Evan before they get here. Joe usually comes earlier than the rest of them to get the best spot on the couch.

I curl up next to Evan with my glass of cheap wine. "Ev, do you think I'm making a mistake?"

He turns on the couch to face me and rests his arm on mine.

"No I don't. You were meant to sing on a stage Leila. You were meant to be seen outside the corners of Hoboken. You are going to be great. I know you worry about your dad and us. We will all be fine. You need to do this and you know it."

I take a deep breath as I let his words sink in. I know he's right and that I have to do this. Basically I don't have a choice after today, but hearing him say it helps my insecurities just a little.

The intercom buzzes making me jump. Evan laughs and gets up to answer the door.

"I'm here!" Joseph yells as he enters the apartment. I'm sure they heard him down the street. I get up to hug my teddy bear. As I am clutching his big chest, Joe chuckles into my hair. "Whoa, what's this Lei? My very own welcome committee?"

"I'm just going to get all my hugs in now, so no comment please." I answer hugging him tighter.

"Even Matt?" he asks.

"Not Matt!" I answer, pulling away and punching him in the gut. "Want a beer?"

"Naah... I want two." He plops himself down on the best spot on the couch, dead center in front of the TV.

Once I grab Joe's beer, he pats the spot next to his.

"How are you doing Leila? Are you trying not to relish in the fact you are going to be a huge rock star and forget all of our names? Even Evan's?" He asks, ruffling my hair.

"I will not forget all your names…yet." I retort as I ruffle what little hair he has. He keeps his hair Marine short.

The intercom buzzes again. Evan answers the door and Logan and Matt stroll into the apartment. Matt looks like he owns the place and Logan comes over to give me a hug. They are early, which means that they are anxious to get this over with or are starving.

"Hey sweet girl, how are you holding up?" Logan asks.

"I'm very nervous, excited, and scared all at the same time." I make my way into the kitchen to return with two more beers. I hand one over to Logan as he sits at my table and the other to his brother, who is already sitting on the far end of the couch. Matt winks as he accepts it but I ignore him and sit across from Logan.

"When's dinner? I'm fucking starving." Matt says like that's the only reason he is here. He is such a jerk. They're attacking the bowl of chips and pretzels I put out for them, so I know they are hungry. Only Matt makes me know it though.

"Soon." I announce dismissively. "So, guys, I want to fill you in on my contract and the details of the tour." I take a deep breath, and start giving them the run-down. This may actually be a bit worse than when I told my dad, because there are four of them.

They listen and occasionally ask questions. With the exception of Evan, they were surprised that Devil's Lair agreed to let me continue with Cliffhangers until we leave on tour. I don't know if they thought I would be gone after this weekend. The relief clearly showing on their faces, even Matt's.

"I also wanted to run something by you guys." I pause to find the words. "I want you to replace me."

"No." Evan barks.

Logan follows. "Absolutely not!"

"No way." Joseph copies.

"Guys, you need someone to pick up keyboards, and to sing alongside Matt. Please promise me you'll think about it. I feel like I'm abandoning you and this will make me feel better. You guys are awesome and it's just a matter of time before you are noticed. By adding back a singer/keyboardist, you can ditch the weddings and bar mitzvahs and spend your free time at band festivals and competitions. You need to get out there." I take a deep breath and am happy that I got it all out.

Evan speaks first. "She's right." He looks around the room. "We need to step it up a notch."

"I'll stop singing for you once you find a replacement. This leads me to the last thing I want to tell you. I know you guys can't afford it, but it may be smart to hire an agent. This agent that Devil's Lair hired is the reason they are where they are. You need someone batting for you, and getting you out of Hoboken. Well, guess what? I figured out the perfect way to do just that."

"Where are we going to find a person, who will accept, hell, beer in payment? To help us become rich and famous?" Logan grins at his own joke.

"Lori." I say. They all look at me like I've sprouted antlers. "What?"

"Lori?" Matt mocks.

"Yes, Lori. Lori Banzini." I respond.

"You must be kidding."

"No, I'm not. I'm serious. Lori can't afford to quit bartending. This affords her to continue to be there with you during shows and not on your dime. She has a very persuasive personality. Most people love her after

113

speaking to her for a few minutes. She is professional, and she loves music. She is gorgeous and people respond to that. She would go the extra mile for you guys and accept little for it, until it paid off. Trust me."

"Have you spoken to her about this?" Logan asks.

"Not yet, I wanted to run it by you all first. But if you are ok with it, I plan on talking to her first thing in the morning. Lori loves to go into the city to see bands play. She knows the best bars to be seen in and what the competition sounds like. She will be good for you guys. Plus she is looking for her dream job. I just know that this is it."

I've been brewing this over since I signed my contract. I was afraid to voice my idea to anyone, even Evan, for fear they would think it was crazy. But the more I thought about it, the more it made sense. For Lori, it would be a social thing as well. She is smart enough to know that schmoozing is necessary to get noticed, and she is just the person to do it. I was a little concerned about her feelings towards Matt. But that brings me to Plan B. I think she and Hunter would be perfect together. I think things could happen between them. If I can get them to meet, then Matt will be a distant memory. I smile at myself for my perfect plan.

The guys are considering this. This is a good time to leave them with their thoughts, and go fix dinner. I busy myself in the kitchen while they are discussing the pros and cons of my brainstorm. Matt is piping in all the reasons it won't work and the others are practically ignoring him. This is good. I can feel them warming to the idea. Hopefully Lori won't think that I'm an idiot once I tell her. I'll worry about that tomorrow.

I announce dinner after I lay out pasta, bread, salad, and more beer on the counter. They all bolt in my direction and pile the food on their plates. I make myself one as well and join everyone at the table. Matt chooses to eat alone at the couch.

I eat silently and listen to their discussion over Lori.

Joseph looks at me and asks, "Do you think she will go for it Lei?"

I look at Joseph and answer honestly, "I hope so. I plan on explaining how perfect a fit I feel she is and I will definitely stroke her ego. I think I'll be able to convince her that this is a good opportunity. It may not pay well now, but there is definite potential."

Evan says, "Let's vote. I say yes." He looks at Logan.

"What can it hurt? I'm a yes."

"Joe?"

"I agree. This could be brilliant." Joseph inhales more of his pasta.

We all turn towards the couch and look at Matt. He has definitely been listening, but acts like he hasn't a clue.

"Matt?"

"What?"

"Cut the crap." Logan barks. "Yes or no?"

He waits a few seconds and then answers with arrogance. "All that chick wants to do is get into my pants. I'm not thrilled with this idea."

UGH! He is so annoying.

"We will all make sure she doesn't try to get into your pants. If that's your only concern, we are counting you as a *yes*."

I smile at my victory and Matt's failure to ruin it. "I will talk to Lori tomorrow and let you know what she says. I know this will work guys."

I serve dessert soon after and the entire cake and all the cookies and brownies are gone in record time. It's a good thing I hid Evan's second batch. Damn, they can eat. They make their way back to the couch to settle in like they are about to spend the night.

What feels like minutes later, I feel a kiss on my cheek and open my eyes to see Evan leaning over me. I must have passed out. It has been an exhausting week and all my sleepless nights must have caught up to me.

"What time is it?" I ask him while yawning and stretching.

"Twelve-thirty."

"How long have I been out?" I hope to God that I wasn't drooling. These guys have seen me in some compromising situations, but my open-mouthed, drool-induced, sleep-coma is not one I'd like them to witness.

He laughs like he knows what I was thinking. "As soon as your butt hit that chair. We watched the game. Logan and Matt left about an hour ago and Joseph stayed long enough to help me clean up."

"You cleaned up? God, I love you so much." I hug him tightly.

"You love that I cleaned up but I love you too." He responds smiling. "I'm gonna go. I'll talk to you tomorrow." He bends to kiss my cheek again and grabs his jacket to leave but stops at my door. "Hand over the brownies."

Locking up after Evan, I prep for bed in less than five minutes. The instant my head hits my pillow I fall into a very deep, very nice sleep.

***

He is shirtless as he plays a guitar and sings to me. We are alone in a room I am not familiar with. When I look around all I see are windows…lots and lots of windows. He stands and very slowly walks over to me, while still singing. Next he puts down his guitar, takes me in his arms, and runs his nose along mine. After penetrating me with his gaze, he bends to kiss me.

I sit up panting.

WHAT THE HELL WAS THAT?

I am sweating, aroused, and upset that I woke up too soon.

I look around to see daylight pouring through my windows and I frantically try to calm my erratic breathing. The alarm clock reads ten-twenty am. Oh crap! I can't believe I slept this late.

I need coffee.

Flipping on the TV as a distraction, I anxiously wait for my coffee to brew. The good news is that I finally caught up with the much-needed sleep I was missing. The bad news is that I can't get Jack out of my mind. The dream was nothing more than a kiss and it was definitely not X-rated, but it may as well have been. There was something very erotic about it. It was a complete turn-on, and left me feeling very unsatisfied.

My raging libido is getting out of control. I may have to take things into my own hands or risk being miserable for the next year of my life. I wanted to get so much done today. Calling Lori will be the most important task. I just can't seem to get my body to move and my mind to think of something other than shirtless Jack kissing me, and what would have happened hadn't I woken up.

Damn it…

I grab the phone and dial Lori's number distractedly.

"Hello?" she croaks into the phone.

"Lori, its Leila. Did I wake you?"

She yawns loudly. "What time is it?"

"It's almost eleven, I think. Call me back later." I am about to hang up.

"No, I'm up, I'm up. No worries. What's up?" Another yawn that follows doesn't make her sound very convincing.

"I wanted to meet for lunch. I have some things I want to run by you. Can we meet at Riverside?" Lori loves Riverside Square Mall. She practically lives there.

"Sounds good. How's one?"

"Perfect. I'll meet you at Cheesecake Factory." Lori loves the Factory as much as the mall. I'm pulling out all the stops.

"Will you call Lis?"

"No, it's just me and you."

"Uh oh…what did I do wrong?" Her tone causes me to laugh.

We hang up and I am buzzing with excitement. I will have a fantastic future to look forward to and will be leaving my boys with a back-up plan if this works.

***

Waiting for Lori to show is nerve wracking. A small hole that is a seed of doubt slowly festers until it's a huge crater. What if she hates my idea? I don't have an alternate plan. It's Lori, or it's leaving my boys without a strategy. That'll mean months on the road worrying and stressing over their well-being. Selfishly, I would like to embark on the tour with the peace of mind knowing the guys will be ok. It may be a false sense of security, but I need it nonetheless.

It's only one-fifteen but I am fidgety and I keep staring at the door. A few minutes later I see the redhead bounce through the doors. She spots me as she nears the hostess podium, and makes her way to my table.

She slides into her side of the booth and smiles. "Hey babe, what's going on? You have me freakin' a little."

"Oh, tons. Don't freak…its all good." I want to fast forward to the part where she says, "YES! I'LL DO IT!" I need to handle her the right way. First, I need to make small talk. Next, compliment her. Then, throw her some gossip I heard about a girl we knew in high school. Once I can't stand the waiting any longer, I begin.

I start off slow by telling her about my new band. I then go into the rehearsals and the tour. She nods a lot, and asks a lot of really good questions, business questions, and "agent" kind of questions. She is perfect for this.

I continue to tell her about my working with Cliffhangers until the tour starts. I tell her about cooking the boy's dinner to fill them in on the contract details. Then I lay it on her. I tell her my idea, except for the part where I want to set her up with Hunter. She stays quiet, and takes it all in.

The waitress comes by and without breaking eye contact with me, Lori quickly comments, "We aren't ready." The woman leaves without a backwards glance.

Lori is staring at me, not moving, just staring.

"Lori?"

When she finally speaks she asks, "Are you high?"

"Lori, you are perfect for this. You know that. You would make a great agent, especially with your personality. How hard can it be?" I'm starting to worry that she won't agree to this.

"I have no experience. None! How can I possibly help those boys in any way? Then there is the small, tiny issue of Matt hating me!" She is getting more and more worked up. I have to reel her back in and *fast*.

"Lor, listen to me. First of all, Matt doesn't hate you, he is a dickhead. Second, you need to get those boys signed on to band competitions and festivals in the New York area. This will get them exposure. You always go to those things anyway and know the best ones that are out there. Once you do that, the rest will fall into place. You know the guys are awesome. They just need to be noticed, and nobody can do that better than you."

She looks at me long and hard. I don't waver or break eye contact. I can tell she is running this through her brain. I can tell she is battling within her head. She knows she can do it, but yet she is afraid that she can't. I patiently sit and let her think it through. She goes to speak, then shuts her mouth. This happens three times in a row.

"You are certifiable." She finally proclaims.

Oh boy.

"Lori, there isn't a risk to you if you take this on. You will still be bartending and earning your paycheck. The upside is you will continue to see them perform every night on Sal's dime. During your spare time you can simply scout out bars and clubs to book them for gigs. This will replace their normal Sunday night bar mitzvahs or weddings. They have a CD recorded that you can use to promote them. You will also start researching band competitions that are happening over the summer. You will enter them in, list your name as their agent, and that's it. You can see if this were something you would even enjoy once things start picking up for them. Then you can decide if you'd want to quit the bar. Win, win for all." I sit back and wait.

"Have you discussed this with the guys yet?"

I nod. "They all voted yes."

"All?" She crosses her arms and challenges me to admit my lie. I'm not lying. I simply won't tell her that we bullied Matt into saying yes.

"All, including Matt. They think it's a great idea. Take Alisa with you. I'm sure she would be thrilled to help you scout out places for them to play. This will give her more time with Logan and help him fulfill his dream too."

There is a very long, very torturous silence between us.

Finally Lori speaks. "I'll think about it."

Score.

Chapter 10-Jack

"Please, please…oh yes…yes, Jack…yes…"

She is naked on my bed and arching her back while I make love to her with my fingers, lips, and tongue. Her long wavy hair is fanned out around her on the pillow. She has the most perfect body. Her chest rises with every breath while her lower half writhes in ecstasy. The skin on the inside of her thighs is as smooth as silk as I grip her to keep her still.

"Please, Jack, don't stop."

I bend back down to taste her again and it causes her to moan deeply. Her moans are driving me crazy.

There's a ringing. What the hell is ringing?

I spring up in bed and the hard-on I am blessed with causes me to slump sideways to relieve the pressure. I reach for my phone with one hand when I realize it's ringing and grip my dick with the other. It's only six am.

Fuck it's early…too early.

Damn it, I'm gonna kill that fucker.

"Hunter, why are you calling me?"

"Is Rachel with you? Amanda is still here. She is trying to reach her, but she isn't answering her phone."

Oh crap… Rachel.

"Um, no, I got her a cab last night. I'm sorry I was supposed to let Amanda know." Damn it, I totally forgot.

"Oh, ok. I'll tell her."

"Hey Hunt, can you call me once Amanda leaves?"

I don't want to run into her and I need coffee. I need to make a gallon of coffee the minute she is out of here.

I lay down and close my eyes so I can replay the dream I just had. So Miss Leila Marino paid me another visit last night. I've had plenty of erotic dreams over the years, but this one seemed so real.

I would have had a very happy ending, instead of sporting uncomfortable morning wood if I wasn't so rudely interrupted.

There is a knock at my door, and Hunter strolls in.

"Fuck! What the hell dude? I could have been jerking off or something. I said to call me, not barge in." I have no fucking privacy.

He shrugs and ignores me. "Mandi is gone."

"Mandi? Already on a nick- name basis? I guess things went well?"

"Yeah, real well." He grins. "I like her. We talked and talked."

"Talked and talked? And?"

"Talked and talked. We made out, felt each other up, but mostly talked."

I gawk at him like he grew another head. "You're shitting me? You finally get a girl up to the roof, and you talk? I endured Rachel and stopped her from interrupting you two last night for nothing?" I can't believe this guy. I know he isn't gay. He is either a hopeless romantic, or a total schmuck.

"We had a real nice time together. She didn't push it further and neither did I. It's kind of a test. No way should you marry a girl who fucks you on the first date." He says this like he has just revealed a trade secret.

"So now you are marrying her?" Throwing up my hands I give him an exasperated look. "Well I hope you are very happy together." Hunter rolls his eyes and leaves my room. The only good thing about our conversation is that it has effectively killed my hard-on.

By the time I get to the kitchen, Hunter is banging cabinets noisily looking for a bowl for his fucking Fruit Loops.

"Jeez, dude. Could you be any louder?"

"What crawled up your ass?"

For some reason watching him standing at the sink, eating his juvenile cereal annoys the shit out of me.

"Nothing crawled up my ass. I'm just annoyed that you woke me up." He gives me a look that says he clearly isn't buying my excuse.

He's right. I've been in a crappy mood lately. I forget Hunter and embrace memories of my dream that provokes a desperate desire to see Leila. Maybe I can convince Hunter to go to Hoboken and see them play? We need to invite her to the party so it would be like killing two birds with one stone. I have wanted to see her band in action, anyway. This would solve that, too.

There are a few minutes of silence as he stares into his bowl and noisily eats his stupid Fruit Loops while I'm drinking my coffee and scheme a plan to see Leila.

Ok, here goes.

"So, I wanted to go out to Hoboken and check out Leila's band. I want to see her perform on stage and all. Want to come?" I try to sound very nonchalant.

He stops eating and looks at me. "When?"

"Tonight. I thought we could also tell her about the party when we are there. We have nothing else to do. Consider it research."

This sounds pathetic.

"I guess. Do you think her band would be upset with us showing up like that?"

"Who gives a crap? We are there to see our new back-up singer working. Screw her band." The truth is that I am more worried about Leila's reaction to us just showing up.

Hunter shrugs and says, "Fine. You're driving though. If I have to go to Jersey, I plan on getting shit-faced."

I can handle that. Feeling optimistic for the first time in days, I decide to try and fall back into the dream I was enjoying so much earlier. "I'm going back to bed, stay out of my room."

"Sweet dreams." He responds, smirking annoyingly.

The dickhead is onto me.

Chapter 11-Leila

"She said she wants to talk to us." I look around the back room of The Zone with an exasperated expression. Three times they have separately asked me if Lori was going to say "yes or no" in the past ten minutes. Each time I've told them that I had no idea.

"I'm sure if it was a no, she would've just let you know and not make such a production about it, right?"

I love these guys, but boy are they *dense.*

I give Logan an exasperated look that screams, "I don't know" and shrug for the fourth time. It's been a few days since I broke the news of my master plan to the guys and Lori. Lori has been absolutely silent on the entire subject. She hasn't said a word and has acted like I never mentioned it. Alisa, who knows all the details because Logan filled her in, thinks it's a great idea and loves the notion of being Lori's sidekick. She is busting at the seams and wants to shake some sense into Lori, even though I promised myself that I would be patient and not try to influence her. Alisa agreed to the same, albeit reluctantly.

The boys promised not to say a word to Lori or to harass her regarding her decision. Unfortunately that gave them Carte Blanche to harass and bother me.

The more the guys mulled over my idea, the more they felt it was perfect. I'm not convinced of Matt's sentiment, but Logan promised me that he was on board. Evan said Logan did admit that he *helped* Matt see the benefits of my plan. I don't want to think about how he went about *helping* Matt. Logan must have ripped him a new one.

Joseph stands and starts pacing the room. He turns towards me and barks, "Where the hell is she?"

Jeez.

Finally, the door opens and Lori breezes into the room looking very calm, relaxed, and stunning. Her hair is loose and shiny and her emerald eyes sparkle. Her curvaceous body leaves nothing to the imagination in skin tight jeans, obscenely high-heeled sandals, and her black t-shirt with "The Zone" spread across her ample chest like a Hooters waitress wanna-be.

"Hi guys. How's it goin'?" She takes the chair Joseph just left and makes herself comfortable. They all stare at her like she is an alien and say nothing. I need to take control of this situation, before I hurt someone.

"They are driving me nuts! Lori, please cut to the chase." I pleadingly grasp her arm.

I think I can hear Logan's heart beating from where I am standing. She stands, lays her hands on the table, and looks at each of their faces while smiling smugly. This is an Emmy award worthy performance and basically I'm going to kill her.

"Well" she remarks in her cocky kind of way. "I have been chewing over Leila's plan. Although I think it needs a lot of work, I feel she is a very smart girl. There isn't a person on the planet that can do this job better than I can." She and Matt really are perfect for each other.

Logan jumps up and hugs her. "Lori, you are absolutely right. I agree that you have exactly what we need in an agent. You are tenacious, smart, ruthless, and you have the biggest set of balls a girl could possibly have."

Lori is beaming and looks over at me for reassurance. I nod encouragingly while smiling myself. Joseph and Evan both move around the table to hug Lori as well, and she enthusiastically returns the gesture.

An awkward silence falls over the room like a wet blanket. Matt still hasn't moved or said a word. A few torturous seconds pass when Lori poignantly looks over at Matt. "Let's address the one issue I'm sure you are all concerned with. I want to say it out loud so there isn't any confusion." She says while pinning him with her emerald green eyes and crossing her arms defiantly. Everyone remains silent, as we are all stare at Lori in shock because she is going to go there.

"Matt, in the past, I know you and I have had some…" She pauses to look up at the ceiling and then looks at him. "Let's call them differences? I'm done. Now that I've made the decision to be your agent, nothing will stop me from the end result. I've decided it's not worth jeopardizing my success or the band's. I've decided you simply aren't worth it." Her apologetic shrug belies the true feelings in her eyes.

Matt and Lori stare each other down. The awkwardness earlier was nothing compared to the tense aura hanging in the room now. We shift our eyes from Lori to Matt and back again like we are watching a tennis match.

Matt stands and folds his arms across his chest to mimic Lori's posture. Something is off. He doesn't look relieved or even accepting of Lori's announcement. In my opinion, he looks stunned. Watching him closely, I can see confusion swirling around in his mind like a tornado. I probably know this man better than anyone else in this room, including his own brother.

It suddenly hits me. I think Matt liked Lori chasing him these past few years. It's a revelation that makes so much sense. His cocky attitude, his better than the rest act, his god's gift to women performance…all of it makes sense. Lori's pursuit was the perfect circumstance for him.

Matt was acting out the role of a rock star.

I am so on to the bastard.

I switch my focus to Lori, who is transfixed on Matt. Either she finally sees him for who he is, or this is a master plan she has hatched up. Either way, they both are holding their cards, and bluffing. Neither of them can fool me.

Finally Matt narrows his eyes and concedes. "Welcome to Cliffhangers, boss." Lori extends her hand and Matt shakes it slowly. Their eyes lock and silently challenge, "Game on."

Of course, the guys are oblivious to this entire exchange. Men.

The chatter in the room becomes deafening with the guys throwing ideas at Lori of different festivals and competitions they want to enter. Lori is bouncing off her own ideas of band image and exposure. It takes all of three minutes for me to see this was a match made in heaven.

Watching my former band and their new agent interacting is such a defining moment for me. I know that she will take real good care of my boys. When faced with a challenge Logan is right...Lori is ruthless.

They are all ignorant to the fact that we were due on stage five minutes ago. Sal will be appearing any minute to find out what the delay is.

"Um...guys. I hate to break this love-fest up, but we're late."

"Let's blow our show and celebrate." Joe says, looking around the room nodding and grinning like a kid in a candy store.

Lori points to the door and says, "Get to work."

Saluting his new drill sergeant, Joe laughs and hugs Lori. "Yes, boss."

The Cliffhangers all file out of the room like good little soldiers. Matt throws Lori one last look before leaving the room.

Lori smirks prompting me to ask, "What are you up to?"

She shrugs innocently. "Nothing."

"Bullshit." A few seconds later, she winks confirming my suspicions.

I watch her closely as she puts on her best poker face. I don't have time to get into it this with her right now.

"I've got to get out there. Thank you."

"What for? I should be thanking you. You were right. Those boys need me."

"Yes, they do. One more thing, I haven't had a chance to tell you some of the details since our chat. I wanted to let you know that I told the guys I feel they need to replace me. They gave me a hard time, and think it's unnecessary. It is now your job to convince them."

"Absolutely." She says without a pause. "I love you Leila, and it will be hard for them to find someone as perfect of a fit as you were, but you're right. This will be item number one on my "to do" list. No worries." She leans in and hugs me tight.

"I know you will take care of my boys and get them where they need to be. I love you." I mumble into her shoulder as my voice cracks from emotions.

Lori chuckles into my hair and hugs me tighter. "You aren't going off to war, Lei."

As we make our way into the bar arm and arm, Alisa spots us and immediately grins from ear to ear. Lori does not miss a beat and accuses, "She knows?"

Oops…

Alisa storms over to where we are standing with both hands on her hips. "Yes I know! Logan told me. I've been dying to talk to you about it for days. Jesus, Lori, what the *hell*? At least a hundred times I was going to bring it up, but this one over here made me swear on a stack of bibles not to say a word. Do you know how hard it was for me to act normal for the last few days? It's been complete and utter torture. Logan was so stressed and every time I would bring it up he would make me zip it. Evan avoided me at all costs so he wouldn't have to listen to me bitching on how unfair it was to keep this in. I could have gotten an ulcer from the stress. Both of you owe me so big for this. I want a spa day with the works, not to mention a percentage of the profits once those yahoo's make it big."

She finally stops only to take a breath and is about to start another rant when I interrupt. "I love you Lis, and yes we owe you one. I know this was very hard on you. I wish I could stay and chat about it, but I have to go do my job now." Kissing her cheek, I bolt towards the stage. Tentatively I look back to see Lori shooting daggers at me. I've just left my one friend alone to get reamed for the next four hours from my other friend with no escape. She is going to kill me for sure.

Evan meets me at my keyboard. "Such a great idea you had. You are so awesome Lei."

"I know."

"Humble as shit too." He kisses my cheek and saunters over to his side of the stage to grab his bass guitar.

I catch a glimpse of Sal standing across the bar and pointing to his watch as Matt hastily addresses the crowd. "Hey, Hoboken. So sorry we're late. I promise we'll make it up to you!" A few girls call out crude, suggestive offers as Matt laughs jovially. He really should laugh more often. It's so sexy. I swear he's like Sybil with his multiple personalities. He ranges from dickhead to dreamboat.

Matt turns to give us his cue and we finally start our first song.

Sal tries hard to look annoyed, but he can't quite pull it off. There is a decent crowd tonight, so naturally the girls are super busy at the bar. I'm hoping this is making it difficult for Alisa to continue her rant on Lori. When

I glance over, though, Alisa is still yapping away and Lori is still rolling her eyes dramatically. I probably owe them both a spa day after this.

Melancholy hits with a violent force. This has been my life for the past few years. Spending many nights a week on this very stage and singing with this awesome group of men with my two dear friends in the same room tending bar makes me realize how much I'm really going to miss this. A lump forms in my throat from the bittersweet events simultaneously occurring in my life. It's bitter because these chapters of my life will all end very soon and sadness doesn't begin to describe my emotions yet sweet because I have landed a job as a back-up singer with a very talented rock band and I'm about to live my dream in just a few weeks.

From my position on stage, I slowly scan the room to commit every single detail to memory. I want to recall where the boys stand at their respective places on stage, the girls at the bar working hard, the back of Matt's body as he suggestively seduces the crowd with his voice, the worn wooden floors and well weathered walls, the view from the stage of the dimly lit corners, and even the faces of the patrons as we perform. I *need* to remember every single detail.

The bar doors suddenly open throwing a temporarily glow into the room from the streetlamps outside. This happens so many times during the course of any given night that it can become distracting. Casually glancing up at the doors just as I do every time they open, I suddenly freeze from panic. I recognize that posture.

OMG…its Jack.

Guardedly I watch as he looks around the bar while taking a few steps deeper into the room. I still can't see his face, but I don't have a doubt in my mind that it's him.

My body starts to tremble from nerves or from being so damn horny. Perhaps it's both?

Jack leans in to talk to his friend. I can't see the other man's face either but spiky hair tells me its Hunter. They move towards an empty table to the right of the stage adjacent to my position. Jack takes the seat directly facing me while Hunter sits next to him. Their table is under one of the recessed lights and affords every female in the bar an unfettered view of his gorgeous face.

Case in point…

Kelly, one of our waitresses, is chatting at another table and turns to tell them she'll be right with them. One look at Mr. Sex God and her mouth hangs open in the most unflattering way.

Lori and Alisa are working opposite ends of the bar. Lori notices him first, quickly followed by Alisa. They both stop in their tracks, completely stunned into silence. It's a definite first.

Every female in the room is gawking at him and either he doesn't have a clue or he couldn't care less. Matt, I'm guessing does have a clue. His head turns towards Jack, probably because he noticed all female eyes are no longer looking at him.

As for myself, I can feel his gaze on me like Superman's x-ray vision. But I chose to keep my head down to avoid staring into his gorgeous eyes. Because once I do, I'm toast. I can feel him watching my every move. It's unnerving. My knees are wobbling, my hands are trembling, and I'm pretty sure I can feel sweat trickling down my back. It's a ridiculous reaction to someone I barely know.

Although he's taken my breath away every time I've seen him, this reaction I am having tonight is different. The onslaught of nervous jitters that are now controlling my body must be because he is here to size up my performance. What if he doesn't like what he sees?

The wobbling, trembling, and sweating go on until the last song before our break begins. It's a duet between Matt and I, front and center sharing a microphone.

That means I need to walk across the stage and pray that I don't fall, or pee my pants, or throw up. In fact, at this very moment I should be standing next to Matt instead of being rooted to the floor at my keyboards.

At ten seconds into the song, Evan gives me the *"what the hell are you doing?"* look.

At twenty seconds into the song, Matt gives me the *"get the fuck over here, now!"* look.

I take a quick glance at Jack, who is leaning forward with his elbows on his knees as if he's waiting for the plot of a murder mystery. Could this get any more humiliating?

My brain starts screaming at my body like a drill sergeant.

"MOVE YOUR ASS AND SING SOLDIER!"

With a deep breath, I turn and make my painful, humiliating way over to Matt as gracefully as I can manage while ignoring his evil stink eye. I pick up the vocals at the chorus, and hope everyone in the room thinks it was planned.

A higher power takes over and bestows me with an outer body experience. As if possessed, I begin to play the role of rock singer somewhat convincingly. Rasping the lyrics in a very seductive, suggestive manner, I place my hand over Matt's while he is holding the microphone stand. His eyes widen slightly at my touch and a slow smile creeps on his handsome face.

I move closer so Matt and I are now a few inches apart, close my eyes and imagine singing with Jack. The image in my mind is breath taking. Jack's face is so close that I can feel his breath. Wanting to feel his lips on mine, I impulsively lean in even closer, as we seduce each other with the lyrics.

I completely lose myself in the daydream I have conjured up in my mind, until I hear the crowd's applause cruelly yank me back to reality. The applause is different than I'm used to. The whistling is deafening!

Despite the crowd's reaction, I think, actually I *know,* that I just made a complete fool out of myself. Evan, Joseph, and Logan are all frozen with shock while Matt is grinning like a fool. He shakes his head and he announces to the crowd we are taking a short break.

Wishing the stage would swallow me whole at this very moment, I walk over to my keyboards afraid to make eye contact with anyone. Evan's loud bark in my ear causes me to jump. "What the hell was THAT?!"

I can attempt to lie, but it won't work. Evan knows me too well. "He's here. Jack and Hunter are both here." I whisper desperately. As Evan tries to look behind him, I grab his face violently. "Don't you dare turn around, I'll kill you!"

He laughs. "Is that who your little performance was for?"

I narrow my gaze and whisper, "I don't know what came over me."

"Why are you freaking out? So he came to see you perform? Don't you think you need to get used to his presence?"

"Yes, but not tonight and *not* in my bar!"

Evan throws me a look. "Lei, don't be ridiculous."

"He makes me so nervous."

"You need to get over it. You are probably looking at him like a celebrity and not your band mate. He's just a guy, Leila, just like me."

"See, here's the thing. I am looking at him like he's my boss. And what if my BOSS hates my performance?"

"Now you're being even more ridiculous."

I sigh and whisper through clenched teeth, "Fine." Then I grab his hand in a death grip and drag him off the stage.

"Your hand is sweating."

"Shut up!"

Matt, Logan and Joseph head straight to the bar, as they do every time we perform. "Guys, come over here when you get your beers. I want to introduce you to my new band mates."

Joe turns to see who I am talking about. One look at Jack and Joe instantly figures out the reason for my new found sex appeal on stage. With a wide smirk he walks backwards to the bar, making obscene gestures with his hips. Jackass.

Matt also figures it out, but he looks annoyed and pissed off.

I ignore him and approach Jack's table. Not realizing I'm still squeezing the life out of Evan's hand. "Ow."

"Hi. What brings you to Hoboken?"

Hunter smiles warmly. "Hey Leila. We wanted to see you guys perform. You sounded great up there. I loved the last song."

"Thanks, Hunter."

I turn towards Jack and I think I hear a whooshing noise in between my ears, as I get hopelessly lost in his smoky grey eyes. We suspend time by intently staring at each other.

Evan attempts to capture my attention by squeezing my hand, but it doesn't work and I effectively zone out. Thankfully he takes control of the situation.

"Evan Miller." He shakes Hunter's hand first then Jack's. Jack gaze flicks over to our clasped hands as he shakes Hunter's other one.

Awkward silence stretches between these three gorgeous men and me. Jack speaks first directly to Evan. "You guys sound awesome."

"Thanks. I've seen you guy's play as well. Congrats on all your success. You deserve it."

Jack and Hunter flash quick, shy smiles at Evan's compliment. My heart swells from the pride I feel for Evan. He's truly a class act.

"Leila, I can never get tired of your voice, but now I have an awesome visual as well. That was hot. You sure know how to work a crowd."

Whoa, what?

All eyes now focus on me.

"Um…thanks?"

With a laugh, Jack follows up. "Compliment. It's definitely a compliment."

He liked it? But more importantly, he thought it was hot? Having Jack Lair tell you something is hot is by far the hottest thing I've ever heard.

Evan squeezes my hand painfully, which causes me to flinch and break eye contact first.

"She says thank you." He speaks for me. My hand is throbbing from Evan's assault. I glare at him and he counters by raising his eyebrows. Without words, we are able to have a very heated conversation. He thinks I'm acting like a complete ass and I believe he's blatantly trying to embarrass me.

"Um…you should meet the rest of the guys." I announce in a pathetic attempt to cover the embarrassing exchange that just occurred between Evan and me. I'm still rubbing my hand as I motion to my fellow band members to come over. This is good. The more people to distract from my absurd behavior the better.

Evan makes the rest of the introductions, since I'm rendered useless. Joe and Logan grab some chairs from a nearby table so we can all sit. They all strike up a conversation effortlessly, except for Matt. He is the only one sitting in silence.

Jack turns towards him and says. "You have a great voice man."

"Thanks." He answers indifferently.

More silence.

He sits there like a total lump and does not participate, in the conversation. Occasionally sipping his beer in complete boredom. Dreamboat is gone and dickhead is back. In spite of Matt's obvious jealous brooding, the rest of the guys discuss their music and future plans.

Kelly sashays over with a pitcher of beer and smiles sweetly at Jack. I've never seen Kelly move her hips that way before. "It's on the girls. I'm Kelly." She thrusts her hand at Jack, then at Hunter. She's talented enough to pour a round for the guys while her eyes remain firmly glued to Jack. It's quite a performance.

Jack looks confused. "Girls?"

Pointing at the bar I answer his question. "Alisa and Lori are our bartenders as well as our good friends."

He turns and like a magic trick both of their mouths drop open at the exact same time. There isn't a doubt in my mind they are both experiencing the crotch clenching at this very moment. Logan raises his eyebrows at Alisa's behavior just as Jack raises his glass and nods a thank you.

He turns away from the girls and misses the best part which is Lori clutching the bar and mouthing obnoxiously, "OH MY GOD!"

Alisa shows more class by resuming her bartending duties, all the while sneaking nervous looks at Logan.

"That's really nice of them. Thank you, Kelly." Hunter says.

"My pleasure." I could swear Kelly grazed Jack's arm with her ass before walking away.

Oh brother.

The guys all interact so comfortably with each other while drinking their free beer. You would think they all have known each other for years. As Jack discusses details of the tour with Evan, his eyes continually find mine. Each and every time, I'm caught staring. It doesn't seem to stop me from staring though. Watching him shooting the breeze with my close friends and speaking passionately about his music is riveting.

Lori waving her arms at me like an air traffic controller interrupts my trance. "Um…I'm sure the girls want to meet you guys. I'll introduce you if you want."

Jack turns and Lori waves at him. "Sounds good."

"We'll catch you guys later. You'll stick around after the show?" Evan asks as he stands.

Hunter nods, "Sure, we'll be here."

"Cool." Evan and Joe both head to the back room and leave Logan and Matt to linger a few seconds longer.

Matt starts to follow as well but then stops suddenly. Almost as an afterthought, he looks over at me and then at Jack. "Take care of her." He says, his tone a touch threatening.

"We fully intend to." Jack responds, taking his challenge.

"Did you hit your head?" I ask, clearly shocked by his comment. Matt pats my shoulder before walking away.

Looking over at Logan, I voice my concern again. "Seriously, did he hit his head?"

"Not recently, but maybe it's finally caught up to him." Logan shrugs. "Let's go meet our lovely bartenders." He adds shooting daggers at his lovely bartender girlfriend.

The girls see us coming, Alisa hides behind Lori to avoid Logan's glare while Lori adjusts her boobs and fluffs out her hair.

"Hey guys, this is Jack and Hunter. They are both in Devil's Lair. Guys, this is Alisa and Lori. They are two of my closest friends, and they both make a mean margarita."

Alisa introduces herself as Logan's other half in hopes of scoring some points with her displeased boyfriend. Lori shakes their hands and adds, "Bartending is a side job. I'm the Cliffhangers agent as well."

Oh lord.

"Hi girls, it's nice to meet you." Jack woos them with his dazzling smile.

Hopelessly I watch as the possibility of setting Lori and Hunter up spins into a fiery crash and nosedives to the ground. She hasn't noticed him because she hasn't taken her bulging eyes off Jack.

Damn it!

"You're gorgeous." Lori announces dreamily while looking at Jack. As an afterthought she throws, "You too, Hunter."

Amused, Jack sneaks a sideways glance at me before answering. "Why, thank you. You gals aren't so bad yourselves." Jack's words have Lori giggling like a schoolgirl and flipping her hair.

Oh for God's sake.

I've had enough of this display.

"Well, ok then…I got to get back to work."

Just as I'm about to walk away, Jack takes hold of my elbow. "Wait." He starts jumbling out his next sentence nervously. "Um, we are having a party Sunday night at our place. Yeah, um, we would love if you ladies could come. Maybe bring the guys, too?" This is strange, as Jack doesn't do nervous. He's clearly uncomfortable and has me wondering why he's bothering with the invite?

Even though Jack is speaking to me, Lori nods her head like a bobble-head and speaks for all of us. "We wouldn't miss it for the world."

The chain of events that occurs next has me staring numbly as if I am watching a car crash in slow motion. Lori gives Jack her best Lori-is-most-definitely-into-you doe eyes. Jack graces Lori with his CCDS smile. Lori fans herself and winks. Jack laughs again. Lori bats her eyelashes.

Ugh. The entire exchange has me nauseous.

Wait. Was his invite a last minute decision once he met Lori? Is my invitation a ruse? Damn it...I *DID NOT* see this coming.

"Lei, we have to go." Logan says with a definite edge to his voice. Before he walks away, he leans over the bar and whispers something in Alisa's ear. Her reaction is one of a kid who just got reprimanded for misbehaving. This is not like Logan. He is not usually a jealous person normally. Jack can single-handedly bring the worst out of most men, and the lust out of most women.

"I have to go. I'll see you guys later." I excuse myself to follow Logan to the stage, where Evan, Matt and Joe are waiting for us to resume our show.

During our second half, I continue to torture myself by watching the flirting duo interact with each other. Hunter has moved back to his table while talking on the phone. Can't say I blame him. He may as well have been invisible. He also didn't react to Lori like most men do when they first meet her. Not like Jack is reacting at the moment.

After Logan walks away, Alisa moves on to help another customer. This leaves Lori and Jack alone to continue their conversation as if no one else existed in the bar, and for me to stew on stage for no logical reason whatsoever.

Matt keeps glancing over at them making me wonder if this is bothering him as well. He is used to being the best looking guy in the room. No doubt his jealousy is simmering even more so now that Lori seems to have moved her obsessions to Mr. Lair. Is this part of her plan or has she truly moved on already? It figures the day she decides to get over Matt Rizzo is the same day Jack Lair walks into the bar. What are the odds? I almost feel sympathy for Matt.

Jack returns to his seat and has a brief conversation with Hunter as they both glance back at Lori while smiling. This totally consumes me. Lori walks over to their table with two beers in hand and is now playing the role of waitress.

Lori sits in a chair next to Jack and leans into his ear.

He leans back and she laughs.

She puts her hand on his arm.

He grins.

She gets up leans in and says something.

He nods.

She gives them both her best smile.

They wave.

She saunters back to the bar and speaks to Alisa.

Alisa responds.

 Lori nods enthusiastically.

Watching this play by play unfold from the stage has my own mind racing with jealous, harpy thoughts. I hardly know this guy so why should this bother me so much? I try to break it down piece-by-piece and figure out why the prospect of Lori and Jack together has me tied in knots.

I am neither attached to Jack, nor do I plan to be. We are co-workers. He is my boss, end of story. On the other hand, I really don't think I can handle living through a budding romance between a man I clearly lust over and one of my best friends. It would be too painful to watch them fall madly in love.

By the end of our very long, very torturous show, I have Jack and Lori married with two point five kids, a center hall colonial, a dog, and a minivan.

Just as they do every night, the boys literally jump off the stage and beeline to the bar for a round of shots. They only do one and it's always tequila and I always pass. As they all turn right, I turn left towards the back room. Fighting the urge to grab my stuff and exit via back door, instead I put on my happy face and walk back out to the bar with my jacket and bag in tow, ready to make as quick of an exit that I could.

Our fun, happy bunch is predictably doing their end of night shots. They invite Jack and Hunter to join their holy ritual. Two lonely shots sit on the tray waiting for my ass to arrive to the bar. "I'm not doing a shot."

Lori rolls her eyes. "God forbid. This one is mine." She picks up the tequila and the last shot that is much lighter in color than all the others. "This one is yours. It's ginger ale." Matt, Lori and Joe all chuckle at my expense. They tease me mercilessly every single night. Why should tonight be any different?

Actually the difference is, that tonight I'm going to kill her.

Evan comes over and throws his arm around my shoulder. "Leave Lei alone."

Lori smiles sweetly at Evan. "Ev, are you going to tour with Devil's Lair, too or is Leila hiring a NEW bodyguard?"

"That's not a bad idea Banzini. Things will be boring around here without Leila to bust on."

Ignoring Lori and Evan, I turn my attention to Jack and Hunter rolling my eyes. "See what I have to put up with? It was really nice of you guys to come see our show." Turning back to my friends, I smirk and wave my middle finger at their laughing faces. "I'll miss you all so much."

"Wait, if you don't like ginger ale, I have apple juice." Lori antagonizes me.

"Bite me Banzini."

"With pleasure Marino. Bend over."

"Ok…I'm outta here."

Evan kisses my cheek as I turn from my ball busting, hysterically laughing friends, Jack and Hunter included.

"Leila, I want to give you our address." Jack calls out as he rushes to catch up to me.

"Oh, ok."

I plug the address he recites into my phone. We stand facing each other, and I'm pulled into the magnetic field that surrounds him.

An awkward silence stretches between us.

"You ok?"

"Yeah, I'm just exhausted." I lie from necessity. I'm not in the mood for small talk at the moment. Jack watches me closely for a few seconds.

"Um, ok, see you at the party Leila?"

"Yes, we'll be there. Bye Jack."

Jack steps closer so we are face to face. My heart skips a beat, then another. "I'm glad we came tonight. Your band is really good. I knew you were talented, but seeing you performing with them, I kinda feel like we've stolen you." It looks like he wants to say something else, but chooses not to.

His presence consumes me.

His words confound me.

I whisper a very quiet thank you. I'm clearly at a loss for words.

"Ok, see you Sunday." Jack looks directly into my eyes, and I fall under the spell of his gaze. He then grips my shoulder as he walks away, leaving me panting and wondering if he is going to wait for Lori to finish her shift.

Damn it!

***

What do I wear to this stupid thing? I stare at my closet hoping that something presents itself to me. It's getting late, and I'm almost out of time. I've dilly-dallied, had three glasses of wine, which was a big mistake in hindsight as I'm now running around trying to get ready while slightly tipsy – another mistake.

Evan and Lori are due here any minute. Logan, Alisa, Joseph and Matt are meeting us there. I was surprised that Matt decided to come. My gut instinct was to un-invite him. Evan assured me Matt would be on his best behavior. My response to Evan was that we'd see.

The door buzzes scaring the crap out of me.

"I need five minutes." I call into the intercom, now panicked. Jeans, shirt, mascara, lipstick, a squirt of perfume between my breasts (I have no idea why, no one will be near them tonight) and I'm done in seven minutes. Not bad.

I take a deep breath and leave my apartment feeling even more buzzed from the adrenaline rush of getting ready in record time.

On my way down three flights, I consider my original plan of setting Lori up with Hunter.

Maybe it's not too late?

Maybe Hunter will capture her attention tonight?

Maybe Lori will become deathly allergic to Jack?

Evan and Lori are sitting in Evan's car waiting for me. The minute I slide into the back seat, Lori starts yapping.

"What a week this has been. Lei, you are the best. First you hand me a dream job on a silver platter. Next you introduce me to the best-looking man I have ever seen. Then he invites us to a party at his place. Life is so good." She reaches back to squeeze my knee.

I feel bad for being angry with her. It's not her fault she is so irresistible to men.

"Evan can you stop at a liquor store? I want to pick up something to bring with us."

"Sure, Lei."

I settle into the back seat. The soothing motion of the car makes me feel very sleepy all of a sudden.

Evan watches me through the rear view mirror and asks, "What's wrong?"

"Nothing. I'm just a little buzzed."

"Buzzed? You? Why are you buzzed?" Lori turns in her seat watching me skeptically.

"Don't look at me like that. I am a little nervous about tonight. I had a glass of wine that led to three."

Evan and Lori exchange a look, which I decide to ignore. They aren't my parents. I close my eyes and drift while picturing Jack's face.

It takes longer than it should to get to Brooklyn, between my brief catnap, stopping for liquor and the tons of traffic we hit cutting through Manhattan. We are over an hour late by the time we arrive at Jack and Hunter's building and my buzz is gone. From the sounds coming from the fourth floor, the party is definitely in full swing. Evan carries the case of beer he and Lori split, and I have the bottle of Tequila that I decided on.

Scott answers the door looking confused until he spots me behind Evan and Lori. "Hey Leila, so glad you could come."

"Scott, this is Evan and Lori. Guys, this is Scott. He's guitarist for Devil's Lair."

Hunter spots us standing at the door. "Hey, you made it" He says walking over. "Your friends got here a little while ago. We were wondering where you were." He is holding hands with a brunette beauty that is partially hiding behind him. Hunter turns to her and says, "This is Amanda."

She smiles shyly and waves.

Well any small hope I had left of Lori and Hunter hitting it off just took a free-fall off the roof without a parachute. That explains a lot.

"I'm Leila. This is Evan and Lori." I turn back to Hunter and shrug. "Sorry, we hit some traffic."

I'm instantly distracted as I spot Jack walk into the room. He notices our arrival, and walks straight over to us looking like a runway model. My mouth goes dry and Lori groans besides me and licks her lips like she is about to have him for lunch.

"Leila, you made it in one piece." he teases.

"Evan drove." I respond defensively. "I was merely a passenger." Evan gives me a look.

"So, it's all your fault Evan." Jack elaborates while fist punching Evan.

"Apparently so." Evan answers sourly.

Jack turns to hug Lori and then me. Man…he smells so good. He feels even better.

As Jack and Evan discuss the route we took to get here, Lori leans into me. "He smells so damn good."

I smile weakly and nod, wondering why she hasn't broken out into hives yet.

God forgive me.

Evan hands the beer to Hunter and I give my bottle of tequila to Jack. "Awesome. We are almost out. Thanks Leila. Come get something to drink."

Jack leads us through the small apartment towards the kitchen. Besides my band, the girls and Devil's Lair, Patti is here. She waves when she sees me. I have to make it a point to thank her. She is the reason I am now a member of Devil's Lair. Also mulling around are Scary Sally, Trey, a selection of pretty girls and a few other guys I don't know. In total there are a few dozen people cramped into this tiny apartment.

The short counter in the kitchen is littered with liquor bottles of all sorts.

Jack helps us select our drink of choice and grabs a beer for himself. Not seeing any white wine, I decide on a rum and diet coke. Jack makes a very strong drink. I casually grab an opened can and add more diet coke to my glass.

Shrugging, I say, "I'm a light weight. I usually drink cheap white wine."

"It has to be cheap?"

"Yes, otherwise it's awful."

He laughs and rubs my back. Lori catches the whole exchange and is unable to hide a frown. I quickly become the least her problems. As we stand in the small kitchen, three other girls appear from nowhere surrounding Jack like sharks circling a seal. Lori slinks over and stands next to Jack, clearly staking her claim. Damn, she's already territorial. I saunter out of the kitchen leaving the four beauties to duke it out as best they can.

Hunter is in a corner huddled close and whispering with Amanda. They make a nice couple. Hunter with his fair spiky hair and adorable smile and Amanda with her exotic long curly hair and warm brown eyes. In hindsight, he isn't a good match for Lori. He is too sweet. Trey is more her style.

Wait… I have an idea.

Wondering if I'm too late with my brand new plan, I look over at Lori who is glued to Jack's side. But in all fairness the three other girls have gotten closer to him as well. One of them is giving Lori a death stare every time Lori opens her mouth. Jack and Lori have been openly flirting, but surprisingly Jack isn't making any moves. Although Lori is very touchy, feely, Jack is not. He's keeping his distance.

This gives me a glimmer of hope.

I search for Trey and spot him across the room watching Lori. He doesn't take his eyes off her. Why didn't I think of this sooner? He is her typical bad boy rocker type, and I know that she will fall head over heels for him if she gives him just five minutes of her attention. I haven't spoken more than two words to Trey since I met him, but I can't let that stop me from putting my plan in motion.

I nonchalantly walk over to where he is standing. He turns towards me to acknowledge my presence.

"Having fun Leila?"

"Yeah, I am." I respond lamely. I don't have a thing to say to this man. Standing side by side in complete silence, five seconds in I am starting to feel uncomfortable. Thankfully, I notice Trey's eyes glued to Lori once again. I seize the opportunity. "Have you met my friend Lori?"

"No I haven't. Introduce us." His request is more of a command.

"Sure, wait here." I walk over to where Jack, Lori, and the trio are all downing shots. Lori always becomes the life of the party without even trying. Nothing intimidates this girl, absolutely nothing. She isn't fazed in the least that the other three are all vying for Jack's attention. She could give a crap.

She looks hot in a simple short red tank dress, her signature heels, and her auburn hair that hangs loosely to the middle of her back. While laughing and holding onto Jack's shoulder, she downs another shot. It's clear that she is beyond buzzed. I need to change her course of action immediately.

I lean over and whisper in her ear. "I want you to meet someone."

"Oh Lei, take a shot. You need one!" Jack looks amused and holds out the shot glass he just had against his own lips a moment ago. Damn that's hot.

Smirking, he says, "I'm afraid we don't have ginger ale."

"Funny." I take it from his fingers, down the shot, and hand him back the glass in one fast motion.

Wow, that burns. I detest tequila. How can they down these things so effortlessly?

Jack laughs at the face I am making. Once the burning stops, I feel a slow, warmth spread in the pit of my stomach that feels nice.

"Want another one?" He asks while staring into my eyes. What I want is to grab his face and shove my tongue down his throat. I really need to have sex before I start working with him or I will be charged with assault.

"No, I'm good. I just need to borrow Lori for a minute. We'll be right back."

I grab Lori's arm and pull her across the room. She protests until I stop her smack in front of Trey. Her eyes lose focus for a second and then she gives him a slow smile.

"Lori, this is Trey Taylor. He is bass guitarist for Devil's Lair. Trey, this is Lori Banzini, my good friend." They shake hands, and it's happening. They check each other out and Trey actually smiles.

Success!

I excuse myself after a few minutes of being completely ignored. Looking around the apartment, I try to decide who would be the lesser of all evils. Alisa, Logan, Hunter, Amanda, Scott and Patti are on the couch chatting like old friends. I guess they naturally migrated together since they are the only couples at the party.

Joseph, Matt, Scary Sally and a few guys are at the table playing some drinking game. Joseph looks relaxed and like he is having fun. Even Matt is smiling and having fun.

Evan has a cute blonde laughing at his every word. He feels my eyes watching him and turns towards me and smiles.

Missing in action are Jack and the blond who was shooting daggers at Lori. I feel a touch out of sorts and amble over to the mock bar to get another drink. Everyone else is buzzed and I am not.

Mixing a rum and diet coke, I feel someone's breath on my ear.

"Are you having fun?"

I jolt around in an extremely clumsy way and spill half my drink. Jack chuckles and says, "Did I scare you?"

"Yes." I respond truthfully. He did scare me. He does scare me.

He grabs a roll of paper towels and bends to clean up the spill.

"I'm so sorry."

"Don't be silly. It's no big deal." He straightens and grabs a half full bottle of Tequila. "Can I show you something?"

Caught in his net, I nod mechanically. There isn't a doubt in my mind that I would follow him to hell. Jack leads me into the hallway and then up a short flight of stairs. He turns to me just as he's about to open a door and I first notice his eyes are slightly unfocused.

Crap. Is he drunk?

This could be a huge mistake. Drunken Jack and Horny Leila...oh fuck.

He opens the door to a beautiful rooftop hangout. I gasp from the view. It's simply breathtaking. Jack smiles at my reaction. There are mini Christmas lights strung along the perimeter. There are a few plastic patio tables with chairs. There is a tacky pleather couch against the wall under an overhang.

"Wow, Jack this is incredible. If I lived here I would never leave."

"I spend a lot of time up here. I love to come up and play my guitar. I become very inspired. A lot of my songs were written up here."

"Why is the party not here?"

"Ssh… this is my secret. I'm not sure we are even allowed up here. No one in the building knows about it or uses it, so I've declared it mine." He smiles devilishly and motions towards the couch. "Want to sit a while?"

He walks me over to the couch and sits close. I can feel every nerve in my body pulsing from his proximity. We quietly enjoy the cool night air and the spectacular view.

"I really loved your show. Your band is very talented."

"Thanks. It's nice to hear from someone who doesn't live in Hoboken. We tend to forget that there's a whole other world out there."

"I get that. The same thing happened to us. Playing the same bars over and over, seeing the same faces. You get very comfortable and complacent."

"Well, things worked out for you guys."

"Us guys." He corrects.

"You guys. I had nothing to do with your success."

"You will. Once we tour and our fans hear your voice, you will be linked to our success."

I quietly contemplate his words. Am I ready for that?

"So what's the deal with Matt?" His question breaks my reverie.

"Matt?"

"Sore subject?"

Matt is who Jack wants to talk about? What the hell?

Laying my head back against the couch I look up at the night sky.

"What's the deal with Matt? Hmmm…that's a loaded question."

"He seems angry at the world." Jack's met him all of five minutes, and he's pegged him perfectly.

"You can say that, sometimes. There are also times when he can be Mr. Wonderful. Not sure what happened there. He is opposite his brother Logan."

"Now that I've met them, it's hard to believe they are even related."

"Yep, it is." I avoid Jack's gaze, I continue to stare up at the beautiful star filled sky. I can't help but wonder why Jack has fixated on Matt.

"You two have chemistry." His blunt statement doesn't squelch my curiosity. I don't see why he would care if we did have chemistry, which we most definitely *do not*.

"No we don't."

152

"From where I sat it sure looked that way." Jack takes a quick swig of the tequila, and leans back against the back of the couch, now avoiding my gaze.

If he only knew that the reason I acted that way was because I was fantasizing about him the entire time. Jack waits patiently for me to continue. I want him to know that I am not attracted to Matt and don't want to be linked to him ever again so I decide to fess up.

"Well he and I dated, twice. Once during high school for less than a year. The second time a few years later for even less than that."

"So you do have chemistry."

"No, we have history."

Taking another drink of tequila he then asks, "Why did you guys break up twice?"

"Damn, you're nosey."

Shrugging, he continues to watch me brazenly, waiting for my response.

Fine, he wants to know details? I'll give him details. I shift sideways on the couch to face him and he does the same, our knees practically touching. "The first time was in high school. I guess I out grew him. He was stuck. The second was a few years later. I thought he matured and gave it another shot. Then he cheated. No strike three after that, I'm afraid. Cheating is a hard limit for me."

Talking about Matt cheating on me spurs my insecurities with relationships. As if possessed, I continue explaining our demise to Jack. "He's ruined me in a sense. Trust is a huge factor in why I'm still single and not attached. Even after almost four years."

Jack regards me quietly, processing my words. "My ex-girlfriend also cheated." That's all he says. He doesn't explain or elaborate in any way.

I just spilled my guts and that's all he's going to give me. He leans back, watching the night sky, dropping his end of the conversation.

"When?"

He waits a few seconds to respond. His pregnant pause is a clear indication he was also hurt. "A long time ago. You can say she also ruined me, in a sense." He says, his tone harsh and filled with resentment. Who the hell would cheat on Jack? What an idiot.

"Well aren't we a pair?"

"Their loss." Jack remembers the bottle in his hand and takes a long swig of the tequila. Turning towards me, his position shifting him closer where our knees are now touching. He makes no attempt to move them away.

"To ditching our cheating exes." He leans closer and offers me the bottle of tequila.

I shake my head and groan. "Ugh, I hate tequila."

"Come on, have one sip. You have to accept my toast. It's bad luck otherwise."

"Fine. To ditching our exes." Taking the bottle I take a small sip. I steal a peak at Jack and note that he is trying his hardest not to laugh.

"What?"

"You are so cute."

My heart pounds noisily in my chest. He's just flirting. I've gotten to know him enough to know it comes naturally to him, but it still ignites my insides.

Suddenly he leans closer and tucks a piece of hair behind my ear. I unconsciously tilt my head and enjoy his warm touch as he caresses my earlobe. I'm falling under his spell and I can't look away from those gorgeous, stormy eyes. I have never had a pull towards someone like I do towards him.

He shifts his gaze down to my lips. "You're also so beautiful."

My breath catches from his words. Slowly, he closes his eyes and moves towards me slipping his hand into my hair, pulling me closer until his lips softly touch mine. His breath smells of tequila and his lips are warm and firm. Surprise, shock, desire all swirl in my head as I accept his kiss. Our kiss lasts for three seconds. It may not seem like a long time, but it's enough time to know I want to continue and now that I've tasted him, I'll never forget it. Three seconds is also enough time for me to subconsciously realize that this is a bad idea...*real* bad.

An involuntary gasp leaves my "*still tingling from his kiss*" lips. Pulling away, his hold prevents me to go far. With our faces still inches apart and Jack's eyes still closed, my deep desire to close the distance between us wreaks havoc on my logical, rational side.

Jack suddenly snaps back to reality. "Shit. I'm sorry Leila. I've had a lot to drink." He pulls further away, but his hand remains at the back of my head, his fingers wrapped in my hair in a desperate hold.

I want nothing more at this moment but to continue kissing him. And if I had a bit more to drink, I may not have been able to stop. Clarity is the only thing that stops me. Clearly seeing my future balanced precariously on this cliff gives me the strength to pull farther away. I woodenly reach up to take hold of his wrist, pulling his hand from my hair. "I should go."

Taking hold of my hand before I had the chance to pull it away, he wills me to look at his face. "I'm really sorry." His apology is genuine, and I believe him. The problem is me I don't trust at the moment.

"I know."

His hand releases mine, but his eyes hold me hostage inexorably and will me to forgive him.

I walk towards the door and look over one last time to see Jack sit heavily on the couch with his head in his hands. I desperately want to go back to comfort him, but that would be as irresponsible as continuing where we left off. Because surely touching him in any way at the moment would open my floodgates.

I quickly make my way back down to the party, which is still in full swing. As I cautiously enter the apartment, I feel like I have a huge blinking sign above my head that says, "I JUST KISSED JACK".

Thankfully, no one seems to notice. Lori and Trey are sitting close in a corner, totally engrossed in each other. The others haven't moved much during my absence either. The couples are still on the couch chatting. Evan has now joined Matt and Joe at the drinking game table. I decide to walk over to the couch and sit next to Alisa. Their conversation stops to acknowledge my intrusion. I pretend to be listening as I smile robotically.

Instead, I become absorbed in remembering his soft, warm, lips on mine. Where would it have led if I hadn't stopped him? We haven't even started working together, and we almost crossed a line already. I'm so lost in thought that I don't even realize Patti is calling my name until Alisa nudges me.

"I'm sorry?" I ask looking confused.

"I asked you if you were having fun. You look like you are going to be sick."

"I'm fine." I lie. "Tequila and I don't mix." To change the subject, I continue, "Patti, I just want to thank you for getting me that audition." The spunky blonde sitting on Scott's lap smiles warmly at me.

"No need to thank me Leila. You got that job on your own. I merely opened the door for you. I knew you would be perfect for these guys." She gives Scott a chaste kiss and jumps right back into their conversation. This leaves me to my own thoughts again, allowing me to slip back into my daze.

I must have been out of it for a long time, because when I glance around the room I notice the crowd has thinned considerably. Trey and Lori are missing, as is almost every girl. But then again Jack is still upstairs, which is probably why every female has disappeared.

Evan comes over and puts his hands on my shoulders. "Are you ready to go? You don't look so good."

"What time is it?"

"It's almost two, I think. I'm ready if you want to leave."

"Sure, I'm sober if you want me to drive."

"Nope, I'm good. I only had one beer."

"Ok. Let me find Lori." Have she and Trey found their way up to the roof or are they behind closed doors? Conflicted, I really don't want to knock on a door that is the only thing separating me from a writhing Lori and Trey. I also don't want to go up to the roof and face Jack, either.

I really should say goodnight to him regardless. I shouldn't leave on such uncomfortable terms. It's not entirely his fault. He may have initiated the kiss, but I willingly participated for three seconds. Taking the steps to the roof, I slowly open the door.

It's quiet, too quiet. Jack is still on the couch, joined now by a blond and a brunette. It takes me a few seconds to realize what I'm seeing. The blond is nibbling on one ear, the brunette on the other. His eyes are closed, and he turns his head towards the brunette. They start making out and I can't stop staring. Getting a good look at them, they are life size versions of Barbie dolls, with long legs and huge boobs.

As the blonde kisses her way down his chest, she slides her hand inside the waistband of his jeans. Jack pulls away from the brunette's lips and watches the blond through hooded eyes. He must sense my presence, because he shifts his gaze and locks eyes with me. I am frozen as he stares for a few seconds and blinks confusedly. Abruptly, he pushes the girls away and stands.

The brunette looks up at him and pouts. "Where are you goin' baby?" Jack stands awkwardly between the fake boob twins with his shirt hiked up exposing his delicious abs and his jeans unbuttoned to reveal he wears black Calvin Klein boxer briefs. Forgetting he was just getting it on with two girls, my eyes drink in every inch of his hard body.

One of the fake boob twins says, "What the fuck?" and breaks me out of my trance. They both look at me like they are ready to take me down if necessary. I clearly interrupted their private party. Jack slowly takes a few steps forward, and I instinctively move back.

What the hell? Does he want me to join in?

Before he has a chance to say anything, I blurt out "We are going."

"Leila...wait!"

Like a bat out of hell I run down the stairs and into the apartment. Evan has already found Lori, who looks completely sated, and asks, "Where were you?"

"Um, I went to tell Jack we were leaving. I'm ready." I hastily grab my bag and wave a good-bye to anyone who is watching. Then I run out the door, down that stairs, and straight to Evan's car so fast that I beat them by a full minute.

"What the hell is wrong with you?" Evan says panting as he opens my door. "I've never seen you acting like this."

"You look like you saw a ghosssssst." Lori slurs. She's bombed. I hope she makes it to Hoboken without hurling. That would be the cherry on my night. "Traaaayyyy is sooo hot!" she says smiling at me. "He is soooooo sweet too."

Sweet? Trey?

"Thanks for into…intro…putting us together. Jack was a waste of time."

Turning towards her I ask, "Why?"

"He kept looking at you." With that, Lori passes out. Evan seems lost in his own thoughts. I almost wonder if I just imagined what Lori said. She has no idea what she's talking about. He was just going at it with two girls at once.

Shit…a threesome? How often has Mr. Lair participated in them? Is that why he kept looking at me? Is that why he came on to me? Is he a man-whore?

Here I thought he was upstairs battling with what happened between us, like I was doing downstairs. Instead he is upstairs about to have a threesome.

Evan glances at me. "What's going on with you?"

I love him, but is simply cannot get into this with him right now.

"Nothing, why?"

"You're acting very strange." He waits a few seconds and asks, "Well?"

"Can we talk about it tomorrow?"

Staring at the road he sighs. "Fine."

He's not going to be happy if I confess everything. I'm going to have to withhold some info or Evan will undoubtedly kick Jack's ass if he hears every erotic detail.

Chapter 12- Jack

What the fuck just happened?

Basically I seduced my new band member and then she walked in on me going at it with two women.

Fucking perfect.

I didn't mean to kiss her. It sounds so cliché to blame it on the tequila, especially since I wasn't that drunk yet, but it did trigger my desire to want to taste her lips. Staring into her gorgeous eyes didn't help with matters either.

Her lips were as soft as I imagined. I could have kissed her all night, if she had let me. That's another internal battle. What if she hadn't stopped me? How far would it have gone? The thought is terrifying, because if she hadn't stopped me I don't think I would have.

Once she ran, I knew I needed to go after her, but I was too much of a coward. So I sat, drank more and then passed out. Suddenly, I felt someone kissing me.

My first thought was she came back. Returning her kiss, I opened my eyes to see Michelle coaxing me awake while her girlfriend Jan giggled beside her. These two are a couple that enjoys spicing things up with men.

I said something like, "Sorry girls, but I'm too drunk to move."

They both saw this as a green light. Jan giggled some more and said, "No need to move baby. We'll do all the work."

I clumsily sat up with the intent to walk away, but they held me down to my spot on the couch, effectively winning that battle. They made out with each other. They made out with me. They felt me up. Tequila or not, my body responded immediately. It wasn't the first time we got it on, but it's been a while. For fuck's sake, our reunion couldn't have been at a worst time. I fully submitted, allowing them complete access, having no clue we were being watched.

Seeing Leila staring at me a few feet away shocked me sober. I pushed away from the girls at once, but she looked disgusted, right before she ran away. Ten minutes later and she would have seen a lot worst.

"Girls I'm done." They laughed at first, until they realized I was serious. I asked them to leave and they stormed off while cursing me out in the process. Whatever.

SHIT!

She was not supposed to see that. How the fuck am I going to fix this?

As I sit glued to this plastic couch, a horrible thought pops into my head. What if the girls are harassing Leila for ruining their good time? I frantically make my way back to my apartment to make sure they are gone. The apartment is quieter now that only a few people are lulling around. No sign of Michelle or Jan. There is also no sign of Leila, or her friends.

Hunter and Amanda are on the couch with Scott and Patti. There are still a group of partiers drinking heavily in the kitchen. Hunter looks up and immediately knows what state I am in.

"Sleep it off man." He says giving me permission to bail. I am going to anyway, but his consent makes it easier to hide away in my room.

"Make sure no one bothers me."

Some of the girls try in vain to get my attention. Taking the tequila with me, I head for my room, locking the door behind me. I try calling Leila's phone, but it goes right to voice mail.

"Leila, it's Jack. I am so sorry. Please call me back tomorrow. I want to talk to you."

I resume my tequila binge until the bottle is empty, puke my brains out and then expertly pass out.

What seems like minutes later, I wake from someone banging on my door. They may as well be hitting me over the head with a sledgehammer. I stumble out of bed with the intent to beat the living shit out of whoever it is.

I scream, "WHAT THE FUCK!" into Hunter's face and take a step closer as he instinctively takes a step back.

He throws his hands up in surrender and says, "Goddamn it Jack, I thought you were dead. I've been pounding on this door and calling your cell phone and I didn't hear a peep from you. For all I knew you hit your head on the toilet and choked on your own vomit."

I feel some remorse for shouting at him. "Sorry Hunt. I didn't mean to worry you." I can't deal with Hunter being mad at me too.

"Just glad you are alive. Based on how you looked last night, my scenario isn't so far- fetched."

"I guess not. Remind me to never drink tequila again. My head feels like it's made of cement." Making my way to the kitchen, I catch a glimpse of the condition of our apartment.

"This place is a fucking mess. Hire someone to clean this up because I'm not doing it."

"Yeah, whatever. How much did you have last night?"

"And don't even think of banging around in this kitchen because I WILL KILL YOU!"

I start prepping the coffee maker hearing him mumble "Christ." while he quietly opens doors to get his breakfast ready.

"What did you ask me?"

"How much tequila did you drink last night?"

"I don't know half a bottle? I lost track."

"Fuck dude. No wonder you didn't hear me pounding. Is something bothering you? The last time you broke out the tequila was when you were telling your parents you were dropping out."

"I just have a lot on my mind." I pour my first cup of coffee and after two sips I'm feeling a little better already.

Hunter is standing at the sink, watching me arrogantly and loudly eating his Fruit Loops.

"Do you have to chew so loud?" Glaring at him, I grab my coffee and head up to the roof to avoid his condescending stare.

"Call Jen and tell her we'll be in this afternoon. I need air."

Hunter mumbles, "What you need is your ass kicked." I pretend I didn't hear him, and shut the door behind me.

Hunter is absolutely right.

Usually sitting on the roof clears my head. Now it's tainted. It holds memories I'd like to forget, specifically the look on her face.

We were getting along so nicely. I enjoyed being with her during our lunch together. The more time I spend with her, the more I want to spend with her. I can't imagine what she is thinking or feeling right now.

Bullshit, I suspect she's thinking what the fuck did I sign on to?

Pulling out my phone, I'm not surprised there isn't a response to my voicemail. This only confirms my suspicions. This is unfamiliar territory for me. I am not used to giving a crap about what someone thinks.

All these meaningless relationships, what the hell was I thinking? I've convinced myself, since the girls I fucked called the shots, that it was ok. I have a nasty taste in my mouth, and I doubt it's from my hangover.

I really do need to fix this. I don't know her well enough to show up at her apartment to talk. A phone call would be more appropriate. My fingers reflexively hit my contacts icon. I sit and stare at her name but chicken out and shut off my phone.

I need some time, a good dose of nerve, and a good ass kicking.

Chapter 13-Leila

The past few weeks have flown by and our first rehearsal is now just two days away. The thick packet of legal documents that are sitting on my dresser is the only proof I am a member of Devil's Lair. Is it normal that I really haven't had much contact from the band? About a week ago Jennifer reached out to so I could sign some papers. She said she would mail them to me so I wouldn't have to schlep into the city.

Just yesterday, someone by the name of Dylan Kressel contacted me. He introduced himself as the Tour Manager and also wanted to meet to also sign some paperwork. We decided on lunch at the studio. I was about to ask Dylan if the band would also be present. But I rather not know. If Jack is there, it's best I don't have time to obsess over seeing him again.

Besides Jennifer and Dylan, the only other contact I received was a text from Hunter that said - *hi, how you holding up?* I thought that was very sweet of him to check in on me.

There was the one voicemail from Jack, too. I was stunned to see his number on my phone the next morning after his party. Actually he called just after we left. On his message he said he wanted to talk and asked me to please call him. At the time, there was no way I wanted to talk, but that was childish of me, because I couldn't keep avoiding him.

So a few days later I called him back. He sounded happy to hear from me. He was most definitely beating around the bush the first few minutes by making small talk. He asked how I was doing, and if there was anything I wanted to discuss. Then he apologized once again for kissing me, and for what I saw that night. I accepted and told him not to worry about it. Jokingly,

I said that tequila was the root of all evil. We ended the call awkwardly and haven't spoken since.

Regarding the kiss, I know that he was drunk. That's the part that's been consuming me. Would he have kissed me otherwise? It's all I've been thinking about.

My logical side tells me, "This is a very complicated situation. You will be living with him, but you'll also be living with three others. You have no business becoming involved with Jack Lair." I hate my logical side. I know she's right, but I hate her.

My passionate side says, "Fuck logic. You have been thinking of nothing else but Jack Lair since the day you laid eyes on him. Go for it."

My life was so simple, so comfortable, and so easy before I signed onto this endeavor. It almost makes me regret auditioning. My nerves have gotten the best of me. My sleep habits over the past few weeks have been horrendous. I've lost weight due to lack of appetite.

Evan noticed and I blamed stress because of the looming tour.

"Bullshit, Lei. You acted weird when he came to the bar. You acted weirder when you flew out of his party. Why don't you tell me what's going on."

"I have a crush on Jack. When we were upstairs on the roof talking, we accidentally kissed." That's all the info I was willing to give him. This was the first time since becoming friends that I did not confide in him. Even with knowing only part of the truth, he still ripped me open a new one. He ranted about how this is my dream, and how he won't let me throw it all away on a crush. He also said to get my head out of my vagina.

He has no idea what is really bothering me. He has no clue that I am so attracted to this man that I can't think straight. Even after seeing him with

166

two girls at once. What the hell is wrong with me? How can I explain this to my best friend?

My dad also noticed my stress levels, yet accepted my excuse easily. He could relate, as the tour looming ahead was causing him to become a bit more neurotic. He's meddled uncharacteristically since I signed. He showed up at the bar a couple times a week and would sit with us during breaks. Our Sunday brunch has become a four hour-long event. I can easily tell him to back off, but I won't. This is his coping mechanism and I can't deny him that.

Besides dad and Evan, no one else has noticed my mood. Lori has jumped head first into her new job. She spends every waking moment doing "band" stuff, when she isn't mixing drinks. She even had business cards made up.

She has a few people lined up to audition as my replacement. The band didn't give Lori a hard time about that at all. They know she won't take their shit like I do. The band wanted me to sit in on the auditions, but I flat out refused. I neither want to influence them, nor see them replacing me. Even though it needs to be done, I don't need to witness it.

Except for my nerves wreaking havoc on my intestines, life during these past few weeks has been normal otherwise. Our shows continued as normal and we hung out as usual. We even went down to Atlantic City for our yearly Memorial Day weekend getaway. Sal closes the bar every year for that holiday as well as The Fourth of July, and Labor Day weekend to go fishing. Make no mistake, the only reason he closes is because Hoboken is a ghost town during those holidays. It costs him more to stay open than it's worth. The only other holiday he closes for is Christmas.

We head down the shore for a mini vacation and we have a blast. We drink, and eat, and gamble, and lay on the beach and it's an awesome tradition.

This year was sadder since the dark cloud of me leaving the band hovered over us. We had a great time, but I'm left feeling unsettled and lonely.

My phone rings as I'm unpacking from our weekend. I debate on answering it, since I don't recognize the number. Realizing it could be someone from the studio, I decide to take the call.

"Hello, Leila?" a sweet voice asks over the phone.

"Yes?" Who can this be?

"Hi, I'm Lizzy…Elizabeth Lair…Jack's sister." I can't imagine why she is calling me. I feel uneasy, hoping it's not bad news.

"Hi Lizzy, how are you? Is everything ok?" I ask her.

"Oh yes, everything is fine. I hope you don't mind me calling you. I got your number from Hunter. I'm planning a birthday party for my brother. He's turning twenty-nine on the Tenth of June. It's sort of a combination *early thirtieth slash good luck on the tour* celebration. I would love for you to come."

Jack's birthday in on the tenth? Mine is on the ninth. I can't believe we are one day apart and both Gemini's. I decide to keep this information to myself since I wouldn't want to give Lizzy or anyone the opportunity to embarrass me at this party.

I am sort of honored she went through the trouble to get my number and to include me. Yes I'll be working with the band by then but she didn't have to invite me. She has no clue who I am. Maybe Hunter asked her to include me or perhaps someone knows it's also my birthday? I feel nauseous at the thought.

"That sounds great, Lizzy. I would love to come."

"Oh I'm so glad. It's next Saturday night at Granite. I can't wait to meet you. Jack has said wonderful things about you."

He did?

"I can't wait to meet you as well."

"Oh, and feel free to bring a friend if you'd like. It's a surprise, so please don't tell Jack."

I don't speak to Jack unless necessary. "No problem. Your secret is safe with me."

"Great. Bye Leila."

"Bye."

It's Jack's birthday. I wonder how he will celebrate a birthday, maybe a four-some?

Ugh, why did I go there?

I'll bring Evan.

***

The studio is very quiet on a Saturday. Even Sally is missing. A young man no older than sixteen mans the phones while his head is buried in his own iPhone. I'm sure it's a studio head's son or grandson trying to make some extra cash.

"Hi I'm Leila. I'm scheduled to meet with Dylan Kressel."

He blushes as he looks up and clumsily drops his iPhone on the floor.

"Oh, I'm sorry. I didn't mean to scare you."

"Um…it's ok."

He is very cute and looks like a rock star in training. Based on his black t-shirt, leather wristbands, and faux-hawk, he definitely has been taking notes watching the many rock stars that walk these halls.

"I'm Ian. Um, Ian Phillips. Dylan is expecting you. Um, he's in the conference room…"

Bingo. He must be Bobby Phillips, the owner of the studio's son.

"Um…I'll show you." His eyes bug out of his head at the sight of my tight t-shirt and jeans. He probably doesn't have a lot of experience talking to girls up close.

"No need, Ian. I know the way." I smile warmly.

Ian's eyes bug out again, and he drops his phone for the second time. He avoids eye contact, after he bends to pick it up and shifts uncomfortably in his chair. He is a mess of nerves and I decide to let him off the hook.

"Bye, Ian. Nice meeting you." Waving, I turn to walk down the hall.

"Bye, Leila. Nice meeting you too!" he calls after me.

I think I have an admirer.

Not concentrating on where I am going, I ram right into a male body. His arms grip mine to stop me from falling backwards.

"Leila, I presume?"

"Um, yes, I'm Leila. I'm so, so sorry." I nervously take a step backwards forcing him to release his hold on me.

"I'm Dylan…Dylan Kressel. It's so nice to meet you. Come on in." He motions me towards the conference room. He is handsome in a very classic way with vivid blue eyes, average height - maybe five ten - sandy brown hair that is parted to the side and is very neatly styled. His best feature is his smile. It lights up his whole face.

He looks like he could be in an ad for an Ivy League university. Especially in his blue sport coat, white collared shirt, khaki slacks and loafers. He does not fit into the rock and roll world he works for. I wonder if he does that on purpose and knows he can't compete with rock stars.

The table of the conference room is laid out with a catered lunch, as well as drinks and a platter of cookies. It looks like he ordered way too much food for just the two of us.

Uh oh.

"Do you like wraps?" He asks while offering me a chair.

I sit and nod, "Yes, that's fine. This is very nice of you."

"My pleasure. I invited the band and Jennifer to join us at twelve-thirty. I wanted to chat and get to know you a bit before they arrive. I hope that's ok."

Dylan's words send a nervous rush through my veins. *He's* coming.

"Sure, that's fine."

Dylan sits across from me, leaving the chair beside me empty. "So Leila, tell me about yourself." Dylan asks, leaning back in his chair.

My leg shaking uncontrollably under the table is the only sign of my anxiety as I wait for the Rock God to appear.

"Well Dylan, I come from Jersey and I sing in a bar in Hoboken."

"Are you ready for all that's about to happen to you?"

"I think I am. I've been preparing for this most of my life. Whether I succeed is another story."

"I've heard your audition tape, Leila. You are very talented. Success is definitely in your cards."

"Thank you. That's kind of you to say."

"Kindness has nothing to do with it."

"Well I hope my nerves don't get the best of me, and hamper my talent."

"You handle the performance part and I'll handle the rest. You will have a support system during the tour and you can leave all the worrying to me. I will be touring with you and the band. It's my job to make sure you are prepared for your performances. I'll be the person you will come to if you need absolutely anything at all. I have an assistant who is extremely efficient. Her name is Cathy, and she is my right hand person. She will not be traveling with us, but she will be in constant contact. If I can't help you, Cathy can."

Relief washes over me. Cathy can be the female confidante I'll need on this tour and Dylan can be the male. I feel relaxed in Dylan's company within the few minutes I've been with him. This is a novelty that hasn't happened with anyone else I've met so far who is connected to Devil's Lair.

"Sounds like I'm going to be best friends with Cathy."

"Yes I'd say you were right. I get there are things you may not be comfortable asking me for. In those cases, Cathy is your woman."

I like Dylan. I really like Dylan. He's seems approachable, and kind and comfortable. I'm feeling a bit better.

"Will you be on the same bus as the band?" I ask hesitantly.

"No, we would kill each other. I am a bit O.C.D. I'm sure five minutes into the tour I'd be throwing any loose articles of clothing out the window as we were moving, and they would throw me out right behind it." He chuckles and I join in.

"Oh no, I'm a bit O.C.D too. I guess I'll have to learn to look the other way?"

"If it becomes too much for you, you are welcome to join me and the roadies. But we'd have to hide you because the band would not be happy if you bunked with us. How do you feel about sleeping in the overhead?"

"Sounds cozy." I respond dryly, and he laughs again.

"I'll be on the second bus with Will Sutter. He is the equipment manager for Devil's Lair, as well as our drivers, and five roadies that you will meet once we take off." He frowns and pulls his phone out of his pocket.

He shakes his head and stands. "Excuse me, Leila?"

"Absolutely."

"I'll be right back. Do you need anything?"

"No, I'm fine." He nods and leaves the room.

Speaking to Dylan these last few minutes helped me forget that Jack is coming. Unfortunately, I now remember that Jack is coming.

We will be in a room full of people. I can handle it. I can handle it. I can handle it.

Dylan is back in less than a minute with Jennifer in tow. "Hello Leila, how are you?" she asks with a phony as hell smile.

"Hi Jennifer. I'm fine, thank you, how are you?" I reciprocate with my own phony as hell smile.

"I'm great. I'm looking very forward to getting started." She looks at Dylan and remarks, "Nice spread."

"I aim to please." He says with a tight smile. He stands between Jennifer and me and now looks uptight and tense. I guess Mr. Kressel and Ms. Baxter aren't BFF's? I like Dylan even more now.

"Hi Dyl." I hear Jack say as he strolls into the room. Noticing me sitting behind Dylan he stops in his tracks. "Oh, hey Leila. I didn't know you were here already."

My heart pounds furiously in my chest, and my breathing becomes labored. I can handle it, *my ass*.

"I asked Leila to come a little earlier so we could chat." Dylan says to Jack while extending his hand. Jack pauses before shaking it. Jack's quite a bit taller than Dylan, enabling him to see over his shoulder and into my eyes. We exchange gazes; Jack's lacking the smolder and heat I'm used to seeing. In its place, remorse and shame.

"Good to see you, Leila." I smile at him not trusting my voice to respond.

Dylan takes the chair beside me. Jack clenches his jaw and moves around the table to sit directly across from me. The tension between us can be cut with a knife. Dylan notices and tries to lighten the mood. "Did you lose the rest of the band, or did you finally fire their asses?"

"You know it wouldn't matter if I fired them, they would keep showing up anyway." Jack responds tightly, while watching me. Jennifer takes the chair next to Jack and scoots closer to him.

Dylan turns to place a hand on my arm. "Hungry?"

I pull my eyes from Jack to look at Dylan. "Yes, everything looks delicious."

He hands me a plate and says, "No need to wait. This is my party. Dig in."

The way Jack and Jennifer silently watching our exchange, makes me feel uncomfortable. The rest of the band finally making it to the conference room lightens the mood. Hunter is the first one in. With a look at the catered trays, he smacks Dylan on the back and asks, "Who the hell ordered sissy wraps?"

"Just trying to please the ladies." Dylan nods in my direction.

"I like wraps." Scott touts as he grabs one without a plate and waves at me with his free hand.

"Of course you do." Hunter responds dryly.

After a quick hello, Hunter and Trey also dive right into the platter of wraps, even though it's sissy cuisine. Dylan spars with them like they have all been buddies for years. He knows how to handle them, and even goads Trey during the course of our lunch. His relationship with the guys is clearly more laid back and relaxed than his with Jack.

Dylan casually shares some details of the tour, specifically luggage requirements and bus constraints. Conversation flows between everyone

174

except Jack. He drinks a coke and only speaks when asked a question, and even then only in monosyllables. If the guys or Jen notice his attitude, they quietly keep comments to themselves and ignore him for the most part.

I haven't been in his company much and I can understand moody, but this goes beyond. I'm having trouble ignoring him, however. His presence across the table is still a major distraction, even in his dour disposition. Dare I say moody Jack is very sexy?

As we are finishing up with lunch, Dylan pulls some paperwork out of his brief case. "I hate to get down to business but this is the reason I did ask you to come. Basically it's the same contract the studio has in place for each of the guys. The contract details my services during the tour as well as the studio's responsibilities." He pushes the stack of papers towards me and offers me a pen.

I skim the pages and sign them where he added cute little flags. I push the stack back towards him. "Well that was harmless. Little do you know you that just gave me all your worldly possessions."

Narrowing my eyes I respond, "Well I hope you and Bessie are very happy together."

"Bessie?" he asks smiling.

"My 2004 Honda Accord. The passenger door sticks a little, but just rub her a bit and she'll open right up for you." His eyes bulge and the guys snicker. I realize what I said could definitely be misconstrued and burst out laughing alongside Dylan. When I finally catch my breath, I notice the room gawking at us.

Dylan awkwardly clears his throat and says, "Ok, well I think we are done. Anyone have anything they want to discuss?"

175

"I do." Jack voluntarily speaks for the first time. "Speaking of Bessie, I want car service sent for Leila every day. We will be working late hours on some nights, and I feel for her safety we should supply car service."

"I'm fine Jack. I can drive myself and I don't need car service." Who the hell does he think he is? My dad?

Jennifer glares at Jack like he has lost his mind.

Dylan nods considerately. "That's a valid concern. I can most definitely offer car service to Leila on any nights you will be working late. She can also park her car in a lot at the studio's expense."

"Thank you." Jack and I both say at the same time as I glare at him.

"Leila, I'll have a copy of this contract mailed to you tomorrow for your records. If you have any questions, just let me know."

"Thanks, Dylan. I will."

Trey chimes in at that moment. "Are we done here?"

"Yep all done. You can all take off." Dylan says.

He stands and says to me, "Say hi to Lori." Then he walks out the door.

Lori? Well that's interesting.

Hunter and Scott stand next and wave to me on their way out. Neither Jack nor Jennifer move.

"Well I guess I'll see you guys on Monday."

Jennifer stands and says, "Leila, nine sharp. We have a lot to do Monday morning even before we start rehearsals." The woman looks at me like I'm an idiot.

"No problem, I'll be here." I look at Jack before I walk out. "Bye, Jack."

"Bye."

176

He remains sitting as Dylan stares at him for a few seconds and finally turns to me. "I'll walk you out."

So this is how he wants to play it? An ache settles in my chest. Why the hell is he upset with me? Maybe because I ruined his good time.

Monday is going to be very awkward unless I do something to break the tension between us. Maybe I'll be the better person and call him later.

Once in the lobby, Dylan turns to face me when we are at the front door.

"Are you and Jack ok?" Anyone could have guessed there was tension between us today, but I'm a bit taken back that Dylan would mention it barely knowing me.

"Yeah, we are fine. Why?" I ask looking away. If he can read people as well as I think, he just figured out I'm lying.

"Just seems like there was some tension between you. If there is anything I can do to help the situation, just let me know. I can talk to him, if nothing else." He offers and I'm touched.

"Thanks Dylan, but I can handle it." This is between Jack and me.

"Handle what?" Jack asks walking over to us. I turn towards him and sigh. How much has he heard?

Without missing a beat, Dylan says, "Just the stress of going on tour." He turns to face me and winks.

Jack stands right next to us at the front door and makes no motion to leave. It's obvious he thinks Dylan is full of crap.

Dylan looks at him indifferently and then turns back to me. "Leila, remember what I said. You can call me for any reason. It was an absolute pleasure meeting you. I look forward to getting to know you." He puts out his hand, and as I shake it he then lays his other hand over both of ours. He walks towards the hallway without a word to Jack.

"You two BFF's already?" Pure annoyance flashes across his face. Is that why he is so pissy?

I ignore his comment and shoot him my own indifferent look before turning to leave.

"Wait, can I walk you to your car? I'd like to talk."

Now he wants to talk?

"Nothing to talk about."

"Please?"

I sigh heavily and turn towards the door.

"Bye, Leila." Ian calls out as I walk out the studio.

"Bye, Ian." I wave and smile.

Jack looks over at Ian then turns to me. "You are here like five minutes, and you already have two admirers?" He tries to sound amused, but he falls short.

What *is* his problem?

We walk towards the lot where my car is parked in total silence, as I quietly stew.

"Can I sit with you inside for a few minutes?" he asks.

My nonverbal response is to unlock the doors. Once inside the car, I barely shut my door before Jacks mutters, "I'm so sorry."

Staring straight ahead, he looks completely distraught. "Leila, I am…I am so sorry." He finally turns to look at me.

"Jack …I…why are you angry at me?"

He turns to me and looks confused. "I'm not angry with you. I'm angry with myself. I'm sorry I'm not handling my feelings very well."

"Oh…I…never mind." I uncomfortably stumble over my own words. I don't know what to say. Watching him, I fail to recall why I was even mad at him. My anger is slipping away, and I wish I could reach over and comfort him.

Why was I so upset with him? He has already apologized for his behavior, but I guess I wasn't ready to forgive him. After the way he acted today, I assumed that he was annoyed with me.

It suddenly occurs to me that the lack of contact from him for the last few weeks is what has me upset. What had me totally freaking out wasn't the tour looming, or the kiss, or even Jack acting like a whore. It was the fact I wasn't hearing from him.

"Jack, it's ok."

"I hate that we started off on the wrong foot. Can we start over?" He pleads.

"I would like that."

He smiles and grabs my hand. "I know you are working tonight, but can I take you out to dinner tomorrow? Sort of a peace offering?"

We do need to feel comfortable with each other. We need to get to a better place, and besides, I enjoy being with him. I now crave it. I would do anything this man asks because, well just because.

Before I can stop myself I blurt out, "Why don't you come to my place? We can bring in or I can cook. We can talk and get to know each other better."

Who am I kidding?

He looks at me with raised eyebrows. "Yeah? Are you sure you are ok with that?"

"Yes, I would like that."

"Ok, I would like that too." He says smiling.

As an afterthought I add, "Bring Hunter if you'd like." I'm not sure I said that to help him feel more comfortable, or for me to.

179

***

Jack arrives alone, explaining Hunter had plans. The way he stands at my door bearing dinner, which consists of a pizza, a six-pack and a box of cheap white wine, makes him look absolutely adorable.

"You remembered the cheap wine."

"Well I was going to get a bottle, but I thought the box would impress you more."

Laughing, I open the door wide for him, taking the wine from his hand.

As we sit eating our meal while making small talk, I can't help but feel he seems a bit on edge with me. As he devours his fourth brownie, I shyly ask, "Are you ok?"

Looking up surprised he responds, "Yeah, why?"

"You just seem quiet tonight."

Smiling warmly, he shrugs and admits, "I just want things to be ok between us."

I reach over to cover his hand with my own, and as I'm doing it I'm aware it's a bad idea.

Looking down he turns his hand so we are palm to palm, and slowly runs him thumb across my mom's wedding band on my right hand. His touch causes the sparks to fly through my body, and causes my logical side to scream for me to pull my hand away immediately.

I can't.

Jack continues to play with the ring on my finger. "This looks like a wedding band." He says, surprising me once again with his candor.

"It was my mom's."

Jack searches my face. "I'm sorry. I didn't mean to…"

"…Don't worry about it." I interrupt, smiling to ease his discomfort. Jack squeezes my hand affectionately.

"Let's relax." He drags me over to the couch while still holding my hand. I sit next to him and consciously keep a safe distance between our bodies. I did not invite him here to worsen our complicated situation…at least I don't think I did. But the yearning to touch him is unbearable now that he is here. Tucking my legs under my body, clasping my hands in my lap, I practically cocoon myself on the couch to prevent any accidental or intentional contact.

Jack doesn't seem to notice my shielding defense, and immediately makes himself at home, flipping around on the remote until he finds a Mets game on TV. Side note, my dad will not be happy that Jack is a Mets fan.

"The Yankees are playing Boston tonight, and it is my TV." Reluctantly I hold my hand out, waiting for him to relinquish the remote.

"We'll compromise. Next inning we'll watch the bums from the Bronx." Sneaking a sideways glance at me he says, "What? They suck."

"Spoken like a true Mets fan." I fold my arms to pretend to be angry, yet the look on his face causes me to laugh.

"And a Yankee hater." He leans over and places a chaste kiss on my cheek, leaving a tingly sensation behind.

We fall into a comfortable conversation as the games move on inning by inning. He tells me about his childhood. He wasn't a jock and preferred the glee club and school musicals to football, plus he was smart. He admits he should have gotten his ass kicked in school. But because he was so popular, everyone thought it was cool.

I relay stories of all the trouble Evan and I would get into and the many girlfriends he lost because of me. He wants to know what my dad is like, and he tells me about his parents. He talks about Lizzy and how gorgeous she is, but more importantly how smart she is. We discuss how Lori and Trey hit it off. He wondered why Trey said to say hi to her. Of course Trey hadn't mentioned it to him but he could see them together. She was definitely his type. I laugh and admit the same.

He brings up Matt once again. I act all cool when it comes to him but truth is he hurt me. I promised myself I would never let that happen again. I fell hard for Matt and that was why I gave him another chance. I was convinced he had matured and changed. All I admit to Jack is that Matt was a dick and he didn't know the first thing about relationships. Surprisingly he defends Matt, and says that he doesn't know all that much about relationships either. I guess he is right. What the hell do I know about them?

I confess that I was not happy with his offer at the lunch with Dylan regarding car service. I tell him he made me feel helpless and pathetic. He is a bit amused at first, but then backs off and says it wouldn't happen again. I then forgive him for being a jackass.

I ask him about the scar on his hand. He says when he was a kid he fell off his skateboard and landed on a broken bottle in the street. I laugh and he says he is glad his injury amuses me. I explain I had a more exciting scenario in my head where he got into a bar brawl, or punched a window in a fit of rage. Now it's his turn to laugh.

He suddenly becomes serious and asks, "What was your mom like?"

"She was perfect." I lean back on the sofa, closing my eyes.

He reaches over and places his hand on my knee. "I didn't mean to upset you." His touch affects me and I stiffen slightly. Jack interprets my reaction as discomfort and quickly removes his hand, turning his attention back to the Mets game.

"You didn't upset me. It's just still hard to talk about her. I miss her every damn day. She would have been so proud of me right now. She always was, but this would have really made her happy because I'm following my dream."

He shifts slightly to face me and smiles warmly. "What did she look like?"

Returning his smile I stand and say, "Come, I'll show you." Jack follows me down the hall to my room. Flipping on the light, he steps in behind me and looks around.

For a few seconds, I watch Jack as he takes in my room.

"Nice room." He smirks. "Very girlie."

He's right. My room is a typical girlie room. I have a pretty white wrought iron headboard with floral patterns on the duvet, shams and sheets, lacy curtains, and a retro princess phone. I tried to duplicate my room at home when I was a little girl because it reminds me of my mom so much.

"Well, I am a girl."

Turning towards me, Jack sweeps my body with his smoky gaze. "That you are."

Damn it! He can't look at me like that with a bed two feet away. In an alternate universe, there is a Leila Marino who pushes a Jack Lair down on his back and has her wicked way with him over and over again. But I want more than hot, sweaty sex with Jack. I also want to connect with him in the most intimate of ways.

All this from one look in my bedroom?

Remembering why we are in here, I walk over to a framed photo of my mom hanging on the wall. Jack follows me and leans in to closely examine the picture.

"You are practically twins."

"A little. She was gorgeous."

"So are you." We turn to face each other.

183

"Thank you."

He nods at my response. I look up at my mom's picture again to break the connection between us. "You haven't met my dad. I look a little like him too. I also have my dad's personality. Mom was such a free spirit. She was so much fun."

"I wish I could have met her."

"Me too. She would have liked you. Believe it or not, dropping out of law school to pursue your dream would have impressed her."

"Really?"

"Yep. She felt you only live once. Everyone should live his or her lives without regret. I think she's the only parent on earth that could care less how I did in school. I take that back, she did care, but if I failed a test she would take me for ice cream." With a small smile, I remember the day my mom did just that. She dried my tears and told me it was no big deal.

Jack focuses on my mom's picture, and then focuses on me. The seriousness in his expression has me wondering what he's thinking.

"What?"

He shakes his head and smiles. "Nothing. You know, I'm really glad we did this."

"Me too."

"I should get going, it's late. I'll see you tomorrow?"

"Yep...nine *sharp*!"

Jack laughs out loud. "You sounded just like her. That's awesome."

"I didn't mean to say that out loud."

"Don't apologize. That was spot on. Promise me you'll do that for Hunter."

"What? No way. She's your agent."

"Our agent."

"Even more of a reason not to." Jack follows me out of my room towards my apartment door.

"Do you want to take the rest of the brownies home?"

"Don't tease me woman."

Now it's my turn to laugh. Taking that as a yes, I wrap the rest of the brownies for him and hand them over.

"I love you." I shove him towards the door and he laughs on his way out. "Sweet dreams pretty girl." He leans in and kisses my cheek, leaving me a quivering mess.

Oh boy…I'm in deep shit

It's just a crush, right? And because my body was denied sexual activity for so long, it took over the cruise controls of my lower half. But it's just a crush and nothing more. That's why I feel like I'm young and stupid and giddy. That's the only explanation for how I act around him. I feel like I'm back in high school.

I lie in bed for hours and I frantically try to think of a way I can ignore it. As the sunlight starts to filter through my window, I come up empty.

Chapter 14-Jack

As I drive Hunter's car back to the city, every street, road, and highway from Hoboken to Brooklyn goes unseen. Autopilot takes over and allows me to twist the steering wheel or accelerate and break when needed. I can handle all the mundane tasks necessary to operate a moving vehicle while completely in a trance, and I spend the entire drive replaying the evening in my mind.

I can't quite pinpoint why I feel so uneasy and unsettled. I made peace with Leila, and I really enjoyed her company. She is easy to talk to, and get along with. She's caring, and also a nurturing person, not to mention gorgeous.

My head is in chaos and I'm irritated by the time I walk into my apartment. Seeing Hunter and Amanda going at it on the couch further annoys me.

"Hey, how did it go?"

"Hi, Amanda."

She looks up and smiles. I can see the draw for Hunter. Not only is she very pretty, she's very shy. She's basically Hunter's perfect woman.

"It went well. I think we turned a corner." I offer no further explanation, as it wouldn't matter anyway. Hunter thinks what Hunter thinks. Prior to heading over to Leila's earlier, I told him that I wanted her to feel more comfortable with me, and for us to become friends.

He didn't buy it and kept harassing me to leave Leila alone. I swore I didn't have a hidden agenda. Well, I lied a little. My agenda isn't just to get into her pants, as Hunter thinks. It's also to spend time with her.

Wait, also?

Their make-out session on the couch resumes and is once again grating on my nerves. "I'll leave you kids alone."

Normally I would head right for the roof but I haven't spent a lot of time up there since our party. Instead, I lock myself in my room and start pacing like a caged animal. I can't figure out what the fuck my problem is.

It's late, and sleep is the last thing on my mind. The unsettled feelings I had earlier morph into complete irritation. A realization hits me full force like a tidal wave just as I grab my notebook to work on some of the songs I've started. I'm jealous of Hunter. I want to be with Leila at this moment on her couch kissing every inch of her.

Fuck…Fuck…Fuck!

While still holding my notebook, I abandon all my current projects to start a new one fueled by the thoughts that are consuming me. Like a man possessed, I frantically scribble down lyrics that pour out of me uncontrolled. My hand cramps from all the writing and my head hurts from thinking too much. I even go as far as strumming some basic chords to the words that validate my feelings.

The result is a heart-felt ballad. I most likely will never let another person hear it because it's way too personal, but it needed to be released from my head.

Surprisingly, even after a sleepless night filled with nothing but tortured romance crap, I'm still wired. What the fuck? I don't *do* tortured romance crap.

I jump into the shower to get ready for the day and the song gets stuck in my head on an endless loop. It continues to play even as I prepare my first cup of coffee.

"You ok?" Hunter stands directly in front of me without Amanda. I was so wrapped up in my thoughts, I never even heard him approach.

I ignore his question and ask, "Amanda's not here?" I don't want to get into this with him. I don't even know what "this" is at the moment.

"Nope, she left last night." He replies as he grabs his breakfast of choice. Hunter helps me forget my own issues by being a romantic sap. I should bet Scott on how long it will take for those two to screw each other's brains out.

Hunter immediately knows what I'm thinking when I shake my head and smirk. "Back off, I know what I'm doing."

"Ok. It's your dick. Just make sure your constant hard on doesn't interfere with playing drums." I laugh at the visual in my head.

"Fuck off." He says while smiling. I'm guessing he envisioned the same image. Even so, he becomes serious all of a sudden and asks, "What the hell were you playing your guitar all night for?"

"Just working on something. I couldn't sleep."

"Just make sure your constant hard on doesn't interfere with singing on stage."

The dickhead is so onto me!

Fuck off." I repeat his words. He laughs annoyingly as I flip him off.

***

Leila is already sitting on a stool when we arrive to the studio. It's before nine, and she looks like she's been here a while. She's texting someone on her phone and barely notices our entrance.

She looks adorable with her hair in a ponytail, tight Levi's, converse sneakers, and a tiny little *Born to Run* concert shirt that hugs all her curves.

She definitely wore it on purpose. Watching her for a few seconds does things to my insides.

"Good Mornin'."

She beams once she notices me checking her out and effectively takes my breath away.

"Hi, guys. I brought coffee and donuts." She points towards a table laid out with a mini breakfast buffet.

"Awesome." Hunter makes a beeline to the box. He grabs one and shoves it whole into his mouth.

"Fanks, Laywa." Crumbs shoot like bullets directly at my head.

I glare at him and punch his arm.

"Owf."

Leila laughs out loud. I love the way it sounds.

"He is such a Jackass." I point out while she still giggles.

"Thanks for the coffee." Walking over to where she is sitting, I look down at her chest. "Nice shirt."

"You like it? I can hook you up with one if you want." She winks.

Leila winking? Who is this girl and what has she done with the real Leila? There is no way she could feel comfortable enough to wink at me after just one night of bonding? This is a huge difference from the bundle of nerves that walked in here a few weeks ago.

I think I like it.

Jennifer strolls in like she owns the place. Leila sits up straighter on her stool making it pretty obvious she is intimidated by Jen.

"Good morning, everyone." She surveys the room. "Ready to rehearse your asses off?" She looks like she is about to walk a runway and not to sit in a stuffy studio for the next ten hours.

From the corner of my eye, I watch as Leila measures her up from head to toe with a very envious look in her eye. I want to shake some sense into her. Leila looks more in place with a pair of jeans and a Springsteen t-shirt, not to mention she is striking.

Jennifer's phone buzzes. "Don't move." She barks and walks out of the room to answer the call. Leila visibly relaxes the minute she is out the door.

"Hey, she doesn't bite."

She looks up embarrassed and blushes. "Is it that obvious?" Her words come out in a whisper.

Leaning in close enough to practically touch her ear, I whisper back, "Yes."

Her eyes widen, and a small gasp escapes her lips causing me to chuckle. "What?"

"She's scary."

"She's harmless." Unconsciously I rub her back to ease her discomfort. She stiffens slightly at my touch. Well maybe she is still a small bundle of nerves.

"She works for you too. Knock it off."

"Yes, boss." She salutes me.

I wave a finger at her and sternly command, "I mean it."

She looks up at me and I freeze. Her lips are totally kissable, her eyes are wide and innocent, and her chest rises with every breath. Damn it. I really, *really* want to kiss her. Imagining the reaction I would get from Leila and Hunter is the only thing stopping me.

This is going to be a long day.

Scott appears next looking fresh as a daisy. I know that he didn't see Patti last night so he would be in top shape for our first day of rehearsals. He can be such a nerd.

"Yay, who brought donuts?" He grabs one from the box as Hunter points to Leila and shoves another into his face.

"Thanks, Leila." He answers copying Hunter. "I'm starving."

Ugh. Except for Trey, sometimes this crew acts like they are five.

Speaking of which, of course he is late. While we wait, Hunter bends to pull out a large packet of papers as well as a few CD's from his duffle bag and hands them to Leila. At least this time he has the decency to pull the donut out of his face before he attempts to speak.

"I printed up all our lyrics as well as our sheet music for each song. We have been working on adding your backgrounds and keyboards as well. For the next few days we will run through our library, song by song, and add your vocals."

Hunter hands Leila the CD's. "These are all the songs recorded. You can take them home and listen on your spare time to become familiar with them."

I admit that he sometimes acts like a child, but he really is a good manager. He ran this by me, and I told him it was a great idea.

Leila looks impressed. "Thanks, Hunter. This is perfect. I really appreciate it."

Jennifer barges back into the room and looks around like she lost something. She looks at Hunter and commands, "Hunter, text Trey to see how far away he is."

"I am two feet away." Trey says from the doorway. "Calm down. I'm on time." He heads for his corner and promptly ignores our stares. Trey is almost half an hour late. His clock runs in half hour increments, so on his clock he is on time.

"Of course you are Mr. Taylor." They exchange sarcastic smiles. Watching Leila watch this exchange wide eyed is comical.

Jennifer flips her hair as she turns and focuses on Leila.

"So Leila, I see Hunter filled you in on what we plan on accomplishing this week. It's important to get you up to speed with the current Devil's Lair library. Please be sure to listen to their CD's as often as possible to familiarize yourself with their songs. We will start re-recording each song to include your voice, once we feel you are comfortable with your backgrounds and keyboard additions."

Leila clears her throat. "I am pretty familiar with most of their songs. I've been a fan for years. I'll be able to record backgrounds in a few days if you want. Regarding keyboards, I'll just need one run through to get up to speed." She sits up even straighter and levels her gaze at Jennifer.

I'm floored. I had no idea she was a fan. She acted star struck at her audition, but I would never have guessed she was a true fan. Hunter is beaming at Leila's admission. He's always been Leila's biggest supporter…besides me, that is. Right now he couldn't look prouder.

Jennifer on the other hand looks skeptical. "Well, that's good news. That will help us keep to schedule as we have a lot to do before September. We will be working in this studio until we are ready to add your vocals to our tracks. Then we will be moving to Bobby's bigger studio in the Village." She glances at her watch as she sits on a stool near the glass partition that separates us from the control room. "I wonder what's keeping Dylan."

"Oh, he said something came up." Leila responds. "I'm sorry I forgot to tell you. He texted me earlier to tell you to he'll catch up with you later." She looks around the room clearly embarrassed.

Jennifer levels her gaze on Leila. "Well then, let's do this."

Dylan texted Leila?

What?

He is so smooth… I didn't see that coming.

Chapter 15-Leila

Our first few days in the studio were exciting, grueling, and had me second-guessing my decision to work both gigs at the same time. Each night I climbed into bed dead to the world, and I haven't hit the weekend yet where I'll have to end my day performing at The Zone. I hope Cliffhangers are close to replacing me.

I worked my ass off, so my new band wouldn't think I was a slacker. Of course I'm not and if anything I ran circles around them, except Jack. His stamina is impressive.

Lunch and dinner were brought in and we basically never left the studio.

He was always conscious of my needs, constantly asking if I needed a break but never bothering to ask the same of the guys.

It's gotten to the point where they each want to kill him.

Hunter was the ringleader in coordinating different ways to annoy Jack.

On day one, Hunter complained he was hungry and wanted to take a break. He griped he couldn't play the drums well if his stomach was growling. Jack of course ignored him. The next day Hunter was prepared. He pulled out a huge punch bowl filled with Fruit Loops from behind his drum set and preceded to slurp them down in the middle of a song. Everyone laughed, even Jack hiding a smirk.

I thought it was hilarious and couldn't keep from laughing.

They would all raise their hands and ask for permission to go to the bathroom. If Jack ignored them, Hunter would ask me instead. "Miss Marino, can I go pee pee?"

We discovered that Hunter had the guys in the control room alter our voices to make us sound like munchkins when we listened to the playbacks. Trey almost pissed his pants when he heard it.

As exhausted as I was at the end of each day, I still loved my new job. I haven't laughed as hard or as much as I did these past few days. My old band members were fun, but watching these guys interact was nothing short of a reality show in the making.

Besides the fun and the whip cracking, there were many moments of clenching on my part. If I thought Jack was sexy on a normal day that was nothing compared to how sexy he looks while playing a guitar and singing.

Oh my *sweet* lord. It was an aphrodisiac of the most dangerous kind.

His handsome face was so intense when he concentrated on the words and his hands were so sexy as they moved among the strings. I couldn't stop staring at his pure perfection. He caught me and smiled shyly. Witnessing him playing guitar will no doubt fuel many, *many* more dreams of Jack Lair.

Jack was thrilled to call me car service at the end of the day. I had to admit it was really nice being driven, especially after the exhausting days we had. In hindsight, his suggestion was thoughtful and sweet. When I regretfully thanked him, the bastard winked at me.

All in all, things were really moving along until today. I woke up with a terrible head cold and my voice wasn't cooperating. Even so, I wasn't going to be the cause of screwing up our schedule. Jack and I argued all morning and got nothing done anyway. He can be so stubborn.

He ended rehearsal early by sending me home and ordering me to rest. I wasn't going to win this fight, so I did just as he asked. I set an alarm just in case I overslept, and woke up feeling cranky and irritable when it went off. The nap did more damage than good. As I'm lethargically getting ready for tonight's show at The Zone, my cell rings.

"Hi, Jack."

"Leila, you sound like crap. Did you do what I said?"

"Yes boss. I had soup, I slept, I took a hot shower, and now I have to get to work."

"I knew it. Leila you need to stay home and rest. I'm sure the guys will understand."

"I'm fine. I feel better. I took cold medicine and I'm fine." Of course it was a big lie.

"Leila…"

"Jack, it'll be a quiet night. I'll play keyboards and…"

"…I'm calling Evan."

Sighing heavily, I begin to lose my patience. "I have a dad, I don't need another one. It's just a stupid cold. Please stop."

The long silence on the other end forces me to ask, "Are you there?"

"A cold that can turn into something worst. Call me tonight. I don't care what time it is. If you forget, I'm coming to Hoboken." With that he hangs up without a goodbyc.

What the fuck was that?

Once I arrive at The Zone, Evan takes one look at me and smirks. "You do look like shit."

"Gee thanks." Obviously Mr. Lair called him. "You are so generous with the compliments."

Evan confirms my suspicion. "Cut the crap. Your boyfriend called. Go home."

"Uh…he's not my boyfriend."

196

"Yeah, whatever."

"Jerk." Brilliant, mature comeback Leila.

Lori walks up to me and smacks her hand against my forehead.

"Owwwaaa."

"You're hot."

"Thank you. You're annoying."

"Hilarious. Go home."

One by one my friends nag me and make me feel like I'm five. Matt is no way sharing a microphone with me. Joe has a party this weekend and if he gets sick and misses it he will kill me. Logan and Alisa both take the liberty to tell Sal I'm sick and have to go home. Sal calls my dad who then precedes to text me relentlessly.

I can't take anymore!

"Fine, I'm going. You are all irritating the crap out of me and that's the only reason I'm going home."

As soon as I'm back in my apartment, I text Jack.

i'm home...they kicked me out... going 2 sleep.

I receive his return text instantly.

good...b there soon...what kind of soup do u like.

no!...can't chance you getting sick...i'm fine...locking door and passing out.

grrr...ur so stubborn....fine...call me 2morrow.

did u just growl?

grrr.

***

My cold turned into an upper respiratory infection. I hate when I'm proven wrong. Evan and dad came by to check on me. Jack took the

197

opportunity to gloat and alternated between texting and calling me. It was bordering on excessive and annoying and it was kinda hot. I felt cared for. It's stupid, because I am cared for between dad and my friends. But Jack's "take control" antics were turning me on.

My phone now buzzes with text number seven hundred and three. This one announces that he is at my door.

open up.

Groaning, I shuffle to the door without opening it. Calls and text were hot and sexy, but showing up at my door when I looked like a zombie out of the *Walking Dead* was not cool.

I'm wrapped in an afghan and wearing mismatched pajamas. My dirty hair is in a messy ponytail, bags are under my eyes and I haven't shaved my legs or showered in two days.

"Go away. I look like crap." Actually, I just insulted crap. I really prefer he didn't see me like this.

"No…open up."

"No."

"Leila…Leila…Really? Open the damn door."

I huff and puff and slowly open the door a tiny crack.

"Hey, Rudolph." He teases.

"Funny. I told you to stay away, you'll get sick."

"Planning on making out with me?"

Wait…what?

"Uh, no…"

"Then how would I get sick? I came to make sure you are getting better." He pushes his way in, and carries two bags into my kitchen.

"What's that?"

198

"Medicine and soup." He begins pulling item after item out of the bags and lines them up on my counter.

"Medicine and soup for a small village?"

"Cute. You're needed back healthy and in singing condition."

"So you're concerned about the recording schedule and not with my well-being?"

Jack stops in his tracks looking highly insulted. "No. Is that what you think?"

"I'm kidding."

"Leila, I don't care about the album right now."

"I know." Jeez, he's so sensitive.

I feel bad about hurting his feelings and allow Jack to play nurse for few hours. I let him feed me, medicate me, and fill me in on what I missed at the studio. He really is a very good nurse who also happens to be very easy on the eyes.

The soup is absolutely delicious. I inhale the entire bowl without stopping and look up to see him scowling at me.

"What?"

"When was the last time you ate?"

"Does Nyquil count?"

"Ha, ha."

"I don't remember. The soup was really good. Where did you get it?"

"My mom made it."

"Shut up!"

"She dropped it off this morning."

"Jack, please tell me you didn't ask her to make me soup."

"I didn't. She did it all on her own."

"Oh my god…that is so nice…and so embarrassing."

"Why? That's my mom. Get used to it."

I can't believe he told his mom I was sick.

I can't believe Jack's mom made me soup.

I can't believe he drove it all the way to Hoboken.

The Lair family can't be real. Gorgeous…generous…caring…it's all too good to be true.

I've been trying to convince myself what I feel for Jack is just a mad crush. Sitting here having Jack take care of me, seeing me at my worst, and killing me with his kindness, makes me realize I've been delusional and in denial.

It's not just a crush.

I am falling for him, hard and I haven't a clue how I'm going to handle this because Jack and I cannot be a together. I can predict what people would say - his back-up singer fucked him to get her dream job. It doesn't matter that I already got the job. That's a small detail that would be ignored. I may as well flush my career down the toilet.

Jack senses my discomfort.

"You ok?"

"Yep, just tired."

To change the subject, he announces, "The guys miss you. They claim I'm a bitch when you aren't around."

Laughing at his admission I ask, "Are you?"

"No comment."

"Tell them I'll be back soon to keep you in line."

"Good." Watching me closely he adds, "I miss you too."

The familiar buzz I feel when our eyes lock takes hold of my body. For the first time in days I don't feel chilled to the bone. I feel very warm. My lower half shows signs of life and I feel my heart pounding in my chest.

My palms are clammy too. My eyes, my heart, my crotch, my body all don't care what would happen if Jack and I got together. They all want him. My resolve is wearing extremely thin and stretched to its absolute limit right now.

Having Jack in my apartment as I'm having this life-altering awareness while under the influence of cold medicine is a dangerous situation.

My brain is the only logical one at this party. It controls my mouth.

"You can go now. I'm really tired." I lie through my teeth.

"Kicking me out?"

With a nod, I close my eyes and pretend that exhaustion hits from the cold medicine. "You are a good nurse. Thank you."

I carefully measure my breathing, as I drift into a fake sleep. I wait as Jack places everything I need within arm's reach.

"Sleep tight, pretty girl." The feel of warm lips on my forehead nearly blows my cover but I continue my even breathing and continue with my charades.

Jack leaves me bundled and cozy on the couch before he quietly exits my apartment. It isn't long before actual sleep does take over.

The bright sunlight wakes me the next morning. Amazingly, I feel better having gotten a restful night of sleep filled with dreams of Jack. We were married and he was taking care of our sick daughter. It was so real and so beautiful and I'm so screwed.

Stretching lazily, my phone buzzes with a new text that puts a grin on my face.

hey pretty girl...hope u feel better...call me when u r up.

So screwed!

***

When I finally got back in the studio, I had to pretend I wasn't at all affected. Let me tell you it's not easy being around someone you love and pretend you don't. Every word, action and facial expression has to be carefully controlled. It's fucking hard as hell and it's exhausting.

I also had to endure endless ribbing from the guys.

"He likes you better. I could lose an arm in a shark attack, and I'd still have to play drums."

"Welcome back, Leila. While you were gone we changed our name to Leila's Lair."

"So glad you're back. We really need to pee and he won't let us."

"He was mean to us."

"He threw out my Fruit Loops."

I'm surrounded by comedians.

Back at The Zone, I now have to endure the reality of being replaced. Lori assures me that Cliffhangers is close to finding a replacement, which means that I will no longer have to work two jobs at once. "You're run down. That's why you got sick. We should have you replaced in no time."

"I got a cold. Happens every day to millions of people. Stop being so dramatic."

"Pifft."

"Very attractive Lor."

"Pifft. So Trey wants me to come to Jack's party." She wiggles her eyebrows and smirks.

"*Really*? How often do you and Trey talk?"

"Every day. Well we either text or call every day."

"Since when? And why the hell haven't you told me?"

"You've been busy. Plus I didn't know what was going to happen so I kept it to myself. But Leila he is so hot and so sweet and I really like him. I can't keep it in any more. I know he's leaving soon, but I don't care. I'll enjoy the ride until then." She pauses then adds. "Literally."

"Ugh, T.M.I."

"I told Alisa and she wanted to kill me. You know how she feels about me keeping secrets." Based on the goofy grin, she can't be all that upset about Alisa.

"I'm really happy for you. Of course you can come to Jack's party with me. I already asked Evan. I worry how both of you will get the night off though."

She stands and starts clapping. "Yay...don't worry, I'll handle Sal and the band. We are going to Riverside to get new outfits. No arguments." She points a finger at me.

Crap...going to Riverside and shopping with Lori is asking for trouble. Our tastes couldn't be more different.

"Yay." I respond sarcastically.

***

Evan, Lori and I decided to share a cab to Jack's party, which is in a swanky bar in midtown called Granite. We didn't want to worry about having a few drinks, and we all plan on enjoying ourselves tonight. I hardly ever get drunk, but I definitely need to get hammered. I should have taken a shot at home to loosen me up a bit.

Lori chose what she called the perfect party dress for me tonight. It's a backless, mini black dress. A long silver necklace, silver peep toe pumps, and my panties complete the ensemble. Because the back of my dress is missing, I couldn't wear a bra. This isn't a problem since I am not very well endowed, but I feel naked…and sexy. If going braless was the worst Lori could have dished out, I'll take it. I bought the dress without argument.

Lori has on a very short emerald green, jersey knit dress that skims her curves leaving nothing to the imagination and no doubt that she isn't wearing panties. She paired it with hot pink patent pumps. Only Lori could pull off this outfit. Her hair is long and lose and her make-up is vamped up. She really looks hot.

She argued I didn't have enough eye make-up on. I allowed her to dress me but there was no way I was allowing her to paint my face.

Evan is wearing a pair of black jeans and a grey button down shirt he left un-tucked. His shaggy hair is messy, he smells good and he also looks hot.

"Thanks for coming tonight."

"My pleasure. I'm actually looking forward to it."

Lori jumps in her seat and grabs my leg. "Lei, I forgot to tell you. I Googled this place and do you know it has a really cool roof top bar and that they hire different bands weekly to perform and there are music producers that attend frequently?"

"I had no clue. That's awesome."

"Yep. I can see Cliffhangers tearing this place up." She looks past me to Evan and winks. "That's how we convinced the guys we needed to be here tonight."

"I was wondering how you accomplished that."

Evan looks over at me. "Yep…research, and getting plastered. That's our goal tonight."

"Me too…on the getting plastered part."

Lori looks at me like I've grown a third eye. "You?"

"Yes, me."

Evan squeezes my hand. "You deserve it. We'll make sure you get good and sauced. What shot do you want to do for your birthday?"

Panic-stricken, I pull my hand from his grip. "Evan please don't tell anyone it's my birthday. I don't want them to know."

He gives me a look and consigns, "Yeah, ok."

Lori snorts and then covers it up with a cough. This is not good.

"What are you two up to?" I ask in all seriousness, turning my head left then right to try and figure out what they are scheming. "Please? Don't embarrass me?"

"What? All I asked was what shot you were going to do? You're paranoid."

"I don't trust you two. I should have come alone." I mumble mostly to myself. They each look out their respective windows pretending to ignore me.

Our cab pulls up to an industrial looking building sporting a small awning with the bar's name scribbled on it. Based on the amount of people waiting on a line that wraps around the block, this must be the place to be.

I hate the club scene. Standing in line forever in hopes that you can get in, paying twenty bucks for a watered down drink, sweating your ass off all night while constantly being hit on by sleazy guys…*ugh*.

Three intimidating big ass men are at the entrance looking bored out of their minds. The one holding a clipboard assesses us as we approach. Once we give our names, without a word he moves the rope aside to let us in. He leans close to Lori and whispers something in her ear, causing a smile to split her face in two. I can only imagine what he said to her. As we walk into the club, the well-organized line becomes an angry mob (minus the pitch forks). Every person is yelling or cursing at us.

"This is so fun." Lori says as she antagonizes the crowd by smiling wide and waving.

"Ok...let's go troublemaker. I can't fight in these shoes."

"Party-pooper." She responds, only half-joking. "Wait I have an idea." She takes a step backwards until she is visible in the doorway and yells out, "Cliffhangers.com!"

"Nice..." Evan says appreciatively.

Lori taps her temple smiling. "Always thinking."

I have to admit, it was a brilliant move.

The elevator opens to a really cool rooftop bar scene.

"Holy shit." Evan mutters to no one in particular.

It *is* gorgeous, absolutely stunning.

There are clear glass awnings above allowing you to see the night sky. The side facing the elevators is a wall of glass that treats guests to a spectacular view of the Empire State Building and everything south of it. A stage adorned with instruments spreads against the wall to the left and a long glass modern bar faces the stage to the right. Scattered, tiny tables surround a large square dance floor in the center of the room and heaters run around the perimeter.

Waitresses sporting black short shorts matching vests are carrying trays of Jell-O shots, beer, and fancy girly drinks. In the corner is an unbelievable birthday cake with the band's logo next to an impressive buffet with all sorts of hors d'oeuvres. Devil's Lair music is being piped into the sound system. Listening to the song, I recognize my own voice. The tracks must be from rehearsals. It's so surreal.

Lizzy thought of everything.

"Is that you?" Evan asks incredulously.

"Yeah. Can you believe it?"

"You sound awesome."

"This deserves a toast." Lori signals one of the Jell-O shot girls over. She grabs two off her tray and Evan grabs two more.

She thrusts one of the shots towards me "Down the hatch."

Shaking my head, I tip back Lori's shot. No sooner do I pull the glass away from my lips does Evan thrust his shot towards me as well. I roll my eyes and drink his too. I quickly recall my goal of getting hammered tonight and I take Evan's other shot out of his hand and pound it back while he gawks at me.

"What? They are very yummy." *Strong too.*

Lori finishes her shot and immediately takes off when she spots Trey, leaving Evan and me in shock.

"She just ditched us."

Evan laughs. "Yep."

There are quite a few people here. Beside the band, Jen is here with an attractive man at her side. Scary Sally is chatting with other girls who look like they could be triplets, and there are rocker dudes interspersed with runway models.

Scott spots us hovering at the entrance. Waving, he drags Patti over to where we are standing. "Hey guys." Patti pulls me into a hug immediately. She's a very touchy, feely person, but for some reason I don't mind it coming from her.

"Scott, how is he getting here?"

"Hunter is bringing him over. We come here a lot. Jack thinks we are all meeting to have a few drinks before we head off to a different bar. He hasn't a clue." Just as he says that a gorgeous girl with long, golden brown hair spots us from across the room and heads on over. She is stunning, wearing a cream colored dress and red heels.

"Scott, is this your lovely new back-up singer?" She asks smiling warmly at me.

Scott turns to look at the beauty and nods. "Lizzy, this is Leila and her friend Evan.

Guys this is Lizzy, Jack's sister."

Wow, she is an absolute knockout. I can see the resemblance, they have the same smile.

"Hi guys. It's so nice to meet you." She shakes my hand first and then goes for Evan's.

I've seen Evan woo many girls during our friendship, but I never have seen him stunned into silence before. My friend is practically drooling. I recognize the look in Evan's eyes. It's the same one I have when looking at Jack.

"Lizzy, this place is gorgeous. You've done such a nice job."

"Thank you. I hope he likes it or I'll kill him." She says throwing us the most dazzling smile. Jeez, the knockout genes in this family are just unfair. Evan's eyes slightly un-focus as he watches Lizzy. I'm sure he is experiencing the male version of crotch clenching right now. Unfortunately it's harder for a guy to hide his crotch excitement. I hope things don't get embarrassing for him.

Evan turns towards me but still has his eyes glued to Lizzy. "What do you want to drink?"

"White wine please."

He offers his arm to Lizzy and says, "Can you walk me to the bar?"

Real *smooth* Evan.

Lizzy smiles shyly and accepts Evan's arm. Watching them walk away arm in arm, I'm left standing with Scott and Patti. Friend number two has now ditched me as well.

Trying to make small talk, Scott fills me in on some of the things to expect on tour when Dylan interrupts. Casually dressed in jeans and a knit long sleeve black shirt, he looks very handsome.

"Hey, guys. Hi, Leila. How are you feeling?"

"I'm all better. How are you?"

"Glad to hear that. I'm good. I hear you guys got a lot done. Based on what I'm listening to I'd have to agree."

"Thanks. We did accomplish a lot. We'll be ready to start recording soon."

"That's impressive. Believe it or not, Jack does have amazing work ethics." The tone of his voice contradicts the compliment he just gave Jack. That doesn't sit well with me.

"Jack is very professional when it comes to his music." I respond very defensively.

Dylan nods and smiles. "He is, and he's extremely talented. I'm going to grab a drink, can I get you one?"

Maybe I imagined the sour tone in his voice.

I feel bad I jumped down his throat because he really is a nice guy.

"My friend is getting me one, but I'll come with you." I don't want to be left standing alone again. Scott and Patti moved on to another group of people and both my friends have forgotten that I'm here. He puts his hand on my lower back as he guides me to the bar. The contact surprises me. Subconsciously I look around to see if anyone is watching. Across the room Jennifer and a handsome man are both talking to a beautiful older woman, and of course she is watching me like a hawk…great.

Evan brings me my wine with Lizzy at his side. "Thanks Ev. This is Dylan, our tour manager. Dylan this is my best friend and former band mate Evan."

"Nice to meet you" he says as he takes Dylan's hand.

"Same here. Hi, Liz."

"Hi, Dylan."

"Evan, I' sorry we stole Leila from you, but we'll take good care of her." Dylan says smiling at me.

"I'm going to hold you to that."

"I promise. I'll keep those guys in line also."

"Thanks. I appreciate it. I worry about the four rock stars she'll be living with."

"That's understandable, but they are really good guys. I can vouch for that. Right, Liz?"

"Yes, they are. There's no need to worry about how they will treat Leila."

Looking from Evan to Dylan to Lizzy, their conversation makes me feel invisible. "Um...I'm standing right here. I can hear you."

Dylan laughs, "Excuse me I'm going to grab a drink." He turns and leaves me with Evan and Lizzy.

"I see a food crisis needing attention. I'll be right back." Lizzy excuses herself.

"I'll help." Evan chooses to follow her with a grin. I sense a pattern on how the rest of this evening is going to pan out since I'm left standing alone once again.

I join Dylan at the bar and wait while he orders his drink. Jennifer follows right behind me with a handsome man in tow.

"Hey you two, did you come together?" she asks, her voice dripping sweetness.

"No we didn't Jennifer. No need to call the paparazzi in." It's nice to see Dylan has no problem giving Jennifer a dose of her own medicine.

"Oh calm down Dylan. I'm just teasing." Striking out with Dylan, she turns her focus to me. "You look very pretty tonight Leila. Glad you're all better. This is Malcolm Reynolds, my boyfriend. Mal, this is our new back-up singer Leila Marino."

I accept Malcolm's hand and can't help but feel he's dissecting me from head to toe. "Hello, Leila. Jen has told me so much about you."

Yeah, I'm sure she did.

Gripping my hand tightly, he instantly gives me the creeps. He is extremely handsome with his black curly hair and vivid blue eyes. His wide smile doesn't reach his eyes and in their depths I feel as if he is hiding something. Jennifer leans over and whispers something into his ear. They excuse themselves to go talk to a rocker dude standing near the stage.

Dylan smiles and says, "Don't they make a lovely couple?"

His comment surprises me and I laugh out loud practically spitting out my wine. Dylan laughs as well and shakes his head. "Malcolm is also an agent. He represents Jared Press and Shelby Sanders."

"You're kidding. They are both two of the hottest pop singers around. He must be a really good agent."

Dylan smirks, "He's a snake…but he can be the snake charmer just as easily. He'd swim the Everglades for his clients and come out wearing a croc suit and alligator shoes. In all fairness though, he is good at what he does. His clients would follow him anywhere."

"Why do agents have such a bad rep?"

"Because it's true?" Smiling at my giggle he adds, "Seriously, Jen is a great agent. Those guys owe her for getting them where they are today. But you need really thick skin and really big balls to succeed in that business. Every agent I've ever met fits the bill."

Dylan's analogy and explanation paints a pretty clear picture. I hope Lori can fit the bill. I nod towards the group Mr. and Ms. Agent walked over to and ask, "Who are they?"

Dylan follows my gaze. "MACE. Do you know them?"

I practically spill my wine. It's dark in the bar, so I really didn't get a good look at their faces. But now that he mentioned that, yes I know them!

"Oh my god, MACE is here?" I squeal like a groupie.

He laughs at my enthusiasm. "Yes, they all became good friends after their tour last year. Do you want to meet…"

"YES!" I cut him off mid-sentence. Dylan laughs again. "Come."

I pull back. "Wait, can I bring my friends?"

"Sure, go get them."

I quickly make my way to Evan, who is deep in conversation with Lizzy. "I'm sorry I need to interrupt. Do you want to meet MACE?" I ask sounding out of breath.

He looks around and spots the band. "Hell, yes." He looks over at Lizzy and says, "I'll be right back…don't move." She giggles at a star struck Evan.

We both interrupt Lori just as she's about to make out with Trey.

"What!?"

"You want to meet MACE?"

"Fuck yeah." Lori leans in and whispers something in Trey's ear that puts a smirk on his face. I'd love to know what she said to him.

Dylan patiently waits and then walks us over to meet one of our favorite bands. I'm so excited to meet them that I don't even care Jennifer and Mr. Agent are watching us like we just broke past security.

Dylan makes the introductions. "Ricky, this is Leila, the…"

"…new back-up singer." Ricky Storm finishes his sentence.

Dumbstruck, I can't believe Ricky Storm knows who I am.

"We've heard great things about you, Leila. Jack also shared your audition tape with us. I'm peeved that he found you first."

Holy shit…

"Um…I really don't know what to say. Thank you?"

"You're welcome. We can't wait to see your first show."

"Now I'm really nervous." I respond while trying to sound humorous but falling flat. My voice sounds high and pitchy. It suddenly occurs to me that people are going to be watching us. Lots and lots and lots of people. Some even famous! I need another drink.

"Um…I know it sounds cliché' but I'm a huge fan."

"Very cliché." He laughs teasing me. "But I do believe you."

"This is Evan and Lori, the drummer of and agent for Cliffhangers."

Ricky introduces us to the rest of the band. Lori immediately jumps into a conversation with MACE, as if they've known each other for years. After a while, I excuse myself leaving Lori to talk shop. She doesn't look at all intimidated, even with Jennifer and Malcolm standing there. Looking over at Evan I give him a "she's perfect" look and he nods knowingly.

Feeling the effects of my three shots, two glasses of wine and these sadistic shoes, I wonder what time it is. It feels like we've been here for hours already. I've been keeping close to Dylan and the longer we chat the more I slur. "Dylan, what time is it?"

As if on cue, Lizzy finally gives the signal Jack is on his way up.

"It's surprise time." He smiles.

Everyone makes their way over to the dance floor with Lori, Trey, Evan, Dylan and I at the very back of the crowd. Lizzy is waiting at the elevator with Jennifer right beside her. Ugh, that woman gets on my nerves.

The elevator doors open signaling the room to yell "Surprise". Jack freezes in place, looking shocked and confused. He scans the crowd, shaking his head. His sister rushes up and gives him a huge hug. While hugging her back he whispers something in her ear. She smacks his chest and pushes him deeper into the crowd.

Jennifer rushes over and gets a hold of him. Kissing him on his cheek she motions for Malcolm to join them and I could swear Jack rolls his eyes.

Jack smiles politely while Malcolm speaks and mid-sentence excuses himself to make his way around the gathered guests. Solidifying my suspicion that Jack isn't a Malcolm fan.

Dylan is making small talk with Evan and Lori, but I'm not paying attention. Instead I observe Jack being hugged, kissed, and passed around everyone in the room. Each time he is passed off, he is handed a shot. Each time he encounters a pretty female, he kisses her cheek and smiles wide. My mind starts reeling.

Are they all past conquests?

Are they all past girlfriends?

Are they all current fuck buddies?

As he makes his way to the back of the crowd, he spots me standing with Dylan. His smile fades for a brief second as he walks straight for us. Damn he looks so good in jeans and a t-shirt.

"Hi." He says quietly, raking his eyes over me and causing my heart to flip instantly in my chest.

"Happy birthday, Jack." I lean in with the intent to give him a quick hug. But as I try to pull away, both his hands move to my lower back holding me close to his. Pressed up against him, his hands on my skin, and his scent surrounding me, cause goosebumps to appear over my entire body.

He notices and whispers into my ear, "Are you cold?"

Cold? Every nerve ending from my scalp to my toes is on fire.

"No."

His glossy eyes connect with mine, and I cannot look away. Dylan interrupts our moment. I clumsily pull out of his grasp, step back, and collide with a nearby table.

"Happy birthday, buddy." He says slapping him on the back.

"Thanks, man." Jack responds. His body is still very close to mine and I can feel his arm against my own. I look down into my empty glass and Dylan notices.

"Leila, can I get you another white wine?"

"Yes, please." I better eat something if I'm going to keep drinking so much.

He walks away heading to the bar. I am so relieved to be standing alone with Jack. "You look gorgeous, Leila."

My breathing is erratic and as my chest rises and falls. I fear he can see right through me to my braless heart.

"Thanks. You also look nice." I don't know if it's the wine, or the dark bar, or the feeling of his hands on my back, but I am completely turned on and this time, I'm afraid I won't be able to hide it. The combination of alcohol and skin on skin has flipped a switch.

Who am I kidding…I'm always turned on around him.

"Jackson, aren't you going to introduce us?"

"Jackson?" I mumble to him. Jackson?

That's *so* sexy.

"Zip it." He says looking down at me smirking.

An extremely handsome man comes up behind Jack, putting his hand on his shoulder. He is with the beautiful woman Jennifer was talking to earlier. Jack turns and smiles wide at the older couple. I can see where both he and Lizzy get their looks. These two look like a pair of super models.

"Of course. Mom, Dad, this is Leila, our new back-up singer." He then steps closer and places his hand on my lower back again. I suck in a breath and he quickly glances down but doesn't pull his hand away. "Leila, these are my parents, Renata and Peter Lair."

His mom immediately pulls me into a hug. "Leila, sweetheart, how are you feeling?"

"So much better. I have no doubt my recovery can be attributed to your absolutely delicious soup. Mrs. Lair, thank you. You have no idea what that meant to me."

"Call me Renata, dear. It was my pleasure. I'm so glad you're feeling better."

During my conversation with Jack's parents, his hand remains firmly attached to my lower back. Does he realize he's still doing that? I am trying to control my breathing, but I can only think of the way his hand feels on my back.

While his parents continue to speak to me I realize that I really need to snap out of it. Dylan returns with my wine and starts chatting with the Lairs. Jack slowly removes his hand but continues to stand close. I am having a hard time concentrating on their conversation.

Jack spots a girl at the bar amidst our chat and excuses himself. He walks over to the petite waitress and bends to whisper in her ear. She smiles at him and whispers something back. I am riveted by what's happening between Jack and this girl. She kisses him on the *lips* and then hugs him hard. During the course of their conversation, they continuously glance over to me. Of course I'm caught staring, each and every time. Suddenly Jack grabs her hand and pulls her towards me. Who the hell is this girl and what does she mean to him?

Jack's parents excuse themselves, leaving me with Dylan. He notices the shift in my posture and turns to ask, "Are you ok?"

"Yeah, I'm fine."

Jack literally drags the waitress over. "Leila, I want you to meet a very good friend of mine. This is Trini. Trini, this is our new band member Leila." He looks at me with unmistakable pride.

Trini grabs my arms and hugs me tight. "So nice to meet you, Leila. Jack told me how talented you are. I can't wait to see your show." Jack is giving me his CCDS smile. I guess they are just friends? Why can't he be a good friend with a girl? Evan is, right?

Watching them interact familiarly is a bit unnerving. These two are very comfortable with each other. Yep…these two are definitely more than friends.

She's tiny, and in my heels I tower over her. With spiky black hair, visible tattoos and a pierced nose, she doesn't look like she would be Jack's type. Oh jeez, if Trini is his type, then Scary Sally must be as well.

"Hi Trini, it's very nice to meet you." It's hard to not like her. Unlike Scary Sally, Trini is so happy and bubbly.

"You're beautiful Leila. I can't wait to see you guys do your thing." She looks up at Jack and winks. Awkwardly I thank her for the compliment. She wishes me luck and excuses herself to get back to work. "Have fun."

"She seems really nice."

Jack watches me for a few seconds. "She is. She's a great friend."

Yeah, I'm sure…a friend with benefits. Jealous Leila is rearing her ugly head once again.

My imagination runs wild with pictures of Jack and Trini when Lizzy takes the mic on stage and asks everyone to quiet down.

"Hi everyone. I'm so glad you all came out to wish my brother a very happy birthday. Someone get him a shot." She smiles wide at Jack as he shakes his head.

"We are also celebrating Devil's Lair being signed!" She starts clapping and everyone follows suit. She raises her hand to quiet the crowd again. "I think we can convince them to play us a song or two tonight if we all plead and beg." The room explodes into applause again. "Guys you have to play now or you'll have an angry mob to deal with."

Oh crap.

I wasn't planning on performing tonight. I rarely get nervous, but I don't know these people. Well I don't know the people we play for at The Zone, but this is different. Plus, I'm drunk!

Lizzy laughs and motions for the crowd to hush down. "Ok, ok, listen up... We have one more thing to celebrate it seems. Our lovely new band member Leila's birthday is the day before Jacks. Happy birthday, Leila! Someone get Leila a shot too!"

The entire room turns to look at me and I almost pee my pants. Oh god. I should have gone to the bathroom earlier. One of the waitresses makes her way over and presents her tray. I pull a shot off the tray and tip it back.

I notice Evan and Lori whispering and laughing in the corner. I have the urge to stab them with a very dull knife. Jack hugs me instantly. "Why didn't you tell me your birthday is the day before mine?"

I shrug and say, "I only found out when Lizzy called. I couldn't ruin the surprise, could I?" I slurred a bit at the end and he looks at me with amusement.

Leaning in, he asks, "You ok?"

Smiling wide, I respond. "No. I'm buzzed and was just summoned to sing in front of all these people. I'm debating how far I'll get sprinting in these heels."

"I'd catch you." He smirks.

Dylan cuts in and grabs me away from Jack, only then making me realize I was in his arms for quite some time. "Happy Birthday, Leila." While he is hugging me, I watch Jack watch us with a forced smile on his face. I pull away from Dylan taking a casual step closer to Jack. I blame that damn magnetic pull he has on me.

We are interrupted with Lizzy's voice again. "Leila, we will all sing happy birthday to you later. Ok, can we hear a few songs guys? Or do we have to become violent?"

Trey, Hunter and Scott make their way up to the stage. They each hug Lizzy and get into position. Jack grabs my hand and pulls me towards the stage. I dig my heels into the floor and jerk to a complete stop. He feels my resistance and turns towards me.

"What are you doing?" He pulls on my outstretched arm.

"I wasn't kidding. I'm drunk. And I am still learning the back-ground vocals." I hiss in panic while shaking my head. "And I have to pee!"

He stops and laughs out loud. Coming closer so we are face to face, he says, "I'm really sorry that you have to pee, but it will have to wait." Looking into my eyes, I get lost in their depths. Amazingly, I feel calmer as I gaze back at him. "You can do this. Besides I'm drunk too." He smiles down at me and further pulls me under his spell. I would do anything for this man at this moment.

I gulp down the rest of my wine before Jack puts it on a table and pulls me towards the stage. He doesn't notice me stumble once.

Once we are with the band, he says to them, "*Committed*, with Leila. Then go into *Nothing to Gain* and end with *You Broke Me*." He looks at me and adds, "Just like we practiced."

I nod and take a deep breath. He is still holding my hand, does he realize that? There is only one microphone, so Jack and I will have to share it. I can do this. This is good practice.

Everyone starts clapping and Jack laughs. "Hey everyone. Thank you so much for coming, although I doubt you had a choice with Lizzy." He glares at his sister who shrugs and raises her glass to him. Evan is right beside her. Lori is next to him and winks at me.

Oh God.

"Ok, you asked for it. Welcome to Devil's Lair first unofficial concert. This here is our newest member, Leila Marino. Leila, happy birthday by the way. She's is a little nervous so let's show her the love." I smile weakly and glare at Jack.

He laughs at me and signals to Hunter. The boys start up *Committed* and I come in at my mark. Jack and I are inches apart, and he winks while I'm singing. I'm going to get real used to this. Being this close to him, feeling as if he is singing only to me, very soon I will be able enjoy this every night. That part of the tour I am looking very forward to. The crowd loves us, and it's pumping me up with pure adrenaline.

By our third and final song, I am no longer nervous. My friends are whistling and cheering along with the crowd. This feels really good.

Jack is beaming and enjoying the reaction we receive. He wraps his arm around me when we finish. "You were incredible. Now you can pee."

Nodding, I sprint down the stage steps and am instantly mobbed by Evan and Lori.

"Lei that was so awesome."

"You guys fucking rocked!"

I nod and yell a little too loudly, "Thank you but I really have to PEE!" As I bolt for the ladies room I can hear Evan and Lori laughing, alongside Jack and a few guests.

That was the best experience of my life. This was totally different than The Zone. It was better. I feel guilty feeling this way but it's true. I can only attribute it to one thing. I love singing with Jack.

I make a left out of the ladies room instead of a right and find a small balcony that overlooks the city. Wow, why isn't anyone back here? It's cooler and the air feels good. The view is gorgeous.

I grip the railing while standing in the overhang, looking down I get dizzy. I am most definitely drunk. Hearing footsteps, I spin around to see who is invading my solitude. Jack strolls towards me holding two more Jell-O shots.

"I found you. I was worried you bolted." He chimes as he joins me on the overhang. His eyes are unfocused, just like they were the night of his party. The difference is, this time mine are too.

He hands me one of the shots and says, "Happy birthday, Leila."

"I think this is number six." Giggling, I down it while he watches me. As I slowly lick my lips, his eyes become heated.

Jack takes his own shot. He transfixes his gaze onto mine and the sparks fly between us.

"That was really fun." I point out in an attempt to distract him. "I can't believe how much I enjoyed that."

"Yep, me too." He takes our shot glasses and puts them on the ledge, and then steps closer until we are practically touching. "You really were fantastic up there. I knew you would be." He strokes my cheek and pushes my hair away from my face. I feel the sensation building below and I want to take this further. I *really* do.

"Happy birthday, Jack."

Jack leans in and hovers over my lips until I can feel his warm breath mingling with my own.

"Thank you. Happy birthday, Leila."

He bends just as I lift up until our lips touch. His are soft, and his kiss is dry and slow. *Really* slow. It's the perfect kiss. We continue to nibble each other's lips until I can't stand it any longer.

I grip his shirt in my hands and pull him into me. My lips part and he slips his tongue in to stroke against my own. He moans and pushes his body up against every inch of mine. My hands reach up and link behind his head just as his hands find my lower back and he grips me hard to his body.

Oh. My. God.

This feels amazing. I don't want to stop.

Jack pushes a leg between mine just as I move my hands into his hair to keep him on me. Kissing him is addicting. I'm sure he can make me climax from this alone.

My enthusiasm is embarrassing. I'm on fire. You would think I've never kissed a man before. His hands move around to my waist and then he runs them up my sides until he skims my breasts. The lack of oxygen has me panting and regretfully I pull away to catch my breath. Jack holds me with his gaze as his thumbs slowly graze over my nipples.

Another groan escapes my lips as I throw my head back, trying to push myself into his hands. I can feel his bulge against my thigh. It spurs me to push my leg against him and now it's his turn to groan.

Jack buries his hands in my hair, holding my head still so he can nibble his way across my jaw to my earlobe. I feel like I'm having an outer body experience.

He trails his lips to my neck, licking and sucking until I can barely stand it any longer. I am about to explode from the sensations he is causing all over my body. We try to consume each other with each kiss to the point that we never hear the voices approaching.

A female clearing her throat and a very familiar voice snaps me back to reality. "Lei?"

Jack closes his eyes and remains still.

"Fuck." He mumbles quietly.

He slowly glances over his shoulder without releasing me. Evan and Lizzy are standing in the doorway in embarrassment.

Coming to his senses, Jack quickly steps away.

"Um, birthday kiss gone wild, I guess." He looks back at me briefly and leaves the balcony, leaving me standing there pulsing all over and mortified at being caught.

Evan tilts his head with pure concern in his eyes. "You okay?" Lizzy is hiding behind him, looking concerned as well.

"Yeah, I'm fine. I just had too many shots. I'll, I'll be inside."

I leave them alone to speculate on what they just walked into.

Holy shit…what just happened? He wanted me as much as I wanted him.

But he left me there. Left me with the aftermath of that kiss while facing Evan and Lizzy. If I were here alone, I would take the elevator down and hail a cab.

Instead, I hide in the ladies room for a while, attempting to fix my face and calm my nerves. When I sneak back into the party, I purposefully walk the perimeter of the room to avoid running into Jack. I just need to avoid him until Evan and Lori are ready to leave. That shouldn't be too hard, since he bolted and left me standing there like a fool.

Dylan finds me at the bar ordering a diet coke.

"Leila you were awesome. It looked like you've been singing with them for years."

"Thank you. I hope you couldn't tell I was terrified."

"Not at all. You looked completely relaxed."

"Helps that I'm drunk."

Motioning to the diet coke, he asks, "Reeling it in?"

"Trying to."

Malcolm strolls over holding a drink. "Well that is quite a voice you have Miss Marino."

"Thank you. I was pretty nervous."

He looks down into is amber liquid, swirling it around in the glass and drones, "If that was you nervous I can't wait to hear when you're relaxed."

Yuck.

He reaches into his back pocket, pulls out his wallet, and produces a business card.

"I'd love to meet with you and discuss all the fantastic things I can do for you and your career."

Is he serious? The only thing missing is a pinky ring, a gold chain and a polyester shirt opened to his navel. He's dangerous actually, because his gorgeous face eclipses his sleaziness.

Trying to be polite, I accept his card. "I'll keep that in mind Malcolm. At the moment I'd like to enjoy my new career with Devil's Lair for a little while."

"Suit yourself. But you should be front and center and not in the back ground." He lifts my hand and kisses it while staring into my eyes. Then he strolls over to his better half and plants a chaste kiss on her cheek.

"What just happened?" I turn and ask Dylan.

"Seems like the serpent just handed you an apple."

Slipping his card into my bag, I throw Dylan a deadpan expression and say, "Lucky me."

The only upside is that Malcolm's sleazy proposition effectively distracted my thoughts off Jack for a few minutes. I try my best to avoid him the rest of the night. Even when summoned to participate in the birthday cake ritual, I kept Lizzy between us the entire time.

As the party winds down, it becomes easier to spot Jack in the room with less people milling around. Seeing him, I unconsciously touch my tender lips. Our eyes lock.

I slightly lose my equilibrium and stumble to the right. Dylan sees me swaying on my feet and leans in to ask, "Do you want me to call you a cab?"

Blinking, I nod. "I need to find Evan and Lori. We all came together." Dylan looks around the room spotting Evan and Lizzy talking to Jack. He grabs my hand and pulls me towards them. Jack and I lock eyes again and he mouths, "I'm sorry."

It's not his fault. I fully participated in our little tryst.

It's the part where he took off like a coward that I'm having a hard time forgetting.

"Are you ready to leave?" Evan says smiling as we approach.

"Yeah, I am ready."

Jack focuses on Dylan's fingers interlaced with mine. I instantly release his hand. Jack says, "Lori headed out with Trey a little while ago. She asked me to tell you she'll talk to you tomorrow."

"Well good for them." Evan turns towards Lizzy. "Walk me out?"

"Sure."

"I'll meet you outside Ev."

He nods without turning.

"Dylan, can I talk to Leila for a minute?" Jack stares at me while asking.

Dylan looks at me and hesitantly says, "Sure. Leila I'll see you soon?"

I nod and he pulls me into a hug. Dylan has gotten very comfortable with me in a very short amount of time. It's strange, every time he touches me I feel like I'm betraying Jack. His facial expressions do wonders to help me to feel that way as well.

As we walk to the elevator, Jack turns towards me to say something and stops himself. The elevator arrives and he holds the door open while I get on first. Just as the door closes, I see Dylan watching us from across the room.

Jack grabs my arms and says, "I fucked up again. I'm so sorry Leila."

"Jack, I am just as much at fault. We both lost control."

"I'm not talking about the kiss. I'm sorry I left you there. I panicked. I wanted nothing more than to keep kissing you, and that's wrong. I don't want to hurt you, but I keep hurting you. Your friendship means too much to me."

Friendship.

The elevator reaches the ground floor and the doors open. I turn to him to say the only thing I can, "Your friendship means a lot to me too." After I kiss him on the cheek, I turn and leave him standing alone in the elevator.

Well there you have it…we're friends.

Evan is waiting in front, holding a cab for us. Lizzy isn't here but from Evan's smile I'm guessing their good bye was special.

"Hey, you ready?" He asks as he opens the cab door for me.

I nod and slide in turning my head towards my window. He holds my hand until I turn to look at him. "You okay?"

"Yes. I'm just very drunk. What you saw were two drunken people losing control."

Evan doesn't say anything, just watches me closely until I look away. "Leila, you'll talk to me if something is bothering you, right?" He says still holding my hand.

There is no way I'll be telling him that I've fallen for Jack. "Yes Evan, I promise. Lizzy seems great." I say, changing the subject.

"She is fantastic, Lei."

I zone out as Evan rambles on about all of Lizzy's finer points. Jack's words are repeating over and over in my head.

The predominant one - Friendship.

Deep down, I knew that was all we could ever be. So why did hearing him say the words out loud, hurt more than I'd like to admit?

Chapter 16-Jack

Damn it! Why do I keep fucking up? I can't stay away from this girl. These last few weeks have been going pretty well. We connected. We've been getting along nicely. I enjoyed taking care of her when she was sick. Then I fucking kiss her again. Shit, kiss her was an understatement. I practically molested her. I could have gone for days. What happened between us was a tease. No, it was fucking torture and now I can't get her lips, her smooth skin, her scent, or her pebbled nipples out of my fucking mind!

I couldn't have been more turned on if she was naked. I wouldn't have mattered if she had on a snowsuit. Her performance on stage, her looks, and how bad I want her culminated in a desire to kiss her that not even an armored tank couldn't have stopped.

I am going to push her to run. I know it. She is the best thing to happen to Devil's Lair. The crowd reaction tonight was fucking awesome. We sounded unbelievable together. On stage she is my other half and our chemistry is undeniable. The crowd eats it up. If tonight is any indication on how good we sound together, this tour is going to be off the charts.

I haven't had sex in days. That's my problem. I'm too damn horny and that combined with being drunk is my downfall. It didn't help that she looked so hot tonight. I feel breathless when I look at her. Still, I can't continue to succumb to my weakness. For once in my life I have to do the right thing. The right thing is to stay away from Leila, and build this band to the level of success I know we can achieve. That's why I dropped out of school and disappointed my parents. That's why I am here.

The elevator doors open to only a handful of people left at my party. My parents left a while ago. My sister is chatting with Hunter, who is still attached to Amanda. Scott and Patti are slow dancing to non-existent music. Jennifer, Malcolm and Dylan are deep in conversation. Trini is collecting cups and bottles around the room. Trini…that's what I need.

I move behind her. "Trin." She turns.

"Hey, did you have fun tonight? You were quite drunk earlier. Did you sober up already?"

Huh…did I ever. Yes I am sober now, *completely* sober.

"Yep, buzz is gone. It was a great night. Sorry you had to work and couldn't enjoy the party." I shove my hands into my pockets, not knowing what to do next. Usually we are very comfortable with each other. I'll tuck a piece of hair behind her ear, or I'll stroke her cheek. Tonight I don't feel like having contact. I thought I did, but I suddenly realize my heart isn't on the same page as my head.

"Leila is great." She says smiling. I nod and give her a half smile back. "Something you want to talk about? You can come over to talk. I am a good listener." Trini knows me so well. I might feel better if I talk to someone about what has been plaguing me lately.

"Yeah, I need to talk. You always know what I need."

"Let me clean up and we'll go."

Walking over to Lizzy and Hunter near the stage, I interrupt their conversation. "I'm heading out."

Lizzy links her arm through mine and says, "Did you like your party, Jack?"

"Yeah, sis. The party was awesome. You outdid yourself." She really did throw me a great party. I was on such a high, until the end that is.

"Good. You deserve it." She suddenly grins. "Evan is nice. How well do you know him?"

Hunter pipes in. "I've only met him a few times, but he seems like a cool dude. He and Leila are very close." Hunter notices Lizzy scrunching her nose and quickly explains, "No, not that close. Brother and sister close."

"Oh, thank god. I wouldn't want Leila to be upset with me." She glances up at me with an obvious look, as she remembers what we were doing less than an hour ago. Knowing my sister, she means it when she says she doesn't want to upset Leila, no matter what she saw. She got all the morals in our family, it seemed to have skipped right past me.

Trini comes up behind me and says, "They said I can take off now. Ready?"

Hunter starts shaking his head and smirks knowingly. Jackass. I give him my own, *mind your own business look.*

"Don't wait up."

I kiss my sister's cheek and turn to follow Trini out of the bar. I guess I can't blame Lizzy for the look she shoots me.

Trini waves as we depart. I, on the other hand ignore everyone. I don't feel like saying goodbye.

***

"So spill it. What happened?" Trini is sitting next to me in the center of her couch drinking a beer. I opted for a coke.

"I fucked up, yet again."

I proceed to tell Trini about the kiss on my roof, how Leila walked in on me with two chicks and how I avoided her for weeks. I told her about making amends and having a really nice night at her place as well as

230

tonight's kiss. She listens the whole time, not interrupting me once. It's cathartic getting it all out.

She finally speaks when I'm done with my play-by-play on ruining my relationship with Leila.

"Jack, it takes two to tango. She didn't exactly push you away tonight, did she?"

"No, she didn't. But she was drunk, very drunk. I think she would have kept going if the circumstance allowed. It's really on me. I keep coming on to her. I know that taking it further would've ruined everything. She doesn't know me or what I am capable of. I suck at relationships. Inevitably, I fear I'll hurt her and drive her away. It may not be intentional but I'll still disappoint her and the guys. I can't have that happen."

She puts down her beer, and leans closer to me. "Jack, you are putting a tremendous amount of pressure on yourself."

I don't see it that way. I'm capable of screwing everything up. I know myself. Plus, I only tell her part of it. I leave out the part explaining the pull I have towards Leila.

"I haven't ever seen you like this. This is tearing you up." She moves to kneel in front of me, looking up into my eyes. "Do you love her?"

The question sends a jolt through my heart. Even so, I shake my head. The motion is a complete contradiction to my thoughts.

I can't stop thinking about her.

I desperately want to be with her.

I picture a life with her.

Fuck...I love her.

"Then there isn't any damage done yet. She's just another chick you have the hots for, and she's a friend. Move on. It's that easy. We both know that you can get your thrills elsewhere. No need to ruin a friendship for a meaningless night of sex." She pauses briefly. "That is unless you love her."

Trini continues, but I'm having trouble focusing. I only hear part of her words. I sit back against the couch and become lost in thought. Trini stands and pats my leg before she leaves the room.

She's right, of course. I need to move on. This could become a cluster-fuck of mega proportions. The ripple effect that could occur from me pursuing Leila would be catastrophic. But I don't think I care about that part, unless it hurts her in the process. But even then, would I walk away ignoring my feelings and try to be content in just being friends? I'm not sure I could.

At the moment, I have no idea if she feels the same way about me anyway. Having an insane attraction to each other doesn't mean it's more. What if she doesn't feel the same way? What if she has no intentions of being more than friends?

Besides, it's not like I can drop to my knees and confess my undying love after only two kisses? Yes, that would work. That would prove I love her, despite the fact she saw me engaging in a threesome just a few weeks ago.

Very convincing, *Jack!*

I let out a troubled sigh. Either way, I need to find out. I can't move on, unless I know.

Chapter 17- Leila

It's been two weeks since Jack's party, and I decided that I need to put him behind me. This job is too important, and I can't screw it up because I fell for Jack. He made it clear in the elevator at his party that he wants to be friends and nothing more. Well then, friends we'll be.

Besides, he was drunk each time he came onto me. When he is sober, he acts like nothing more than a friend. I can kid myself into thinking he has feelings for me, which I'm sure he does, but definitely not in a romantic way. I'm sure he is very used to girls falling at his feet, and has lumped me into that same category. I have no doubt I am just another conquest to him. Based on our working relationship, I think he realizes that I'm not worth it. He has worked too hard to get his band where they are today. There is no way in hell he will risk that for sex.

Since the party, we have fallen back into our friendship. Things appear normal when we are together. We kid around and he teases me. I pretend I'm mad at him until he wears me down.

We worked our asses off on my birthday. I thought everyone forgot. Thankfully, no one mentioned it all day. Jack ordered a few pizzas during our lunch break. We were waiting for them to arrive when a very cute delivery guy walked in holding the pies.

"Hi, I have pizza for Leila?"

I instantly felt I was being set up. I tried to run for the door but Jack grabbed me around my waist.

"This here is Leila." He responded while carrying my squirming body and sitting me on a stool in the center of the room.

Jennifer and Scary Sally were there to witness. Everyone looked like they were in on his little prank.

The delivery guy put down the pies, and stripper music started playing. The guy proceeded to take of his shirt and pants and began gyrating in front of my stool in nothing but a tiny Speedo. I was mortified.

I glared over at Jack. "You are so dead."

He laughed at my discomfort and came over with a stack of singles.

"Here, use these." He thrust them into my hand and abandoned me to my hell.

Jack wanted to take me out for dinner that night. I already had plans with my friends, though, and so declined with mixed feelings of disappointment and relief. I'm not sure I could spend a dinner with Jack alone.

I got even with him on his birthday the next day with my own little prank. You could tell that he was on edge and anxious for my retaliation. I made him wait all day. I didn't tell any of the guys about my plan, not even Hunter. I did confide in Scary Sally, though, and she was all for it. It effectively helped my relationship her.

At the end of the day when nothing happened, Jack assumed he got away with it. We were wrapping up when there was a knock on the studio door. His eyes flew over to me and I stood crossing my arms.

"Your turn." I said and went over to open the door. In walked a huge biker dude named Axel holding a birthday cake. Behind him was Scary Sally with a camera.

He was decked out in a black leather vest and black leather chaps, with only the tiniest black g-string under it all. Now it was Jack's turn to try and bolt when Hunter and Scott grabbed him and held him in the center of the studio. Axel gyrated expertly for Jack's pleasure, taking off his vest and

234

chaps in the process. Sally snapping away with her camera. It was priceless, and it has set the tone for our friendship. He said he would get even with me. I acted like that didn't bother me, but inside I'm terrified.

Later that evening, as we were all having dinner together I was on pins and needles. Every time a person even passed our table I'd jump thinking he or she was a plant. Jack watched in amused enjoyment of my paranoia.

I also have been building a friendship with Dylan, although it's a lot different than the one I have with Jack. He and I have had coffee a few times after rehearsals. He drove me home one night instead of calling car service. He even took me to dinner on our way back to Hoboken. Conversation with Dylan is always easy. I really feel comfortable with him, and enjoy his company.

We have gotten to know each other these last few weeks, and it feels good to talk to someone who is part of my new world. He told me things I can expect on tour and during performances. There will be cities that we will be staying in a hotel overnight to rest and most importantly have our laundry done. That was a relief, I couldn't imagine us pulling up to a laundry mat in the bus or arguing over machine space with rock stars. I am also happy to hear there will be a few breaks during the tour where I'll get to sleep in a real bed. He gave me Cathy's phone number and arranged for us to meet. Getting to know Cathy will be a great help to me.

Jack noticed my relationship with Dylan. One morning we found ourselves alone in the studio while waiting for the others to arrive. He didn't seem himself.

I asked him if he was ok and he answered, "You and Dylan are getting close."

His comment surprised me. "We're just friends. Like us."

An odd expression passed over his features but it was gone as quickly as it came. The rest of the band filed and effectively killed our chat. But I thought about it all day and well into the night. Does it bother Jack that I am becoming friendly with Dylan? Why would he care? That one little comment has been consuming my thoughts.

Despite my Jack infatuation, life has been good otherwise. Lori has seen Trey often since Jack's party. One night she hung out with the band and filled me in on their antics. I was supposed to be there as well, but had plans with my dad. She has no idea how I feel about Jack, so she didn't hold back any details regarding stories that were told that night. Unfortunately Trey told her all about Jack's indiscretions. She jokingly said Jack is definitely not a one-woman man. Hearing this should be the validation I need to forget about him… at least you'd think.

Evan has also been in contact with Lizzy. Their schedules have been crazy but they made plans to go out to dinner as soon as they can. I am so happy that they met, and hope that their relationship grows while we are on tour. Lizzy confided in Evan that Jack was surprised they have been talking but that he is also happy they met. Jack said he thinks Evan is a great guy. I felt that was really nice of him to say.

Lori found a replacement for me. Her name is Nina Parker and she has been rehearsing with the band for the last week. Being petite and blonde, bubbly and outgoing, and funny as hell, she is my complete opposite. Our only common characteristics are the singing and the ability to play keyboards. I feel Lori chose well. In just a short time, Nina has already won over all the guys. She gets along with them effortlessly, even with Matt. She has a boyfriend who lives in the city, and the guys all like him as well. The guys feel she is almost ready to take over.

With Nina assuming her new role perfectly, we all decided on a date for my last performance with Cliffhangers. It saddens me every time I think about it.

Lori booked the band to play down the shore in a band competition on July 4th. This is huge for them and will get them a ton of exposure. The boys are bouncing off the walls with excitement. Trey has been a huge help to Lori and has been giving her information on where she should focus her attention for Cliffhangers. She has been gushing about it.

Jack and Hunter decided to have a barbeque at their place for Devil's Lair. Jack made sure to repeat this ten times. Scott wasn't happy that he couldn't bring Patti. Trey was fine with it since Lori will be down the shore with Cliffhangers at the competition. Hunter's girlfriend Amanda was going out of town as well, so Scott felt he was being punished because their "chicks" weren't around. Jack told him to get over it, and to concentrate on what he was going to cook for us. I laughed at the look on Scott's face.

Hunter suggested inviting Jennifer and Dylan but Jack immediately shook his head at the suggestion.

While looking at me, Jack said for the eleventh time, "Just *us*."

Hunter dropped it.

It's Sunday and I am waiting for dad at our usual brunch diner. It's not like him to be even a few minutes late, nonetheless twenty. When he finally comes through the door and spots me at our table, the look on his face has me concerned.

"Hey sweetheart. I'm so sorry I'm late. I needed to drop Barb off at Evan's house."

"You should have called me. That's closer to Hoboken. We could have eaten near my place today."

"Nope, I like this place. I don't mind driving back this way." He opens his menu and stares at it intently. It's funny because he orders the same exact thing every week.

"Why did you have to drop Barb off?"

"Just because." He continues to study the menu, without looking up. My dad isn't a good liar. Something is most definitely up.

"Do you have plans for the fourth?"

"Um, I'll probably spend it with Barb." He progressively looks more and more uncomfortable.

Concerned, I ask, "So what's going on with Barb? Everything ok?"

"Yeah, she needed to talk to Evan about something." He responds without looking up.

"Dad, what's wrong?"

As he puts down the menu, my mind instantly starts racing.

He waits a few seconds before he responds. "Barb needs to talk to Evan about her illness."

"What illness?"

He exhales slowly. "Leila, Barb has breast cancer. She found out a few weeks ago. I've been accompanying her to her doctor's appointments. Thankfully, it's very early and only stage one, but she is scared and needs support right now."

I am stunned. I am obviously concerned about Barb, but I can't help but worry about my friend. He is going to need me, more than ever and I'm leaving.

Dad grabs my hand across the table. "Hey, she's going to be just fine. She is under the care of a very good surgeon. She will have her surgery and start her treatments. She will beat this." As he speaks, I don't detect any doubt in his eyes. It makes me feel slightly better.

238

"I'm worried about her, and Evan. How long have you known?"

He shrugs. "A few weeks. She wanted to get her full prognosis and speak to the surgeon before she told Evan. I can't blame her for that. She now has her treatments all planned and it will help her to reassure him she will be ok."

I feel awful. I've been so self-involved while my dad and my best friend's mom have been going through hell.

The rest of our brunch is somewhat subdued. We talk about things I need to get done in the next few weeks. It's all nonsense, if you ask me. Compared to what he just told me, why would I give a crap if I will be forwarding my mail to his house?

As dad is paying the bill, I get a text from Evan.

where r u?

brunch w dad. R u ok?

please come here w/ ur dad

When my dad returns from paying the bill, I say, "Evan wants us to come to his place."

Dad looks a bit uneasy, but I'm sure he is not looking forward to the emotions we will find there. Dad doesn't do emotions well.

I follow in my car as we make our way to Evan's place. I barely ring his bell when he immediately buzzes us up.

We walk in to see Barb sitting in a chair, and it's obvious she's been crying. Evan also looks distraught. He gets into my dad's face and barks, "How long have you known Anthony?"

"Calm down Evan." Barb says standing in the process. "This isn't his fault."

"Evan, what is going on?"

He glares at his mom. "Enlighten her mom."

This is bad…very bad. Evan never acts like this. He is the most even-keeled person I know. I feel weak in the knees as he sits in a chair and looks down at the floor. I move over and take a place on the couch. My dad follows and takes my hand.

"Leila, we never wanted to hurt you, either of you." He glances at Evan and me.

"Dad you're scaring me."

Evan still doesn't speak and just continues to look at the floor.

There is an unbearable silence in the room.

Barb finally speaks first. Her voice is shaky and weak with emotion. "Leila, your dad and I were very good friends when we were kids. We also dated for a short time, but that didn't work out for us. Our friendship, however, remained constant. Your dad met your mom, and fell madly in love. It's obvious why that happened as quickly as it did, your mom was spectacular. Not only was she beautiful, she was a saint. Your dad knew instantly that she was the one.

"I was dating Doug at the same time. Your mom was in nursing school, and younger than us. Even though she loved your dad, she felt she needed to focus on her career and didn't want to hurt your father. She felt he was moving too fast. It scared her, so she broke up with him in hopes that he would move on." She looks over at my dad and then back at me.

"Your dad was devastated. He was distraught and hurting. My relationship with Doug wasn't all that great. He came to me and we both tried to forget our problems. We got very drunk, and what we did was a huge mistake." She sits and starts to sob. Dad gets up and moves over to her. He rubs her back and tries to console her.

She smiles at my dad through her tears. Evan hasn't moved his position at all.

"I told no one, not even your dad. His future was with Marie. He needed to be with Marie. I told Doug I was pregnant with his child. He threw a fit, of course. We weren't meant to be together. I told him that I rather raise the baby alone, than to force him to be with us. He said he wasn't going to run out on his responsibility. It was wrong of me to make him think that the baby was his, but I was afraid that I would expose your dad if I confessed that it was not Doug's. He knew I spent a lot of time with your dad and would have figured it out. Your parents did not deserve that fate."

*Oh my God…*Evan is my brother.

When Evan looks up at me, his eyes are bloodshot and wet. He comes over to sit next to me on the couch and holds my hand. Barb watches us and says what I already know. "Evan is your brother."

Hearing it out loud isn't any less shocking. Evan squeezes my hand at the sound of my gasp.

"Leila, your dad didn't know. He did get back with Marie, and they did get married. Your mom became pregnant almost immediately, and your dad was so happy. He always cared for me and your mom did as well. They knew my marriage to Doug was in jeopardy, and they both always made sure Evan and I were ok. I was planning on asking Doug for a divorce because I couldn't continue with the lie that was my marriage. I already had another lie that was consuming me. Then Evan became ill and that's when Doug found out the truth. He took off without a backwards glance. I quickly came to realize that was the best thing he could have done. He would've told your mom the truth just to hurt your dad and me and I couldn't risk that happening. I *had* to confess to your dad once Doug knew. I made him swear not to tell Marie. I couldn't hurt her, or you. Your dad was devastated, of course. He wanted to acknowledge Evan as his son. I threatened if he told your mom I would leave and take Evan with me. I felt that was the right thing to do. Evan and I were fine. I couldn't destroy your family. Your dad did all he could to ensure we had everything we needed. Marie being the person she was had no problem with all your dad did for us."

She stops and looks like she can't continue. She waits a few seconds, and starts again.

"I sometimes wonder if your mom knew the truth, even though we never told her. The older Evan got, the more he looked like your dad. She always showed us nothing but kindness and love. Sometimes I felt she would understand and forgive us because she was that type of person, but I couldn't take that chance.

"Then Marie died. You needed your dad more than ever. I felt that the way I handled the situation was best for all of us. Obviously the longer we waited to tell you, the more difficult it became. I would have taken this to my grave, if I hadn't gotten sick. If anything happens to me, I need Evan to know the truth."

She gets up and walks over to kneel in front of him. He never once looks at her.

"Evan, I love you. All the mistakes I made were to protect you, Anthony, and Leila. I felt I was doing the right thing. I'm so sorry."

I'm torn. I want to hate this woman, but she is sick, and shouldn't be dealing with this sadness and pain right now. She honestly thought she was doing what was best for all.

My dad looks at Evan and speaks next. "This isn't entirely Barb's fault. I should have fought harder for you. I was selfish and scared. I couldn't lose Marie, so I sacrificed you instead. When you and Leila became best friends, I was so happy. I got to be involved in your life. I love you Evan, more than you will ever know."

Evan continues to sit emotionlessly on the couch.

"Did you know Barb was going to tell Evan this today?" I needed to know.

My dad shakes his head. "No."

"I decided to do this on my own. I needed my son to know the truth." She takes Evan's other hand in her own and addresses him. "Evan, I know this is a shock to you. I've let you feel your father abandoned you all these years. In truth, I did."

He pulls his hand out of his mom's grasp and replies, "I need time. I can't be with either of you right now."

Barb starts to cry and nods weakly. She stands and says, "I love you, Evan. Please never forget that." She grabs her bag and moves towards the door.

My dad looks at me and pleads, "Stay with him. We love you both."

With that, they walk out of the apartment and leave me in shock.

"Do you want me to go?"

"No. I need you, please stay." He pulls me into an embrace and starts to sob.

How can life turn on a dime so quickly? Our world has just been rocked to the core. Evan found out in one day his dad is Anthony who has been within arm's reach for years, and that his mom is sick. How can life be so cruel to someone who doesn't deserve it?

What seems like hours later, Evan suddenly stands and starts pacing the apartment. "How are we going to handle this?" he says looking at me with panic in his eyes?

"I'm not sure." I respond honestly.

"I can't have anyone know yet. I need to process this. Leila, our parents played with our lives. What would they have done if we met and fell in love? How can they do this to us?"

He's panicking and I need to calm him down.

"Evan, no one needs to know. We have each other and we will get through this. I understand you are upset right now but your mom needs you."

My words agitate him.

"Please, Evan …you are not a cruel person. Please just understand why she did it." I have to help him understand why his mom did what she did.

He sits heavily on the couch. "I don't know if I can Lei. I'm not who I thought I was. My whole life was a lie."

He needs time.

"I'm being selfish. This affects you too." He says looking sadly at me.

"We will get through it together."

He looks so lost. Yes, this affects me too, but I need to keep it together for my friend, my brother. I love him.

***

I spent the night with Evan, making sure he ate and slept. He put up a good fight, but then finally allowed me to take care of him. I woke early and am sitting in his kitchen holding a cup of coffee. I can't bring myself to drink it, I feel no nauseous.

Evan shuffles into the kitchen looking like he didn't sleep at all. "Lei, you have to get to the studio. Please don't worry about me, I'll be fine." He comes over and kisses my head.

"You don't look fine. You look like death warmed over."

He grabs a mug from the cabinet. "Yeah, well, I can't always be the stud muffin I was born to be." His comment makes me feel slightly better. Evan will be fine.

"I do want to keep this from the guys for now. I'll understand if you need to tell someone, though."

"Evan, the only person I would want to tell already knows. This is no ones business."

He comes over and pulls me into a hug that I energetically return. Of all the people on Earth I could be related to, I thank God above it is Evan.

"Hey, we were always brother and sister in our eyes. Now our bloodline proves it."

"My kid sister got the brains and the looks."

I hug him tighter. "Now get out. Go to work."

"You're so bossy. I don't have to listen to you, you're not my dad."

Evan literally pushes me out of his apartment. I don't put up a fight. I still have to get to my apartment, shower, dress, and drive to the studio. I'll need to text Jack to let him know I'll be late.

hey, so sorry... will be late... on my way.

He texts back immediately. *no worries...r u ok?*

yes...see you soon.

Truth is that I look like death warmed over myself. I didn't sleep all that much last night. I have dark circles under my eyes and they're still red and blood shot. I'm not even sure makeup would help me at this point.

As I am getting ready, my phone rings.

"Hello?"

"Leila, I love you. Please tell me you are ok."

"Dad, I'm ok." I feel awful; in the midst of all our angst and anger, I forget to understand how my dad must be feeling. He had a son he couldn't acknowledge or wouldn't at least. "Can I call you later?"

"Yes. Please call me as soon as you get home. We need to talk about this. Promise me."

"I promise."

"Should I call Evan?"

"No, dad. He needs time. Please let him be."

The silence tells me how he feels about my advice. "Ok." He hangs up at once.

I do my best to look normal and fifteen minutes later I am on my way to the studio. I still can't bring myself to eat or drink anything. I feel sick to my stomach. I unfortunately have time to think during my drive and my thoughts get the better of me. I think what has me the most upset is the fact I'm leaving. I'm leaving Evan to deal with this alone.

When I finally arrive to the studio, I'm almost an hour late. The guys are discussing whether they should start the show with *High Life* or *Committed*.

"Hey, guys." I walk straight to the corner to put down my bag.

"Hey, is everything ok?" Jack asks.

With my back to him I nod, not wanting to look at him for fear I will lose it.

He comes up behind me and rubs my back. "Do you want to take a walk?" he asks quietly so no one can hear.

I shake my head and busy myself with searching for something in my bag. He isn't buying it, and I am irked I can't keep my emotions in check. As I take a deep, shaky breath he first catches a glimpse of my face and frowns. He grabs my hand and pulls me towards the door.

"We'll be right back." He says to the guys as he drags me out of the studio. They don't seem to notice, except for Hunter. He looks up at me with concern.

I should insist I am ok, but I can't even get the words out. I am completely choked up and am angry with myself. I feel like I'm betraying Evan.

Jack pulls me into the small conference room and closes and locks the door.

"Leila, what's wrong?"

"It's nothing to worry about. It's just family stuff." I try to sound convincing. He regards me for a few seconds and pulls me into a hug.

I can't take it. I unleash sobs into his chest. He doesn't speak. He just strokes my hair patiently letting me get it all out. What the hell is wrong with me? I must be PMS'ing.

When I finally calm down, I pull away and wipe my tears from my cheeks. Without a doubt I look a mess right now.

Jack pulls out two chairs and forces me to sit. He holds my hand waiting for me to speak.

"I found out something yesterday that was a shock. I really don't feel comfortable talking about it yet. Please bear with me?"

He holds my face and wipes a tear away from my cheek with his thumb. Like a magnet to metal, I lean into his touch. I've missed it.

"Is your dad ok?"

I can hear the genuine concern in his eyes and nod but I don't respond otherwise.

"I understand. I'm here if you need anything, ok?"

I simply bob my head and try a smile. He returns the gesture and pulls me back into his embrace and I don't fight him.

Chapter 18- Jack

Two monumental things have happened over the last few weeks.

First and foremost, it turns out I can't move on. I live for the moment I get to see Lela in the studio. I relish every moment we're together. I go home, lock myself in my room, and live for the moment I get to see her again.

So that brings me to the second thing. I'm miserable.

Except for when I'm with her, I've been in a perpetual mad mood. In my mind, I try to hash a way I can be with her and fuck the consequences. Since my birthday party, I've been on the verge of an emotional meltdown too many times to count. I've turned into a romantic sap. Basically, I've turned into Hunter. Hunter came right out and asked me what my problem was. I made up a lame excuse, which I know he doesn't buy.

He also noticed Leila's been emotional lately and insinuated that it was my fault. I couldn't even get angry with him. I simply told him that she has some family stuff she's dealing with and he didn't ask questions. I am worried about her. I feel like reaching out to Evan to make sure she is ok. I'm not convinced that she feels comfortable to talk to me about anything that is bothering her. For that I have no one to blame except for myself. I'm the ass that kissed her, twice.

Today is our July 4th barbeque. Honestly, I wish I could ditch the guys and just spend the day with Leila. I would love to take her out of the city, and drive to a quiet beach alone. Since bonding with her in her apartment, I now see us together doing couple things and not just having sex. My thoughts about Leila started with hot, mind-blowing sex yet have most definitely progressed. It's really freaking me out even more than the sex dreams did. Sex I understand. Relationships I don't.

I haven't shared this with anyone. So it eats away at my confidence, and my ability to act like Jack Lair is supposed to act. Hunter has taken over my roof, and has been hanging out with Amanda a lot lately. She has a roommate, so he prefers that she come to our place. From the looks of Hunter's face, they have finally turned a corner. I should be happy for him, but it pisses me off. He gets to be with someone he cares for openly, and I don't. Every time I see them together in the apartment, I want to hit something.

Amanda spent the night again last night and I'm standing in my usual spot in the kitchen, consuming my third cup of coffee. They both emerge from his room and Amanda blushes the instant she sees me.

"Hey Jack, you're up early." Hunter comments while dragging her into the kitchen. She looks like she wants to run out the door.

"Hi, Jack."

"Hey, Amanda." I plaster on a saccharin smile. "You kids have fun last night?"

Amanda looks down and blushes even deeper, and Hunter turns to pull her into a hug. "We did. Lots of F.U.N."

"Hunt."

"What?" He kisses her cheek. Ugh, they are making me sick.

I tell them as much, "Ok then, you two lovebirds are sickening." I turn and make my way into my room. "Bye, Amanda."

As I shut my door, I hear Hunter saying to her, "Don't be mad."

Robotically, I work out, shower, dress and wait in my room. I feel like a prisoner, until I hear the apartment door close. I'm guessing Amanda took off and I can finally emerge again without feeling like a third wheel.

Hunter is busy in the kitchen pulling crap out for our barbeque. He looks up and without beating around the bush he asks, "What the hell is going on with you lately?" My gut instinct is to tell him to fuck off.

"Nothing, why?" I try to act indifferently. I don't really want to tell him the truth, but this charade I have going is exhausting.

"You're full of shit and you know it. You haven't had a chick here in weeks. You haven't been with Trini. What the fuck is going on?"

He looks completely pissed off. Why does he car so much about my social life?

"Why does it matter to you if I haven't picked up a chick?"

"Because it can affect the band." He thunders arrogantly.

"Why do my fucking habits affect my band?"

"It's happened already. You haven't written a song in weeks. You are completely impassive during rehearsals. The old Jack would argue for hours over d sharp versus f sharp. The old Jack wouldn't let us stop to take a piss. So I'll ask you again, what the fuck is wrong with you?"

"I don't want to talk about it."

"Jack, cut the shit. Just tell me what's going on."

We stare each other down until I crack. "I'm fucked up."

"What do you mean you're fucked up? Are you on something?"

"Jesus, Hunter…no, I'm not on something." Walking towards the couch, I sit heavily while pondering how much I should admit to Hunter. He watches and waits for me to speak. After waiting several minutes, his patience wears thin.

"Damn it Jack…what the fuck is going on?"

I pinch the bridge of my nose while squeezing my eyes shut and murmur very quietly. "I think I fell in love."

Hunter starts laughing his ass off. He just loses it, cracking himself up. It takes every fiber of my being to not pummel him through a wall.

"Fuck you." I stalk towards the apartment door. I'm going to kill him if I don't get away from him.

"Wait, you're shitting me right?" He says trying to get me to stop. Ignoring him, I slam the door behind me.

I'm on the roof all of three minutes when he shows up. "Leave me the fuck alone." I say, wanting nothing to do with him. I really don't want to be here at all. Maybe I'll borrow Scott's van and take off for a day or two. I need to get away from everyone and everything.

He pulls up a chair and sits facing me. "You aren't kidding?"

I feel my blood boiling over, and instinctually clench my fists. "No...I'm not fucking kidding." I say with my jaw clenched so tightly, I feel like I can crack a tooth.

Hunter watches my body language and smirks, "You gonna hit me?"

"Shut up."

He sits back and scratches the back of his head. "Hey man, I'm sorry. I really thought you were fucking with me." He tries to sound contrite, but the smirk on his face is giving him away.

"Yeah, well I wish I were."

"Shit. How did this happen?"

"I have no idea. I can't stop thinking about her. Hell, is this even love? How the fuck should I know?"

"When did this happen?"

"I don't know, the last few weeks? I think I realized it the night of my party."

He looks confused and is trying to process in his head who I was with that night. "Trini?" he asks with disbelief.

"No."

"Do I know her?"

"Yeah, you do."

"Who?"

I can't say it.

After a few minutes, he barks, "WHO!?"

"Leila." My heart is pounding from admitting it out loud.

He looks at me like I've lost my mind. Then realizes it and reins it in. As he leans forward with his elbows on his knees, he stares at the ground.

"Leila?"

I nod my head and mimic his posture. We sit like this for the longest time, until Hunter finally speaks. "Did you two hook up?"

"No. I kissed her, twice. That's it."

"And you fell in love?" He sounds incredulous.

"I know, it doesn't make sense."

"Damn man, I don't know what to say."

"Yeah, thanks." Sitting back against the couch, I suddenly feel exhausted. "I really would appreciate it if you kept this to yourself."

"I'm not telling anyone. How is this going to work Jack?" he asks calling me out on all the issues I have been dealing with myself.

I want to say, "I'm going to tell her."

Instead, I say, "I've been ignoring it."

Hunter lets out a single belly laugh.

Great.

"Come on Jack, ignore it? Because that's worked out so well for you so far."

Sighing my concession, he continues. "There is no way you can continue being celibate. How long has it been since you fucked someone?"

No, there is definitely no way I can continue being celibate.

"Rachel." Yep, that wacko was my last fuck. So fitting.

"You haven't even been with Trini since then?"

"Nope."

"Damn. Are you sure it hasn't shriveled up and fell off?"

"Screw you."

Chapter 19 – Leila

I promised Jack that I would be at the barbeque today. I've made excuses the last few times the band went out after rehearsals and he called me out on it. He said he would drive to Hoboken to come get me if necessary. I just haven't been in the right frame of mind to play the "we are friends" act outside the safety of the studio.

Plus, I've been worried about Evan. I would cancel any plans in a heartbeat if Evan needed me. The problem is he doesn't. It's an excuse I conjured up in my head. He and the boys are down the shore at their first band competition. Lori and Alisa are with them and Nina has resumed my place. My former life has gone on without me. It's a good thing, they need to move on, and so do I. But it still stings not being part of my old entourage any longer. This is a huge milestone for them, and I wish I could be there just to witness it. However, I'm no longer a member of Cliffhangers, and they don't need me tagging along.

Since there has been no dire emergency requiring my presence, I will be spending the day with Devil's Lair. Today I will have to deal with Jack and my feelings for him without the distraction of work. It had to happen sometime, with the tour weeks away and the fact I will very soon be living on a bus with him twenty-four-seven. I guess there's no time better than Independence Day. It's pretty symbolic of my life right now.

I baked a bunch of my brownies and bought a case of beer. It's really hot outside and after spending way too much time on what I should wear I decide on shorts and a tank top. I don't want to look like I tried too hard, but

I don't want to look like a slob either. Truth be told I did spend a little extra time on my hair and make-up.

I'm on my way and thinking to myself, "well, here goes nothing".

Schlepping the four flights of stairs with all my crap has me sweating my ass off already, and wilting my hair-do. These guys better have their air conditioning cranked up.

Hunter opens the door, smiling from ear to ear. "Hey Leila, missed you." He says pulling me in to the cool apartment…thank God.

"I saw you yesterday. You are so much like my Evan." I grin until I realize what I said. Hunter doesn't seem to notice, and grabs the beer and brownies out of my arms.

"Wait. Are these your homemade brownies?"

"Yes, why?"

"Oh my God. I had one bite of the left over's you sent home with Jack. First of all, I love you. Second of all, he almost beat the crap out of me for taking just one bite and it's left me craving them since."

"Well it's a good thing I made a double batch. I won't tell him if you want to hide some."

Hunter takes the platter of brownies into the kitchen, wraps a bunch of them in foil, and runs to his room, leaving me in hysterics.

Trey is on the couch watching TV. There is no sign of Scott or Jack. "Hey, Trey." I say walking past him.

"Hey." He simply says. He is a man of few words. I don't buy a thing Lori tells me about her and Trey talking for hours and hours. She must be delusional.

Hunter comes out of his room grinning like he has a mad secret. He leans in and whispers, "I owe you one."

"You owe me fifty bucks or I squeal like a pig." Trey quips, never taking his eyes off the TV.

"Worth every penny."

Giggling, I follow Hunter into the kitchen and ask, "Where are Jack and Scott?"

He turns to look at me and waits a second before he responds. "Um, Jack and Scott are on the roof, no doubt arguing on how to start a grill." I smirk at the image of a rock star trying to start a grill.

There are burgers and hot dogs on the counter as well as different salads, chips, and all the necessary trimmings. I nod at the spread laid out. "I'm impressed. You boys know how to throw a barbeque."

Hunter smiles and says, "It's all Scott. He is a bit of a foodie. We could give a crap about...pesto pasta salad?" I laugh out loud as he points to the green concoction and is obviously repeating what Scott told him it was called.

Scott walks over holding a long spatula and says, "Fuck off. You never complain while you are shoveling my food into your face." He turns to me. "Please tell me you appreciate my pesto pasta salad, Leila."

I smile back and say, "Hell yes. This one looks better than mine. I may need the recipe."

"See? She knows food too. Jackass." He says to Hunter.

Hunter simply says back, "She's a girl."

"Quit yapping like women over the menu. I'm fucking starving." Trey pipes in from the couch.

"Then get your ass up and go explain to Jack how to light a grill or we will be ordering in pizza." Scott retorts, making me laugh again. "He is so fucking stubborn." These guys need a woman to take control.

"I'll go." I say to Scott.

Hunter immediately says, "I'll come with you."

We both head for the roof, and as soon as we are on the stairwell Hunter stops and holds my arm. "I haven't had a chance to talk to you alone, but I want you to know if you ever need to talk, I'm a good listener."

The look on my face prompts him to explain. "You've been…quiet."

"Has it been that obvious?"

"Not to them, but I noticed. I did ask Jack what was wrong. All he said was you had some personal stuff going on. I just wanted you to know I'm here if you need me."

I'm touched by his concern. He truly is a nice guy. "Hunter I really appreciate that. It means a lot to me."

"I mean ever word of it."

He pulls me into a hug…a warm, friendly hug. "Let's go check on him before he burns the building down."

Giggling at that visual, I follow him up to the roof.

The second we step outside the smoke assaults us. We can barely see Jack in the corner from the plume of smoke surrounding him. Incessant coughing clues us into his exact location. Hunter turns to me with his raised eyebrows and says, "I told you so."

Jack turns towards the sound of my giggling with tears streaming from his eyes.

Hunter and I walk up to the grill. "Where's the flame?"

Jack looks annoyed, hot, and sweaty and like he is going to slug Hunter. I bite down on my lip to stop from laughing. Once he looks at me, his face breaks out into a smile. "I'm working on it."

Hunter shakes his head and says, "We'd like to eat before Labor Day. I brought a professional." He turns towards me. "Leila, please start our grill."

Jack waves towards the grill and says, "Have at it."

"Such pressure." I grab the lighter fluid and matches from Jack's hand. "You've over saturated the briquettes. Do you have newspaper?"

They look at me like I'm speaking a foreign language, then turn to look at each other, neither of them moving. Finally Hunter huffs, "I'll get it." He stalks toward the door.

"What's a briquette?" Jack asks. I shake my head and openly laugh at him. "They have no faith in me." He adds.

"Gee, I wonder why?"

"You can start it and we can always tell them I did."

"You want to take the credit for lighting this grill?"

His head bobs up and down.

"You know they won't believe you."

"They'll believe you." He counters with a seductive wink that causes my insides to flutter. "I'll make it worth your while."

"Hmm…sounds very tempting." With that Hunter comes back with newspaper, hot dogs and hamburgers. "Oh well…opportunity over." I shrug and pretend to be disappointed…with *pretend* being the key word here.

"My loss." Jack pins me with his gaze that now causes my insides to ignite. Who needs lighter fluid with Jack Lair nearby?

They both watch in awe as I effectively light the grill. "Did you boys pay attention?"

Hunter shakes his head. "I don't do grill prep. I do beer prep."

"Did you, Jack?"

"Nope. We'll just have you over every time we grill."

"Good plan." I smirk. "Just give me a day's notice so I can drop everything to accommodate you."

"Sounds like the *perfect* plan."

Oh god.

"Go away, I have work to do." This man is killing me.

Somehow it becomes my barbeque as I take over the meal. During my grilling duties, I delegate Hunter to get all the drinks, Jack to get the plates and utensils, Scott to get the sides and trimmings, and Trey to drag over the large table in the corner.

All the burgers and hotdogs are cooked in no time. As I'm flipping my last burger onto the platter, Jack comes up behind me and touts, "Now you are just showing off."

I shrug. "Maybe." Adding the burgers and hot dogs to the table, it finally looks like a barbeque.

Trey, Scott, and Hunter all start applauding when they see everything laid out and ready to eat. As I take a bow, Jack takes one as well and I shove him away. "You're riding my coattails."

He bends and whispers, "You do have adorable coattails." As he walks towards the food, he leaves me dazed and confused and squirming.

He's just flirting. He isn't coming on to me. It's just the way he is. I need to stop flattering myself and stop taking every comment he makes so literal.

By the time I take some food, the only seat left available is on the couch next to Jack. I put as much distance between us as the couch allows. No one speaks, except for the moaning coming from their filled to the brim mouths.

"Scott, everything is so good. This pesto pasta salad is to die for. Patti is a lucky girl."

He blushes and looks thoroughly embarrassed. "Thanks." He ignores the way the guys start snickering at him. "These idiots take me for granted."

We fall into a comfortable conversation about how much we got done in the studio, and the approaching tour. I'm starting to feel more like one of the guys, and I'm glad I came.

At one point Jack excuses himself and leaves the roof. He returns quickly with a chilled bottle of white wine.

"I hope it didn't cost more than six bucks." I point out. "Otherwise it will be awful."

"Nope, five-ninety-five. It's even a screw top." He pours a cup full and brings it over to me on the couch.

"It's delicious, especially in a red Solo cup. Good job." Jack sits next to me so our thighs are practically touching. I catch Hunter watching us but he quickly glances away when he notices and resumes eating his food.

Once we are done eating Jack orders, "Trey, clean up."

Trey gives him a fuck off look. Jack looks at me smiling wide, causing the clenching to commence, and the wine's not helping in the least.

We make our way back down to the apartment after we all clean up and it feels so good to be in the air conditioning. Trey, Scott and Hunter immediately plop themselves on the couch and start watching a ball game on TV. Jack pulls up two chairs for him and me.

So this is what a Devil's Lair does on their free time. It's comical actually. If all those screaming fans could see them now. The only thing that would make this scene funnier is if Trey was to stuff his hand into his waistband and Scott was to belch.

"What's so funny?" Jack says watching me grinning.

"You guys are such party animals." This draws their attention to me. *Uh oh.*

Jack takes the first jab. "Are we too boring for you Miss Marino? What would you like to do, play strip poker?"

"Um, no. Baseball is fine." I motion towards the TV. "Resume watching baseball."

Suddenly Trey lets out a laugh. As we all look at him, Jack starts laughing too.

"Oh no. Keep your fucking trap shut." Hunter threatens. Scott immediately starts to blush profusely.

Jack and Trey persist until I can't stand it any longer. "What? Was it something I said?"

Jack shakes his head and looks at his roommate.

"Don't." Hunter warns.

"Oh, come on Hunt, it wasn't that bad."

Trey chokes on his beer.

Hunter stands up and walks into the kitchen, mumbling under his breath. Jack takes this as a sign to enlighten me on what has them cracking up. He tries to speak but cannot stop laughing.

"You are killing me…" I point out as I patiently wait for him to tell this story.

He wipes his eyes and continues, "Ok…ok. We were on tour with MACE. We were in Detroit?" He glances at Trey for confirmation. I've never seen Trey smile this much, nonetheless laugh.

"We were in Detroit and there was an after party in a hotel near the arena. We met some girls at the bar who were in town on business. After a few drinks, they invited us up to their room." He sees my discomfort and shakes his head. "It wasn't like that. They convinced us to play strip poker."

From the kitchen, Hunter mumbles, "You two are such dicks."

"Oh come on Hunter, did you honestly think this story wasn't going to come up eventually?"

Jack looks at Trey nodding in agreement and continues. "So we are losing our asses to these girls, except for Trey. They hustled us. We lost every single piece of clothing we were wearing. Thankfully they had mercy on us, and let us keep our underwear." Trey chokes out a laugh again.

"Oh my *God*." I say getting a visual.

Jack nods. "They kicked us out. I had nothing on but my underwear. Trey lost one shoe. Scott had on…" He bursts into a laughing fit and can't finish his statement. Meanwhile, Scott curses their antics and gets up to join Hunter in the kitchen.

Jack composes himself and blurts out, "Scott had on Sponge Bob boxers!"

"They were the only clean pair I had." He is still flushing beet red. "I love Sponge Bob."

I almost pee my pants.

Jack takes a deep breath and wipes his eyes before continuing. "Wait…it gets better. Unfortunately Hunt decided to go commando that night."

"Oh no…" I look at Hunter who is clearly reliving that experience in his mind. He looks mortified. "Poor Hunter."

"We had to walk through the hotel lobby, and there was a wedding going on." Trey loses it, and his entire body begins to shake uncontrollably.

"To make matters worse, MACE was still in the bar hanging out at the after party. We never saw Hunter run so fast in our lives."

Hunter curses them out again. Ignoring him, Jack continues, "Someone got a picture of Hunter running through the lobby, and made a ton of copies. The next day our tour bus was plastered with them. Let me tell you, his ass was *very* pale."

Trey falls off the couch, I'm bent in half holding my stomach, Jack is on the floor shaking, and Scott even starts in until Hunter slugs him in the arm.

He looks at Jack like he is trying to be angry and fires back, "Sure, laugh at my expense. Trey was fully clothed and you looked like a friggin' Calvin Klein underwear model."

Wow, I just got another visual, and a hot flash.

"I never leave home without my Calvin's."

"I'm sorry Hunter. That must have been traumatizing for you." I try very hard to gain my composure, yet fail miserably. Biting my lip barely helps.

He looks at me shaking his head. "You have no idea. It was freezing out and a long run to the bus."

It doesn't help matters when Jack offers to pay for a spray tan session for Hunter's ass or when Trey starts singing, "Who lives in a pineapple under the sea." Fifteen minutes pass before we finally calm down.

During the course of the night they proceed to tell more stories, but none are as funny as the strip poker story.

After the boys attack the rest of Scott's pesto pasta salad, as well as every last brownie, we head up to the roof to watch some fireworks. I really am having a great time and am disappointed that it's already past ten. Jack stands so close that I could feel the warmth of his skin. The familiar sensations take hold once again, and I responsibly decide it is time to go.

"I should get going."

He nods somberly and admits, "I feel bad you have to drive all the way to Hoboken. I probably should have told you to pack a bag. Why don't you stay and leave tomorrow?"

My heart skips a beat at the thought of staying here with him overnight. "I'll be fine. Thanks guys, I really had fun today." Trey and Scott both wave, and Hunter comes over to give me a hug.

"I'm sorry I laughed at you." I confess.

He shakes his head. "I'm used to it. Drive safe. I'll see you tomorrow. And I meant what I said earlier."

"I know. Thanks."

Jack says, "I'll walk you out."

He walks me to my car and opens the door for me.

"I really did have a great time. Thanks for including me."

"Of course we would include you. You are one of us now." His expression becomes serious. "Let me drive you home. I'll take a cab back."

"Jack, don't be ridiculous."

"It's late."

"And?"

"Leila."

Here comes the possessive, dominant Jack who surfaced when I was sick. I would like nothing more than to have him drive me home and stay with me all night. My brain quickly takes control of the situation, reminding me that I don't have hairy legs, mismatched pajamas or Nyquil numbness as a deterrent. I can't allow him near my bedroom or me tonight. I'm all fired up and horny as hell from all the clenching, fluttering and heart stopping that occurred today.

"I'll call you as soon as I get home. I promise."

"Are you ok to drive? Are you sleepy?"

"Nope. I'm totally awake."

"Fine. Don't forget to call me or I'm driving to Hoboken."

Smiling at his threat, I nod. "I will. I promise." He bends and kisses me lightly on the cheek, leaving a tingling sensation from the touch of his lips.

I quickly get into the car, putting much needed distance between Jack's lips and me. My emotions are swirling inside me like a whirlpool as I drive off. I'm happy I finally feel like a true member of Devil's Lair. I'm excited for the tour that's a few weeks away. But mostly I'm scared that these past few weeks haven't lessened my feelings for him at all.

Not. At. All.

***

I am dying to talk to Evan. It's been a few days since they got home from the competition and a brief phone call and a few texts were all I got to let me know they did fantastic. I need details. I'm glad he has had this distraction from what's happening with his personal life.

Our schedules have prevented us from hanging out and catching up. Today is Sunday, and he said he was coming by my place early. Then he wants to join dad and me at brunch. I'm very nervous about this. Not that I think Evan would pull anything, but I love these two men very much and it hurts me that they aren't on good terms right now.

I've had a few conversations with dad since that fateful day. He told me that there were many times when he wanted to tell Evan the truth, especially after mom died. However, he thought if he revealed the truth and Barb still took him away, it would hurt Evan and my mom unnecessarily. It took many years for dad to build a friendship back with Barb. He resented her for what she did although he began to understand it over time.

The day Evan and I became friend's dad felt it was God's way of sending a message. When it was clear we were getting closer and closer, dad and Barb actually had a sit down. I'm not sure Evan is going to be happy with this information. I told dad that he might not want to share that with him.

My doorbell jolts me out of my thoughts.

Evan walks into my apartment looking happy and carefree. "Hey sis, I missed you." He has taken to calling me sis, which tells me he is more comfortable with our situation.

"Hey. You look good. Are you ok?"

"Yep, I'm great."

I grab his hand and drag him to the couch. "Tell me everything." I plop down beside him.

"It was so awesome, Lei." He proceeds to tell me every single detail of the competition, the crowd, and the great job Lori did in getting them seen and noticed by some of the local radio deejays. She had a bunch of CD's made and handed them out to record producers. The best part was they came in third place out of ten bands. Third place at their first competition, I am so proud of them.

"Hey, I didn't mean to upset you. We missed you, Leila. It would have been even more perfect if you were there."

"I know. Things do happen for a reason Ev. If I didn't get the job with DL it wouldn't have caused the chain of events that got you to the competition."

"DL?" He questions and I shrug. "You're right. You're always so smart."

"I know."

"Humble as shit, too."

"I hate to bring this up but we have to go."

He nods.

"Did the competition help you forget what happened?"

"Yes, and no. I've done a lot of thinking. It is what it is, and I've gained more than I lost."

"I'm so proud of you."

"Don't be so proud yet. I'm not ready to forgive her."

"Evan, she needs you."

"And I'll be there for her. But it still hurts when I remember her lies." He runs his hand through his hair. "Hell, my name shouldn't even be Evan Miller. Evan Miller never existed."

He's right.

He has a lot mottling up the possibility of forgiving Barb right now. He needs to work through this his way.

We reluctantly set off for brunch with Dad.

As we sit and wait for my dad to arrive, Evan fidgets manically. I don't say much and leave him with his thoughts. He keeps fiddling with his silverware and glancing towards the door.

My dad finally arrives and looks like he's aged since I last saw him. My heart goes out to him, as this must be so hard for him as well.

He kisses the top of my head and pats Evan on the back.

Evan doesn't beat around the bush and comes right out with it. "I don't forgive what she or you did, but I'm slowly beginning to understand your reasoning." He pauses while my dad simply nods.

"I've already spoken to my mother. I told her I would be there for her during her treatments and her recovery process. I love her. I am grateful to you for also being there for her. As far as our relationship goes, I hope we can get back to the point we were at. I loved you like a father and I think that I still do, but I can't just pick up where we left off. Not yet, at least."

Dad's eyes well up with tears and he nods again. He looks over to me, and I feel my heart breaking for him. Evan follows his glance as well. "The only part of this whole mess that I am completely at peace with is the fact I gained Lei as a sister."

The tears that have been threatening all morning finally spill from my eyes. I know Evan will get to a better place because it's just the kind of person he is. I hope he can rebuild his trust and his love for dad. We all just have to give him his time.

***

Time has taken a speed pill, and flies by without showing me any mercy. Tonight is my last official performance with Cliffhangers and that chapter of my life is now closing. It's extremely bitter sweet for me. I will miss the guys, the bar, and the girls all terribly. Things are changing not only for me, but for my former band mates as well. We are all growing up.

I spend a little extra time on my hair, make-up, and outfit. I want to relish in every moment of tonight. Even my drive over to The Zone has me reminiscing of all the times I've taken this route while battling with the nervous butterflies I always got before performing. I'll be taking these memories with me and pulling them out when I'm missing everyone so much.

The Zone parking lot is almost full, and there are only a few spots left. I know tonight we will have a huge crowd but it's still fairly early. All our regulars know that it's my farewell show and many have promised to be here for me to say goodbye. Why are they here so early?

I also wonder why Ace isn't on his usual perch. I approach the doors and notice it's unusually quiet inside the bar. Just as I pull open the door it occurs to me why.

Oh crap…but it's too late to run.

"SURPRISE!"

The bar is jammed and every single person in it is facing the door, every pair of eyes looking at me.

Someone is going to pay for this.

Mortified doesn't begin to describe what I'm feeling, as I am passed from person to person. Some I know, others, I have no clue who they are, and a few hug me a little too intimately. I now know how Jack felt at his party. I never had one thrown for me, and I remember thinking that night I wouldn't ever want one. My friends mean well, and I'm going to have to grin and bear it. I wanted a nice quiet send off, maybe having a drink or two after the show with all my best buds, but they obviously have other plans for me.

Above the stage is a huge banner that reads:

LEILA MARINO once sang here.

Shaking my head and frowning, I walk over to my friends who are standing near the bar waiting for me. Jack, Trey, Hunter and Amanda, Scott and Patti are all congregated with my former band mates. Even the girls, Ace, Kelly, and Nina are here. I'm stunned into silence.

Evan moves forward and pulls me in for a hug. "Lei, you mean a lot to us and we wanted to give you a proper farewell party."

Lori appears with a tray of shots and starts handing them out. "Bottoms up Lei-Lei."

I warily look at the small glass filled with amber liquid and ask, "Um, is this tequila?"

Lori nods and says, "No Ginger Ale for you tonight. This is the only way to properly get plastered." She grabs a shot for herself. "To Leila, we are going to miss the fuck out of you, and we all love you." She focuses on my new band members and says, "You guys better take care of her or I will have your dicks for lunch with a side of your balls."

She smiles sweetly and then downs her shot in one fluid movement. There is some laughing, but my new band mates look uneasy and smile weakly. I would be nervous if I were them. Lori means every word.

I guess Lori's comments turned Trey on, because he moves over to suck her face. I look away totally embarrassed and mumble, "Ugh...get a room."

Lori stops enough to say, "You're just jealous." Ironically, she is spot on. My eyes find Jack, and I tentatively down my shot. As I make my tequila face, Jack openly laughs at me then drinks his own shot.

"Crap. I hate this stuff. Damn it Lor, couldn't you make our shots something sweeter?"

She shakes her head, and passes me another.

"I need to perform tonight, are you trying to kill me?"

"Drink it!" she barks and I obey. I'm here five minutes and I'm buzzed. This is going to be a long, night.

My dad shows up looking somber and like he just lost his best friend. He's hovering in the corner as if by avoiding us, he's eluding what we are actually celebrating.

I need to snap him out of his funk. "Dad, smile."

"What for? My daughter is leaving me for a year."

"It's not a year."

"It might as well be. My son barely speaks to me and the Yankees are three games behind the Sox. Life sucks."

270

There isn't much I can say to that. "Maybe you need to pick a different team?"

He gives me a look. "Are you drunk?"

"No, not yet. Almost though." I giggle. "Come meet my new band."

He gives me another look.

"Stop sulking, and try to be nice."

He allows me to drag him over, while his facial expression sets the tone for the introductions. The guys look like they want to bolt. Instead I wander towards the bar, putting distance between my dad, my new boss, and me.

Jack takes control and engages my dad in a conversation. Within minutes, dad is smiling and chatting and no longer sulking. Jack Lair and his endless charm know no bounds. I hope that dad likes him, and isn't just acting. I don't know why, but it's suddenly important to me that they get along. I also hope that he isn't giving him the third degree right now, or threatening his life in any way. Even if they are both smiling, that could be a total front.

As I'm about to walk back over to them just to be sure, Matt comes to stand next to me and pushes into my shoulder. "Hey."

I push back. "Hey."

"I'm real proud of you. I may not show it or say it, but I am. I just wanted you to hear it."

I turn to face him totally stunned. "Really? Are you drunk?"

"Yes, really and no, I'm not drunk...yet. I'll wish you luck, but Leila you don't need it. You are going to be great out there. Just don't write harsh things about me when you publish your first autobiography."

"I can keep it to myself for a price." He pulls me in for a hug and kisses my cheek. While in his embrace, my eyes land on Jack, who is watching us intently.

Pulling away from Matt, I ask, "What just happened?"

He strokes my cheek slowly. "I realized what I lost."

With that, Matt walks away and moves over to the bar to say something to Lori. She flips him off jokingly and he laughs. Seriously, a planet must have careened of its axis tonight or the apocalypse is coming.

As I am trying to figure out Matt's atypical behavior, Jack strolls over and says, "Hi."

"Hi. Was my dad nice to you? He's a bit depressed."

"Yes, very. He's not happy that I'm a Mets fan though." He chuckles. "How are you feelin'?"

"Buzzed." At that moment, Lori chooses to come over with another shot.

"Oh, no." I warn while backing up. "Stay away from me."

"One more, for luck." She smiles sweetly and holds the shot out for me to take.

Jack starts laughing, but then turns it into a cough when he sees my face. I shove him and sulk, "You're no help."

With a heavy sigh, I drink more of the awful medicine she continues to inflict on me, and immediately make my ugly face.

"You're such a drama queen." Lori huffs. "Its just tequila, not battery acid."

"Go away."

They do get easier to handle, though, probably because they numb your taste buds. I won't admit that to her. The third shot immediately reacts with my brain cells. How am I going to do our show? I hope I don't fall on my ass up there. That would be quite an exit.

I giggle at the visual and Jack asks, "Want to share?"

I forget that he was standing right next to me. "I'm gonna fall on my ass up there."

Jack moves closer and whispers, "I'll save you if you do." His lips brushed up against my ear, causing me to break out with goosebumps all over my body. I slowly turn my head and we come face to face. I stare at his lips while licking my own. He smiles slowly, setting off all my triggers. Self-consciously I take a step back because his aura is numbing my brain.

"You can't do that to me." I pant. The tequila fuels my honesty.

"Do what? Save you?" He smirks knowingly and my eyes once again fixate on his lips.

"You know what. You're like a vampire. You glamour me."

"Good to know…for future reference."

"I…I gotta go…um… I gotta…I gotta go sing." I stupidly respond, fumbling over my words.

His stare is intense and serious and fucking hot. "That's a shame." He brushes his lips against my ear again and adds, "I'll be here when you're done."

Holy fuck.

I'm not sure how I managed to walk to the back room without breaking my neck. Alcohol gets me into trouble with Jack. What game is he playing? That bastard absolutely knows the affect he has on me. Does he enjoy watching me act like a complete idiot?

The first time he kissed me he was drunk. The second time he kissed me we were both drunk. Well he's completely sober right now…so what the hell is he pulling? I'm coherent enough to know Jack wasn't just flirting with me out there. That was an invite.

As I'm storing my bag in my locker, trying frantically to calm my breathing, Sal enters the back room.

"Hey princess, how's my girl doing?" He gives me a hug. "You ok sweetheart?" I wonder if it's my beet red cheeks, erratic breathing, or pounding heart that tips him off.

"Yes, I'm fine. Lori is getting me drunk."

"That girl is too much." After a pause he says, "So, um…I haven't had a chance to congratulate you Leila. I am so proud of you, and I want you to know you always have a place here if you need it. I say that fully knowing you'll never be back."

"Unless I fail miserably and come begging for my old job back."

"Not gonna happen. This joint is in your past. You are on your way, pretty girl. I'm honored to have been here during your start." I start to well up with tears from his words.

"Aaww, don't cry. I'm not trying to upset you. I just wanted to let you know how I feel. And don't you worry about your old man, I'll keep him busy. He won't have time to miss you." He embraces me again. We both know that would never happen, but it is nice to hear dad will have so many people looking out for him. Between my boys, Sal, and Barb, I know he'll be just fine.

"Sal, I'm going to miss you. You're like my favorite uncle."

"Get out there and do your thing." He wipes away my tears, then turns and walks out the door. I'm sure this is his way of saying goodbye and I doubt I'll be getting another one from him before I leave. Sal is a man of very few words.

As I'm about to finally get on stage, Lori strolls into the room holding a margarita.

"Why are you crying?"

"Sal said goodbye."

"Oh. Here." She holds the margarita in front of my face.

"Nah ah."

"Oh relax. It's still tequila, so you aren't mixing. Besides, you love my margaritas. One for the road?"

"Lor, I'm gonna make a fool out of myself up there."

"So? After tonight you'll never see those people again. Besides, you've made a fool out of yourself in front of us plenty of times."

"You. Are. Exhausting." I take a tiny sip, but then proceed to gulp the entire drink down.

Lori laughs obnoxiously. "See that wasn't so bad?" She takes my glass, kisses my cheek and turns to get back to the bar in five seconds flat. She's like the stealth enabler.

I'm plastered by the time I get my ass on stage.

Our show is awesome…I'm lying. It's our worst show ever. We screw up and we make mistakes and we laugh but it is still awesome. During our show I somehow consume two more of Lori's lethal margaritas and I have no clue how they even found their way to my lips. The boys sang *Jersey Girl* to me for our last song and the entire bar joined in. The alcohol I've consumed coming in handy at that moment, because a sober Leila would have been mortified. Instead I cried, laughed and sang along with them all. It was the perfect ending.

The walk from the stage to the bar takes forever. Almost every patron stops me every few steps to say goodbye and or wish me luck. Some asked for my autograph. Some of the guys wishing me luck try to get frisky.

Jack appears out of nowhere and escorts me to the bar himself while murmuring, "Fucking idiots." Possessive Jack is a complete turn on.

By the time I get to the bar, I need a drink. "Lor, margarita me!"

"Babe…I think you've had enough."

Babe?

Oh God. Jack calling me Babe is a complete turn on.

Stretching on my tippy toes, I bring my lips to his ear. "It's so hot when you call me babe and I think I need one more." My seductive move might have been very effective, had I not stumbled and fallen right into his arms.

"My hero." I gaze into his eyes, sending obvious "kiss me" signals.

Jack mumbles under his breath. "You're killing me." Before I can formulate the words to ask the question why, he lifts me onto an empty bar stool.

"Sit."

"You're so bossy, Jackson." I giggle from using his real name and decide to test it on my tongue. "Jackson. Jacksonnnnnn."

"Only my mom calls me that."

"And me."

"And you."

"What's your…" Wow he smells so good. His body is pressed up against my back, and, wait, is that a bulge I feel on my ass?

After a few seconds, he asks, "Yes?"

"Huh?"

"You were about to ask me something."

"Oh…um…I forgot." I take a long sip of my margarita. "Lori, this one is the yummiest yet!"

My friend gives me a thumbs up from across the bar. "Stop yelling!"

"Was I yelling? Wait, I remember. What's your middle name?"

Chuckling he answers, "Henry."

"Jackson Henry. Jackson Henry. Jackson Henry Lair."

He places his lips directly on my ear and says, "Ok, zip it."

Shit I could do him right here, right now, right on the bar.

I tilt my head back at the thought and plant a big, wet kiss on his neck. "When you whisper in my ear, it makes me hot!"

I said that too loud, based on Jack, Evan, Lori, and my dad all gawking at me.

Screw it. I blatantly ignore them, choosing to enjoy Jack's body some more. Moving back until I press against him, he groans so only I can hear. His groan jump-starts my groin. In my perfect world scenario, I would be facing the other way and I would be making out with Jack at this exact moment. Even drunk, I'm not that brazen. Instead I snake my hands behind me and grip the back of his thighs.

"Crap…you're killing me." Jack laces his fingers with my hands, the ones that are molesting his thighs, and pulls them forward resting them on my lower back. I have to hand it to him. It's a brilliant move. I'm now unable to reach my margarita.

"Release me."

"No."

I look up at him pout, "You hate me."

"I most definitely don't hate you." He brings my earlobe in between his lips, tugging before releasing it. My whole body ignites and puts me on the verge of a sexual conniption.

"Fuck."

"Hey, Miss Potty Mouth."

By the time the bar empties, and our party comes to an end, I'm horny as hell. Not the tingly, pins and needles, hot flash, kind of horny that I've gotten used to. It's more like the *fuck I can't stand it any longer and even the inside of my underwear is turning me on and I'm on fire,* kind of horny. Granted, most of it is my own fault. Jack has released my hands, and I don't know what to do with them. I can touch his hard body some more or relieve my own. I know he's worked up too. I can still feel his excitement pressing into my backside. A quick trip to the ladies room and I could...

"I need to go home." I mumble to no one in particular.

"You ok?"

"Huh?" I look up behind me at Jack, again forgetting what I said and wondering why he is laughing.

Chapter 20- Jack

Everyone within a ten-foot radius now knows how plastered Leila really is after her outburst that I make her hot. Her dad is the most observant and starts calling for cabs. While angry dialing, he grumps and mumbles under his breath. Most of his words are inaudible.

"There is no way you guys are driving home." He mutters to the wall he is facing, as he dials the phone.

One by one, my friends all assure him they are ok to drive home. After a quick assessment, he releases them. For a second I thought he was going to make them walk a straight line while touching their noses with outstretched arms.

"I drove here!" Leila yells and follows up with a very loud belch. Laughter rises and causes my chest to shake from trying to hold it in, causing Leila to giggle.

One minute Evan is serious and contemplative, the next he is hysterical. Leila's giggling turns into a full blown laughing fit, her entire body shaking uncontrollably, her hands holding my arms that are still circling her. This is better than TV. I'm rarely the sober one in a bunch and it's very entertaining watching drunken Leila and her friends.

Leila loses her balance and makes me tighten my grip around her waist to prevent her from falling off the stool. Evan suddenly becomes serious and says to no one in particular, "I couldn't tell her to cab it. That would've ruined the surprise."

279

The look on Evan's face makes me crack up all over again. Even her dad tries to hide a smile and fails miserably. He turns his back to us and resumes his phone call to the cab service.

"Mr. Marino, I'll drive her home. I'm fine."

Her dad now judges what state I'm in. I could practically tell what he's thinking. He's not going to allow me to drive her home to an empty apartment after watching me touching her in one way or another all night. But after a short moment he relents, "Um... Leila, are you ok with Jack driving you home?" She nods her head up and down, causing Evan to lose it again.

"Ok, Jack. I'll be there as soon as I get these boys taken care of. Thank you."

Hunter saunters over. "Jack, what are you doing?"

Ignoring him, I wrap an arm around her waist and help her off the stool and to the door.

"I luuvv uuu guyyyss." She calls out waiving at her friends. Most of her friends yell good-bye back, except for Evan. He is still hunched over in hysterics.

"Ok, let's go party animal." I walk her out the door.

Leila leans her body weight against me, mumbling randomly. "Funny...so good...can eat him." Turning towards my chest, she suddenly sniffs me.

"Did you just sniff me?"

"Nooooooo. Nope."

She makes me laugh. I love this girl.

"You're killing me."

"Why do ya keep ssssayeen that?"

"Cause you are." I respond while smiling wide.

"I jussssssssssssssssst luuuv your Cee Cee Dee Esss smile."

"My what?"

"Huh?"

Oh boy…this is getting nowhere.

Getting her to her car, folding her in to the passenger seat, and buckling her seat belt are not easy feats.

She turns towards me just as I'm snapping in her belt and commands, "Jack…kissssss mmeee." She has a death grip on my t-shirt, and rubs her nose against my neck.

No sooner do I pry her fingers off my shirt than I hear her snoring. She's out cold.

I'm glad she had fun. She needed this release. She is an adorable drunk. Of course I don't know what's going to happen when I wake her up. She may hurl all over me.

Minutes after leaving the bar I pull her car up to her apartment. There isn't parking in front so I have to circle a few times until I find a spot that's two blocks away. Going to her side of the car and opening her door doesn't even wake her up.

Sighing heavily I reach in to pull her out and get her to a standing position. As she slumps against me, I can feel her soft breasts pressing against my chest. She is complete dead weight. There is no way she will be able to walk two blocks. Doing the only logical thing I can think of, I bend and throw her over my shoulder…still nothing. Tomorrow is not going to be a good day for her. Tequila hangovers suck ass.

With her bag in my hand, I carry her home on the deserted streets of Hoboken. Thank God the streets are deserted. I look like I'm kidnapping a drugged girl, not to mention her skirt is hiked up exposing her thighs and part of her ass.

So our little display tonight was a bit obvious. Her dad was on to us. Her friends were all just as drunk so I doubt they noticed. The ones who weren't, like Lori or Alisa, or Hunter, hell they saw every move she made on me, and I on her.

Shit...I could care less if an announcement was made. It's her I worry about. She will not be happy when she hears how she came on to me tonight, or how I responded with so many witnesses.

While carrying her up the stairs, she starts mumbling incoherently. I set her down and dig for her keys when she starts to come to.

"Where are we?" Her words come out in a slur.

"Your place." I respond while trying to hold her up and open her damn door. I finally get it open and walk her inside. Just as I flip on some lights, Miss Marino catches her second wind.

"You staying the night?" she asks seductively. She pulls away and stumbles slightly, but she still manages to pull her shirt over her head.

Oh my God...

As if in slow motion, she reaches behind and unzips her skirt. It falls and sweet Jesus, what the fuck is she wearing? She is practically naked in a pink lace bra and matching boy shorts! I love those damn things. She's still wearing her heels, too. A raging hard-on immediately springs to life in my jeans.

Oh fuck.

"Leila, stop." I say moving towards her.

Just as I bend to pick up her clothes, she grabs my face and shoves her tongue into my mouth.

She is killing me...she is fucking killing me!

When I pull away, she pleads, "Hey I want to kissssss you some moore. You always taste sooo good Jack."

Aw, fuck…

Holding her head, I wait until she looks at me, forcing her to focus on my words. "Let's get you into your room."

She smiles wide and saunters towards her bedroom. The sight of her walking down the hall in her bra and sheer panties gives me a nice glimpse of her fantastic ass and causes my dick to twitch.

I adjust myself and follow while thinking this is the worst form of torture. It's worse than kissing her at my party, and then having to walk away. The second I flip on her lights, she turns and starts to unhook her bra. I know if I just get her in bed, she will pass out. I frantically start opening drawers, looking for something to throw on her body…her practically naked, smoking hot body. Finding an oversized sweatshirt just as her bra falls to the floor, I grip it in my hands, dumbstruck from the sight of topless Leila.

I can't stop looking at her. I've had plenty of sex dreams about Leila these past few months, but nothing…nothing compares to her in the flesh. She is absolutely gorgeous. Her breasts, her tight stomach, the slope of her hips, her legs are all perfect. The best part is her sheer panties afford me a glimpse of her smooth shaven pussy. Holy fuck, this is another complete turn on for me.

She's fucking perfection.

I can't do this.

"Jack." She says looking at me like she wants to attack. "I love you. I want you and I know you want me too." Her gaze is smoldering as she focuses on the obvious bulge in my pants. Smiling wickedly, she seductively licks her lips and then sways unsteadily. I'm smart enough to know she's too drunk to know what she's saying. But her words still have an immediate effect on me.

"I do babe, but not like this."

"I love when you call me babe." She steps closer, gripping my t-shirt in between her fingers.

Fuck.

I quickly drag the sweatshirt over her head, maneuver her arms through the sleeves, pull back the comforter, lift her onto her bed and cover her to her chin in record time.

As I turn to walk out of the room, she sits up. "Where are you going?"

"I'll be right back." I respond while flipping off her light and moving towards her living room. If my calculations are correct, she will be passed out in less than sixty seconds.

Hopefully.

Her phone suddenly rings and I jump up to grab it off the coffee table.

"Hello?" I keep my voice low.

"Jack? It's Anthony Marino. Is Leila ok?"

"Yes sir. I just put her to bed. She's out cold."

"I just got all the boys in cabs. I'll be there in a few minutes to stay with her." He probably doesn't trust me and I can't say I blame him.

"That's fine, but you don't have to. I'll stay tonight and make sure she's ok. I'll leave in the morning. I promise I'll take good care of her, sir." I hope that I can convince him to trust me.

There's a pause, until he answers, "Ok. Please tell her to call me as soon as she is up. And um, thanks Jack."

Waiting a few minutes, I quietly walk down the hall to peek in. Thankfully, she *is* out cold. As a parting gift, she suddenly flips off the comforter and turns on her stomach with her gorgeous ass totally exposed in her sexy lace panties. Soft snores are the only sounds she makes.

"Fuck, this is torture."

I have two options -rub one out or cold shower.

Unfortunately rubbing one out may still leave me with a hard-on and a bad case of blue balls. The cold shower is my only option. Sighing heavily, I step into the ice-cold stream of water and kill my hard on instantly.

Fucking torture.

***

All night I've drifted in and out of a very depthless sleep. All the admissions she subconsciously released in her drunken state swirl in my head.

"You make me hot."

"I love when you call me babe."

"Kiss me, Jack."

"You glamour me."

"I want you and I know you want me."

"I love you."

I feel like I found a key to her diary and shamelessly read every secret she wrote down. This night felt like it was twenty-four hours long.

Once I finally hear her use her bathroom, or more specifically emptying her stomach into her toilet, I get up off the couch, throw on my jeans, and go into her kitchen. I consider checking on her but I'm sure she would prefer her privacy at the moment. I have her coffee maker running by the time she emerges from her bathroom.

Leila slowly enters the room wearing a tank top and short shorts. Her hair is adorably messy. Other than looking a bit green, you wouldn't know she's hung over.

"Hi. How do you feel?"

"Sssshhh!"

"Sorry."

"It's ok." She points to her bathroom, "I'm sure you heard. I do feel better now. My head hurts, and I have cotton mouth but otherwise I think I'm ok." She walks over to her table and sits down. Her eyes rake over my shirtless torso while she fiddles with the hem of her tank top.

"Where do you keep your aspirin?"

She points to a cabinet in the corner. I retrieve two pills, and then turn to her fridge to pull out a bottle of water and a Diet Coke. Opening them, I walk over and pass them to her.

"Drink and take these, Coke first."

She doesn't argue and does as instructed. "Thank you for staying."

"You're welcome."

I walk back into her kitchen, open her freezer and pull out frozen bagels. She looks at me with raised eyebrows.

"You need to eat some bread." I explain as I drop a bagel into her toaster. While waiting for the toaster to pop, I watch Leila sitting quietly and struggling with her own thoughts. I pour myself coffee, butter her bagel and carry them over to her at the table.

"Eat." I demand.

"Yes, sir." She takes a small bite out of her bagel. "You have a lot of experience with tequila hangovers?"

"You could say that. Did you have fun last night?"

"Yes I did, I think. I don't remember a lot of it." She gets very quiet again and begins to gnaw on her bottom lip.

"What's wrong?"

"Jack…um, did I…um…did I try to seduce you last night?" She looks totally embarrassed.

"Yes." I respond truthfully.

"Did we do anything?" she asks looking up at me.

I wish I could say I wanted to or that we did and it was mind numbing. Instead I say, "No, we didn't, just a lot of flirting at the bar. Once we got here, you tried to kiss me, and I saw you in your underwear but that's it." I'm unable to hide the anguish I felt last night in my voice.

"Flirting at the bar? Oh crap." She slumps forward, putting her head in her hands. I understand why that's what upsets her the most. She is a very private person, and I can only imagine how she feels right now.

Trying to lighten the mood, I say, "You snore."

"I do not." She defensively retorts.

"Yes you do. You snore like a lumberjack and you curse like a sailor. You have a real bad potty mouth."

"Liar."

Laughing I watch as she nibbles on her bagel. "I used your shower last night. I hope that's ok."

"Of course. I hope that couch was ok."

"Yes it's actually very comfortable."

"The boys love that couch. I can't get them off of it when they come over."

"I can't say I blame them." I can picture four guys sprawled on her couch. "I take it that the chair is your favorite spot?"

She looks over her shoulder. "Yes, it's the only corner of my apartment that has a view." I stand and walk over to admire it.

"It is beautiful. I guess this your roof?"

She understands my reference. "Yes. I guess that it is."

"Oh, I almost forgot. Your dad wants you to call him." I say remembering my instructions.

"My dad? You spoke to my dad?" she asks looking confused and worried.

"He called last night. I think he was checking on me more than he was checking on you."

She shakes her head and grabs her phone. Her conversation is only a few minutes long. She doesn't leave the room and I'm flattered she feels comfortable to talk to him in front of me. She asks if he checked on Evan and listens while he talks for a few minutes. She agrees to something he says and at the end of her conversation she says, "Yeah, he is." while looking over at me and blushing. She tells her dad she loves him and hangs up.

"Yeah, he is what?" I ask dying of curiosity. She looks at me confused and I ask, "You said to your dad *Yeah, he is*. What am I?"

"A great guy."

My heart skips a beat.

"Oh...I thought you were admitting that I was still here."

"Oh. Well he didn't ask but if he did I probably wouldn't lie." She admits giving me a dazzling smile.

She takes my breath away. I need to spend time with her. I just can't leave yet. I walk back over sit at the table and ask, "What are your plans today?"

"Nothing exciting. I need to get my car from the bar. Saturdays are laundry days, and since I'm no longer a member of Cliffhangers, I'm off tonight."

"Want to show me how great Hoboken is?" I ask.

She smiles wide. "Sure, I'd love to. Do you like cannoli? We have the best there is." She says proudly.

"I love cannoli."

"Give me fifteen minutes to get ready."

"Wait. Finish your bagel."

"You're so bossy." She finishes her bagel and heads for the bedroom. For two point five seconds I'm left wondering if this is a good idea. Then I argue with myself that I simply don't care.

After I use her bathroom to freshen up, I send a quick text to Hunter to tell him I'm hanging out with Leila today.

Of course he responds immediately.

jack...what are you doing?

i'm hanging out with Leila

yea, you said that...dude?

bye hunter

Fucking Hunter...I should have never told him my secret. I'm already regretting it. His text resurfaces my qualms, and my brain tells me to listen. I should tell her that I couldn't stay and leave before I do something I will regret.

I'm about to do just that when she comes out in her shorts, pink top, hair in a ponytail, and tan legs...and my brain goes numb.

You would never know that she was drunk off her ass last night. She looks so gorgeous, effectively causing me throw all logic out the fucking window.

"You clean up well. I look like death after a tequila night."

"You're blind. I do look like death. Ready?"

***

After retrieving her car, Leila showed me every inch of Hoboken. It's a quaint town, and I can understand the attraction. We spent hours sitting in a park on the Hudson, watching the boats go by. We laughed at all the countless dogs and their owners who morphed into look-a-likes. Late in the day, we decided to grab a pizza, some of Hoboken's famous cannoli and go back to her place.

As I set her table, she pulls out a beer and some cheap wine for herself. It feels so natural to be with her. We really had a nice day, and there were times I wanted to hold her hand as we were walking along the river. I could get used to this. I enjoy being with her. This realization no longer scares me. What scares me more is being apart.

Chapter 21-Leila

"I probably shouldn't be drinking so much today. My body just recovered."

"The second best hangover remedy besides aspirin and Coke, is to keep drinking." He taps his beer can to my glass.

I giggle and respond, "Good advice."

I feel so relaxed and comfortable sitting here with him. His arm is stretched along the back of the couch, and he is lazily playing with my ponytail.

After relentlessly grilling him to tell me how I acted last night at the bar, he finally gave me details of my over the top flirting. Crap, I told him he glamour's me! I grabbed his thighs! I kissed his neck! From the look on his face, he was purposefully withholding some other details.

No more tequila for me.

I will most definitely have some damage control to deal with when I see Dad and Lori. I'll worry about that tomorrow. Evan was plastered, so I doubt he remembers my behavior.

He playfully tugs on my ponytail and asks, "Where's my cannoli?"

"Oh yeah, cannoli time." I bounce up and run to the fridge to grab the box.

He laughs at my enthusiasm as I bring them over to where we are sitting. "Prepare yourself, these are life altering."

"Can't wait." He reaches in and picks up two of them, one of which he hands to me.

We both bite down at the same time. "It is delicious."

Savoring my bite, I close my eyes and moan. "MMMmmm. It's so good."

When I open my eyes, I'm surprised to see Jack staring at me with a heated look on his face. Reaching over, he slowly wipes his thumb across my bottom lip, sending a jolt right through me. He brings his thumb to his mouth and sucks off the cream he removed from my lip. The cannoli I am holding is the last thing on my mind as I drop it back into the box, and it lands with a thump.

"Delicious."

We continue to stare at each other for what seems like an eternity, and with each passing second my heart beats louder and louder in my chest. He removes the box from my lap, drops his cannoli in and puts the box on the table. He holds my face and slowly pulls me in until we are inches apart. In slow motion, he pulls me in closer until our mouths touch.

Our kiss starts off soft and slow. When he slides his tongue along my top lip, I open my mouth giving him complete access. Accepting my invitation, his slips in further to taste me slowly. We make out like teenagers and it's the best make out session I've ever had in my life.

I finally gasp for breath and pull away. "I need to catch my breath."

He releases my head and takes my hands. "Leila, if you want me to stop, I'll stop."

"What happened to being friends?"

"It's not enough."

"I'm scared things will get complicated between us."

"I won't let it."

He pulls me into his embrace and kisses the top my head. "Leila, I want you to know something before anything happens. I can't stop thinking about you. Since my party, you have consumed my thoughts. You have taken over my life."

I turn in his arms so I can see his face better. His confession has me reeling. "Jack, don't say things like that to me."

"Why?"

"Because I won't recover."

"Baby, I mean every word."

Tilting his head down, he kisses me softly on my lips. Weeks and weeks of holding back, of hiding my feeling, of denying my feelings for him all come flooding to the surface. I kiss him back harder, clutching his shirt between my fingers to force him to move his lips against mine and respond to my kiss.

Jack does respond by drawing me into his hard body and making love to my lips with his own. He lays me back on the couch and slips his hand under my tank. Slowly, he moves it up my body until it reaches my breast, skimming his thumb on the underside of my bra. He pulls away and watches for my reaction.

"I want you Leila. I can't fight this any longer." He stops and waits for my consent. "Please, I want to be with you."

"I want that too, but it's complicated. Our working relationship, the tour, it's all too complicated."

"Stop over thinking it."

When I remain silent, he starts kissing me slowly at first but then it quickly builds, escalating to the point we are writhing against each other on the couch.

Breaking our kiss, I rasp, "I know what you're doing."

He stands and pulls me off the couch, wrapping his arms around me. His hands find my lower back.

"What are you afraid of, Leila?"

"What will be left of me when it ends."

"Why does it have to end?"

He's right. Who goes into a relationship already worrying about how it will end. I can't continue down the friend path anyway… while living with him, or being with him. That is no longer an option. In my mind, I've crossed over that line weeks ago. I had no idea he had as well.

Bottom line, I want him. I need him.

"Leila, I want to be with you. Do you feel the same?"

As he continues to wait for my response, my decision is already made. What I'm about to do will change everything. I'm done hiding how I feel. I'm done playing games. Pulling him down to lightly kiss him, I whisper, "Yes."

Taking his hand, I lead him to my bedroom.

Once inside, he embraces me, desperately gripping me to his chest as if afraid to let go. When he does let go, he lightly strokes my cheek before pulling me in for a kiss. Slowly, he pulls off my tank and then grazes his right thumb over my bra and across my erect nipple. How can such a simple touch wreak absolute havoc on my insides? I can't stand it any longer. If I don't have him soon I'm going to die.

I pull his shirt up and off his body, unfasten his jeans, and slip my hand in to feel him. His size is impressive, and I stroke him from base to tip, smooth skin over steel. He pulls my hand away and takes a few steps back.

"I want to go slow."

My heart is pounding in my chest and I feel desire spread through my entire body. His eyes never leave mine as he slowly peels away his clothes, leaving him bare. He takes my breath away, and he is absolutely stunning. The muscles of his chest, his arms, and his stomach are all so well defined.

He's perfect from the pronounced v on his hips to the thin trail of dark brown hair that leads from his belly button to his obvious arousal.

Jack moves closer and quietly undresses me. It is so erotic as he devours me with his eyes. Once I'm naked, he steps away to admire my body.

"You're so beautiful."

I subconsciously move towards his body to touch his skin. The pull I feel in undeniable, like a tether holding my heart to his. He steps closer at the same time. It was only a few steps, but it may as well have been miles.

Laying my hand on his chest, I can feel his heart pounding. Succumbing to the incessant urge to touch him, I run my hands over his chest, abdomen, and hips. Tracing his erection with my fingertips, he closes his eyes and moans, completely lost in my touch. I take his hand and lead him toward my bed.

"I've dreamt of you…of kissing you…of tasting you." He says as he travels down my body, placing kisses in between his admissions. Stopping at my breast, he pulls a nipple between his lips and tugs gently while his fingers begin stroking me below. His lips and touch, cause my back to arch and my hips to follow his rhythm. The ache below becomes agonizing.

Pulling his hand away, he leaves me bereft.

"Jack."

"Ssh, baby." He grabs each of my ankles and pushes them up so my legs are bent at the knee and spread wide open. He runs his thumb up my sex very slowly, causing me to shudder.

His head disappears between my legs, his lips teasing, touching everywhere but where I need them to be. Once they touch my most sensitive part, I become unhinged. As I bury my hands in his silky hair, he relentlessly tortures me, running his tongue through my folds and slipping his finger inside my entrance.

"Please… don't stop."

Jack complies expertly, causing sensations I've never felt before. He covers me with his mouth. I buck into him to quicken his pace. He sucks forcibly while stroking relentlessly with his fingers inside of me. My legs begin to tremble as he brings me to an intense orgasm causing my whole body to jerk. Weeks of pent-up desire come to fruition through my release.

It's been so long since I felt these sensations. Fighting to catch my breath, my head is spinning from the pulses that continue to manipulate my body.

Once I lay motionless, he states, "You taste better than I imagined."

He kisses his way back to my breast, pulling my nipple with his lips. I feel a throbbing ache in between my legs as if I didn't just have a mind blowing orgasm seconds ago. Remembering my initial hungers, I grab his head and pull him up until he is looking at me.

"I need you."

He bends to kiss me. I can taste myself on him as I greedily suck on his tongue, causing him to groan loudly.

Suddenly he breaks our kiss. "Don't move." Climbing off the bed, he pulls his wallet out of his jeans and retrieves a condom. Watching him roll it on to his erection is the sexiest thing I have ever seen.

The minute he gets back on my bed he stretches over me, his length is positioned and teasing. I am one pulsing nerve ending. My entire body is aching for him.

Linking our hands together, he slowly pushes himself into me, without breaking eye contact. I can feel every inch of him fill me and I never want this to end.

"Leila, you feel so good." His words are raspy with raw emotion and give voice to my own thoughts.

We move together and it's pure bliss. I clench around him, as he moves excruciatingly slow.

"Jack…faster." I tighten my legs around his waist.

He flips us around so I am now straddling him. His hands are at my hips and he pulls me down so he can plunge in deeper. The sensation he is causing inside my body is mind blowing. He sits up and the shift causes me to gasp, as he presses against the perfect spot inside.

Burying his hands in my hair, he pulls me down to kiss my mouth. I inhale him, taking him every way I can, taking control and moving myself over him even faster. My second orgasm quickly builds. He is right there with me as we climax together, our bodies trembling concurrently.

"I've dreamt of this." He admits as I clutch him to my body.

All I can do is nod to his admission. Words aren't presenting themselves to me at the moment.

We stare into each other's eyes as we sit panting, nose to nose, still connected.

"My God." He says kissing my face all over while I cling to him.

Still unable to speak, I simply nod again. I want him inside of me forever. Now that I've been with Jack, I'll never get enough.

***

As we lie in bed holding each other, Jack plays with my hair. "You smell so good."

"Jack?"

"Hmmmm?"

I can't bring myself to say what I want to. I chew on my lip and he turns my head to look into my eyes.

"What?"

"Um…have you ever had sex without a condom?"

He smiles and understands why I'm so nervous. "No, I never did. Have you?"

"Um, no, never. I'm on the pill." I offer. He smiles the CCDS, making my heart skip a beat.

"Leila, I trust you. Thanks for telling me because I hate condoms." He kisses me, and I settle back on his chest.

As he draws circle patterns on my back, I call his name again. "Jack?"

Chuckling he says, "Yes?"

"Aren't the guys going to wonder where you are?"

"For a second I thought you were going to ask me to go again." He replies with disappointment. "Hunter knows I'm with you."

"What?" I sit up unable to hide my shock.

"What? Hunter won't tell anyone. We can trust him."

"*We* can trust him with what?" I start to panic.

He sits up and shrugs. "I told you, I've been thinking about you a lot. I also wasn't acting as myself. Hunter noticed and called me out on it. I confided in him. He thinks I should stay away from you, and he's right…I should. But I can't. He won't tell the other guys how I …" He's stops mid-sentence, then adds, "He won't say anything."

"Jack, you don't need me as a distraction right now."

"Leila, not being with you will be the distraction." He says kissing me. "Do you remember what you said to me last night?"

"No, what?"

He hesitates for a moment, and then runs his nose along the length of mine. "Forget I mentioned it."

"Jack, what did I say?"

"Nothing."

"That's mean."

"Still not telling." He says kissing my shoulder and making his way towards my breast. "Now ask me to go again"

He effectively helps me forget what I was just freaking out over.

Jack and I have sex again and again before we both fall into an exhausted sleep. He is so tentative and I've never had better sex in my life. I woke a few times to feel his arms around me and his body pressing up against my back. It feels like a dream having him here, with me.

Of course I want to continue this. Of course I also feel this is a huge mistake.

Waking first, I can't help but stare at his beautiful face. He looks so peaceful and content. I can watch him for hours. I slip out of bed and slip his shirt over my head to go and make coffee.

He wants to keep seeing each other. How will this work? If Jennifer or Dylan gets wind of this or if this doesn't work out between us, this could be a disaster.

While I'm lost in thought, Jack comes into the kitchen completely naked. I blush and point to the windows. "Jack, I have neighbors."

"So? Oh good…coffee." He grabs a mug and helps himself. "You'll need to know I'm a coffee-aholic."

He laughs when he sees me gawking at him and brings me closer. "You like?"

I shake my head. "You are so conceited."

Pushing one hand up under his t-shirt to touch my breast and putting the other on my bare ass, he whispers in my ear. "No I'm not. I just like that you like looking at me."

We start to kiss and once again it quickly builds. We can't even kiss without wanting to screw each other's brains out. How are we going to keep this discrete? I pull away to tell him my concerns.

"I'm not going to lie, it's going to be very hard" He kisses my shoulder.

"But think of how good it will feel when we can be together." He kisses my neck.

"In a bunk." He kisses my chin.

"Or backstage." He kisses my cheek.

"Or especially in a hotel room." His lips find mine for a long, passionate kiss.

That does sound nice.

He pulls back and smiles wide. Running my fingertip through his dimple, I admit, "God, I love your smile."

"That reminds me. When we were leaving the bar, you said you loved my CCS something. What did you mean?"

Oh crap. I really have to stay away from tequila.

"Um...I don't know?"

I try to pull my hand away, but he grabs it quickly. "What did you call my smile?"

"Damn it...I wasn't supposed to say that out loud." I admit very flustered. "CCDS is the acronym I use for your smile. Crotch Clenching Dimple Showing smile." Shrugging, I add, "Dimples are one of my turn-ons."

"Fuck, that's hot. Crotch clenching? Is that happening right now?"

Still looking thoroughly embarrassed, I confess, "Yes, there is always clenching when I see your dimples."

"God, I wish I knew that sooner. I would have used it to my advantage."

"I may have been fired as your back-up singer if you knew."

"You would not have been fired. I would have definitely caved in to your charms sooner than I did, though."

I need to change the subject or I'll end up having him for breakfast. "Um, do you want me to drive you home? You've been wearing the same clothes for two days."

"Are you trying to say I smell?" His arms are wrapped around me and he bends to nuzzle my neck. "Besides now you're wearing my shirt, and it looks great on you."

He is driving me nuts. "No, you smell delicious and so does your shirt. I just thought you wanted to go home to change. I have brunch every Sunday with my dad, but I can cancel."

He shakes his head and points out, "I don't want you canceling on your dad."

"What will you do while I'm out?"

"I'll wait for you here and hang out until you get back. Do you mind?"

"I may be a few hours. If you are ok hanging here, then I'll drive you home later."

"Sounds good. I'll shower and sit here naked. I don't want to dirty up my only set of clothes." He starts to laugh at the look on my face. "Kidding."

Kidding, my ass. He is in my kitchen naked as we speak, and the fact that he is naked and aroused is extremely distracting. I rub up against him and we end up on my kitchen floor helping him out with his predicament.

***

"He seems really nice. He called me sir." My dad says in between bites, smiling. He's been asking a ton of questions about Jack and I'm having a hard time deflecting them, and a hard time to keep from blushing.

"He is dad."

"Anything going on between you two?"

Oh crap…

"Um, we just flirt a lot."

"From where I was standing, it looked like that boy is in love with you. Wouldn't let anyone near you all night."

My dad's admission has my heart stammering. I vaguely remember sitting at the bar, and Jack's body shielding me. My dad probably just misinterpreted his possessiveness for something else. In either case, I'm not ready to talk about my relationship with Jack with my dad, or anyone.

"You're nuts. So, I can't wait for you to see my new band in concert. They are really good." I try to steer him in a different direction. It seems to work as he starts rambling on and on. He starts discussing the tour and my last show. He wants to see my first show with DL and I promised him I would get him tickets. He brings up Evan and how they had a nice chat at my party before he got plastered, and Barb and the fact she has a date for her surgery. It's like the flood gates have opened and he's trying to get it all out. He yaps and yaps while I smile and nod.

As we leave, I hug my dad very tightly. I only have a few more brunches before I leave. "Dad, what will you do on Sunday mornings while I'm gone?"

"I was hoping I could convince Evan to take your place."

"Oh…Dad don't push him. He'll come around eventually when he's ready."

"I know. You keep telling me that."

Kissing my dad goodbye, I drive back to my apartment lost in thought of replaying every intimate, fantastic detail of last night. By the time I park Bessie, I'm horny as fuck again.

I unlock my door to find Jack sitting on my couch in only his Calvin Klein briefs watching a Mets game. It's a site I can easily get used to. The visual I've tucked away of Jack wearing Calvin's is nothing compared to him in the flesh wearing them. Hunter was dead on…he should be their model.

I smile at him and voice my thoughts from earlier. "Kidding huh?"

"What? I'm not naked." He gets up and immediately comes over to pull me into his arms. "Missed you." He bends kissing me deeply. Jack is a very sexual person. He's also very affectionate and I can get very used to this.

I break our kiss, panting, "You're killing me." He is so freaking sexy I can't stand it.

"That's my line." he retorts. "I've been waiting for you." Pulling me towards my bathroom, he strips me naked, without saying a word he then turns on the shower. He strips off his briefs and steps in holding his hand out for me.

"You're very presumptuous." I tease.

"Get used to it." He immediately starts kissing, stroking, petting, and touching me. A minute later he has me up against the wall with my leg hooked over his shoulder and his face buried between my legs on the brink of a fantastic orgasm.

Once my body stops shaking, he stands, watching me seductively.

His hair is slicked back and his eyes appear even grayer. Drops of water run down his sculpted cheekbones, perfect nose, and square chin.

I run my hands over and down his chest, trailing my fingers along his happy trail towards his erection, before taking hold of him. Jack intently looks into my eyes the entire time my hands roam his body.

I kiss his chest and slowly stroke his length. He buries his hands into my hair as I graze my way down until I am kneeling in front of him. I look up into his hooded eyes before bending to lick him from base to tip. His groan courses through me, heating my skin as if he were touching me with his own hands. I tease, but never fully take him into my mouth. I then run my tongue up the slit in slow motion. When I finally pull him into my mouth to devour every inch of him, he shudders.

Hollowing my cheeks, I suck heartily while stroking his length with my hand. Losing myself in the process, he responds to my efforts by rocking his hips in rhythm to my movements. Releasing my hair, he leans forward and holds himself up with his hands on the wall behind me. His forehead is resting on his left bicep. His eyes are closed and his breathing is shallow. It's all so sexy.

Giving him oral sex is a complete turn on. My own body pulses and quickly responds to his pleasure. Not long after, his muscles tighten and he stills when I feel his warm release at the back of my throat. It practically causes my own orgasm.

Jack doesn't move a muscle and instead remains in the same position, panting, and hands up against the wall. He slowly opens his eyes to look down at me. I love that he is completely undone. I stand and link my hands around his neck, pulling my body flush into his. He bends to kiss me, wrapping his arms around me, holding me tightly to his chest.

He suddenly grabs my legs and lifts me until I am straddling him, my back against the cold tile wall.

With one fast thrust, he buries himself inside me. It's exactly what I need at the moment. I clutch his back and dig my heels into his butt while his hands grip my thighs, and he buries his face in my neck. His grunt puts me over the edge. Once I clench around him and call out his name, he thrusts one last time responding with a guttural moan.

It was intense and hard and so good…so fucking good.

I release my legs and lean on him for support, since they are unable to hold my weight.

With one hand still around my waist, he shuts the water and then grabs a towel. He wraps it around me before reaching for his own. Then he climbs out of the tub, and carries me out of the bathroom and into my bedroom.

As I am getting dressed for the second time today, I turn to see he is watching me. "You like?" I ask as I pull on my panties.

"Very much." He confesses. His look causes my whole body to ignite, but I need to drive him home, otherwise I'll hold him prisoner forever.

"We need to stop."

"Says who?"

"You're going to kill me."

"Death by orgasm?" He smiles wide. "Sign me up."

***

Once Jack sees no one is home, he grabs my hand and yanks me into his apartment. "Hunter must be out." He pulls out his phone and texts his friend. "Want to see my room?" He wiggles his eyebrows, making me roll my eyes. "What?"

Pulling out of his grasp and putting my hands on my hips, I try to be the more responsible one.

"It's been like an hour. You are insatiable." I really am a hypocrite, because at the moment I want nothing more than to throw him on the ground and ride him for hours.

"Your point?"

"Jack, we are out of control. We need to be around each other without foaming at the mouth. This isn't good."

He is about to respond when his phone buzzes. Frowning, he pulls it out and says. "Looks like you're off the hook. Hunter and Amanda are on the roof." Grabbing my hand again, this time he pulls me towards the apartment door.

We are about to expose ourselves to Hunter. I am really not ready for this. My heart pounding as we climb the stairs towards the roof.

"Jack!" Tugging on his arm, he jerks to a stop on the top step and looks at me like I've lost my mind.

"What?

"I'm not comfortable with Hunter knowing yet."

"So then we won't tell Hunter." He says studying my face.

Feeling like I have to explain, I add, "I hate deceiving him, but I'm not ready, I'm sorry."

"Ok, don't stress." He lifts my hand up to his lips and gives it a soft kiss. "Done." Dropping my hand, he turns to open the door and walks out onto the roof as I follow.

Hunter and Amanda are cuddling on the couch.

"Hey, what are you doing here?" He asks looking surprised to see me.

Jack responds for me, "She drove me home."

"You could have put his ass in a cab and not drive all the way to Brooklyn. You're too nice to him, Leila."

Jack gives me a sexy smirk. Ignoring him, I try to act as nonchalant as possible. "I don't mind. He took good care of me after my night with Jose Cuervo. I owe him one."

Matching Jack's smirk, Hunter says, "I'm sure he did."

Jack then clears his throat, the bastard.

Throwing Jack the evil eye, I turn away to grab a chair, but mostly so Hunter doesn't see my face blushing profusely.

"Hi, Amanda." I say changing the subject as I drag a chair closer to the couch, and away from Jack. "I hope we aren't interrupting you guys."

"No, we were just relaxing. We had a late night last night. My roommate had a party."

Hunter gives her a chaste kiss. They are so adorable together. "What did you guys do?" Hunter asks while looking at Jack suspiciously.

Jack quickly says, "Leila showed me around Hoboken to try and convince me it has merit. Then we just hung out and talked and talked."

Hunter raises his eyebrows. "Talked and talked?" I notice Amanda subtly nudge him with her elbow.

"Yeah, you know how that works, we talked and talked." It's like they are speaking in code. Curiously, I watch as Jack gives Hunter a bug-eyed look, and Hunter gives Jack a fuck off look.

Ignoring the jackass twins, I turn back to Amanda. "Um, Amanda, where do you live?"

"I'm in SoHo. I've been there about five years now."

Hunter pipes in. "Her apartment is only a few blocks from the studio."

"That's a great area. Where do you work?"

"Mid-town. So my commute is fairly easy. I'm in advertising. You two should come by my place one night. We have a fantastic Thai restaurant around the corner."

"We'd love to." / "Trey & Scott should come too."

Jack and I speak at the exact same time, and then quickly look at each other. We couldn't be more obvious if we tried.

Hunter notices our exchange and adds, "Sure. We'll have them bring Lori and Patti and make it a date night." He is so on to us. "Leila, did you have fun at your farewell show?"

I chance a glance at Jack. "It was fun and I'm sure you saw how much of an embarrassment I was."

"No you weren't. You are an adorable drunk." Jack admits with a smile. Unable to control myself, I instinctively smile back, until I notice Hunter watching us like a hawk.

"You're very different when you're drunk." Hunter teases.

"Yeah, I've heard that."

After spending some more time chatting with Hunter and Amanda, she reminds him that they need to take off. That means I will soon be here alone with Jack. I'm going to rip him open a new one and then ride him for hours.

Hunter comes closer to give me a hug. "See you tomorrow, Leila." Amanda says a goodbye as well, and they both head towards the door. Hunter suddenly stops and adds, "Be good kids."

Once they are gone, I look over at Jack to see he's grinning like a fool. "Talk and talk? That's what you come up with?" I ask raising my eyebrows. "What the hell?"

308

He laughs and says, "I was just throwing his own words back at him. The night he met Amanda they came up here and she spent the night. The next morning I asked him how it went and he said all they did was *talk and talk.*"

He shrugs and stands to pull me out of my chair. Wrapping his arms around me, he starts sucking on my neck.

"Jack, he could come back, and plus, I'm mad at you." At the same time I turn my head to give him better access. I'm such a freakin' hypocrite.

"What did I do?" He asks in between kisses.

"Um…Can you stop so I can think?" He's driving me wild.

Jack chuckles and steps away. "Ok, what's freaking you out so much?"

"Do you think he…"

"Yep." He moves closer until I push him away. The *what the hell* look he gives me makes me lose it.

"Jack…I…he…I…damn it!" I take two steps, turn back towards him and try again. "He can't know!"

"Can you dial down the crazy please?"

Huffing loudly, I can't respond because he's absolutely right. I'm babbling like a complete lunatic.

He grabs my hand and pulls me towards the couch, sitting me on his lap. "Listen, Hunter could speculate all he wants. He'll ask me and I'll admit nothing, unless you want me to." Shaking my head, he continues, "He'll drive himself crazy with whether we did anything or not. So let him. We will be careful, and after a time, he'll drop it."

Digging his hands into my hair, he lowers my face towards his. "In the meantime, we will be good, unless he isn't around. It is what you want, right?"

"Yes."

"Ok, then we will keep our relationship a secret, for now. But if you change your mind, I'll tell him in a heartbeat."

He would have made a great lawyer, as I immediately forgot what I was worried about. I also forgot I was mad at him, and start making out with him like a teenager…a horny teenager who wants more. He's made me ravenous.

"Now can I show you my room?"

"Yes, please." I would have done it right here on this couch, but I realize that it is daylight, and people could be watching.

Jack drags me by the hand in lightning speed, all the way down the stairs and straight to his room. He opens the door and presents it with a "Ta da…" Giggling as I walk in, I can't see a thing. It's very dark until he flips on a light.

"It looks like the middle of the night in here. Are your windows painted black?"

He walks over and pulls back the blinds. "Room darkening shades. I like it dark. Your room is entirely too sunny."

"I'll get you an eye mask. A pink satin one."

"Funny."

It's a typical guy room. His guitar is propped in the corner. His dresser is littered with change and journals and CD's. There are clothes on the floor in clumps and shoes in the spot where he must have kicked them off. His bed is unmade. There are free weights and a bench in the corner.

"You're a slob."

"I wasn't exactly expecting company when I left here Friday night." He watches me as I walk around the room inspecting things.

"You don't belong to a gym?"

Walking to the weight bench, I sit on the edge and picture a shirtless Jack, lifting weights. The visual instantly turning me on. Noticing my smirk he reads my mind.

"I hate gyms. This way I can work out naked."

"You're lying."

Laughing, he adds, "Ok, not completely naked. I wouldn't want to hurt myself."

Shaking my head, I smirk at his comment. Neither would I.

I move to his dresser to pick up a framed picture of his parents and sister.

"You all should be super-models." I say staring at the picture. It's not fair that one family can be so gorgeous.

He comes up behind me and wraps his arms around my waist, resting his chin on my shoulder. "Looks aren't everything. They are really good people. My mom and sister are saints. They both keep me grounded." Once I replace the picture, he turns me around and gives me a look that says he is done with the small talk.

Jack and I spend hours rediscovering each other in his dark messy room. As he holds me in his arms, I giggle.

"What?" he asks looking down at me.

"Never saw this coming. I can't believe we are here, when just two days ago you were my boss, who I had a tremendous crush on." I admit.

"You did?" he asks smiling.

"Oh, come on. I acted like a complete idiot the first time I met you and probably every time since. You had to have known." I say incredulously.

He laughs and admits, "You didn't act like an idiot. It was more like a deer caught in headlights." He kisses my nose just as I wrinkle it.

"Such a great, *flattering* visual." I say, moving to lie on his chest. I run my hand across the smattering of hair he has in the center of his chest and I start tracing his tattoo with the tip of my finger. I move his arm so I can see it better. "This really is cool."

We shift so we are facing each other. "Can I convince you to get a mini version?"

"Um, no…"

"Oh come on. How sexy would a mini version look right here?" He traces a spot over my left breast, then bends to kiss it. "Or here." He traces a spot on my left hip, then bends to kiss that. "Or here." His finger moves to a spot on my inner thigh very close to my sex. "My name here would look so hot." He bends to kiss that spot, lingering there longer than the others. He positions himself between my legs. "Yep…this is my favorite spot." He bends and sucks the skin of my inner thigh between his lips, until he leaves a mark and then moves to my center to torture me with his tongue.

"You are very convincing." I gasp out while he continues his torments.

He brings me to an immediate orgasm. Then starts again and doesn't stop until I lay limp. He kisses his way up my body to my breast, stopping there for a few seconds then moving up to my lips. He immediately takes me, sinking into me slowly. I enthusiastically respond by arching my back to get him deeper. I can't get enough of him, and the thought terrifies me.

Lying together, entwined in his bed, I ask a question I've been dying to know the answer to. "Jack?"

"Yeah, babe?" I instantly forget what I'm about to say. He's called me babe before but it still causes my breath to catch in my throat. I reach over and stroke his hair. It's so soft to the touch. He smiles and leans into my hand. Blinking, I then remember what I was about to ask. This man makes me feel like I have A.D.D.

"Have you slept with Trini?"

Jack turns his head to look into my eyes. His pause confirms my suspicions.

"I thought so."

"Babe, Trin and I have a very convenient relationship. We are really just good friends."

"Who screw."

"I care about Trini, but I don't love her. She knows that and she feels the same about me."

My heavy sigh causes him to frown. "Are you upset?"

"No. Yes."

He leans down and kisses me gently. "There is nothing for you to be upset about. I've told Trini how I feel about you."

He did? His admission softens the blow, just a tad.

"Can I ask you another question?"

"Anything."

"Did you ever sleep with Jennifer?"

There isn't even a second pause when he says, "Absolutely not." I look back at him and am instantly relieved because that would upset me more than anything. He watches me intently. "Why?"

"I was just curious. She is very possessive of you and not in an agent-client kind of way. I needed to know if you two have a history, since she hates me."

He reaches over to stroke my cheek. "She does not hate you. Jennifer is just ruthless when she wants to achieve her goal. She wants us to reach fame, and will make sure nothing stops us. Don't take it personally." He kisses me, and pulls away to add, "Besides, she's really not my type."

"You have a type?" I ask surprised.

"Yeah, I have a type. Why?"

"Well I've witnessed Mr. Sex on Legs flirting with all types…brunettes, blonds, redheads, even Goth chicks. It's hard to believe you have *a* type."

"Mr. Sex on Legs? Is that my nickname?" He's clearly amused.

"One of many." I respond purposefully ignoring his gaze. He lays me back onto the bed and starts a torturous interrogation with his lips. He starts to nibble on my neck. When he is doing this to me I would confess to a murder without question, and I think he knows it.

"What are the others?"

"So what's your type?" I ignore his question, trying to steer the subject back to that. I need to know if he prefers blondes. Maybe I don't want to know. That could cause a lot of agonizing for no reason.

"I asked first. What are my other nicknames?"

"Let's see…mmmm…Um… so there is Mr. Sex on Legs… mmmm…and Mr. Rock-Star-Sex-God Extraordinaire…um…Mr. Pretty…oh, and then Panty-Soaking-Rock-God." This one makes him smile as he lifts his head to look at me.

He resumes his attack on my neck. "Any others?" He is driving me insane.

"Man whore." I breathe out.

He stops and looks at me. "Man whore?"

Uh oh…

"Yes, um, you earned that title the night I saw you on the roof with the fake-boob twins." I answer, sounding a touch apologetic. I look into his eyes, and see he is hurt by that nickname. I guess it's a sore subject, which doesn't sit well with me.

He moves away and lies on his back, staring up at the ceiling, folding his arms behind his head.

"Hey, I was mad at you, and extremely jealous." I grab his chin to turn his head towards mine. "How many have there been?" Do I really want to know this?

"I don't have an exact count."

"That bad, huh?" I laugh out yet Jack doesn't look amused. "It doesn't matter. Jack, I don't care about your past, ok?" I bend to plant a tender kiss on his lips. He responds hesitantly, and then I slowly feel him coming around by the way his lips start moving over mine.

"How many for you?"

"Three, counting you."

Jack sits up in shock. "Three? Have you been living in a convent your entire adult life?"

"No. I don't sleep with men unless I care about them. There have only been two others."

Jack pushes his hand through his hair, sitting quietly, lost in thought. "Damn."

"So, you have a type?" I ask again trying to get his frame of mind back to where it was before I ruined it with my big mouth.

"Yes, I do." He repeats, turning on his side to look at me.

"Is Lori your type?"

"Lori?"

"Yes. The first time you met, I was convinced you would be a couple."

"What?" Here goes my big mouth again.

315

"Weren't you into Lori?"

"No and NO. I was being nice to Lori. That night, you captivated me. Your performance with Matt, watching you in your own environment surrounded by your friends, I couldn't stop staring at you. Didn't you feel it?"

"No. I was so nervous you were there, I zoned out a lot that night. I was convinced you were flirting with Lori and invited us to your party to hook up with her."

Jack leans in and kisses me softly. "Leila, you couldn't be more wrong."

"Am I your type?" I ask nervously.

"Ugh, no, you I find repulsive." He responds with a very serious face. Then he puts me on my back and dips to take my nipple in between his lips to emphasis his disgust.

"Jerk." I say while pushing him onto his back. He laughs and takes me with him, positioning me over his body. He then sits up so I can straddle his hips.

"You are most definitely my type." He says seriously. "Baby, I adore you." He buries his hands into my hair and pulls me closer to kiss me sweetly on my lips.

Oh my god...he *adores* me!

Our kiss quickly turns into something else. We make love again, but this time it's a bit more hurried and fervent.

Exactly five minutes later, we are both physically exhausted, panting, lying flat on our backs trying to catch our breath. I can't get enough of him. I want nothing more than to stay in this bed and having more mind-blowing sex, for the rest of our lives. He turns on his side to look at me. His hand instantly finds my breast, as he stares at me. My body is a magnet for his hands, as is his for mine.

Still lying on my back, I am totally spent and fight desperately to keep my eyes open.

I collide with a warm body as I turn mine, causing me to sit up in confusion, looking around the room.

"Hello there. You passed out on me."

"I did? How long was I out?"

"Thirty minutes maybe?" He laughs when he sees my face.

"What's so funny?"

"I fucked you unconscious." He is very proud of himself, and it makes me laugh too.

"Yes, it seems you did, rock star." I lean over to kiss him for his accomplishment, and he tries to pull me closer.

"What time is it? What if Hunter comes home?" I ask, starting to freak-out.

I have no idea what time it is. During one of our love sessions, his phone buzzed a few times in the pocket of his jeans that were still lying in a lump where he removed them earlier. We both ignored it every time it buzzed.

Another round of buzzing causes me to ask, "Don't you think you should answer that?"

"Nope." He simply says while kissing my shoulder. He is behind me, my back flush to his chest. He has both arms are around me and our legs are intertwined.

"Jack, maybe the guys are worried. Or worst yet, maybe it's Jennifer."

"Whatever anyone wants, it can wait until tomorrow. It's probably about the photo shoot Tuesday."

"Photo shoot?"

"Oh, yeah. We have a photo shoot Tuesday for the album cover." He says shrugging.

"When were you going to tell me this?" I ask, my voice high and pitchy.

"Um…now?"

"Thanks."

He looks up at me and notices the panic on my face. "What?"

"Why do I have to be on the album cover? Can't you just have the band's name or something?" I ask.

"You're gorgeous…why can't you see that?" Rolling my eyes at him, his tone gets snippy. "You are going to be the best fucking thing on that album cover!"

"Don't yell at me."

He turns me around so we are facing each other. "I'm sorry I yelled at you. But I meant what I said." Jack kisses his way from my lips to my ear to my exposed breast, pulling my nipple in between his lips, swirling his tongue around my peak. This always seems to be his method of choice to initiate more sex.

"Um, what were we talking about?"

Smiling against my skin, he kisses a path down my body. Just as he makes it to my stomach, it growls very loudly. He looks up revealing his beautiful CCDS smile.

"It sounds like I need to feed you?"

I personally could care less about food, especially now…but my stomach betrays me by growling again. I look down at him and shrug.

He kisses it and says, "You are so freaking cute. We can go out. I can show you the merits of Brooklyn."

"Ok…I'm starving." I admit. Also, I really fear Hunter walking in on us at any moment.

***

It's the middle of the night and I can smell him on my sheets. It's such torture, causing me to toss and turn. I want him here with me and he isn't. He's in his own apartment in Brooklyn, and I miss him terribly.

After we finally made it out of his bed, and out of his apartment, he took me to a quiet little place nearby for dinner. We talked about how difficult it was going to be now that we've started this. Well I talked about how difficult it was going to be, and he kept assuring me we could handle it. I admitted to him I was not a good actress and just thinking about pretending had my stomach in knots.

He broke it down for me. We can avoid that and tell them. Otherwise, if we must keep it a secret, well Trey pays attention to anyone but himself so there is no need to worry about him. Scott is too shy and embarrassed to bring anything up so there is no need to worry about him. Hunter thinks what he thinks so there is nothing we can do about him.

Makes sense…

Jennifer is extremely intuitive. She, I worry about. Dylan is also going to be a challenge. Jack reluctantly admitted that I needed to act the same way with him. I never told Jack that he and I have had a few dinners together or that I feel that Dylan is interested in me. I don't know why I kept it from Jack. I guess I worry he would do something stupid like show him we are together, just to stake his claim.

Jack made me promise to call him when I got home. He kept me on the phone for a very long time. It helped to hear his voice, as he said all the things he wanted to do to me, but it was a poor substitute. We finally hung up around two am, after deciding to meet at the studio in the morning.

I should have been able to fall fast asleep. But when I see daylight filtering through my curtains, I throw the covers off and get out of bed frustrated. It's still way too early, but I can't keep lying here thinking, and sleep is definitely not presenting itself. It's not surprising, given all the things I have swirling in my head. Remembering intimate moments with Jack kept me up half the time. The other half was consumed by thoughts of Evan, and whether I should confide in him.

Normally I would without question, but I haven't been completely honest with him regarding my attraction and feelings for Jack. I also feel it would be very selfish of me to dump my problems with all the crap he is dealing with at the moment. I know he has plans to see Lizzy this week, and I really hope they hit it off. Lizzy would be just what Evan needs right now.

The only good thing about my insomnia is that I am able to catch up on the laundry and cleaning I neglected this past weekend. I've practically put in a full day's work by most people's standards, by the time I leave my apartment to drive to the studio.

Since we have gotten so much done the first couple of weeks, the band's starting hour has been getting later and later. On most days they stroll in around eleven. If Jennifer isn't around, they'll show up past noon. Jack cuts them slack, sometimes. Usually, he curses them out for a few minutes. It annoyed me having to wait around until the three princes graced us with their presence so Jack started texting me with an estimated time of arrival. Today's text said to come at nine.

It's a little after nine, when I park my car in the lot. A new text message comes through on my phone as I walk to the studio.

where r u?

walking into the studio.

good.

He must be here already. I plug in the lock combination code, and I notice lights on in the hall. As I lock the door behind me, warm lips attach to my neck and muscular arms wrap around my waist.

"You're late." He walks us forward towards the studio.

"No one else is here? Jennifer may show up any minute." I say as he pulls me into the dark room. He flips the lights and closes the door behind him, then decides to lock the door and turn the lights back off.

"She has to meet with the photographer today to review wardrobe."

"Wait, I didn't have to be here at nine?"

"No, I wanted you to be here at nine."

"Oh…"

We are going to have sex in the studio? This is going to give me a visual I am sure to clench from every time I think about it.

The only lights illuminating the room are the two EXIT signs above the doors. He pushes me into a corner, where nobody can see if they were to be at the door.

Jack starts sucking on my neck as he pushes his hands under my shirt. "I can't get enough of how you taste." He says moving lips until they slant over mine. I love kissing Jack, and can make out with him for hours. Usually his kisses set my crotch on fire, so I haven't been able to test that theory and even now I'm already reaching for the button of his jeans.

"You missed me too, I see." He unbuttons my shorts and slips his hand into my panties.

The second his fingers reach me, I forget what I was doing prior. My hand is still on the zipper of his jeans, but I'm not able to move it. He traces a line through my sex and circles around my most sensitive spot. Throwing my head back, I clutch at his shirt while I pant from the sensations he is causing in my body. He slowly slips inside of me, bending to kiss me simultaneously. He mimics the same patterns his fingers are making below with his tongue in my mouth. I can do nothing but pant open-mouthed, while still clutching his shirt in my grip.

He brings me to an intense orgasm. Having to break our kiss because I am gasping for air, he slowly pulls his hand out of my panties to suck on his fingers. "Like I said, I can't get enough of how you taste." His admission makes my body instantly throb and I forget the severe orgasm I just had.

This man is going to kill me.

I continue with what I was doing before he distracted me, and lower the zipper on his jeans. Firmly I take hold of him as he lowers my shorts down my legs. He lifts me and sits me on to a stool in the corner. Standing before me, he pushes in one inch at a time.

"Jack…faster." I say in between pants. He smiles and complies. It isn't long until I feel another orgasm and I wrap my legs around his body to hold him inside of me. He buries his face in my neck and groans as I feel his release.

"Fuck…fuck! You feel so good." His voice is throaty and raw. "You are going to be the death of me."

"Death by orgasm…sign you up." I gasp.

He laughs and gives me a sweet kiss. "You're right."

By the time the boys stroll in, Jack and I are sitting at a table having coffee and chatting. After the guys finish with their normal morning arguments of whatever the topic is for the day, we start recording our last few songs for the album. It becomes an exhausting day since Jack is being relentless in the amount of work he wants to get done. We still have a lot of time before our tour begins, but the engineers need to mix and cut each song, which will take some time.

Jack acts totally normal and teases me as usual. I caught Hunter watching us a few times, but other than that I didn't notice anyone else letting on they know what we have been up to.

Our tryst is all I can think about the entire day. It fuels my performance and adds sensuality to our duets and my back-ups. Jack smiles knowingly when Jennifer says, "Well Leila, no need to re-record that one, you were spot on."

"Thank you."

At the end of our day Jennifer makes an announcement. "Make sure you are all at the photographers at nine sharp. I know this is the middle of the night for you guys but suck it up…especially you, Trey."

He gives Jennifer a look that clearly says, "Bite me."

Jack secretly told me the session doesn't start until ten, but Jennifer made him promise to not let the boys know that small detail.

As I'm gathering my things to get ready to leave, Scott says to Jack, "Let's go to Granite. Trini has been asking for you." I sneak a quick peek at Jack and he stiffens slightly.

"Oh, I don't know. I'm not in the mood." He shoves sheet music into his bag.

Scott asks, "Do you have other plans with the brunette from…"

"You don't know her." Jack cuts Scott off before he can finish his sentence. He looks at me and adds, "I'll see you guys at the shoot tomorrow. Don't be late." Then he strolls out of the studio.

Scott turns to Hunter. "He's such a dog."

Hunter nods and looks over at me. He catches me biting on my lip and I quickly turn my back to grab my bag.

A few minutes later I say my own good-bye. The guys respond, which I barely hear. I can't get out of the studio fast enough.

Was Jack serious? I'm a little stunned at what I just heard and it stings more than I'd like to admit. He has a date tonight? What the fuck? I get that he has to act normal in front of the guys because it was my idea after all, but he could have warned me that we would be continuing with our private lives. He never claimed to be exclusive. Even so, there is no way I'll be ok with him sleeping around while he's sleeping with me.

I take a deep breath and walk to the lot where my car is parked. As I approach Bessie, I see Jack leaning against the driver's side door and it catches me off guard.

"Hey." I say, slowly walking towards him.

"Hey." He grabs my bag from my hand.

"What are you doing here?"

"Um, I packed some things. I didn't know if today would work as I planned, but since it has, I'd like to come home with you tonight."

"You're a good actor. You had me convinced you had plans."

He pushes my hair off my shoulder and touches my ear lobe. "You should have known it was an act." When he kisses me, I drop my car keys.

Laughing, he picks them up and says, "I'll drive."

Chapter 22- Jack

"Damn woman, this is delicious." I point out as I scoff down my third helping of penne with vodka sauce.

"I don't cook a lot but I can make this well." She answers with a smile. "I've had a lot of practice since the guys love this dish. It's all they want me to make for them."

"It's really good. I'm stuffed." I push my plate away. "I'll clean up."

She looks at me suspiciously. "You'll clean up? Why do I feel this is gonna cost me?"

"I don't know what you are talking about." I grab our plates to bring them to the kitchen. She follows and watches me like I'm crazy.

"What?"

"Do you know you have to use soap, rock star?" She says as she grabs a dishtowel to dry.

"Smartass." I say as I flick water at her. Giggling, she hides behind her dishtowel. Not being able to resist, I turn the sink hose on her full blast. Her screams make her that much more endearing as she hides in the corner.

"I love the sound of your laugh." I also love the way she looks down when she is embarrassed. I love the way she wrinkles her nose when she doesn't like something I say. I love the way she mumbles in her sleep. She has said my name a couple of times already, and I have to stop myself from waking her up to devour her.

I want nothing more than to do that right now. As she stands in her kitchen, her t-shirt clinging to her breasts, leaving nothing to the imagination,

I am throbbing with need. I lean forward, tugging her towards me by her wet t-shirt and bringing her wet body up against mine.

"Jack, I'm drenched!"

"Just the way I like you."

Her heated gaze focuses on my lips. We manically remove each other's clothing and literally try to consume each other. I can't get enough of her. She's like a drug to me. Just one hit causes me to spiral out of control.

I lift her and carry her to her bed, devouring her mouth on the way.

Wasting no time, I drag finger up her leg and straight to her clit. The process causes her to shiver. My fingers stroke and caress her slowly as I take her nipple into my mouth. I mimic the motion of my tongue on her nipple with my fingers below and I sense her building. Her hands holding my wrist in place as she moves against it.

"No… not yet." I say removing my hand.

"Jack, please."

I slowly kiss my way down her body and she grabs my shoulders to pull me up. Shaking my head, I continue my path. "I need to taste you." She surrenders and lies back allowing me to reach where I need to be.

I bend her knees and open her up to me. I place a single kiss on her, causing her to inhale sharply. She's so smooth, so soft. Dragging my tongue over her, I taste her like it's the first time. She fists the blanket beneath her hands as I try to consume her savagely.

"Oh god…Jack. Please, please." She pleads as I pull away. I could taste her for hours, but I need to be in her, looking at her when we connect.

She huffs in frustration, and I smile against her skin as I slowly move up over her body. I lace our fingers together and lift our hands above her head. I'm positioned at her entrance, and I slowly sink into her. She closes her eyes, but I can't look away from her beautiful face.

"Open them." I command as I move slowly in and out of her body. She feels like heaven. She clenches around me and I'm fighting to remain in control.

She finally opens her eyes, and they are moist with unshed tears. I kiss her and grip her fingers tightly with my own. The sensation is unbearable, and I'm quickly building. I won't be able to hold off any longer.

"Leila, please get there. I can't hold back." She wraps her legs around me in an effort to get me deeper. I pull out and slam back in, causing her to gasp. Removing my hand from one of hers to slide it down between our bodies, I begin to touch her where we are connected.

She pants my name and I feel her coming apart beneath me. I watch her face as I bring her to the edge of reason. Her shuddering body immediately causes me to let go as well. I look directly into her eyes as I moan with my own release. Our orgasms roll on wave after wave. I still feel her tremors as she continues to clench around me.

Once my body stills, I can't look away, pull out, or move, afraid of breaking the connection. We remain this way until our pants subside, and our breathing returns to normal. I then pull her into my arms and hold her tightly until we both fall asleep.

The next morning, I wake first. Watching her sleeping so peacefully simply leaves me breathless. Her long brown hair is fanned out around her naked torso, with one perfect pink nipple peeking through. Not being able to help myself, I slowly skim a fingertip across it, and it instantly pebbles beneath my touch. Even in her sleep, she reacts to my touch…as I do to hers. She stirs slightly, her tongue poking out to lick her perfect lips. I can watch her for hours. But I really should wake her, though, since we need to start getting ready to leave for the photographers.

Running my fingertip over her nipple again, she stirs but doesn't wake. Bending, I pull her pebbled nipple between my lips, watching as she slowly moans and opens her eyes.

"Mmm, nice wake up call."

"Like that?"

"Mmm…yes."

"We need to get up sleepyhead. It's getting late."

She rolls away from me. "Can't we stay here, and skip the photo shoot. I'll make it worth your while."

"Nice try."

She moves over my body, kisses me erotically, causing my excitement to instantly grow. "You're playing a dirty game, Miss Marino." I smack her on her butt. "Time to shower."

"I don't wanna."

Jumping off the bed, I walk over to my jeans, still laying crumpled on the floor, and bend over to fish out my phone.

"Well we hafta."

Turning, I see Leila on her stomach, kicking her feet behind her in the air, her head on her hands, blatantly molesting me with her gaze.

"You like?" I ask, raising my eyebrows suggestively.

Nodding, while grinning like a fool, she says, "Uh huh."

"And you say I'm insatiable." Walking back towards the bed, I grab her hands and pull her up until she is up on her knees and our bodies are pressed up against each other. Bending, I pull her bottom lip in between my teeth and tug.

"Shower time." Turning, I reach behind my back to grab her thighs and pull her up to give her a piggyback ride. Squealing, she wraps her arms around my neck as I carry her into the bathroom. Setting her down long enough to turn on the water, I take her hand, helping her climb into the shower. As she watches me, I join her under the shower's steady stream.

"I thought we were late."

"We are. I'm saving time…showering together and making love to you all at the same time. Smart idea, right?"

"Brilliant."

Standing behind her, I wrap my arms around her waist, my cock is pressing into her lower back. Pulling her hips towards me, I then reach for her hands. Entwining our fingers, I raise them up against the wall in front of us. Positioning myself, I slowly slide in.

It's way too soon before we climax together, our hands tightly entwined. Our pants are competing with the steady sound of water hitting our bodies. My pounding heart is pressed up against her back while her head rests on my chest. This is exactly where I want to be…forever.

Fifteen minutes later, as we are hurriedly getting dressed and ready for the shoot, I notice we move around each other like we've been together for years. It's strange. I'm so comfortable with her. I would never have imagined feeling like this with anyone. It wasn't something I wanted or craved. Now that I've experienced this with Leila, I never want to go back to live the way I used to. It sickens me to think about all the women I've been with. They didn't care for me, and I sure didn't care for them. Except for Trini…she always has my back. I should call her. I haven't spoken to her besides a few texts since the night of my party. She will be happy that I'm happy.

Moving towards her, I wrap my arms around her as she tries to get dressed. "Ok…out! Now!" She says, pointing to the door.

"You're no fun."

Sitting in her favorite chair, I'm waiting for her to finish getting ready. I'm totally lost in thought when my phone buzzes with Hunter's name on the screen. I can ignore it, which would probably send him into a panic thinking I'm passed out at some chick's house sleeping right through our appointment. It's annoying, because I've never given him any reason to have to check up on me or keep tabs on me. Whatever, he's in manager mode and all.

I decide it's not worth the trouble and I answer my phone.

"Yes?"

"Just making sure you are alive." He replies. "Where are you?"

"I'm on my way." I know what he meant...he meant, who am I with?

"Ok, just double-checking. See you there." He says hanging up.

"So annoying." I mutter aloud.

"Who?" Leila asks as she walks into the room. She looks fantastic. She is wearing a dress that shows off her tan legs, her hair is loose and down, she looks so good.

"You look really nice." I mention appreciatively. She smiles and comes to sit next to me on the couch. "Thanks. Who's annoying?" she asks again.

"Oh…Hunter. He's checking up on me and it's annoying." I kiss her cheek. "Ready?" She nods and we leave her apartment.

She is very quiet on the drive to the city. I can guess it's because she is nervous about this photo shoot. Eventually I grasp her hand and tell her to stop stressing.

"I'm not stressing."

"You are an awful liar." I admit squeezing her hand.

At five minutes to nine, I pull up in front of the building to drop Leila off. "I'll go park your car, this way you can go inside well before I do."

Just as she is about to get out of the car I see Dylan walking towards the building. I grab her hand again and she looks over at me confused.

"Dylan." I say nodding towards the building. She gasps and turns her body so her back is to the door.

"Oh crap. Do you think he saw us?"

I watch Dylan head through the doors and shake my head. "No, he didn't. That was a close call though." She nods with relief. "Go ahead, I'll see you upstairs."

She turns and opens her door. I watch her look left then right, and bolt to the front doors. I hate this…it shouldn't be like this. I should be able to proudly be with her and not have to hide. I need to convince her that if no one else, our inner circle should know about us. There is no reason we should hide.

***

Ok, this fucking sucks!

We have been manhandled, our hair has been done, our faces made up, and we were forced to try on a dozen different things until the photographer approved. We are all dressed casually in t-shirts and jeans. After an exhausting argument, thank God the photographer finally allowed Trey to keep on his shades.

The said photographer is named Pierre and is very eccentric. He has a small army of staff at his beck and call. He keeps fiddling with my hair and I want to slug him. We are now sitting in a studio waiting for Leila, and I'm done.

"That chick put lipstick on me. This sucks ass." Hunter says wiping his lips with the back of his hand.

"It's necessary for the camera to capture your faces properly." Jennifer explains as she paces the room again. She is getting on my nerves.

"Can you please sit down? You're driving me crazy." She scowls and sits in a chair.

I don't mean to be so harsh, but I'm in a bad mood and I'm not hiding it well. My day started out great, until we were almost seen by Dylan. Then as I'm parking the car, distracted by thoughts of hiding my relationship with Leila, I answered my cell without checking to see who was calling. Big mistake!

Jessa, my high school girlfriend was calling to let me know she would be seeing our first show. She asked to see me afterwards and I told her absolutely not. She said one way or another she would see me. We were on the phone all of two minutes, when I wanted to put my fist through a wall. The phone calls and texts have been coming daily, and I've been ignoring them. I can't stand it anymore. I have no doubt that she wants something.

Hearing a commotion in the corner of the room, I snap back to reality and remember where I am. What is taking so long? We are sitting here for almost an hour and we are all getting really cranky.

The door finally opens and my mouth drops.

Holy shit!

Leila stops at the door and she doesn't look happy at all. Every person in the room is staring at her and it's making her uncomfortable, as well as me.

I slowly walk over to her and ask, "What's wrong?"

"I look ridiculous." She agonizes.

She doesn't, of course. She looks fucking hot. They have her in a dark, red leather lace-up thing and the tightest pair of jeans that leave nothing to the imagination. On her feet are black fuck me pumps. Her hair is wild and looks like she just had sex. Her eyes are smoky grey. He lips are red, but not a trampy red, more like she has been kissed for hours, red. I am completely turned on.

I shake my head and refute, "You look unbelievable Leila...trust me." Even so, her expression says that she wants to die.

Dylan comes over. "Leila, you look great." He says rubbing her back to comfort her. I clench my jaw at the sight of his hand on her bareback.

Jennifer stalks over without sympathy. "What is the problem here?"

"Sorry, they kept changing my outfits and hair until they were satisfied."

"Relax Jennifer, we're ready now." Thankfully, Jen walks away in search of Pierre.

Looking at Leila, I tease, "Stop biting your lip."

As Pierre makes last minute lighting adjustments, my band-mates openly gawk at the girl I'm in love with. This is not helping my mood. Her pants are so tight that you can see the smooth curve of her ass. Instinctively I stand between Leila and their line of sight. Trey has the balls to look around me.

The photographer arranges us in front of the backdrop. He takes dozens of shots, moving us and facing us in different directions. I look down at Leila at one point when he is adjusting his lights and ask if she's ok.

"I will be when this is over. My boobs are sweating."

I am so surprised by her comment that I let out a loud snort, prompting the entire room to look at me. I turn towards her and she shrugs nonchalantly.

The last picture, Pierre had me remove my shirt. The guys are behind me to my right. Leila is pressed up against me on my left while whispering in my ear, and my head is turned away from her seductively.

Pierre yells "Perfection. That's a wrap." At once all his minions scatter in different directions.

I feel Leila visibly relax next to me. "You did great." I say rubbing her arms. Then I bend to whisper into her ear, "See if you can keep this outfit."

I move over to Jennifer, before I can get myself into trouble and pretend I have questions regarding this week's schedule. From the corner of my eye, I see Dylan walking up to Leila, causing my hackles to rise. Watching from across the room, Leila smiles at something he says. They stand and chat for a few minutes, when he leans in and says something to make her laugh. She quickly glances over at me and turns back to Dylan before he walks out. Giving me a shy smile, she then turns to walk out of the room herself.

I need to talk to her. I haven't heard a word Jennifer said for the last five minutes. She finally shuts up and says, "I'll see you tomorrow. I have a meeting with Bobby."

I walk over to Hunter and ask, "Jennifer has a meeting with Bobby, are you heading over to the studio?"

He grabs his jacket. "Yeah, Scott has his van. Are you coming?"

"I'm going to drive down with Leila so I can talk to her." I say innocently.

"Ok. See you later." He pats my back and leaves me dumbfounded. What? No words of wisdom?

I leave the room in search of Leila, and finally find her in a small dressing room by herself. "Can I come in?"

She is sitting in front of a vanity staring into space. She is back in her regular clothes, her face is clean, and her hair is brushed. She must have bolted to this room and stripped down immediately. As hot as she looked earlier, this is who she is and she is beautiful.

"Sure." She says looking over at me in the doorway.

"Did your boobs cool off?" I ask as I close the door behind me and walk over to her. I put my hands on her shoulders and look at her reflection in the mirror.

"Wouldn't you like to know?" She glances up at me in the mirror. "Well that was a bit embarrassing. I guess I need to get used to people gawking?"

"Based on how you look, prepare for lots of gawking."

"Yay. I can't wait." She says with sarcasm dripping in her words. Nodding toward a bag that sits on a chair, she adds, "They said I can keep it."

"Well yay for me."

She suddenly gets serious and frowns. "Um, Dylan asked me out to dinner tonight." She looks up and starts biting on her bottom lip.

"Why?"

"Because he had fun the last time we went out?" she responds with a question. She comes closer when she notices my clenched fists. "Listen, he's just a friend. It would look weird if I refused his invite. You said yourself to act like I normally do. The Leila I was a week ago would have said yes."

"Remind me why we are keeping us a secret?"

"Because you want to make me happy?"

She's right.

Fuck.

"Oh, yeah...I forgot." I pull her into my arms and kiss her head. "Its just dinner, right?" She nods quietly.

"Ok. Its just dinner...nothing else." I repeat, more for my own sake.

Chapter 23-Leila

Life has been a whirlwind since our photo shoot. The album cover has been chosen, the track order has been set, and the songs are cut and mixed. Our tour kicks off in a few days and I'm a bundle of nervous energy.

Jack and I have stolen time together whenever we could, but it's been very hard since we've been so busy. He has continuously voiced we could spend nights together if we just told Hunter. I almost caved a few times during the throws of passion, but I'm just not ready. I don't know what's keeping me from going public.

Actually I do know. I don't want to be judged…especially by Hunter or Evan. Jack had a very active sex life before I came along. He promised he hasn't been with anyone else and I believe him. I just can't process in my brain why he would want to go from having a hot girl almost daily to stolen moments with me. That's just what they are - moments.

I try to tell myself that's a stupid mentality, but unfortunately his track record speaks volumes. What if he gets bored and moves on? If our relationship was common knowledge, even if just to Hunter or the guys, and he was to end it to go back to his philandering ways, the humiliation at this point in our success would be fatal to me.

As far as going public to the rest of the world, again it's stupid, but if I read one negative comment on the Internet claiming I got job because I was screwing Jack, it would be even worst. That's not why I got the job and I know the truth, but reviews like that could kill my career before it even got started.

That being said, I love being with him. I love everything from having a quiet dinner, to rehearsing, to having sex…whatever it is we are doing. Our time together goes way too fast, and it always leaves me wanting more.

Dylan and I have been have gone out to dinner a few more times during these past few weeks. It's only platonic. I assured Jack that we were just friends. I did not mention that Dylan alluded to wanting more than friendship. That little tidbit wouldn't help matters.

Friends or not, I truthfully enjoy his company. It's easy and comfortable between us. During the times I'm left with nothing but my own thoughts, I can sometimes visualize a relationship with Dylan. If Jack weren't in the picture, Dylan would absolutely be someone I could be with. It's not fair to any man I meet from here on. As long as Jack walks on this earth, he is and will always be my weakness.

I've been spending a lot of time with my dad and some time with Evan these past weeks. On rare occasions, Evan would join us for brunch. There is still a strain between them but it's definitely improved. I hope Evan will make the effort to become closer to dad again, while I'm gone.

Evan has seen Lizzy a few times. He gushes about her and I've never seen my friend acting this way over a girl. I asked Jack if Lizzy has mentioned Evan, and he said that it seems she is into him as well, but Lizzy has priorities and her career means a lot to her. She has worked hard and will not have anything interfere with that. Evan mentioned the same information to me as well, so I was glad to hear she is being honest with him.

Cliffhangers have been playing bars in the city one day almost every week. Lori has been booking them on nights the guys are off from The Zone. She said she wants to pick her battles with Sal and only when a once in a lifetime opportunity presents itself, will she insist on having the weekend off for the boys. Lori has proven to be perfect for them.

According to Lori, she and Trey have been having a "fucking fantastic time". She isn't looking for a relationship at this point in her life. Her obsession with Matt helped her to realize that. She wasted too much time on him. She wants Cliffhangers to be a success, and she wants to prove this is her purpose. Trey has been a nice distraction. The orgasms are off the charts…again, Lori's words. She said they both decided to end things during our tour. She feels it's best not to pine away for a rock star while he is off crossing the country and she'll be too busy with her career. I agreed with her. Besides, I have no doubt that she will find someone else in a heartbeat, especially now that she has moved past Matt. I also feel if it's meant to be with Trey, it will happen once he gets back.

Dylan's assistant Cathy has been a godsend. Since exchanging cell numbers, she and I have been chatting often. I love the fact that the guys have to go through Dylan, but I just need to call my newfound friend Cathy to get what I need. She requested a list of *must haves* from all of us so she could properly stock the bus. She also has my *personal* list and said not to worry about anything and she would take care of it. I sent her a large bouquet of flowers to thank her for all she has done for me these last few weeks. She argued that she hasn't even begun to help me yet, but I quickly told her she has tremendously already.

Yesterday we were taken to the tour buses so we could get an idea on living conditions and storage space. This was quite an experience. We were in the bus all of ten minutes and the four hulking men I'll be living with were making me feel claustrophobic.

There is a living area in the front of the bus, directly behind the drivers. It contains a u-shaped booth that could seat four. Directly across is a long couch with a TV mounted on the wall in the opposite corner. The kitchen area has a small sink, a microwave, coffee maker, and four cabinets, two above and two below. I opened one of the cabinets to find it filled with boxes of Fruit loops.

"What's with all the Fruit loops?" I asked Jack who was sitting watching me explore.

He shakes his head and says "Friggin' Hunter has the diet of a five year old." I laughed out loud as I opened another cabinet to reveal Pop Tarts and Blow Pops. I do thankfully see my pretzels, yogurts and Diet Cokes in the fridge. These are my only must haves in life. There is a single serve coffee maker on the counter, and at least ten boxes of coffee k-cups squeezed into one of the other cabinets. I look over at Jack and he shrugs.

The bathroom could be compared to that of an airplane bathroom, only with a small stall shower in the corner. Under the sink is a cabinet with removable bins that are labeled with our names. This is where we could store our personals. When I took a look inside the cabinet, I cringed. I wasn't off the mark when I worried where I would hide my tampons.

A curtain separates the living space from the bunks. There four on each side, each containing a little nook to hold personals, a drawer below the mattress, a built in light above, and a very flimsy curtain for privacy. At the back of the bus is one small bedroom. The whole room consists of a full size bed and a built in closet on one side. We will all have to share this one closet. Our suitcases would be stored under the bus in the luggage compartment.

The bed discussion has been an uncomfortable one. The guys were trying to diplomatically create a schedule. During their argument Jack threw me a heated look. Later that day, he tried to convince me once again of the benefits of exposing our relationship to the guys, a bedroom to ourselves being the latest one.

Physically, I am completely ready to leave. I've forwarded my mail, made a set of keys to my apartment for Evan and stored Bessie safely in my dad's garage. I've cleaned out closets, cabinets and drawers to get rid of anything I didn't need. I am even somewhat packed. It's hard to fit everything you could possibly need in one suitcase. I've pulled things out and replaced them, only to put them back dozens of times. The one thing Jack insisted I take was my photo shoot outfit. He wants me to wear it on stage opening night and I'm not entirely comfortable with that. I do have it packed, but I'll need a lot of convincing or alcohol to sport that outfit on stage. Those jeans are so tight I could barely walk.

So now I have nothing left to do before we leave, but think. Mentally, I am not ready for this tour. This has been my dilemma since joining DL, because I'm not sure I'll ever be ready. We open the tour in two days in the city. We all received a nice strip of tickets for family and friends. All my guys will be there, the girls, my dad, even Sal is coming. To say I have butterflies over this is an understatement. They are more like bats wreaking havoc inside of me. I just need to get through opening night and I feel I'll be ok…I think.

Today I spend a few hours with my dad. He made me lunch and now we are looking at old family pictures. Our few hours go by way too quickly. I already gave him my complete itinerary as well as Jack's cell, Jennifer's cell, Dylan's cell…hell anyone's cell that I will be traveling with.

Dad drops me off at the restaurant where I'm meeting my friends. I hug him super tight and promise that I will text or call as often as I can. He frowns and wells up with tears. I am going to miss him terribly but I know he'll be ok.

"I'll see you tomorrow at the show?"

"Yes, sweetheart. I'll be the one in section three, row two bawling my eyes out."

"Dad…"

Shrugging, he draws me in for one more hug. "I love you, Leila."

"Me too, dad." No sooner do I close the door than he literally peels out of the parking lot, never giving me a second glance.

Once inside, I realize I'm the first one here. While waiting for my late friends, I order a few pitchers of beer and a cheap bottle of house white. Evan arrives a few minutes later and takes a seat beside me.

"Watch my bag I have to run to the ladies room." I quickly kiss him on the cheek and leave the table. As I'm walking back towards our table I hear a familiar ringtone playing from my phone, and I see Evan holding it while smirking.

Oh crap.

I grab the phone away and say, "Hello."

"Hey babe." He replies and my heart stops. It is so sexy when Jack calls me babe or baby, so damn sexy.

"Hi. What's up?" I try to remain as casual as possible under Evan's steady glare.

"How long do you think you'll be out?" He asks.

"Don't know, why?"

"I'm coming over, is that ok? Hunter is out for the night, wanting to spend as much time with Mandi as possible."

"Yes, that's fine. I'll text you that info once I have it." I hope he decodes my words.

There is a two second pause. "Not alone?"

"Nope."

"Got it. Ok, text me when you are done. Give me about an hour warning. Oh and babe, I can't wait to go down on you." He hangs up before I can respond.

Holy shit…

Avoiding Evan's gaze, I hang up and silence my phone. I don't want that ring tone blaring once the rest of the gang arrives. As I start pouring myself a glass of wine, I look up to see Evan gawking at me.

"What?" I ask trying to feign innocence.

"*Tie me down?*" he asks referring to my ring tone.

Crap!

"Spill it, Leila. What's going on?"

"Nothing. You know I've always had a crush on him. It's a joke. I set it as a joke." I casually read my menu.

I blatantly ignore his stare when he scolds, "I hope you know what you are doing. If you want to talk about it then just bring it up." He reaches over and takes my hand from the edge of the menu. "Ok?"

I feel completely torn. I really can't burden him with this right now. Furthermore, I worry what Evan would think of our situation. I never want his opinion of me to change. That may be shallow of me, but he has held me on such a high pedestal that I can't disappoint him. I'm not concerned about his feelings of me being with Jack. I'm more concerned he will think I'm selling myself short and hampering my career.

I nod and lie. "Of course I will."

Evan continues to assess me with concern in his eyes. I'm not sure that he bought my lie. It's shortly after that our friends start filing in. Thankfully this distracts Evan. We are a loud, happy, obnoxious group of seven. As we place our orders and are waiting for the food to arrive, Matt informs us that he is dating a girl named Gina who he met at the bar. So that's why he's been nice to us. I closely watch Lori for any sign of distress and sure enough, she frowns for the briefest of moments and then plasters a sweet smile on her face. She catches me watching and changes the subject to the last bar the guys played in. She's thinks she's so slick but she's not over him.

A little while later, Logan stands and clears his throat. He beams down at Alisa and she jumps up presenting her hand out for all to see. "We got engaged last night!"

Lori and I start screaming with her while the guys congratulate Logan. This is a big deal. They are the first of our group to take such a plunge. The wedding will be in a year, and she wants Lori and me to be bridesmaids.

The group teases Evan over his "phantom girlfriend". They aren't convinced that she exists, and Evan summons for Lori and I to attest the opposite.

Joseph announces he is most definitely still single and may join Match.com soon. By the end of our night, I have laughed so hard my cheeks hurt.

I brought a copy of DL's CD containing a personal handwritten message for each of them. It's not an ego thing or that I'm leaving behind my autograph. It's more of a dedication because I would not be where I am today without them. They took the opportunity to tease me mercilessly. I knew they would.

"Wow Leila, this outfit they have you in will have guys drooling over you." Joe says smirking. He looks up at me, a new lust in his eyes that was never there before. "When you get back, can we go out to dinner or see a movie?"

Shocked by his comment, I'm speechless until he smirks.

"Shut up, you idiot."

"You're so easy to bust."

I chose to drink more wine and ignore them as they continue to laugh at my expense.

I threaten after a few minutes, "That's it, no tickets for any of you."

"Will you be wearing this outfit opening night? Then I'll need a few more for the guys at my gym."

"You're hilarious, Matt."

I hand out the tickets as the backstage passes they will need for the after party. Jennifer is sending us off with a bang.

I know our night is coming to an end, and I quickly text Jack to let him know. They surprised me with a small cake and an embarrassing rendition of *Layla*.

We congregate in the parking lot with rounds of good-lucks, hugs and kisses before each going our separate ways.

On the short ride to my apartment, Evan admits, "I love you, Leila. I don't want you to worry about a thing. I promise I'll look after Dad and my mom. I'll keep you well informed with what's happening here and we'll talk every few days, ok?"

The sobs I've held in for most of the night finally escape. He called my father Dad!

"Why are you bawling?"

"You called him Dad." I smile through tears.

"I did? Huh…"

Evan pulls up to my apartment and turns to face me in his seat. "Please be careful."

"I will, I promise. I love you, Ev."

"Me too. Just remember what you've dreamt about your whole life." He raises an eyebrow poignantly, and I get his message loud and clear.

Smiling, he adds, "If you need me, I'm a plane ride away."

He leans over and hugs me tightly, kisses my head and releases me. I wipe away my tears as I get out of the car and walk away from my best friend.

I'm lost in thought when I climb my stairs to hear a familiar voice say, "Hey, gorgeous." Jack is sitting on the top steps near my apartment door looking all sorts of gorgeous himself.

"Hey. You got here quick. How did you get in?" I sit close to him so our bodies touch. It's been a while since we were able to have a whole night together, and truth be told, I'm thrilled that he is here. I missed him in my bed.

"I couldn't wait for your text. I've been here a while and I have my ways."

My guess is that he wooed one of my female neighbors.

"How was dinner?" He leans into me and kisses my shoulder. It's like eighty degrees out but his lips on my hot skin still manage to cause goosebumps to sprout all over my body.

"Fun, sad and depressing." I answer truthfully. "Matt has a girlfriend, Logan and Alisa are engaged. I'm going to miss those guys."

"We'll take good care of you." He says with a smirk.

"Yeah, I'm sure *you* will."

"What's that?" He motions towards the take out container I'm holding.

"Leftovers. Are you hungry?"

"I can eat." He wiggles his eyebrows at me. I can't hide my own smirk, as I understand his double meaning.

"So you've mentioned."

He stands, taking my hand and pulling me toward my apartment. Once I open the door he responds, "Time to follow through."

We are through my door for about three seconds, when he starts undressing me. "I feel so used." I say smiling until I see his smile drop. "What's wrong?"

"Do you really?"

"I'm kidding." Part of me always feels it's just about the sex with us. But I enjoy him as much, if not more than he enjoys me. I'd be a hypocrite to say I didn't.

His mood has completely changed. Grabbing one of his hands, I wait for him to look up at me. "Jack, I'm really glad you're here." He searches my eyes and wordlessly pulls me into an embrace. Something is bothering him, I can tell.

"Are you ok?"

"It's not just the sex."

"I know."

Bending towards me he places a sweet, tender kiss on my lips. "Ok, so what'd ya bring me?" He grabs the container out of my hands. Wherever he just went, Mr. Mercurial is now back.

Jack heats my leftovers and devours them while standing in my kitchen.

"When was the last time you ate?"

He looks up with a face full of pasta and questions, "Food or you?" He smiles wide and I want to attack. I'm not usually the initiator but when he says things like that, my lower half ignites. Plus, I feel bad I hurt his feelings.

I walk over to him and take the container out of his hands. Leaning up to kiss him deeply. He makes pasta primavera taste even better. I groan as he takes over and my body starts to pulse from just a kiss.

He pulls away and admits, "I love the sounds you make." He bends to pull my earlobe in between his lips and I moan pathetically. "Like that. It's so fucking sexy."

I grab his hand and drag him into my bedroom. He has me in my bra and panties in record time. I wasn't expecting him so my underwear is functional and definitely not meant to turn someone on. He fingers the little satin bow in between my breasts.

"I like this." He says and reaches behind me to unfasten it and soon throws it to the floor. He turns me around and runs his hands down my back until he reaches my white basic panties.

"I like these too. They are very school-girl like." He slowly pulls them down my legs, as I feel a tremor from his words and his hands. He crouches behind me removing my panties one leg at a time, and I can't stand the anticipation.

Jack trails kisses up my legs, my ass, and my back until he is standing and pressed up against me. I reach around to cup him through his jeans, feeling his arousal in the process.

"Why am I the only one naked?"

"It's more fun this way." He runs his hands over my breasts, pulling and rolling both of my nipples at the same time. As I throw my head back and make one of my noises he loves so much, he whispers into my ear, "You're so fucking sexy."

Then he starts kissing and licking my exposed neck, slowly running his hands down my body until his fingers find my aching sex. He doesn't stop as he explores and strokes me intimately.

"Jack you are driving me crazy." I say in between gasps.

"Good." He touts arrogantly. Removing his fingers, he runs his hands around to my ass and then up to my lower back. He pushes me gently until I fall forward and land on my hands with my ass is in the air in all its glory.

He kneels behind me and runs his tongue over my exposed ass until he reaches me from behind. My hands clutch the comforter as he proceeds to drive me to the brink with his lips and his tongue. He pulls me into his mouth and sucks on my most sensitive part. It doesn't take long for me to tremble from my orgasm.

I bury my face to muffle my screams. He continues until he feels the last quiver leave my body. Then he stands and I hear him unzip his jeans. I can't move. I know I must look ridiculous with my ass still in the air, but I can't move. It works well with his plans, as he enters me from behind and groans deeply.

"God, Leila. You feel so good." He says while pulling out and then back in torturously slow.

He still hasn't undressed, and it only adds an erotic element to the crudeness of our position. His hands are gripping my hips as my body starts to respond to the sensations of Jack sliding in and out of me. He is working us both up to into frenzy, when my phone rings and stops him in his tracks.

"Don't stop...the machine will get it." I push backwards to prompt him to continue. He slowly starts moving again until he hears Dylan's voice on my answering machine and then he completely stills.

Oh fuck...

"Hey Lei, its Dylan. I meant to call you all day. I'm sorry about last night. I was hoping I could come by so we could talk about it. I don't regret what happened. I just wanted to let you know that. Please call me when you get in. Bye."

Jack hasn't moved the entire time Dylan was rambling on my answering machine. *Fuck...*

He pulls out and sits on my bed.

"Jack..." I say sitting next to him.

He stands quietly, zips up his jeans, and walks out of my bedroom and out of the apartment, slamming the door behind him. Instead of talking to me, he just storms out.

What the hell?

Is this a glimpse of what he'll be like in a crisis? When he gets upset, he'll bolt?

I can't have dinner with a friend? Dylan had dropped by, and I had forgotten to mention it. And yes, the message may have alluded that something happened between us. That something being a kiss. But don't I get a chance to explain, without him assuming the worst?

The more I sit, the more I stew. My anger is off the charts by the time I throw on my clothes and storm out of my room.

Chapter 24- Jack

I'm beginning to hate this guy. He needs to back the fuck off!

Is that why she wanted to be discrete? To hide our relationship from Dylan? Last night she said she was home finishing up with packing. She never told me she saw Dylan. I couldn't get over here, but what would have happened if I showed up without warning? What would I have found?

Fuck.

I'm assuming that I know something happened between them. I may not trust Dylan but I trust Leila. Besides, its not like he knows I fell in love with this girl. Hell, it's not like she even knows I fell in love with her. I've never told her.

Sitting out here on her stoop brooding is definitely not the smartest thing I could be doing right now. I feel like a complete ass, by the time I climb the stairs to her apartment.

I knock on her door and wait for her let me back in. After a few seconds, without a response, I knock again. "Leila, open up."

"Just go away."

"I will stand here all night. Please open the door." More silence follows my request. "Please, Leila?"

She finally pulls the door open but doesn't move aside to let me in. "I'm sorry."

"What exactly are you sorry about Jack?"

"I guess for acting like an ass mostly?" The look on her face tells me that was the wrong answer.

She stares me down while waiting for a better excuse. I try again. "I'm sorry that I assumed the worst?"

"I've told you nothing is going on between us. It hurts that you don't trust me."

I cut right to the chase. "I do trust you, but Dylan wants more, doesn't he?"

She shrugs but doesn't answer.

I suspected Dylan intentions, and her confirmation causes my blood to boil.

That *prick*.

"Do you?" There is double meaning to my question. Does she want more with him or with me?

She looks over at me and doesn't respond immediately. At last she says, "Jack, he's just a friend."

"Can I ask you one more question?" She nods. "Has he kissed you yet?"

Taking a deep breath, she practically whispers her response. "Last night. He stopped by with dinner. I was surprised to see him. He only stayed an hour because I told him I had a lot to get done. As he was leaving, he kissed me."

We look into each other's eyes for what seems like an eternity. I can't hide my displeasure.

"Jack, I don't have feelings for Dylan. I don't."

At this point she lets me take her in my embrace. "Thank you for telling me. I do trust you."

She pulls away and shakes her head. I cannot read her thoughts and as I bend to kiss her she stiffens in my arms.

"Leila?"

"Jack, you stormed out. You never even gave me the chance to explain."

"I acted like an ass. I'm sorry."

She watches me for a long time. She finally takes a deep breath and speaks. "Jack, you don't think it's hard for me to see you with a girl, and wonder if you've fucked her? Or if you want to?"

"Leila, I haven't been with anyone since…well it's been a long time. Believe me."

"This is only going to get harder once we leave tomorrow. I need to concentrate on adjusting to my new life, and on my career while you need to focus on yours. Maybe we should stop."

"No." Crap, why is she doing this?

"Jack…"

"Leila, this isn't just a fling for me. I can't just turn this off. I'm in this."

Releasing her, I walk over to the couch. Its time I told her what she means to me.

"Leila, please come here. I need you to listen to everything I am about to say." I guess she senses the unmistakable resolve in my voice and doesn't attempt to argue with my request. She slowly walks over and sits next to me on the couch, but purposefully leaves a distance between us.

"Leila, I started to have feelings for you the day you walked into the studio." The look of surprise on her face doesn't deter me at all. "Of course I didn't know that at the time. My feelings for you started off slow. I would wonder what you were doing at that moment or picture you laughing in that adorable way of yours. I yearned to share something with you that I thought was funny, just to see and hear you laugh. Then it became something more consuming."

I look down at my hands. "I have never felt like this in my entire life. I had no idea why I was acting the way I did. I was in a constant bad mood, instead of walking on clouds from the tour and the album. I was falling in love with you and subconsciously I knew I couldn't be with you. The realization of both hit me like a baseball bat to the head. It was the night of my birthday party. I tried my damndest to hide it. I felt if I admitted my feelings, inevitably I would screw things up and you would run. I haven't been with anyone else. Once I felt you, I couldn't think about another woman.

"I tried to stay away from you, Leila but it wasn't possible. It made me angrier that I had to deny what I felt. The kiss we shared first at on my roof, and later at my party were the cruelest forms of torture. Once we spent such a great day together after your farewell party, I needed you like I need air to breath. Now…now I want nothing more than to show everyone we are together. You aren't ready for that though, and I don't want to push you or pressure you. Even so, I want the world to know I love you."

She sits stunned.

"Why didn't you tell me that sooner?" She asks very quietly.

"I've only known you for a few weeks. At first I just wanted to be with you, in any way I could. The more time I spent with you, the more I realized friendship wasn't enough. Falling in love with you doesn't make sense to me. It's never happened before and I didn't handle it well. I'd convince myself to stay away, then one look at you and I'd kiss you. Then I'd convince myself it was a mistake, then one look at you and I'd kiss you again. Then I'd convince myself we should just be friends. Then I'd convince myself maybe we could be together, and maybe I should tell you how I felt. But I was scared you wouldn't believe me. I barely could believe it myself.

Or what if you didn't feel the same? I still have no idea what you are feeling. I was tormented by these confused feelings."

She leans forward and takes my hands in hers, yet she doesn't speak. She remains motionless, stunned into silence.

"Baby?" She looks up almost forgetting I was sitting next to her. "Am I scaring you?'

"No...yes..." She looks lost as a few tears slowly slide down her face. A tiny seed of doubt festers in the pit of my stomach. What if she doesn't feel the same?

"Babe, talk to me."

"Your words don't scare me. It's how this'll work that does."

"Why?"

"Jack, I think I fell in love with you the first day I met you. My feelings weren't a slow build. Mine were like a freight train running through my heart." She stares at me, nodding slowly, her eyes still moist from her tears. "I've been dealing with very similar emotions. I wanted to be with you so badly yet knew it wouldn't be the smartest thing to do. You're like a drug to me. I can't stay away from you."

"Jeez, Leila."

Closing the distance between us, I clutch her body to mine. We cling to each other like neither of us want to let go. Eventually she pulls away with the lost look still obvious in her eyes.

"You're holding something back. Leila, tell me."

"Jack, I am terrified of what people will think."

"Who cares what people think?" I respond angrily.

"Let me rephrase it. I'm terrified how this will look." I run my hand through my hair. I'm sure the frustration I feel is written all over my face.

"Let me explain. I've wanted nothing more than to become a rock singer since I was a little girl. I still do. I don't want you to think it's more important to me than you are, but it's part of who I am. I worry of the backlash we would get if we went public. Others might think that I only got the job because we're together."

I never thought of that. There would only need to be one negative comment, to cause rumors to run ramped all over the Internet. How would that affect her career?

"I understand." Taking both her hands in mine again, I tug until her gaze meets my own. "We don't have to go public. I get how vulnerable you are in this situation, but I don't think we need to deny our feelings and not live our lives."

Leila sits quietly as she processes my words.

"Babe, I would never let anything hurt you. Everyone we know is aware of why you got this job. The world will know, too, the minute we go on tour. Your talent is undeniable."

I take her face in between my hands and bend to kiss her gently. "We've wasted so much time fighting this. I'm done with that. We love each other and that's all that matters."

I kiss her a second time and profess my love once again. I'll say it every minute of every day so she knows and never forgets it.

"I love you."

Smiling wide, she has never looked more beautiful. It's seems almost impossible, I know. How can someone who is perfection, be even more perfect? It's the love in her eyes that makes her even more beautiful.

I never want to forget the look of pure love and joy on her face at this moment. I know it will be forever etched in my memory, but I still want evidence that this magnificent woman loves me.

Pulling out my phone I snap a few pictures of Leila.

"What are you doing?" she asks while laughing.

"I want to remember how you looked at the moment we professed our love."

Blinking, she sits motionless for a few seconds looking stunned again. "That is the sweetest thing I've ever heard."

I kiss her gently and snap a few more pictures. I notice a tear falling slowly down her cheek. Using my thumb to brush it away, I kiss her gently before saying, "Why are you crying?"

"Because I love you."

"I love you too."

Chapter 25-Leila

My heart swells with the love I feel for this man. His admission causes my body to sag against him like I am suddenly boneless. He is everything I ever wanted. Caring, kind, gentle, funny, romantic, passionate, sexy…all my wants and needs rolled into one perfect man. This seems too good to be true. How could I have gotten so lucky?

I clutch him without wanting to let go. I'm afraid that this is all a dream. Our embrace is a symbolic culmination of what we have been stupidly holding back from each other.

Jack bends and kisses me again, probing my mouth open with the tip of his tongue, and I allow him complete access. When he pulls away, the sudden space between us causes me to want to sob.

"Leila, I am overwhelmed by this." A slow smile spreads across his face, causing me to suck in a breath from his beauty. "I'm never letting you go." He crushes his lips to mine, transferring his emotions through his kiss.

I have one nagging thought that I can't ignore. This man just confessed love to me, how am I going to bring up my concerns with his past? Being dishonest wouldn't be fair to me or to him. I need to admit how much I worry about him cheating on me. I could not handle that again. And I refuse to be put in that position.

Pulling away, I gulp and venture, "Jack, can we talk about something else?"

"Anything."

I take a deep breath and try to begin but I can't seem to get the words out. I'm not sure if it's fear, or I'm afraid by voicing my fears they may come true.

He squeezes my hands and wills me to continue with apprehension etched into every line on his face.

"Jack, you know Matt cheated on me. What I haven't told you is that I actually walked in on him with a mutual friend of ours from high school."

Realizing where I'm taking this conversation, Jack sits quietly until I continue.

A vivid image appears in my mind as if it happened yesterday. "I stood frozen, unable to move. When they finally realized I was standing there, I felt sick to my stomach. He made me look like such a fool. I defended him over and over to anyone who tried to convince me Matt was cheating on me. It was pathetic how much denial I was in.

"What I'm trying to say is if you have any reservations of being faithful, I need to know now. I will not, ever put myself in that situation again. I'm not asking for a signed contract stating that you'll never cheat. I'm not dumb enough to believe that would be reality. I'm asking if you think you'll cheat, please end it before you actually do."

Jack sits quietly, somberly returning my gaze. "Leila, I've had only one girlfriend in my life. I was in a two-year relationship during high school. I thought it was love. Now that I know what love actually is, I see that we weren't even close. I did care for her, maybe too much. She cheated on me several times during the course of our relationship. I don't cheat."

"Thank you for telling me that."

"I love you. I want nothing but to be with you and be completely committed to you in every way."

I pull his face down to mine and kiss his gorgeous lips over and over and over.

He stands and holds his hand out for me. As we walk towards my bedroom, the anticipation I feel is different than all the other times we were together. I think it's because this time, we will truly be making love. All the sex I've had up to this point, with Jack included, really was just sex. Once one admits to love someone, a sudden change occurs. The physical act is no longer the focus. I want to connect to him like we've never connected before.

Jack undresses and then slowly removes my clothing. "You are gorgeous...inside and out."

He bends to kiss me passionately. I am one huge nerve ending and I feel the sensations in every cell of my entire body. He stares at my exposed chest before pulling my erect nipple in between his lips. My fingers find the hair at the nape of his neck, as I arch my back, forcing myself further into his mouth. I throw my head back and slump against him while he kisses and sucks on my breast until it drives me to the brink of an orgasm.

He slowly unbuttons my shorts and then hooks his fingers into the waistband to pull them down my legs very slowly. As I place my hand on his shoulder, he lifts each leg to release them. Dressing in haste after he stormed off, my bra wasn't the only thing I skipped over. I also didn't put on my underwear and am now standing completely bare.

I hear him gasp and he takes a step away from me to get a better look.

"Turn around." His voice is husky yet soft. I turn, with my back to him and he immediately slides his hands over my belly, wrapping his arms around my body. He finds my ear with those magnificent lips. I don't think I'm going to make it much longer as he kisses me slowly from my ear down to my neck. I groan while he continues to kiss my neck, using his tongue to lick me in the most erotic way. He skims his hands over my body and slowly slides them down my legs. As he squats behind me, I can feel his lips against the small of my back. It sends jolts through me and into my crotch.

Without standing, he slowly turns me until his face is at the apex of my thighs and then plants a kiss low on my abdomen. He is so beautiful as he knees before me. Running my hand through his silky hair, I feel my heart will burst from the emotions he triggers inside.

"I want to make love to you for hours, Leila." He says smiling while looking up at me.

I smile back at him and simply say, "I want nothing more."

Jack stands and lifts me into his arms, placing me dead center on the bed.

The journey he makes down my body with his lips causes pulsing sensations to spread through me like a slow smoldering fire. He stops at my breasts, kissing and suckling them, caressing and holding them, taking his sweet time. The sensation is now unbearable.

"Jack, please." I gasp, trying to pull him back up to my face.

"Not yet." He smiles against my skin.

The next stop is my belly button, where he torturously dips his tongue and it feels unbelievable. I relax back onto the bed and try to accept the slow torture he is determined to unleash on me.

He slowly moves one hand down to lightly stroke me, and then his lips follow as he kisses his way down my body. When Jack reaches his target, I lose all conscious thoughts. Relentlessly, he licks and sucks me in the most perfect of ways. I immediately come and come and come and come. It's doesn't end. He lets me ride my wave, and then he starts all over again. He takes me in between his lips, his hands spread on my inner thighs while his thumbs trace patterns close to where his mouth is.

He repeats the entire process again. As he slowly slides two fingers inside me, he laps at me in very long, slow strokes. He is a master at oral sex. I feel my body clenching around his fingers. He pulls them out and replaces them with his tongue. The wave of ecstasy goes on and on as he makes love to me with his tongue.

Only after the last spasm subsides does he then slowly make his journey back up my body.

"Jack, my God." I say, as he once again sucks on my nipple. He moves up my neck, and kisses his way to my mouth. I pull him over me so we are flush up against each other. I feel every muscle of his body pressing against mine with the most important one pushing into my thigh.

He starts to kiss me slowly, while his hands are on either side of my head. Staring into each other's eyes, he reaches for my hands and laces our fingers together and shifts so his erection is positioned at my entrance.

He slowly sinks into me as I close my eyes from the intensity of the overwhelming emotion he is causing inside my heart.

"Open your eyes and look at me."

I obey, although it's hard to do so. I only want to close them and relish these sensations. The intimacy between us is overwhelming. We've done this plenty of times before, but this time is different. I know he feels it too.

We move together over and over, until I feel the familiar tightening. He kisses me, pushing me over the edge and then he releases seconds after I do. I can see every emotion he is feeling cross over his features, and in his dark grey eyes.

"I love you, Leila." He assures me while our bodies are still connected. Neither of us wants to break the connection.

"I love you too." I say losing myself in his eyes.

**

"Can we talk about something?" He asks while sipping his coffee. He spent the night, and we have a few hours before we need to be at the arena.

361

"Sure."

"Can we tell the guys?" He watches me closely and waits for my response.

I move into the kitchen to refill my mug. "It means a lot to you that they know?"

He comes to stand with me, taking the mug from my hands and placing it on the counter. "It means I can love you the way I want to."

Well when he puts it that way…

"Leila, we are all going to be together night and day. I understand you aren't ready for the world to know. But to keep this from the guys would be torture for me. I want to be able to hold your hand, kiss you, love you without hiding it in front of them."

He's so romantic…and loving. How can I deny him something so profound? "Ok."

"Ok?"

"Yes."

He crushes me to his chest without warning. "Jack, I can't breathe."

"Oh…sorry." He releases his hold, but only slightly. "Leila, you have no idea how happy I am right now."

"I know exactly how happy you are." I subtly stroke his excitement.

He shrugs sheepishly. "It has a mind of it's own."

Jack loves me over and over for the rest of the morning. In the kitchen and in the shower and in my bed.

"I'm going to have a limp on stage tonight." I tease as we get dressed and ready to leave.

"Fuck, that's sexy." He says coming behind me to kiss my neck. His tongue slowly traces a line to my ear.

"Jack, we are out of time. We have to go. The cab will be here any minute."

Sighing he releases me. "Fine. You're a buzz kill though."

I walk into my bathroom and call out, "I'll make it up to you as we pull away from the arena tonight while on my knees."

His eyes are smoldering as he walks over to me. "Fuck. You can't say things like that to me." He kisses me like he wants to leave his mark on my thoughts. It's the kind of kiss that has me panting and gasping for air.

"You don't play fair." I huff as he walks away chuckling at the condition he's left me in.

Jack helps me lock up my apartment and carries my bag down all three flights of stairs. On the cab ride to the city, I am a bundle of nervous, excited, and over the top happy energy. I can't sit still, constantly tapping my foot or jiggling my leg. Jack holds my hand the entire time, smiling wide every time he looks at me, clearly entertained by my nerves.

When we arrive at the concert hall, the limo pulls around to the back entrance to let me out first. "I'll circle the block, and then come in." He kisses me before I exit. "I love you."

"Me too."

Once at the arena door, a security guard asks for my pass. I've never been back stage in my life. It's thrilling to know that some great performers have walked these halls.

A pretty girl with a clipboard and an earpiece greets me, she introduces herself as Stephanie our event manager, and leads me down the hall a large room.

Dylan is the first to see me and walks over to grab my bags. "You excited?"

"Um, yes excitement is somewhere on the list of things I'm feeling now…but I think it's towards the bottom." I admit with a smile. "Dylan, I'm sorry I didn't call you back last night. I got in pretty late."

"No worries. I just wanted to see if you were ok."

"I'm fine. Let's just forget about it, ok?"

"Yep." He pulls me into a hug. I look over to see Jack walking in time to see Dylan's arms around me. He smiles warmly and my heart skips a beat.

"I'll see you before the show?" He asks.

"Yep." He nods and passes Jack on his way out.

Hunter comes over and grabs me by the waist. "Leila it's here. It's finally here." He says while swinging me around.

I'm laughing at his enthusiasm when Jack orders, "Put her down or she's going to throw up on you."

Hunter puts me down and says, "For real?"

I nod and smile, "For real. I definitely feel like I could lose my lunch right about now."

He immediately obeys and Jack laughs.

Jennifer walks in with a burly middle-aged man. His name is Will Sutter and he's our equipment manager. There are also five young guys with him who are all wearing Devil's Lair t-shirts. I am wondering if these guys are fans when Will informs us they are our roadies and will be traveling with us.

He and his staff are in charge of setting up and breaking down the stage and making sure all of our belongings get on the bus after each show. A shy redhead in the back is staring at me as the blonde to his right stares at Jack. Jack and I both notice at the same time, trying to hide our smiles.

We are then all whisked away by Stephanie. She leads us down a long dark hallway that takes us right to the stage. The guys sprint up the stairs all hooting and yelling like they are at the Super Bowl. Jack follows me up and stops when he sees my feet are planted and not moving.

"You know no one is here yet."

I nudge him with my elbow as I take it all in. The lights are on in the theater, and no one is obviously in the seats, but there are a lot of freaking seats.

Stephanie introduces us to someone named Bruce, who is our sound check manager. He explains what we will rehearse and then leaves the stage to make his way towards the sound booth.

We run through four songs and stop occasionally for adjustments. Bruce then calls out over the PA system that all is a go. From my own ears we sounded really good. Singing along with Jack is euphoric and our chemistry on stage is undeniable. By the look on his face I know he feels the same way.

After our sound check we are then brought back to the holding room where they set up deli platters and drinks. There is no way I can eat so I grab a plain roll and a bottle of water, and I excuse myself to my dressing room. I need to settle my nerves. Jack must know I'm really nervous, as he doesn't stop me from leaving.

I take my time with my make-up and getting dressed for the show. I decide to surprise Jack and wear the photo shoot outfit he loves so much. I can't get any more nervous than I already am, so what the hell.

As I'm just about finished getting dressed, a voice comes on over the PA system announcing that we are on in ten minutes.

Oh my *God.*

The announcement immediately causes me to break out into a cold sweat.

Frantically, I start pacing the room, fanning myself to cool off. As I'm walking back and forth, over and over, there is a knock on my door.

"Come in." The door opens and Jack walks in. He looks so good in dark jeans and a tight black t-shirt. His hair is perfect. I forget my nerves as I gape at him. He gapes right back.

"You wore it." He shuts the door and walks over to where I'm standing.

"It's an opening night present, but don't get used to it. I wasn't kidding when I said this makes me sweat more than necessary." He laughs and pulls me into his arms.

"I love you so much." He says kissing the top of my head. He smells so good I would love to just stay in this room and hug him all night.

He pulls back slightly to look down at me. "I love this thing." He says as he runs a finger down the lacing of my bustier. My pulse quickens from the look in his eyes and the feel of his fingertip touching the skin between the laces.

"I came to wish you luck. You'll be great, Leila. Just remember this is what you do." He rubs my arms and then adds, "I also came for a good luck kiss." He continues to look down at me but he doesn't move.

This is probably a mistake. Kissing Jack before having to perform is like an alcoholic taking one tiny sip of wine. His kisses leave me wanting so much more...but fuck it!

I lean up towards him and he meets me half way. Just as always, our kiss starts out slow. He nibbles on my lips. Before you know it, one kiss turns into a full-blown make out session.

I pull away and gasp, "You are killing me." I reach up and wipe the lipstick from his lips and he closes his eyes and takes a step back.

"Maybe that wasn't such a good idea." He reaches down and adjusts himself through his jeans. His hard-on is visible, clear as day.

"Jack, you can't go out there like that."

The voice announces that we only have five more minutes and Jack takes a deep breath. "Ya' think?"

I bite on my lip to keep from laughing and say the first thing I can think of.

"Hunter's pale ass."

He looks down and his bulge visibly shrinks before our eyes.

"Brilliant. Thanks." He moves closer to me, as I take a step back.

"No…no more kisses."

"Buzz kill." He sits in a chair as I resume my frantic pacing. He looks so calm and collected like he's about to walk into a party and not about to sing in front of a few thousand people.

"Aren't you nervous at all?"

"Nope."

A two-minute announcement comes over the PA system.

"Let's go kick ass." He grabs my hand and tows me out of the room. We walk to the stage where the guys are all assembled, pumping themselves up.

As we wait, Dylan comes up behind me. "Good luck, Leila."

It's dark backstage and he doesn't notice Jack is still holding my hand. But at the sound of Dylan's voice, I drop his. He looks down at me while frowning. I thank Dylan as he pulls me into a hug before he strolls away.

Stephanie gives us our cue and the guys run up the stairs. Jack waits and holds his hand out for me. I love that he isn't going to let me go out there alone. We walk on stage together.

The crowd goes wild and Jack drops my hand expertly as the spotlights go on and illuminate us for all to see. I look out into the crowd, not seeing anything but a mesh of faces. I can't see my friends or dad because the lights are too bright. At my suggestion, my keyboards have been moved up so that my walk to the mic wasn't as long. Now I wish I were farther back, hidden in the shadows.

Jack grabs the mic and exclaims, "Good evening New York City!" The theater erupts with cheers. He thanks them for coming and tells them we are so honored to start our tour in such a great city. He introduces our first song, which is one of the fan's favorites, and the crowd goes wild. This really is fantastic. Jack engages them and saunters around the stage like a natural.

We go into our second song without stopping for air. Right before our third song Jack introduces us. He starts with Hunter. Hunter takes the opportunity to do a drum solo and he calls him an attention whore.

Jack tells the crowd there is no need to introduce his next band member. Trey lifts his shades and nods to the crowd prompting ear-shattering screams to erupt. I could swear I hear Lori's voice among them.

Jack teases Scott that he must have gotten lost on the way to choir practice, and Scott flips him the finger before doing his own solo, prompting Trey to retaliate with a third solo. "I'm surrounded by attention whores." The crowd loves it and eats up the fun ribbing that goes on between them all.

Jack moves back to center stage and replaces his microphone. He takes a deep breath and looks around. I'm going to kill him. Standing dead center, Jack continues to scan the masses, allowing the cheers to get louder and louder. While laughing, he shakes his head and then finally says, "So…I'm sure you've heard we added a beautiful member to Devil's Lair."

He puts up his hand to quiet them down when more noise erupts from the fans. My legs are shaking from the attention.

"We *thought* we were adding a back-up singer." There is more applause and more laughing from Jack. "What we didn't know was we would actually be turning our souls over to her or that she would be owning our asses. We didn't have a clue that she would become the devil in our lair!" He looks back at me and grins. I know I'm beet red from embarrassment. I shake my head and smirk back.

"I suggest you show her the love, or she'll own your asses too!"

I wish he would get on with this so we could move on with the show, but it is exciting to hear all these screaming fans are screaming for me.

It's pretty loud in here but yet Jack still eggs them on, "Oh, I don't know. You don't sound convincing enough to me." The screaming and applause becomes deafening. He laughs and shakes his head.

Turning to the guys he adds, "She took over our fans!" More yelling ensues. "Wow! Ok, ok. I'd like to introduce you to Miss Leila Marino."

He motions for me to come forward and the crowd continues to go wild. As I approach Jack, he bows down to me, the jackass.

As I pat the top of his head and wave to everyone, he stands up straight and holds his heart. "Didn't I tell you so? She is pure evil."

Only after I put my hands on my hips in a threatening stance does he follow up. "Ok, so are you guys ready to be Committed?"

He grabs my hand and pulls me towards his center mic. With a quick signal, Hunter starts with drums. Jack puts a hand on my bare back, and looks into my eyes. During the duet parts, our lips are practically touching as we share the same microphone. I'm completely turned on.

The crowd is eating it up and it sets the tone for the rest of our show. The way they sing the lyrics with us makes it is one huge party. I can see the pride all over Jack's face. It must be amazing to write a song, and have thousands sing it back to you.

Jack doesn't believe in taking breaks. He feels the fans pay good money and shouldn't have to sit around waiting for us to take a rest, so we play straight through for over two hours. By the end of the show I am drenched, exhausted and loving my new job.

After our encore all the guys move forward for a bow. Jack holds me close to him and whispers into my ear, "You were fucking fantastic." I smile at him as we take our final bow. The lights dim and we make our way off the stage leaving our fans chanting the band's name. They want more.

Jack stops and looks towards them. "Let's give them one more…follow my lead." The guys all run back onto the stage and Jack and I follow. The screaming and cheering has not let up.

"You guys haven't had enough?" They respond with enthusiasm. "How would you guys like to hear a song that is real special to us? We don't play it often, so this is a treat for the city we love!"

When the crowd quiets down, he says, "We can't take credit for this one. One of our inspirations is Aerosmith. This one is called *Dream on.*"

I'm touched he chose this song to play. He wants to showcase my voice. I smile wide and nod.

Despite how good it was during my audition, it's a million times better tonight. It was like Aerosmith wrote it for us. He lets me take over and becomes my back-up during most of it. The crowd sings along and he is beaming from the energy in the room.

When we are done Jack says a final goodbye. We all bow one last time. I feel like I just ran a marathon. My adrenaline rush is off the charts. As I come down the steps he grabs me, picks me up and spins me much like Hunter did earlier.

"How awesome was that?" He sounds so happy. I hug his neck as he continues to spin me.

"I know. I had so much fun!" There is nothing like the high I'm feeling right now. The rest of the band all hug each other and Stephanie appears to whisk us back to the holding room.

The minute we all walk into the room, Jack pulls me into his arms and gives me one of his mind-blowing kisses. When I pull away to breathe, I first notice two sets of eyes gawking and Trey smirking while nodding.

Jack starts to laugh, and pulls me to his side.

"Um, so guys, this would be a good time to tell you that Leila and I are in love." Their expressions change after his admission as if we both just stripped naked.

"I want to be with her and I'm tired of hiding it. You guys have a problem with that?"

Scott looks shocked. Trey looks like he could give a fuck. Hunter is sneering.

Trey is the first to speak. "Why would I give a shit?"

Scott blushes profusely and shakes his head. It looks like he's afraid to open his mouth to say anything at the moment.

Hunter starts to clap in a very slow, annoying manner. "Well, it's about fucking time."

Jack laughs. "Good. So now that you all know, there's one more thing. We aren't going public with it yet. So you are the only ones who know. Keep it to yourselves. Got it?"

All three heads nod simultaneously, just as Jennifer walks through the door. Jack casually releases his hold on me.

"You guys blew them away." She admits with a wide grin as she hugs each of the guys. She looks even more beautiful when she smiles. She should do it more often. Jennifer makes her way to me. "Leila, you really were fantastic tonight."

I'm shocked to my core. I thank her and she smiles warmly. This must be an act.

Malcolm appears with two cocktails and hands one to Jennifer. "Hello, Leila. It's so nice to see you again."

Jack turns towards me with raised eyebrows. Feeling the need to explain, I say, "Malcolm and I met at your birthday party."

"How are you, Jack?"

"I'm great, Malcolm. Fucking great."

Malcolm throws him a patronizing grin and turns his focus back to me. "So have you given our last conversation any thought?"

What the hell? This guy is pushy and I don't respond well to pushy.

"No, I'm good, thanks."

Jennifer slinks an arm through Malcolm's and takes on a very territorial stance. She can just relax. I want no part of her boyfriend. Thankfully, Malcolm clarifies his statement to Jennifer and Jack.

"Jeez, Malcolm. She's been a member of Devil's Lair for all of five minutes. Can you back off please?" Jack looks pissed as hell.

"I merely pointed out to your talented back-up singer that she is too talented to be a back-up singer." Shrugging he adds, "She's not ready. But I'm patient and I'll wait." Focusing on me he says, "You have my card. You know where to find me. I can make all your dreams come true."

Jack mumbles an epithet under his breath, which Malcolm ignores. "Jen knows how competitive I am, don't you baby?"

Jennifer doesn't look upset in the least that her sleazy boyfriend is trying to take one of her clients. That makes me wonder if this is a little plan she hatched up to get rid of me. She hasn't liked me since day one. "I know baby. You'd steal a client from your own mother. I'm not offended."

She smiles at her man and he bends to kiss her lips.

This is beyond ridiculous. Ignoring them I turn towards Jack and ask, "Do you want to go get a drink?'

"Yes!"

He drapes his arm around my shoulders. See you guys later. Malcolm, stay away from my band member or I'll hurt you."

Giving them his CCDS smile, he steers me towards the bar.

Jack looks down at me. "He's right, you know."

"Jack, I'm not going anywhere. I have no idea what I'm doing. This is all so new to me. I really want to tour with you guys. I believe in you and you're about to explode. I want to be part of that."

He skims his thumb along my cheek. "I would never hold you back. I just thought we could enjoy you for a while. But I would never stop you from excelling in your own career."

"I know." I lean in closer and add, "I love you."

He smiles warmly. "Me too. Let's celebrate."

The room has been set up with food and drinks. The boys take advantage and head right to where Jack and I are standing at the bar. Hunter orders a tray full of shots and I feel a little uneasy when I realize its tequila. Jack laughs at my expression and holds one out for me to take. "Do you want me to order a girly shot for you?"

He winks and downs one in a single quick motion.

"No." I down mine effortlessly. I'm actually getting used to tequila.

Raising his eyebrows, Jack smiles cunningly. Leaning in, he whispers, "You said you loved me the last time you had tequila."

"I did not." His mention helps me to vaguely remember that. "Oh my God."

"What? It was hot."

Our friends end our conversation by piling in. My dad is the first one through the door.

"Lei!"

I look up to see him smiling from ear to ear. I run towards him and can tell he's been crying when he catches me in mid-air. He hugs me so tightly that I can barely breathe. "You were so amazing tonight. I am so proud of you."

Evan embraces me next. "You were awesome up there. You guys rocked this place."

"Thanks, Evan. I have never experienced such an adrenaline rush in my life."

"I'm sure. This tour is going to sky-rocket you right to the top."

Lori and Alisa grab me next. Lori says, "Oh my god Lei, that was so fucking hot. You and Jack should totally do it." I let out a nervous laugh while catching Evan's eye.

As the night progresses, our guests are having a great time. Evan and Lizzy are already attached at the hip. As he is introducing her to my father, he sees me watching and winks. I blow him a kiss. I'm happy he is coming around. Lori and Trey are attached at the lips. Matt, Gina, Logan, Alisa and Joe are all drinking and mingling. Matt introduced me to Gina, and she's a sweetheart. That will *not* work out.

Jack has been by my side most of the night. "Your outfit has me throbbing."

If we were alone in this room, I would have him naked by now. Huffing out a breath, Jack looks at me deviously. "You ok? You look a little flushed."

I mutter *bastard* under my breath just as his parents walk over.

"Hi, guys." Jack greets them with a tight hug. His dad whispers something and pats his back while his mom grabs his face and kisses both cheeks.

"Mom, stop." He says as he pulls out of her grasp. It's so cute and funny. Rock star or not, he's a momma's boy.

Jack's dad pulls me into a warm hug. "You are the perfect addition to this band, Leila."

"I'm flattered. That is really a nice thing for you to say."

Renata grabs me away from her husband and hugs me tight. "Leila I can't wait to get to know you better when you guys get home. You'll come to the house, and bring Evan?"

"I would love to." She smiles and kisses my cheek. I can see where Jack gets it. It's heartwarming to know that he comes from a very affectionate family.

"Ok, stop man-handling Leila." Jack scolds. She gives him a look and hugs me tighter.

Our party is going strong. I am having so much fun mingling with my friends, reliving our performance on stage. My face is nearly splitting in two from all the smiling and laughing. That is, until I spot Jack frowning at his cell phone. Hunter is beside him, holding Amanda's hand and shaking his head. Amanda looks very uncomfortable. Jack says something else and Hunter shrugs. Their conversation looks like an argument. I wonder what's wrong.

My dad calls me over and forces my attention away from Jack. As I walk over, I worry over what just happened. No sooner do I turn towards my dad, than a gorgeous brunette walks into the room. She looks around, spots Jack, and seductively strolls right over to him. This woman is stunning. She has a tall, killer body and hair like a black, silk curtain. I watch Jack's facial expression change when he sees her and he meets her half way. He looks upset as he grabs her arm and yanks her into the hallway, while many of us watch. Who the hell is she?

His parents exchange a few words just as Lizzy makes her way over to them, and immediately begin an animated discussion. A weird hush fell over the room that's hard to ignore. Plastering a smile on my face, I try desperately to ignore what just occurred, and I'm failing miserably.

I really need to use the bathroom, but I don't want Jack to think I'm following him. I decide to wait a few minutes before I walk down the hall hoping not to run into Jack or the brunette. I'm so lost in thought that I barely hear Dylan calling my name. Smiling wide, Mr. Harvard walks towards me and is clearly a bit tipsy.

"What so funny."

"I've been wanting to get you alone all night and it figures it's when we both have to pee. Go and meet me back right here." He says and takes off. He is most definitely drunk.

A few minutes later I come out of the ladies room to see Dylan leaning against the wall waiting for me. As I walk over to him, he turns his body so I am now against the wall and he is in front of me. I'm really not in the mood for Dylan right now.

"Dylan, I want to get back inside."

He doesn't speak. He just bends and kisses me. It's soft and sweet and I instantly feel guilt.

I'm so confused and annoyed, it takes me a few seconds to realize what's happening before I push him away.

"Dylan, I thought I made it clear I don't have feelings for you." He steps back and nods. "I'm sorry."

"No, I'm sorry. I really shouldn't have done that. I was so overwhelmed with pride and, I don't know I just got caught up in things."

"I value our friendship and wouldn't want anything to ruin it, but…"

He cuts me off. "No need to continue." Shrugging, he adds, "Leila, I'm dense. It was really a stupid move on my part. I'm really am sorry." He smiles at me and his eyes are full of longing.

"I need to get back in there." He nods and motions for me to go first. As soon as we get back into the party room, Dylan heads right for the bar.

I finally see Jack come into the room alone like fifteen minutes later. My heart sinks as I see the look on his face. Where was he? Did he see us? He moves to Hunter and starts talking to him in the same agitated state, as he was earlier.

I continue to search his face but he doesn't make eye contact with me.

I'm unable to enjoy myself any longer. Something happened to cause him such pain. It's written all over his face. Our eyes meet when he starts to walk towards me. I close the distance between us.

"Are you ok?" I ask hesitantly. I want nothing more than to ask him who that girl was, why was she here and what did she want. But I need him to want to tell me. I need to trust he will.

"I am now." He steps a bit closer so our arms touch. My skin tingles instantly from his touch. "Is everything ok with you and Dylan?" He looks down at me anxiously. He must have seen us in the hall. Is that why he's so sad?

"He kissed me again. I set him straight."

Jack's posture immediately changes as his gaze flies to Dylan across the room. His glare is cold as ice and his fists clench automatically. He looks livid until he looks at me, and then his eyes soften immediately.

"Do I need to kick his ass?"

"Please don't. I don't want you spending the night in jail. I have plans for you."

"I love you." He whispers, so only I can hear him.

"I know." I squeeze his hand and walk away. I'm disappointed he didn't open up to me. He may need time. As the party winds down, I'm consumed with theories and speculations.

Saying goodbye to my dad and friends distracts temporarily. I'm exhausted from the continuous goodbyes so I decide to end the pattern. I tell them so, as I hug everyone I love and say that I would see them soon. No more tears.

My dad surprises me and says, "Ok kiddo…see you later." He hugs me, kisses my head and walks out. Evan and I look at each other stunned.

Evan kisses Lizzy and says he'll see her next week. Lori and Trey try to get months and months' worth of good-byes in before they separate. Hunter and Amanda are whispering in a corner. Scott is holding a sobbing Patti. Jack is hugging his parents. The merriment we were feeling a short time ago now completely gone.

Once everyone leaves Dylan comes over and says he'll be meeting up with us in Boston. He reminds me to call him or Cathy if I need anything.

He runs his hand down my arm and offers, "If you change your mind…"

I move away from his touch. "Sorry, Dylan."

He nods, and walks over to Jack. He says something and Jack's jaw clenches at whatever it is. Dylan looks back at me and leaves the room.

Jack is very quiet as we make our way to the bus. The guys start sitting around the bus reliving highlights from the show. He takes my hand and walks straight to the back.

"I want to get out of this sauna suit and shower. I'll be a few minutes."

"Ok...find me when you're done."

As I'm getting ready for bed, I can't shake the feeling of dread that is coursing through my body. Something is very wrong. My concerns are confirmed when minutes later I find him in his bunk staring into space.

"Hey." I say

"Hey" he says back. "Did you have a good time?"

"I did. Are you ok?" I ask.

He shrugs and says "Not really." I walk over to his bunk and look up at him.

"You were awesome tonight, Jack." I say.

He leans forward and caresses my face. "So were you."

Sitting up he takes my hands in both of his. "Can I talk to you?"

Bile rises, making me feel sick to my stomach. He jumps off his bunk and takes my hand leading me to the bedroom. Once inside, he closes and locks the door.

"Leila, I need to tell you something." His words cause my knees to give out, and I sit heavily on the edge of the bed.

"Is this about that girl?"

"Yes. She's my ex." He says watching my face. I wasn't expecting him to say that.

Pathetically, all I can say is, "Oh."

I try to shake the thoughts that immediately come to mind. I remind myself he loves me and he wouldn't do that to me.

"Babe, we need to talk."

I feel I'm about to have my heart broken. Panic takes hold and it leaves me ice-cold and shaking.

Chapter 26–Jack

I was literally on top of the world just a few hours ago. We couldn't have had a better start to this tour. We were in our hometown, the crowd loved us, Leila rocked their asses off, and even the after party was the perfect way to celebrate with our friends and family.

That is until she came.

When I got her text I wanted to punch something. She is relentless. I didn't take her seriously when she admitted she would see me after the show. Fuck, she has no boundaries.

Why was she showing up now? Actually, it's because she smells success. When I was nothing, she could easily fuck me over and move on. Now that she sees us on the climb to fame, she wants in. The news she dropped on me though, shook me to the core.

When I saw her walk in, I dragged her ass into an empty dressing room so fast her feet barely touched the ground.

"Jess, what the fuck are you doing here?" I asked inches from her face.

"Nice to see you too, Jackson." She replied sweetly.

"Cut the crap. How did you get back here?" She yanked her arm free of my grip and walked a few steps away from me.

"One of the stage hands here is an acquaintance of mine." She strolled around the room pretending to be interested in it's décor. "I miss you. You've been avoiding me."

She has got to be kidding. She couldn't be serious. "I was very clear during our last *mistake*. I am done. So why are you here?"

"Several reasons, the first one being that I still love you." She walked closer to me and put her hands on my chest.

I grabbed her hands and she smirked, assuming victory.

I practically spat in her face as I hissed, "Love? You are delusional. You think what happened between us was love?"

Her smile faltered slightly but she recovered quickly. "Yes, I absolutely love you and you love me, too."

I pushed her away forcibly. "I now know what we had was not fucking love." Turning my back to her, I attempt to walk out the door.

"You *now* know? Jackson Lair, you love someone *now*?" Her words halt me in my tracks.

I neither turned around nor responded. "Oh my God. Jack Lair *thinks* he's in love."

I clenched my fists as she continued. "It's her, isn't it? It's that new singer you hired. I can tell you want into her pants. Or have you already? Is she pulling you around by your dick? Are you confusing that with love?" She stopped to laugh again. "Wait, did she fuck you to get into your precious band?"

I was instantly in her face and she took a step back. "Get the fuck out of here before I have you thrown out."

She immediately composed herself. Leaning up, she kissed me briefly before I pulled away. "I hit a nerve." Ignoring my outburst she moved to the couch and calmly sat down. "The second reason I came is to warn you."

"About what?" I ask through clenched teeth.

"I've tried to call and text you, and you've been ignoring me. I needed you to know before you left on tour. Regardless of what you think, I do care about you."

My patience was wearing thin, quickly. "Jessa, just say what you have to say and get the fuck out." My entire body was shaking. I would never hit a woman, but I wanted to put her through the wall. I haven't been this angry since high school. Ironically, Jessa was the reason back then as well.

"I ran into Danny."

"Danny? Danny Sorenson? So?"

"He was pretty upset when he saw me and wanted me to give you a personal message. He said you stole his career and he's definitely not over it. Jack, he scared me. He looked and sounded so angry. It was definitely a threat."

What the hell was I supposed to do with this info? Danny Sorenson was the bass player we hired and fired a few years ago. What Jessa told me sent a tiny prick through my body. He is a degenerate drug addict and he could definitely be dangerous. Danny is a dark person. I sense that he wants what he thinks he deserves, especially now that we are on our way to fame. We could take care of ourselves, but if anything happened to Leila because of that maniac, I would kill him with my bare hands.

"Consider me warned. Now get the hell out."

Jessa stood and walked over to me. My fists were still clenched. She grabbed one of my hands and pried it open. "In spite of what you think Jack, I don't want anything to ever happen to you."

I pull away. "Thank you. Are you done?"

"No, there's one more thing." She paces the room without speaking. When she finally does, my knees almost gave out on me. "I'm pregnant."

I felt like I swallowed shards of ice.

This can't be happening. I won't let this happen.

Recovering quickly, I arrogantly said, "So?"

"It may be yours."

Letting out a snort, I said, "Yeah, ok. I'm supposed to believe that."

"It's true. I'm about three and a half months along. Do the math. I wanted to tell you sooner but you've avoided my texts and calls. So here I am." I wanted to wipe the smirk right off her face.

"We used a condom. It can't be mine."

"Not the second time."

I was drunk that night, but there is no way I didn't use a condom. "You're lying."

"No, Jack. You took me against the wall, while we were in the middle of an argument. I'm not lying."

I vaguely remember that. Ironically, with everything she just dumped on me, my thoughts go to Leila instead and the fact that I lied to her about always using a condom.

"I want proof."

"I'll have a paternity test, although it's not necessary. You're the father."

"Prove it."

"You have a lot to digest. Take what I said about Danny seriously. I'll be in touch regarding a paternity test." With that she strolled out the door.

How could my life go from fucking amazing to fucking disastrous in a matter of minutes?

I can't lose Leila over this. We are just starting out our relationship.

I'm going to have to tell her.

I run into the bathroom in time to empty my stomach into the toilet.

As I walked back towards the party in search of more alcohol to replace the amount I just purged, I turned to see Leila and Dylan intimately close to each other.

Her hands were on his chest as she spoke to him. I turned back to the room I came from and grabbed a chair to throw it against the wall.

When I did come back to the party, I couldn't bring myself to look at her. I wanted to cross the room and grab her, claim her, show everyone here she was mine. Instead I cowardly avoided her. I watched her from across the room. Every so often her eyes would search for mine. She knew something was wrong and kept her distance, also giving me mine.

I walked over to be near her and she took the few steps to meet me half way.

"Are you ok?" She asked with concern evident in her eyes. I'm sure she was curious who that woman was and why we were gone for so long. But yet, she didn't say a word.

She deserves so much better than me.

"I am now." I stepped a bit closer so our arms touched. Her skin on mine dulling the crushing pain I felt inside myself. "Is everything ok with you and Dylan?" My stupid curiosity caused the question to pop out. I had nerve to worry about her and Dylan with my situation looming above us like a storm cloud that was about to wreak havoc.

"He kissed me again. I set him straight."

My eyes flew over to the bastard, standing in the corner. I wanted to cross the room and beat the living crap out of him. I was unconsciously clenching my jaw and my fists with the vision of doing just that.

I looked down at her gorgeous face watching mine closely. I paused and remembered how she reacted the last time I jumped to conclusions. The bottom line is I trust her, completely.

She, on the other hand, had no business to trust me…especially with her heart, because I was about to shatter it.

"Do I need to kick his ass?"

"Please don't. I don't want you spending the night in jail. I have plans for you."

"I love you." I whispered.

"I know." She smiled shyly, letting me know with her eyes she loved me to. She squeezed my hand and moved over to be with her friends.

All the success we have will mean nothing without her. My life would be the worst kind of hell if I had to live every day with her within arms' reach, but not being able to have her.

When the party came to an end, I watched Dylan stand close to her, as he whispered to her. I had to look away when he touched her. To make matters worse, he had the nerve to tell me on his way out, "She isn't the kind of girl to screw around with."

Why would he say that to me? There is no way she confided in Dylan with details of our situation. He must have figured it out on his own. Leila watched our exchange from across the room. She mouthed, "I love you." I smiled weakly, wanting to rewind the last hour of our night and make it go away.

After the party was over we all boarded the bus to begin our tour. Leila knows something is wrong but she hasn't asked me to explain myself yet. I need to tell her the whole truth tonight. I can't start this journey until I tell her everything.

As I'm cowering in my bunk waiting for her to get changed, I run through my conversation with Jessa, and wonder how I will be able to find the courage to tell her. When she approaches, her face reveals that she knows something bad is about to happen.

"Hey."

"Hey. Did you have a good time?"

"I did. Are you ok?" she asks.

"Not really."

"You were awesome tonight Jack."

Caressing her face, I silently a say a prayer that she forgives me. I can't lose her. I just can't...

"So were you."

I sit up and take her hands in mine. "Can I talk to you?"

She nods weakly and I lead her to the bedroom.

Once inside, I close and lock the door.

"Leila, I need to tell you something." She sits heavily on the bed and doesn't meet my eyes.

"Is this about that girl?"

"Yes. She's my ex."

"Oh."

"Babe, we need to talk."

The color drains from her face. She outstretches her arms as if holding on to the bed will prevent her from collapsing.

"Jack, you're scaring me."

I need to touch her. I feel like an hourglass filled with our time together, is down to its last few grains of sand.

I can't bring myself to say any of the words I've been iterating in my head. I gently sit on the bed next to her and take her hand.

"Lei, she came to warn me about our old bassist who is pissed that we kicked him out of the band years ago. She felt it was necessary to tell me about his grudge. He's a lunatic, and I don't take her news lightly."

Leila brings our hands to her lips, kissing mine gently. "Jack, is he after you?"

"I'm not sure, but I'm more worried about you. I'm glad you and I haven't gone public yet. I don't want him even putting you on his radar."

Leila's relief causes the bile to rise in my throat. She thinks this is all I have to say. What I've admitted to is nothing compared to what I still need to admit.

"Babe, Jessa also came to tell me she's pregnant."

Leila predictably pulls her hand out of my grasp. "What?"

"It may not be mine. I was with her a few months ago. It was a huge mistake. I told her I want proof."

Tears immediately fill her eyes and slide down her face.

"Baby, I'm so sorry. This changes nothing for me…nothing. I love you more than anything and I …I can't lose you." Holding her hand again I plead for her to stay. "Please babe, please don't give up on us." I try to pull her closer but she shrugs away from me. My heart feels like someone is driving a steel rod right through it.

"I don't…Jack …please don't touch me. I need you to let me be…please. I need to be alone."

I nod and stand reluctantly. Even so, I ignore her plea and step closer. I wipe away her freely falling tears and place a soft kiss on her lips. "Please promise me that you won't shut me out. We have to talk about this."

A simple nod is all she gives me as she steps away from my touch. I leave the room and close the door to give her the space she asked for. Hours later, sitting on the edge of the bed, I watch her toss and turn in her sleep until daylight starts to filter in through the slats of the blinds. I quietly close her door and return to my bunk.

***

I've been up all night, recanting all the mistakes I've made that led to this. I can't bring myself to leave my bunk. I can hear the guys all chatting up front, reliving details of last night. I don't hear Leila's voice in the mix.

"He emerges." Hunter calls out when he sees me.

I ignore him and knock on Leila's door. She opens it slowly, barely looking at me when she does. It's obvious she's been crying. My heart breaks from the pain I'm causing her. I can't lose her. I would give everything up to avoid losing her.

"Can I come in?"

She moves aside and opens the door to allow me access. I move to the bed and immediately sit in preparation for the heartbreak I'm about to feel.

"Leila, I wish I could un-do what I did. It was a huge mistake and now the person I love the most has to pay the price. I'm so sorry."

Without warning, she launches herself onto my lap and into my arms.

"I love you, Jack."

I cling to her as if I was drowning and she was my life vest. I'm afraid if I let go she'll change her mind.

"I'll support you, no matter what the results are." She pulls away from my embrace. "Jack, I'm not going to lie, it hurts more than anything I've ever felt before, but it's because I love you so much. I don't want you keeping anything from me. No matter what it is, I need to know. No matter how bad. I'll need you as much as you need me during this nightmare."

"I promise, no matter what." I tighten my hold on her. "Leila, I don't deserve you."

I've never thought how blessed my life was until now. I would move heaven and earth to make her happy. I would do anything, to keep her safe, *anything*.

I love her.

Leila and Jack's story continues in Front & Center, coming soon.

Acknowledgements

Writing this book seems very surreal to me. Reading romance novels is definitely something I happen to be a professional at. The books I've read, allowed me to escape the stress and daily struggles of my busy life.

I am a textbook hopeless romantic. I am also a stickler for realism. I love all the books I've read, but many left me thinking, "That would never happen."

So I began imagining a love story that could happen. I filled it with all the factors I love in a romance, specifically, hot rock-stars. But most importantly, I wanted to create a book that was filled with fun, compelling and realistic characters that you could fall in love with.

The story of Back-up began in my head. Once I got serious and put words to paper, they flowed relentlessly. Every spare moment I had was used obsessively writing this book. Laundry, cooking, and other chores took a back seat, and I apologize to my family for the un-intentional neglect.

I have so many people I want to thank for helping me finally put my dream into motion.

I thank my fantastic husband, who has been my best friend for the last twenty-six years. I thank my boys, who encouraged and rooted me on once they "accidentally" discovered my new project and obsession. I love these three men in my life more than life itself.

I thank my family who unknowingly supported me through this process. Their love is a constant in my life. Thank you to all my friends who are the best group of people one could ever know. You have touched me in ways I'll never be able to express. I love you all, and you all know what you mean to me. A huge thanks goes out to my reading buddy and romance novel confidant. Your opinion and advice during this process has been invaluable to me.

Thank you Tres Cunningham at custombookcover.com, and Sarah at Sprinkles on Top Studios for creating covers that captured my feelings perfectly. Thank you to Kathleen Y. at Swept Away by Romance Book Blog. Your advice and pointers are priceless to me. Our relationship began as a blogger who loved this new author's book, but it blossomed into a true friendship. I adore you girl. To Nikki B. at Bookaholics Blog, Geri at Ever After Romance Book Blog, and Kathy at Panty Dropping Book Blog, thank you all so much. Not only were you the first to read and review my book, you all gave me invaluable advice. To Jake Bonsignore at Five Star Editing, I stumbled upon you and it was kismet. Thank you for editing Back-up. To all the authors who have fueled my love for a perfect romance, thank you for writing stories I became lost in. There are too many to name, but each and every book I've read touched my life in one way or another. Some helped in my own romance department, and my husband thanks you for that as well.

Thank you to all the musical inspirations that are a part of me. Bruce Springsteen's music has influenced me since I was twelve years old. My Darkest Days, Linkin Park, Every Avenue, Journey, Pat Benatar, Led Zeppelin, you music and lyrics helped me get through my long commute, every day for over two decades.

Finally, thank you to my readers. If you walked away feeling as if you knew Jack, Leila and all the others, if you fell in love with them as much as I did, and if you enjoyed their story, then my goal as a writer has been met. I can't wait to continue their journey with you. Please remember to leave a review at the sight of purchase.

~ A.M.

www.ammadden.com

Made in the USA
San Bernardino, CA
17 May 2014